RIVERSEND

Also by Sylvia Kelso

Amberlight

Everran's Bane (Book 1 of The Rihannar Chronicles)

The Moving Water (Book 2 of The Rihannar Chronicles)

The Red Country (Book 3 of The Rihannar Chronicles)

RIVERSEND

Sylvia Kelso

JUNO

Juno Books
Rockville, MD
www.juno-books.com
info@juno-books.com

For Lois McMaster Bujold, early reader and source of encouragement
And Orlanda Endicott and Widge Rowden, for even longer-term
friendship, and this time, inspiration as well.

Acknowledgements:
With thanks to Paula Guran for her more than sterling
efforts in getting this manuscript edited.
And to Helen Merrick for early encouragements.

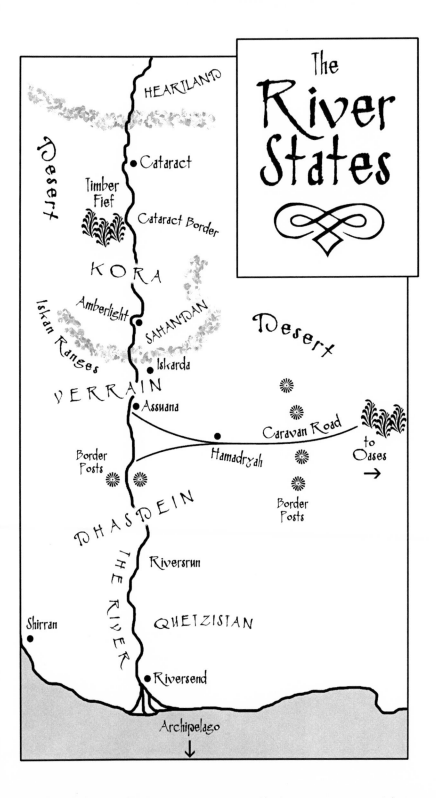

PART I

DIASPORA

I

The Diaspora. Week 1.
Tellurith's Diary

HOWEVER IT FEELS, this is not a dream. I will not wake to my life's remembered walls; to that Uphill view through wide glass widows, the House around me. The City beyond. I am already wide awake. Perched by a makeshift fire amid miles of dry rice paddies, in the heart of the Sahandan, with half a pilfered archive scroll and somebody's old silverpoint; planning to make a record. Of where we are going. What we have begun.

But it is hard to begin this journal without turning it into a requiem. For how shall I go on without remembering all those who are gone? All my peers, my fellow House-heads: Damas and Eutharie and Ciruil, my rivals; Maeran and Denara and Sevitha, my enemies; Zhee and Ti'e and Averion, my allies; my friends. Averion above all, my lovely general.

And the women who followed them, the House and Craft-folk, the cutters and shapers and troublecrew; so many bringing their men as well. The Downhill clans, the workers and guilds and merchant folk. Even the guerilla raff who came for us or against us out of River Quarter. All the folk of Amberlight. All left, lost, gone.

But how shall I mourn the greatest loss of all? My dear, my darling, the surety under my heart, the life rising to my fingertips, the light in wall and statuette and mother-face, the voice to my silence, the measure to my song? The heart's blood, the treasure, the bane of Amberlight. The city-killer, the king-maker. Pearl-rock. The qherrique.

Blown out of existence, with the armies that besieged us. Never to know, to feel, to share that unhuman answer's mystery, ever again.

Yet who am I to complain? When I surrendered, at that mystery's behest? When my—our—House survived, and relatively intact, after other Heads died with theirs? When most of my folk are here, to shape that House back round me? Safe out of Amberlight, bound for the Iskan marble quarry. Telluir House's traditional holding; a fresh life, a new world. Above all, when I, unlike so many on either side, have brought both my men live out of the wreck?

Both of them. Ah. There begins the difference. We—I was used to sharing, yes, in old Amberlight. By House custom, four, five women take—took—a single husband, who dwelt modestly in the men's tower, while we managed House and Crafts. Sharing a man, I am used to.

But not to two men sharing me.

If they *will* share. I am House-head still. I can command it. Will that make it happen? Two men together, not in the tower now, no rules laid down for them. Two such men as these?

Sarth, so much the pattern of Uphill Amberlight. I see him still, in those bronze silk trousers, gold-dusted muscles shaped in the tower gymnasium, bronze hair in waist-length lovelocks, gold-shaded eyelids, bronze-gold eyes in that perfect face. Tall, splendid, polished as his tower skills of music and conversation and love.

And the words, the delicate, drawling poison, that he could plant, surer than a Navy gunner, in my heart.

Jealousy, oh, yes. There is an abundance in Sarth of both bile and balm. Sweet work-Mother, how he could make me cringe in those days, after the boys—after I lost my children. After we lost our children; for a man in Uphill Amberlight, children are the only pride. And the worst disaster: a first-born son.

Bitter, deforming, hideous decorum: that only after a House woman's first girl might her male children live. That cost me my first, and second, and third-born child; and with them my husband's love.

Small wonder he compounded that poison on Alkhes. To Sarth, no doubt, in his very person as much insult as antithesis. Small and black-avised and wearing what comes handy. No polish, except in warfare. Outlander. Worse than outland; rankless, nameless, certainly spy, probably mercenary, possibly renegade. Taken in, street flotsam, to our infirmary, our men's tower; named, by the qherrique itself, for the Dark, the holy quarter of the moon. Prisoner, sparring-partner, lover. House-head's favorite, suave in silk and rubies. Troublecrew, lithe and lethal in killer's black. In my bed, in my love; twined into my House.

Or was that Assandar? Before he lost his memory along with his money to that River Quarter gang? Coalition general, top-flight mercenary; imperial officer, caravan guardsman, with ties only to soldiery. Deadly in brawl or battle. Deadliest in his wits.

Resurrected with those memories, and locked in battle against me, the House, Amberlight. Is there any dividing them, troublecrew and mercenary, beloved and enemy, Alkhes and Assandar? Less one man than two at once.

And how will Sarth understand that?

Any more than he will understand Sarth?

But for the future, all our futures, that I glimpse—that I am trying to see—the men, these men, are the keystone. They have to understand. What do we have, if they cannot?

As I WRITE THIS, it is quiet; camp pitched at last, after more hours of chaos with folk who never had to find a new home every night. Fireglow on the patched dun Dhasdeini tent wall behind me, on shadow and motion I know better than the rhythms of my heart: Hanni with the handful of slates and tallies she already calls Head's records. Shia yet again stirring pots. Shapes that come and go, prowling our perimeter, Zuri, Azo, Verrith. Troublecrew at work. A snatch of acid voice out in the dust-light. Iatha, stewarding my House.

And the shadows that move inside my tent.

What are they doing? What do they say to each other? Twin shadows, one tall, one small; one with a stately elegance, one with a weapon's tempered grace. If not now, with a slung arm and three ribs in a cincture of bandages, with bruises, grazes, contusions everywhere, from the huge black eye to the blisters in a stranger's boots.

I tallied that damage this afternoon. All of it. When he caught us up. Obsessed lunatic, escaping, chased clear of the—catastrophe. Whatever the price. Salving, then abandoning his army, his conquest. Leaving a letter of resignation to the Emperor, before he cast himself, knowingly this time, on his enemies' mercy. Riding, doubly outcast, incurably stubborn, after us.

And there was water in the last, bigger stream our ramshackle caravan labored over; an upstream pool, relatively clear of stagnance, sheltered by plumes of gold-tinged poplar and clumpy silver-gray hellien. A place to water a horse, and tie it up. And then, behind the shield of Zuri and her troublecrew, strip down my restored man; to purge away travel, battle, an old life.

I put the borrowed soap and towels on a tussock. He had halted, his back to me; trying to decide, forespent and one-handed, what to tackle first. But when I walked up and put both arms around him, he sighed, and leant back into my embrace.

His good hand covered mine. I locked the other over it. How to speak, in the body's language, of joy beyond what had been mortal loss? I am too tall to burrow in his shoulder; he turned his face, burying it in my neck.

"Oh, Tel . . ."

Loss, and killing grief, and thankfulness, for what we had never thought to have again.

A long time after, he whispered, "I missed you so much . . ."

I started to undo the acrid, mud-smeared laborer's shirt. Miss him, yes. What words can shape the truth of "miss"? The ache, the physical ache of it, like a cancer, night after night?

"All down the River—in Dhasdein—in the siege—all I could think was—I have to get back . . ."

He was fumbling, one-handed, with what had been an infantryman's belt.

"Not just you—or this. I never understood what it meant, Tel. The— the House. I never had it before. Not belonging. Not like that."

House-folk. Community, fellowship. Precious beyond all empathies. Except one.

The sword-ties had trapped his hand. I freed it. Pulled the heavy buckle loose. Undid the trouser strings beneath, found the hard, sunken belly muscles below that, and he caught his breath and pushed backward, twisting to find my mouth.

"Oh, gods, Tel—"

He was dirty and bristly as a porcupine, I could not even hold him tight. And when I let go he swayed, pressing a hand into his side.

"We better stop." It was breathless as the shaky laugh. "Sorry—no good for any more. Not right now . . ."

I worked the shirt off, to bare the wad of soiled linen, wide as a packhorse's surcingle, that girdled his ribs. He slid down on another tussock and scrabbled at the ties of the heavy, cross-laced cavalry boots. But when I knelt and set his hand aside he battled it, catching his breath. "No, don't—Tellurith!"

The knots were solid. Drawing the boot-knife unearthed from some Verrainer's tent-kit, I felt his hand brush my hair.

Breast-long, crinkle-curled, brandy-brown hair of Amberlight. He had undone it, releasing its mazes, that first night.

"I thought—you'd send me back . . ."

It was less than a whisper. I looked up. Our eyes locked. I could have stayed forever, his hand on my shoulder, my arm across his thigh, he bending over me, gathered between his knees.

"You should have known better than that."

He lifted the hand to cup my cheek. I touched the splint's edge, luckily not unseated by zealous handling, and murmured, "I'm sorry. Back on the road . . . Zuri was—upset."

"I expected it."

"Eh?"

"I thought they might kill me. Before I got to you."

"Kill you! Sweet Mother—"

"They had the right."

I let go the boot, half-off. He stared past me, mouth set, that silky black wing of hair, matted now, falling in his eyes.

"I was troublecrew." He said it harshly. "One of them. I betrayed the trust."

"And you'd have let them finish you. For that?"

"I betrayed the House."

I worked one boot off. Started on the other. We both knew there was no reply to that.

"I had to go, Tel. Nothing could have stopped it. They'd made up their minds. All I could do was go back and try to get some say in it. Try to hold off the worst . . . Gods, do you have any idea what it took to get that command?"

I had to go back, he had said to me, at that first parley, after his troops sealed Amberlight. I had contracts, I had obligations. I couldn't break them, and keep myself.

It made far more sense this time. Far harder, less noble, more likely sense, that our destruction was already destined, that Dhasdein and Verrain and Cataract had fixed on it, that he had indeed fought tooth and nail for the general's command. Not to have his revenge on us. Simply, as he had tried, over and over, to protect his new loyalties. To save as much as he could of Amberlight.

I pulled the second boot off. Stood up and held out my hands. When he reached his feet again, I touched his cheek and said, "I can guess."

Some of the strain went out of him, a long, soundless breath. Carefully, I worked the trousers down his hips. We were close beside the water. I gave him a hand down the stones.

It was evening, autumn, and a stream off the Iskans. He was out in two shaken gasps and I picked my way over him with the soap. When I took up the bucket he said, "I can get in again."

"We're upstream."

"Yes, of course—"

He stopped.

In some ways that was the worst moment of all. Worse than losing him that first time, thinking myself betrayed. For this was the new life. I had taken him into it. And now I saw the gulf between us: that he, even he, who had begun as a foot soldier, who could feel a child-bereft woman's grief, could so simply think—could just assume—it did not matter if we fouled the water.

With a camp of three hundred people downstream.

What woman of Amberlight could forget? Could act, were she the veriest stevedore, as if they were not part of her? Sweet work-Mother! I nearly shouted. You accused us of injustice! And you want to be part of us. Coming from a world like that: where even generals like you can't see the people underneath.

"Tel. Tel. I'm sorry. I didn't think. I'm not used—Tel, give me time. I'll work at it. It won't happen again."

And he would work at it, fast as he had understood, it needed no pledge beyond those inimitable wits.

He was huddled over, clutching the bad arm, shivering as hard as his chattering teeth. I yanked the bucket over and sank it with one vehement swirl, heaved up and ran it to his side. "Hold on. I'll be quick."

When I had him dry, a pair of someone's leggings, a Dhasdein infantry tunic and some cameleer's coat on him, the shivering had almost stopped. He picked up the dirty clothes himself. It was true, he would work at it. Azo took the horse. Walking back into camp, I touched his cheek again. "I don't have a razor, myself."

"There's one somewhere." Meaning his own makeshift kit, slung in a knapsack at the saddlebow. "Only I can't manage it . . ."

But someone else could. I pushed his hair back, clean now, if not so finely scented as once. "Will you let Azo take you wherever they've put me? I'll be back as soon as I can."

I had been Head when he first knew me. When did he not have to compete for my time? He moved the right arm to put it round me; winced. Tried to smile. "I won't be going anywhere."

AFTER FOUR NIGHTS on the road I could hope my target would be at his self-appointed work; hence out of my camp, and handily open to approach. I caught him just walking from the pair of Dhasdein five-man infantry shelters that had become Ahio the shaper's tents.

"Sarth?"

He broke stride; swung round, mallet dangling. He smelt of cow dung and sweat instead of hyacinths, there was grease on his green and brown troublecrew shirt, his beautiful hair was tied back in a tail under yet another rascally straw hat. His features looked naked, without the men's house-veil, his exquisite skin was sunburnt. But he could still make my pulse jump with that smile.

"What brings me this honor, Tellurith?"

Once it would have slid malice like a stiletto, straight between your ribs. How can I say what it was, to hear honest amusement instead?

"I need you for something, of course." I smiled too, putting my hand on his arm. No hardship in either move. He was still so splendidly tall. And to him, fresh from the tower, there could be no greater compliment.

"A double honor. Might one ask . . . ?"

It had all come so happily, it was so logical, so apt. But now, of a sudden, there was a constriction in my breath.

"I just wanted you to—ah—"

He was waiting, brows up, that lovely new, open smile.

"Ah—"

Trust, warmth, love renewed. And I was going to smash it. With my own two hands.

"What is it, Tellurith?"

The voice had changed. In his own way he was as redoubtably shrewd as Alkhes. Just trained in a different field.

I looked up the five inches to those topaz eyes. So warm, so kind, so wholly concerned with me; the way he had used to ask, when nothing mattered more than solacing my woes.

"It's Alkhes."

I said it baldly. There was no other way.

"I see."

"No, you don't, Sarth, wait!" He had not moved. It was in himself he was going away from me, the warmth running like blood. "He didn't get killed, he came after us, he—"

"He's in your tent."

"Sarth . . ."

How much explanation, how much plea, can you put in a single word?

"I'll get my things out, now."

"No! Listen to me! That's not what I want!"

He stood there. Stone to the very eyes.

"You're my husband—"

"Just temporary."

The stiletto never cut so deep. I actually put a hand to my side. His muscles flexed to turn.

"Blast it, wait! It's *not* temporary! That's what I'm saying!"

It stopped him dead. All he could do was stare.

"He's your lover—"

"I told you—!"

"Your favorite."

I actually shook him. "Sarth, will you listen? This is *not* the tower and it's *not* Amberlight. We can do what we want now. I can do what I want. You're my husband and I've got you back. And I'm keeping you. I'm marrying him as well!"

For a while I thought he really had died. But eventually his face shifted. He started breathing again.

Looked down, and then, one by one, loosened my fingers from his arm.

"Tellurith." He actually sounded groggy. "Even for you, this is—"

"For me it's just good sense." I had not meant to break it this way, but there was no going back.

"But you can't—"

"We're on our own now, and I can!"

He shook his head. "I don't—"

"Do you *want* to go?"

People and beasts squirmed by us in the alleyway, children skirmished round our legs. The sky had gone ice-pink and lavender between the silhouettes of tent. I knew there were people, a whole camp's routine waiting on me. But for that moment, we were alone.

And at last, so slowly, he shook his head.

I felt my breath go out. "I know it won't be easy. I know I'm asking far too much. But if you could try . . ."

He was still looking at me. Those topaz eyes had darkened with the twilight, but he could not seem to blink. Then, once more, he shook his head.

My heart stopped. But he let the mallet drop. Groped for my hands. Held them, a clumsy blend of schooled grace and pure feeling, against himself.

"You want the craziest things." He was trying, like a man trying to walk with a broken leg, to smile. "And I can't imagine how to—but I'll try."

"Oh, Sarth." What sweet thankfulness, to come into his arms as Alkhes had into mine, to rest in safety, however briefly, my head on his chest.

"Oh, Tellurith." He smoothed my hair. "And now; what is it you want me to do?"

"I just thought—it was just an idea—"

"Just thought what?"

"We had this problem—"

"What problem?"

"I, ah— Tell me, can you shave someone else?"

"Naturally, we all learnt." The hidden smile was dying. Too much like recall to that frivolous, pointless life. Then his voice changed. "You don't mean—"

"Sarth, he's broken an arm and three ribs and he's been riding after us four days— Somebody has to do it! And I don't know how and outlanders are funny about depending on women at the best of times, and I thought—I thought—it would be a start . . ."

His muscles jerked and I nearly cringed. I had feared Sarth in malice. I had never felt him approach rage.

"Forget it, it was stupid, I'll think of something else . . ."

"No." The anger checked. Then he sighed and let me release myself. "I'll do it. You have enough to think about."

I kissed him. He held me gently, but close. When I stood back this time, the bystanders read it as conclusion, and moved in from all directions. I did not see him walk away.

The Diaspora. Week 1.
Journal kept by Sarth

HE WAS SO blasted small. I stamped into that tent ready to bite him in half and spit out the bits, and he was huddled up on the floor against a saddlebag. Like a twelve-year-old bridegroom, just brought into the Tower. So blasted small. Nothing to spit.

He must have been half asleep. He felt me come in, jumped up, hit his arm—or the ribs—and doubled up. I grabbed him, down on my knees, before I thought. I've seen so many children come into the Tower. Little. Uprooted. Afraid.

"Steady," I think I said. "It's all right."

We were staring, a foot apart. He has these enormous eyes. Far too big for a grown man. Black as pitch. A whole night sky, in one human face.

He knew me, without a doubt. He tried to straighten—or stand up, outland soldiers have pride but absolutely no wits. "Whoa," I said. I had been prodding draught-bullocks all day. "I've seen Tellurith."

The last time we met he had seemed twice my size. An avenger, a demon with a dagger who filled Tellurith's rooms to the roof. And he threw me out. It should have been pleasant, to know we had exchanged boots.

I felt the bones in his shoulder move. Below its padding the faded roan infantry tunic bulked awry; the bandage round his ribs. His fingers clamped the bad arm's wrist.

"What did she say . . . to you?"

The ribs had pinched his breath. It came out ragged. Masking the intonation. Telling me more about damage, and exhaustion, and being here alone, an exile, than Tellurith had explained.

I could have retorted, I imagine you know, or even, Don't *you* know? I could have said, Another of Tellurith's crazy ideas. She wants to marry us both. Or, She expects me to open gates with you. Somehow. But the first two were war-signals, and the next friends' talk. And the last was franker than I could manage. Then.

We were still staring, all but nose to nose. The eyes had got bigger. Or the face had shrunk, under the beard-shadow, the bruise. A scrap of a man, hurt, tired, hunted into a corner. Cold. Afraid.

I had moved before I knew it, too. As if he were just another new, unkempt boy. I pushed the hair out of his eyes and drew my palm on down the black bristle on his jaw.

"She asked," I said, "if someone could help you shave."

He froze solid. I should think his very heart stopped. And in that moment, I understood.

Just as he took a great breath, and clutched his ribs and got out through it, ". . . never know—how m-much . . ."

The ribs pinched him on the stammer, that came from his chattering teeth. The sense was clear as a flag. Relief; apology; thankfulness; gratitude, decently controlled.

I found the cameleer's jacket they had given him, and put it round his shoulders. Outside it was quite dark, and the sound of Shia's pots said supper was close. "It's warmer out there," I said, "though you may not believe it. And I could do with supper first."

We did not wait for Tellurith. He was past keeping a House-head's schedule, whose one certainty is Late. Azo, of all people, dour scarcheeked troublecrew, cut up what meat Shia missed, so he fed himself. My own razor was in the camp gear. Imported ivory handle, chased Dhasdein steel. Shia let me thieve hot water. We went back inside, for the steadier light, he splashed water and worked up a lather one-handed. I took the razor, and gathered myself up.

And he shut his eyes and lifted his face like a child ready to be washed. Offering me, offering the razor, his unprotected throat.

TELLURITH WAS BACK before we finished. A shadow against the coals, head tilted from the papers in her lap. Bronze-crinkle Craft plait, every hair etched by firelight, the high cheekbones and arrogant jaw. Features I can shape from memory, in the dark, in my sleep. Like the question, the anxiety, the dawning, vindicated, once more successful gleam in those narrow chestnut eyes.

"There you are." Scrambling up to meet us, a hand on my chest, on his intact arm. A smile for me. For him a scrutiny, then a butterfly, multiply significant touch on the cheek.

And then to me, "Do you want the last hot water, before we turn down?"

Old House usage. Dim the qherrique, that was both light and heat, for the night. Not so subtle reminder that they had bathed, as I had not. Horrifying signal that she was going to throw us all in bed together. Right now.

I think I managed not to gulp. Hot water? I wanted a full, hour-long bath. I wanted skin softener and hair wash and perfume, a manicure, my eye make-up, a face-veil and jewelry, sheets on my bed. Not to wash and shave by guess behind a wagon in the cold and dark, then fall into dirty blankets with my hair still stinking of sweat. And not, Mother save us, with another man!

One is grateful, at times, for the discipline of the Tower. I was thankful, at least, that she waited for me by the coals rather than give him first possession of the tent. Even if she waited in his arms.

The tent was a Verrain subaltern's, built for one man and his servant, and that only while he dressed. It was actually an honor that Tellurith had one, technically, to herself. Otherwise we would have bedded down in the big infantry shelter. Figure such antics under the eyes of Shia and Azo and Hanni and her husband, and the Mother knows who else.

The Tower taught me, long ago, the dance of entry and apportion in shared territory, but it is always so delicate. This one was damnably delicate. And I was so tired. So tired I sat down like a peasant on a pack-bag and left arrangements to Tellurith.

So it was my own fault we wound up with a blanket on the ground canvas under us, and two beneath the Dhasdein officer's cloak atop. And Tellurith nearest the door—"in case there's trouble in the night"—and me against the wind-side wall. And the third between us: on his side to protect his broken ribs, and his bad arm, if you please, pillowed on my chest. "Because you're the right size, Sarth. And you don't thrash about."

It is true, she sleeps like a net-cork in a gale. And true too, though she does not know, that I have learnt to tender fragile bed-mates in my sleep. How many times, in the Tower, has a boy with homesickness or some direr fever ended in my bed?

Outside the Tower, rumor has some nasty words for it. And sometimes, they are true, whether from lust or loneliness—too often you sleep solitary, even with five wives—or from honest love.

Perhaps such shadow territory stretches beyond the Tower. Certainly, no boy inside it ever made such a fuss.

The Diaspora. Week 1.
Meditations. Alkhes-Assandar

HE WAS SO damned big. I'd dropped off when they left me alone. Three nights huddled in ditches with the bridle over my arm . . . I was still on hunt alert. So I jumped up the minute the shadow moved and there he was, right on top of me. Ten feet tall.

And so damned *handsome*. Built big, but perfect shape. Long legs, broad shoulders, narrow hips. Face like a temple sculpture. Not pretty. A man's model. And those cursed lion's eyes.

I remember him from Amberlight, got up like an artist's whore, all gold-dust and jewels and paint. The sod's better-looking without. Even with his nails broken and his hair uncurled and axle grease all over his shirt.

I expected him to hit me. Or to snipe. He's got a tongue like a Heartland poison dart. I don't know why he shut up. Or why he touched me, but it scared me dumb. If I'd been less cold, and less damaged, and less—daunted—I would have hit out myself. There are plenty of those around the court. In Dhasdein. Even in Cataract, sometimes. And they seem to like my looks.

And then Tellurith had to put me in bed with him. Like a damned woman, plastered all over his chest.

I have been in bed with men before. *Not* at court. In the field, on picket, or a retreat, you can get caught without blankets. Or even a cloak. When a raid hits the caravan, and you wind up on a sandhill with your gear on a camel thirty miles away, in one of those freezing Verrain desert nights. Or you can have wounded, and sometimes, to keep warm's their only chance.

But I do not, not, not expect to wind up beside a man who looks like the River-lord's statue, with the woman I'm supposed to have married on my other side.

May I be hung if he doesn't look better in bed than Tellurith as well. All that hair—longer than hers, *and* thicker—spread out over the saddlebags like black-bronze silk. Profile like a cursed—statue. Plenty of muscle to fill out the blankets. And of course he'd never dribble or break wind. I doubt the bastard so much as snores.

Not that I had a chance to find out. If the rest hadn't done for me, Tellurith did. Dropped sleep-syrup in the last tea we had, waiting for—Sarth—to wash. I knew by my next morning mouth. But after that, I hardly got past, "I can't sleep in there, wait, listen, Tellurith . . ."

And part of it, gods know, was the relief. Oh, gods, to have that pain stop. To rest a broken bone on something not too hard, not too soft, just the right height. And not have to move again. To know yourself back in friendly lines. Safe.

The Diaspora. Week 2.
Tellurith's Diary

THE OLD POET WAS RIGHT, when she said that leaving your City is only to take it with you somewhere else. But even with it half a moon dead behind you, on what else do you pattern your life?

Which may be why, along with grief, and loss's aftermath, and remembered ruin, not to mention wrestling these Mother-forsaken bullocks and more forsaken wagons along this most forsaken mule-track, I have had to break up a war tonight.

Two women. Two cutters. Cousins of Charras, my senior power-Crafter, married amiably ten years to the same man. Coming to blows, to woken cutter blades, over who should bed him first.

It must be memory that terrifies me so, to see a cutter woken like that. Memory of the great light-guns, that I designed, that Diaman and Keranshah built along with us, shearing through wood and metal and flesh and bone on the glacis of Amberlight. Of that sick jerk as the blade in my own hand met naked flesh. But to see those white beams clash in the twilight, and know they threatened my own kind . . .

I broke it up, of course. House-head skills, ingrained House discipline. A couple of bellows, and Azo and Zuri were there to back me. If they had not stopped.

If they had not stopped . . . Azo or Zuri with an arm gone, a thigh slagged, a foot cut off. If they had not stopped . . .

It will be better once we arrive. When we can shed the nightmare of pursuit, of fresh massacre along this pestilent bog-rut. When we can settle into the new life.

A relief to know we are expected; that it is all right—or as all right as three hundred strange mouths at the heel of autumn may be. The light signal came back today. I sent Iatha, House steward, with Hayras and Quetho, the closest I have to Craft-heads, and Desis: troublecrew, sometime raider, scout. All well, the signal said. Report follows. Desis will be riding back with it, firsthand information, right now.

A TIDY enough village, it sounds. Forty to fifty permanent houses, perhaps four hundred souls. Mother bless, room to spare; quarters for the summer quarrymen. And a negotiable ascent. Better than this pig-wallow where we have had to shore every bridge; Desis is developing an engineer's eye.

I could have sent a genuine one, but Alkhes is still not fit to sit a horse. And to judge from Desis' words, I was wise.

"The Ruand, ah." Hunkered on her heels, sipping the last tea by my fire. "Reckon she's a bit of a character." A pause. A shake of her alert, cropped, troublecrew head. "They stick to the old ways, up there."

Troublecrew, so she will not warn me outright: Ruand, we are headed for the backwoods, where they make myths of Dhasdein and an ogre of Cataract. Where men's rule has not merely never threatened, but is still undreamt. Where newfangled revolutions might be more danger than they are worth.

I was considering that . . .

No. I was still refusing to consider that when, behind me, someone spoke.

"That water's getting cold."

The last hot water of the night. Saved with love's care, with steely determination. Offered in Sarth's dark velvet voice.

With Sarth himself hunched at my back, one hand thistledown-soft on my shoulder point.

From Alkhes it would have been nothing, but from Sarth? Bred and trained in the tower, in Amberlight, where men are taught from birth not to ask?

Six nights I had been sleeping with them both, too tired and too tense to think of anything more. After this news it would be worse. As he, with the remnants of that men's gossip-net, would know.

The bath would warm me, the other would help me sleep. That too, he had long known.

The rest had to begin some time.

I got up, and offered him a hand. When he took it, I said, "You can come and scrub my back."

The Diaspora. Week 2.
Meditations. Alkhes-Assandar

THE BASTARD! The scurvy, sneaking, double-crossing *whore*!

I should have thought. Should have expected it. She said, Both of us. She took him back. He fought for her. She was with him while I—was blowing up, tearing down her life. She even loves the bastard. I can tell that. She has a right. She has every right!

But oh, gods, it hurts.

I thought I could manage it. Whatever happened, I have to wait. You can't please yourself, let alone a woman, when every stray move folds you up like a busted tent. And I'm so tired. Not just the damage. Trying to stay on my horse, trying to make these stubborn, lamebrain, deaf-and-blind women do *some* things right—gods, with two pentarchs and some discipline, I could cut five days off this march. If I even had a sapper who'd pay attention at the creeks! But Zuri's are the only ones who listen. Most are shapers or power-crew. They don't know me, they don't trust me, they damn well don't like me. I betrayed their Head and wrecked their House. And blew up Amberlight.

And Tellurith, I could shake her, leaves me stuck with—him. Not enough he has to help me dress and shave and even *eat*. He heaves me on the blasted wagon. When things go wrong and I try to swing a pick for them—if the ribs catch, *he* has to pick me up!

I can bear with that. I can bear his nursemaiding. I can bear to *sleep* with him. But gods above, how dare the dung-eating bastard slip in and sleep with *her*!

I could swipe his head off. I could cut his guts out. I could kill him. One good kick in the throat.

But the look on her face. When they finally came in. Hand in hand. With that whore smirking from ear to ear. And Tellurith—not worried for once. That smile. That look.

Oh, gods, it hurts.

The Diaspora. Week 2.
Journal kept by Sarth

IN THE MOTHER'S NAME, if I must endure exile, have I to suffer barbarity as well? Am I not perpetually unbalanced by a man who acts like a House-head and looks like an injured boy? Have I not the right, after shepherding him from every piece of mischief in the day's march, to offer comfort to my own wife? And if, for the opulence of an upper level Tower room, with its cushions and rugs and drapes, the elegant artistry, the leisured music and conversation, all by the glow of the qherrique, I can substitute only a quick cold tumble in the dark, must I bear a ruffian's tantrums at its end?

Bad enough when he refused to sleep between us that night. No explanation. No manners about it either. Mother, he could use a spell in the Tower. Worse when Tellurith went off early, without a word, so I had to help him dress. And when I offered it, he tore the shirt out of my hands.

I am Tower-bred. I said only, "What is it, Alkhes?"

"You slime!"

"What?"

"Bed her while I can't—slip off with her—you cheating *thief!*"

No time for bewilderment. Less for shock. Had he been whole, I would already have died. As he started for me, I said, "So predictable. Your only art."

"You—!"

"And for me, one hand will be enough."

It stopped him like a fist. Tellurith says I have a stiletto tongue.

"You might consider," I was less angry but just as ashamed of myself, "what *Tellurith* wants."

He was trying to get his breath. As if I had struck him in good truth.

"Will it please her, if you kick my face in? If we go brawling like a pair of dogs? Do you ever think about what she feels? Did you consider how she felt, last night?"

His lips moved. Nothing came out. If those eyes get any bigger, I was thinking, I will drown.

Blessed Mother, why did you curse me with Tower training? Why do I lack a soldier's cruelty? A soldier's callousness?

I took the long step forward to grasp his shoulder and said, "I mean the news Desis brought."

There must be discipline in soldiery after all. He was still linen-white, but the lips, however stiffly, could move.

"What news?"

"The Iskans. The village. They're traditionalists."

"What?"

"That means women rule. There'll be a matriarch."

I might as well have told him camels could fly.

"So," I said patiently, "she may well doubt folk who've decided to pull the Tower down. To let the men out. And put two of them in the Ruand's tent."

The lips moved. Maybe it was, "Oh."

"Don't you think, last night, Tellurith might have been a little— concerned—about that?"

The eyes had got bigger. Too big, far too black. I am a total fool as well as Tower-bred. I put both hands on his shoulders as if he were a compatriot, a cousin, a new young bridegroom. A friend.

"I didn't mean to distress you." At that moment, it was the truth. "I was thinking about her."

He put the good hand to his side. There are times I have seen Tellurith do that. With just such a look on her face.

"I'm sorry." Sometimes it is easier than you would imagine. "Now and then my words are sharp."

His breath jerked, almost as if shaken into a laugh. Then he took the hand away. Looked up in my eyes and said, "No. You were right."

I tightened my grip. Fine-twisted muscle, slender bones, steely tendons. Frail as his soldier's pride. His exile's confidence.

"I have to—"

He stopped. Took another sip of breath.

"We have to—sort this out."

I let go. Sort what out? I wanted to say. You are an outlander, a killer, a barbarian. In Amberlight, no decent woman would put you in her Tower.

But we were not in Amberlight.

And you, said another, more accusing voice, have Tower skills, if he does not.

And you promised Tellurith: I'll try.

"*You are there for the woman,*" I said. "That is what I learned. *What she wants, when she wants. Be ready, be waiting. Be patient. Learn to read her wish. Learn about her friends, her work. Remember that they matter more to her. Never ask. Never importune. Always, put the woman first.*"

Teach to learn, Sethar used to say, wisest of men, in my own youth. I seemed only to have struck this one dumb.

I picked up the shirt. He caught and checked my hand. The eyes were alive now. Enormous, but no longer dazed, sparking like midnight qherrique.

"You're telling me this—you're not telling me this because it's what you want. But to explain how it was. Because you don't understand me. But you do understand yourself."

"No," he read my eyes, "let me try . . . I was raised outside Amberlight. It's—the quickest way to say it is: men come first."

He produced a bleak little smile. "Yes, reverse everything you said. Well, almost everything. Women out here do have more freedom than you. But men . . ."

He paused, and frowned. "It doesn't reverse properly. Because Tellurith's always shared. But men out here—don't share."

I let the shirt fall. He gave a quick, jerky nod.

"I didn't expect—I didn't think I'd feel like that. I never meant to—unload it on you. On anyone. It just—hurt too much."

He thought she was his property. No, he had been taught she was his property. His sole property. So his response, instilled as mine, had been the opposite.

"I thought I could handle it. But . . ."

I put a finger to his lips. Warmth, breath, the soul of him, alive under my touch.

"Let me try. It was a knee-kick, both sides." The jerk the physicians tap out to test if your nerves are sound. "We were both at fault."

His eyes spoke. I pressed the finger tight. *Now,* something within me said. You took one step to save yourself and another to rescue him. Take a third, for us both. For us all.

"I don't understand you, yet. But I promised Tellurith. I will try."

I took my hand away. He blinked.

"Try?"

"To make this—us—work."

Something happened to his face. Then he put his own hand up, as if to feel my touch, on his mouth.

But he was still the outlander, the soldier. Among whom, I find, treaty terms and boundaries must be spelt out.

"So can we agree," for an instant he shut his eyes, "that whatever— whoever—she wants, she gets?"

She has never, I did not say, operated on any other terms.

"And that we—let her make the choice?"

What would be different?

"And," he swallowed, "that we don't—compete?"

There I finally woke to sense.

"We can agree whatever we like. The question is, what does she think?"

He clapped his hand back over his face. I caught at it in alarm, and he lowered it, with another long, shaken breath.

"I keep forgetting. I keep fouling it up." He looked up at me with eyes where rage and jealousy were weirdly entangled with guilt. "And I used to think you were a—a—"

"Clothes-horse?" Whatever was in my smile, he winced. "That you're outland doesn't make you a fool."

He started to speak. Stopped. Then he shook his head.

"And the code *you* talk . . . I'll try to remember that as well."

Then he thrust out the good hand and looked me straight in the eye.

"We let her make the rules, then. We try—I'll try—not to fight over her. Not to—lose my head again. Not to," a wry, bitter smile, "put it off on you."

What use to recall the Tower, where he would have learnt to manage all this, or to let it out mannerly, from birth? I took his hand. When he let go, I decided he was chastened enough for the risk. I picked up the shirt for the third time and enquired, "And now, would you consider getting dressed?"

Mother be blessed, he laughed.

WITS, THEN, despite being outlander. Sharp enough to learn, perhaps. Certainly to encourage me in idiocy. So at the first hold-up that day, when half a bridge-span's edge caved in under Zariah's bullock-cart, and he scampered down to embroil himself in the uproar, I dared to touch his arm.

"What the—!" He had spun so fast I jumped back myself. "Oh ... Gods, be careful doing that!"

It takes no troublecrew to know a killer's reflex. But he was past that already. "What is it—uh—"

A fresh cascade of diggers and riggers poured round us, halfway down the flattening track past the bridge bastion. Good solid Iskan stone, with dry grass, and shadow, at its foot.

Following me into it, wary, almost suspicious, he repeated, "What is it—ah—Sarth?"

Another giant step. One, pest on him, I could only match.

"Uh—Alkhes. May I suggest something?"

The eyes focused. The eyebrows flicked. A gesture down into the creek, where they were wading about, disputing and quarrelling, around the debris. "About that?"

"Um. Yes."

He waited. He was going to listen. More than you can say for Zuri's lot, whose best response is a courteous pat on the rump.

"Let them get on with it. It may take time. But it's what they need."

The eyes sharpened. "Need?"

I was far outside decorum. Far beyond my place, to explain women to an outside man. "Ask Tellurith. I have to get back—"

"Wait just one moment!" He actually caught my sleeve. The eyes skewered me. "Need what?"

"Ask her. I can't explain it. It's not my place—"

"What do they need?"

"It's not my business, Alkhes!"

"All right, I'm sorry." He came the step back with me. I have never seen the general, or the outlander, or the Mother-forsaken, terrifying wits of him, so clear. "I'll ask Tellurith. I'll think about it. They need their way. And," the eyes sharpened, "it isn't mine."

He came with me up the bank, back to Charras' bullocks, which I was trying to help drive that day. He held cups when I heaved the water-jar down for her three children; boiled water, to keep them from disease as well as the creek. He listened as we talked. Settled beside me, quiet, and willing, attentive as any novice, and terrifying as a leashed tiger-cub, in the shade where we decided to wait.

He would have been an ornament to a Tower after all. He does not learn by questions. He listens, and looks.

And thinks.

The Diaspora. Week 2.

Tellurith's Diary

"Tel, what is it that you—your folk—need to do, that I can't help?"

He had waited for that precious after-dinner lull, with last reports made, trouble sorted, Iatha and even Hanni gone; the space before baths and men's time, the time I have kept for myself. He sat on his heels, a slight, lithe shadow in the ember-glow; the falling wing of hair crossed his eyes with paler night. I slid a hand through it, living silk under my fingers, while I thought.

"Why do you ask?"

Darkness folded. A frown.

"When the bridge collapsed today. He ..." An almost audible gulp. "... Sarth—said I should stay out of it. That they 'needed' it."

I did not exclaim, Sarth? Probably I will never know what happened this morning. But a truce was miracle enough.

"Alkhes ... Caissyl." Incongruous to love-name this one Sweetness, yes. Unwise to say, You've been talking. I'm so glad.

"You're a soldier. A general. You've probably forgotten more about marches—and road-making—than we'll ever know." He did not trouble to nod. "You think I ought to use that; and I would. Except ... do you remember the soap?"

The black brows came together. A moment's pause. And then a softly indrawn breath.

"If a general wants to spoil the water, he can. No question. But you thought—remembered—considered—everyone else."

Never, yet, have his wits failed me. Never, yet, have they failed to exceed my aim. But when I nodded, I felt the renewed frown.

"So what's wrong with considering—trying to help?"

"Two things. First ..." I held out a hand. He eeled closer, into my arm.

"First. You still try to help like a general. You want to—go in from the top. Give orders, arrange, direct things. Do it as clean and fast as anyone can."

The hurt was clear as a cry. He had been so sure he was doing better, paying attention, thinking of other people. I gave his shoulder a little shake.

"The second thing ... I've pulled them out of the City. Out of places, and crafts, and ranks that were settled, fixed, longer than their lives. And

I've pulled down the towers. They have to fit the men in now, some way—altogether new. And the men have to fit. Do you know what Sarth's gone through, just learning to swing a mallet? Have you seen his hands? And do you notice the way the women still have trouble hearing him? When he does have something to say?"

His head was bent, his eyes on the fire. After a moment he said very quietly, "Damn, how much more have I missed?"

"I doubt you could have helped that. Even with Zuri's crew. Not yet. But . . ."

He turned to me this time. Swinging on his heels to put the good hand, light, if without its usual feather deftness, to the haft of my plait. But he did not urge, Go on.

"And there are all the—people who—died."

Craft-heads, Navy captains, clan leaders. Mothers, sisters, daughters. All the gaps in the great web of kin and craft and custom that had been the House.

"They have to—put the House back together. Most of all . . . most of all, they have to do it from the bottom. You can't *tell* them, even if it's a better way. They have to do it for themselves."

The coals spat. A palpably more bitter wind skirled round the tent. Elsewhere in camp people talked, cattle bawled, a baby cried.

"So your way of organizing—is to let them organize."

He read my relaxation. His fingers flicked my plait, a tactile smile. "With a few gentle prods, and arrangements when they're asked for. And godforsaken—endless—waits."

Never have his wits failed me. And never have they failed to reach beyond my aim.

"But, Tel—if they—we—put it all back together, the old way—what will change?"

I could not help the little laughing gasp. "What!" Nor the yank on his hair. "Just why do you suppose, dangle, that you're here at all?"

"Ouch! Tyrant . . . you mean it'll shift, just having men out of the tower?"

"Hasn't it?"

This time the silence was arrested. To break on a jerk half upright, a grunt. "The cursed—slime!"

"Eh?"

"Tel, this is—past crude. But who asked who, last night?"

My own muscles set. Then I said, "*The woman comes first?*"

His back transmitted the little, shaky sigh. "You are so quick . . ."

"Did you," yet more indecent, but it had to be said, "did you two—argue?"

"I never got a chance." A sharp little snort. " I was ready to kill him, and he put five words between my ribs." A more difficult breath. "And then he told me—his way—what you've been saying tonight."

"You think he lied?"

"I didn't think —I thought—the way he explained, it all made sense." Now there was bitterness. The taste of betrayal. "And all the time—"

"No." It was clear now as the ground-plan of Telluir House. "Not by intent. He knew I was upset. Worried. It was the one way he could help. To him, asking me . . ."

When I stopped, he finished for me. "*Men never ask.*"

However they are needed. I had been astonished, I recalled. And thought again, and shook my head.

"He's changing too. He just hasn't realized; hasn't admitted it, yet."

Silence, longer this time. Easier. Then a shift of position. A hand slid down my back; a silent, impudent, envisagable smile.

"If he can ask—so can I."

The Diaspora. Week 2.
Journal kept by Sarth

LUCKY, AS OUTLANDERS DO NOT SAY, that there are more ways of making love than one, and that Amberlight women know—expect—to use them all. So I daresay she made him happy, whatever he did for her. I do know I gave them time for it, fool that I am, trying to look busy, and easy, and dodge Azo's eye, cowering over the deadened embers. Trying to guess, without prying indecency, when it would be safe to go inside.

Trying, harder than I have ever tried, not to let jealousy eat my heart in coals hotter than eternal fire.

I thought I could handle it, he said. So did I. I thought I was used to sharing. So I am. But not of my wives.

No doubt Outlanders would consider it barbaric, barbaric as the female harems they keep in Cataract. In fact, three of my five were dead: Sfina, head-Shaper, Wyen, second in the power shops, Khira, Captain on the Navy vessel *Wasp*. Lost in the River battles, killed defending the House. And Phatha, head of a Telluir sub-clan, chose to stay in Amberlight.

And yes, now I can admit it, that though they shared my bed and my marriage, and I—worked—as hard to cushion and tend and pleasure each of them—

Even so, even when she left me, there was only one who mattered. Only one whose step I knew a stair away, only one I was ever waiting for.

At first it was the honor. Fourteen years old, fresh from flute and dancing school, crammed with the economics and politics of the River as of Amberlight, all the knowledge a man must carry, to understand, to sustain the woman's talk, and never, never flourish for yourself—and Sethar walked in, that bright, sharp spring morning, with grandmother Zhee in person, upright and keen-edged as a blade in her plain leggings, the eccentric silver-worked black coat. The eyes, keener than any stiletto point, running over me as I stand, just dismounted from the vaulting horse, heart plunging, ribs heaving, but instinctively, reflexively, struggling for the perfect pose. Her slow, yet far sharper drawl. "You think he'll do us grace."

To me, as ever, unreadable. But for all his skill, Sethar cannot hide from me. My heart too leaps into my throat.

"Ma'am." So calm, so deferent, so perfectly disciplined, the model of my life. "This is our best."

She prickles me with that stare again. Then puts up the stiletto points, and frightens all excitement out of me. "We have a marriage offer," she says. "From Telluir House."

Not merely from Telluir House, ally, neighbor, glamorous, notorious, the Thirteen's scandal and cynosure. From the Head of Telluir House.

How many nights was it that Sethar had, like a homesick baby, to sing me to sleep? How many mornings, like a woman pregnant, did I spend throwing up? Mother, when they brought me in the great House doors, double-swathed in the silk trousers, the gem-embroidered coat and shirts and face-veil and the great diaphanous outer cloak that took the summer breeze like a huge saffron flame—how did I keep my legs straight, and my heart unburst, and breath in my throat? When we reached the courtyard. And there at the Tower foot, she took my hand. And smiled at me. Tellurith. Brilliant as a star in gold-worked ivory, in the heirloom jewels of the House. My dream. My terror. My wife.

Of course, as Sethar had drummed into me, I did not have to finish the ordeal by fire that night. At fourteen, barely two years younger than she, I was not expected to play the man for another year or two. Time to learn my place, my House, my Tower. To be confident and calm. So the night she did come, I could offer my Ruand her husband's suite, and a light supper, and music, and some intelligent comments, and even, forewarned by the Steward at mid-afternoon, manage to look my best.

And later, to do my best. And best of all, to meet, to match—to be her heart's desire.

The good times—no, I cannot think of them. I *will* not think of the bad times. I *will* not remember how it felt, when they told me about *him*. Mother preserve me, do you know how it is to hold your face still, while dogs eat out your bowels? While every fiber of you cries, Oh, Mother, only let me die?

But I will write this down, as I never could, never would have dared before. Men's trivial records, men's paltry thoughts. Huddled here by the coals with an old slate and Hanni's chalk-end, where no-one would look for such a thing. I will set it down, to cement the vow.

I survived all that. I can—I will—survive this.

II

Arrival. Week 3.
Meditations. Alkhes-Assandar

THIS CANNOT GO ON.

Three days it took to get up here. Three—whole—gods-forgotten days. When the accursed quarry is no more than a spur and a foothill and a last one-in-five gradient from the actual plains. When we have a bare thirty wagons, and a bunch of push-barrows, and ten or twelve mule-carts. And two hundred—count them, two hundred able-bodied women, give or take a pregnancy or two—incapable of rousing their brains.

I've never written, except for reports. But however awkward the scratches and pot-hooks on this excuse for paper, with my clumsy left hand, I have to write now or burst. The things with Sarth, to begin with. But now, because I deserve commemorating. Because in these last three days I have not said a *word*. I have not *thought* a word. I have sat on the roadside. Or at the bridge-ends. Or with the children. Or wherever Sarth went. And I don't know how my teeth aren't ground to stumps.

The village is well enough. I remember it now, laid across the hill along a single street. Under the crest, facing north, to dodge wind and snow. Houses above the road, stock-barns, transient-quarters below. Timber and shingles, two-storey houses with high-canted, gargoyle-pointed roofs, weathered blue or scarlet paint. At one end, the curl around the ridge of this carthorse track. At the other, the gnawed prow of rock that marks the quarry gate.

I remember that too. Silvery grass, pale clouds, silver-gray mountain helliens. Bark of gray and steel. Silver and blue-shadowed snow. Silver, cream, mottled and veined and buried amid cross-cuts and dirtheaps, the jagged stairsteps of the quarry face, the marble itself.

I don't remember the—Ruand. Village-head. Almost, I thought, Ruler. I could have made it, Queen.

She met us at the street-head. Most of the village with her, I should think. A shield-wall of women, dour sun-dark mountain faces, tricked out in their best. Silver-thread leggings, embroidered coats. Picks, surveyor's levels, ox-goads, skis, hafts beribboned, edges polished like swords. Men somewhere behind them. And Darthis, the—Ruand—in the midst.

She looks big. I keep thinking, massive, and then, seeing her, am shocked. Old, yes. Old enough for jowls and grayed hair, and a sag under her heavy upper arms. It must be inside. The stillness, the weight, the sheer—resistance—of compacted stone. A boulder. A great, sentient rock.

She spoke a ritual welcome, ushered the Telluir entourage down the street. To the safe-come sacrifice. Being only a man, I missed that. Incense, Sarth says, burnt on the village altar, lit by Tellurith's own cutter. The qherrique's, the Goddess's holy fire.

The altar is—alarming. I don't recall that, either. A bulge in the street, the market-place, I do recall, and the tavern either side. The spring at the hill-face falls into a culvert, we had to help clear it once.

Good stone work around the head, where the village men bring their jars. And out in the middle, this other great—rock. Smooth as silk, though unshaped. Probably, Dhasdein's earth-scholars would say, a glacier boulder. Fawnish cream, but not sandstone. With a dark, stained, polished hollow at its heart.

They burn the incense there. And pour wine, no doubt. And it has gone on for centuries. I never felt this place's age before. Or that disturbing kinship. The Ruand and her altar. Both of them ancient. Immoveable. Heavy—and menacing—as stones.

Stupid thing for a soldier to think. Silly, superstitious, womanish thing, they would say, in Cataract. In Dhasdein. Not in Amberlight. There it would have been a message, from the city's, the House's core. Given to the Head, as answer, direction, warning. By the qherrique.

Ineffable, unanswerable surety. Not to judge, to guess, to wonder. To ask, and to *know*.

As I—I myself felt it. Once. Just once.

NOT A STUPID THING to be still boiling over, gods help and succor me, about this!

Arrival. Week 3.
Tellurith's Diary

I SHOULD HAVE known better. After asking Alkhes to deny his nature these interminable ten days, while the House's struggle to re-assemble itself has maddened me as well; then, with broken bones still paining him, to dress in Azo's good trousers and Zuri's best black coat, with the emerald ear-stud Iatha found in the Cataract mercenary's kist . . . Then put him with Sarth, looking like the Mother's choice in a Dhasdein officer's mulberry velvet overtunic, and take them both, with my steward and shop-Heads and their own husbands, may She pardon my imbecility, to supper. With Darthis.

Not an official banquet; Iskarda is too small. A good householder's courtesy, to save us the meal's work. In her own house, all dark panels, old, heavy furniture, polished, fragrant with years of beeswax and unrelenting use. Decorous as only a provincial upland house can be. Supper laid in the dining chamber, by men who were back on the men's side, invisible, before we approached the house.

So we pulled the heavy bronze chime at the defense gate, and trooped up the step, and Darthis' own daughter opened to us, acme of courtesy. And I led the men inside.

A Head's daughter, dark, stocky Eria is prenticed in protocol. But I should have known from the way she stuttered, before she got us into the dining chamber, and passed the introductions to Darthis.

Who had waited at the table's top, beside the big carven family-head's seat. Already I could understand Eria's consternation, and foresee an almighty counterclash.

Because there were eight guests, already. And the table was set for seven.

Thank the Mother, Eria remembered the women's names. When she stumbled, I beckoned the others forward, and said, "May I present Roskeran, Iatha's mate. And Huis, Hayras' mate. And these are my husbands. Sarth. Alkhes."

Tall, stooping, gentle Roskeran, self-effacing Huis had no idea where to look. Alkhes produced an officer's salute. Making himself troublecrew, on duty for the night. Sarth is acquiring my brazenness; he tendered a tower courtesy: to an unrelated woman entering. Eria . . .

Darthis, at least, did not swell. She simply seemed to solidify, without moving a muscle. Turning that lined, jowled, old-bronze face to adamant, thrusting at us the full force of a House-head's puissance. Overpowering refusal. Solid obloquy. Silent disgust.

"We have opened the tower," I said.

Had Zhee ever given me such a look, in the days when she mentored an un-mothered twenty-four year old, just catapulted into Head-ship, I would have died.

"It was a bad, cruel, unnatural way to live. It has cost too much hurt. Too many innocent ... children's lives."

Her eyes went past me. Up and down. Sarth is tower-trained, I only felt him catch his breath. Alkhes ...

Alkhes bristled like a Heartland tigercat, head back, jaw outthrust. "Some problem, madam?"

Bad enough he looked her in the eye, let be with such insolence. To address her outright, making the title an obscenity, in that voice ...

Mother bless, how that woman snubbed me! In retrospect, it was magnificent. She never bothered to retort. Just turned to Eria, and commanded, curt, majestic, "Call more plates."

To her bones she is traditionalist. Iskarda is a Telluir client village, she is my vassal. She kept her oath immaculate. She fed me at her table. She conversed. She never said a word against my policy, my unutterable perversion. And she kept her other trust. She ignored the men utterly. With armor-clad, earth-moving willpower, she made them not be there.

BY KICKING HIM under the table, I managed to gag Alkhes while we ate. A pincer grip above his good elbow smothered the after-blast, but on our own threshold it burst.

"Gods *damn* it, Tel!"

A passage splits Iskan houses into men's and women's sides; we were hard by the main dining chamber, filled by Zuri, Azo, Verrith, my personal troublecrew and their kin. Shia, her sister, Hanni and two nieces were next down, Iatha's family among the looms in the men's work-room opposite. I hissed at him like a viper.

"Shut up!"

I knew it was wrong before it came out. The silence hit like a slap in the face. His face.

"Caissyl ..."

He tore his hand away.

"Oh, how dare I talk? A bird-brain man. What would I know? Of all the fool stupid thoughtless—Tel, you idiot!"

"Then what would you have done? Backed off before we began?" I was too furious for explanation, let alone control. "Do you want to be back in the men's rooms, hauling water and peeling onions for the rest of your life?"

"I wouldn't insult my local command and outrage the whole village the first night! Gods, a drunken pentarch could do better—!"

"*I* could have done better! If you'd shut your stupid mouth—!"

"*My* mouth!" Suddenly it was quiet as I could ask. "You hear me, Tel. If she treats me like that again I'll ram her dinner down her throat!"

"Stop!"

We could not have been struck dumber by a lightning strike. He towered over us, in the fat-lamp's flutter looking ten feet tall.

"Tellurith?"

As ever, he was quiet. At his cruelest, tower manners never eluded Sarth. When we quarreled it had been by omission, in frigid malice. A glacier's ice.

"Oh, sweet Work-mother . . ."

I could not go on. It had been exhaustion in his voice. Distress. When all I wanted was to throw off my good clothes and forget the day's cloven dilemmas and the procession tomorrow would have waiting, and fall into bed.

But how are they to understand, if I never spell out what I think?

"Coming here, I thought about all this. And I made up my mind. We're going to change things, and not just leaving Amberlight. Or settling here. We'll bring men out of the towers, for good. We'll have a—a different life."

Silence. Fulminating, absorbing? Stubbornly resistant, in the dark?

"And this—now—may outrage the village, and upset the Ruand, but it's the strategy I chose. I thought it out before we went. And I decided—for your sakes—" it was hard to keep my voice steady, "that I would begin as I mean to go on. No compromise. And no backing down."

It was suddenly so quiet I could hear them breathe.

"There are other men here. If you want to renege—you can. But even for you—I can't."

Silence. Mother, I thought, and my soul ached. They don't see it. And if they don't . . .

"Tel . . ."

Alkhes' voice. Husky. Suspiciously soft. Head down, guilty as a beaten dog. Not daring to grope for my hand.

I caught at it, pulling him round. Catching Sarth, as in turn I heard the breath that spoke clearer than words, deciphered through years' experience. Equal shame. Equal guilt.

"*Don't* blame yourselves. And *don't* make any more of it. Can we just," suddenly I was more than bone weary, "go to bed?"

Settling. Week 5.
Journal kept by Sarth

So MUCH that Tellurith does I miss. Or misunderstand. That supper. What she has already done, here in the House. Not just settling the women into new precedences, new trades, no longer shaper and power-worker, but surveyor, timber-cutter, carpenter. Stone-mason, builder, child-carer, cook.

But including men as well.

Perhaps it is that everyone who came was already disposed to, determined on change. But it still astounds me, that Charras trusted me to yoke and drive her bullocks today. That burly taciturn Quetho should pass on the adze when she took a break and just grunt, "Down that end there. Watch the knots." It still amazes me, that muscles trained in the gymnasium prove effective for anything else.

And I have only just fathomed all those extra delays on the road, negotiating with Korite farmers at what I find, now, were holdings of Telluir House. Source of winter provisions, grain, hay. Timber. And young folk, free after harvest, trickling up for hire.

Paid from our folk's loot in that chaos when the hill fell, shattering three armies along with Amberlight. Which spoils include, I learn, ten chests of Cataract silver: mercenaries' pay.

But I understand too why from dawn to dark Tellurith has been out with us, men and women, hire and House-folk alike. Using pick and cutter on a foundation, guiding timber over the sawpit; helping unload logs, adding the day-wages with Hanni. Not leading, not obvious, but unrelentingly there.

She is using Iskarda's ways against them. I recall those sentences clipped in half, those eyes dropped in mid-glower. Traditionalists, to their back-teeth. Obdurate, therefore, against us: the men. Especially us. Alkhes and me. And as obdurate in their loyalty. They are Telluir vassals. It would break their honor, to flout her in person. To throw us out.

Trouble, therefore, has stayed minor. A broken wheel, slipped loads, a worker hurt. Except in our own bed.

The Mother knows, it is big enough. An old four-poster with corners thick as unshaped trees, it could sleep six uncrowded, and possibly it has. There are linen sheets, furs, a brazier, if not the permeating qherrique, that could leave you in shirt-sleeves at mid-winter. And trouble underneath.

For me, to swing an axe for firewood is exhilaration. To peel a turnip, to mind a child, is liberty. Tellurith remains a leader, if not in a House. But Alkhes was—is—a soldier. A general. Bred to that strange world where men rule. The first time Zariah asked him to stir a cook-pot—

By the Mother's luck she had already turned away. I had time to set chopped onions aside and murmur, "Did you jar that arm?"

His eyes whipped round. Slitted, blazing black. I think he nearly spat. Words, if nothing else.

"I can do it, if it's too bad."

He gave me that trademark lightning glare and snatched the spoon in his left hand.

I chopped onions and tried for words to defuse the hush: Your arm is still splinted. You aren't fit to use a kitchen knife, let alone an axe. Your own trades are lost. Not only is there nobody here to command, there is nobody to kill, and almost nothing to fight. To do this is not ignominy. It's value, use, respect.

"It's getting late," I said. "Zuri will be looking for you." He can patrol and consult with the troublecrew, if nothing else.

I tried a glance, and earned myself another glare. And then a furiously presented back.

I can bear it for myself. But if he looses that venom on Tellurith …

Give the Mother thanks, not yet. Sullen, sour, unkind between the sheets as a thundercloud, but nothing more. She must know, from the way she suffers it. He resents his limits, I expect. I know he resents me. And I think, somewhere he cannot yet look, he resents Tellurith.

Most of all, he resents sharing her.

Am I so different? How long is it since she would lie in my arms, curled in the big Tower window, and pour her heart out half a night? Shared trouble and decision, sweeter than union of the flesh. He and I have both known that. And can no longer be her one ear, her sole confidant.

And with minds' sharing goes the body's. Including sex.

LITTLE CHANCE OF THAT while all of us were dead on our feet. But with half a moon gone, the plots and work-crews are settled, new houses planned, folk beginning to find their place. We took a break at the moon-turn, for hirecrew to visit home. And it left Tellurith with energy too.

So in bed last night, the house quiet, the moon's great silver blossom in the narrow window, she turned over and began to caress Alkhes.

I gave fresh thanks for Tower discipline, and prepared to re-smother the snakes in my own flesh. We sleep now with Tellurith between us. But when I muttered about fuel for the morning and began to ease out my side, she rolled back and caught my hair.

"Wait, Sarth."

I froze. He'll kill me, I thought. At a stroke.

"I said I'd marry you both. I meant what I said."

Any Tower boy knows before puberty that he may be bedded by more than one wife at once. And many of us, to say it again, have shared with other men. Not, evidently, Alkhes.

He gave one snort and leapt clear out of the furs. "Curse it, Tellurith!"

"Alkhes!"

It stopped him in his tracks. She came upright, furs cascading, all chemise and naked breast, the merest hiss, but the voice of a Head.

"I said we'd change things. I meant this as well."

He managed three steps before she spoke again.

"Caissyl," it was so quiet, and it froze my backbone. "If you walk out now, you walk out for good."

The moon-shadow sketched his pale, quivering shape. Her hand trembled on my hair. My own heart was in my teeth. No, I wanted to cry, do anything but this with him. Don't push him in a corner. Don't make his pride the price of your bluff.

"Alkhes?"

Who but a Head could juggle that intonation, a knife-edge between command, plea, threat? Who but a Head would have the timing, at the precise moment before one of them broke?

He spun on his heel. His breath flew, a sharp white gust. "Gods *damn* it, Tel!"

"CAISSYL, TRULY, it's not difficult." She had him in her arms, coaxing. I could feel his outrage clean through the bed. "I want you both. Is that so very bad?" A thread of laughter now. "Your imagination's never failed me before . . ."

"Tel." He was still shaking, but it had a frail, steely quiet. "I can sleep like this. I can cope with—wanting you and not—with—missing out. I can't," it started rising, "make love to you with an audience like a g-goddamn whore!"

Her silence should have been a slap in the face. I did feel him twist.

All three of us breathed. The moon laid its silver path across the boards.

Very softly, she said, "Caissyl—"

"Oh, Tel . . . No . . ."

In a moment they would be severed past recovery. Already it was beyond words. I rolled in behind her, laid my lips against her neck, through the storm of copper-brown hair. Slid my arms around her, and prayed to the Mother as I cupped her breasts.

She curved back against me, memories of that movement waking like a burn. Then she caught his head and pulled him to her, and before she kissed him, whispered, " . . . just like this."

Even then, it might have been all right. Had he not, as he calls it, failed.

WHEN HE PLUNGED from the bed she let him go. The door slammed to shake the king-stones, she just sat up. A stir all down the passageway, snap of crossed challenges with troublecrew, the outer door's diminished Bang! She flung the covers back and for the first time in my life I baulked a woman's will.

"No." I caught her wrist at the limits of a snatch. "Let him go."

Her breath went in and my backbone quailed. After everything, she is a Head.

So at such a moment, she remembers difference. Policy. Change.

"Can you tell me," level, more dangerous, "why?"

But not abuse, denial, a wrench away. Mother knows, grandmother Zhee would have . . . I could only say, stupidly, "Tellurith—he's not like us."

Silence. The words in process. Not like us, Amberlight, men in Amberlight, she and I? Therefore I did not, she did not understand him? So I could give orders, could not give orders? Could, could not explain?

"I can't—say if it's right. Why it's right. I just feel—let it be."

Still breathing. Weighing all that, my possible truth, my possible interest, the shape of my intuition. Not, after all, an answer from the qherrique.

Then stiffening, disengaging, a quick, "Wait," as she went to the door. Summons to Desis, the night's sentry, soft words. An endless pause.

I could not bear it. I was behind her when Desis came back, cat-foot, breathing from the darkness, "They saw him go into the byre."

Where we keep three bullock teams; and his horse.

I felt her stiffen, the jerk of breath. The long, long hesitation before its release.

"If he comes out . . . Let me know at once."

She swung around, clutching for my wrist, a shadow in the moonlight, with undone rivers of hair and great shadow pools for eyes. "Oh, Sarth." Pressed against me, head on my chest, her whole weight in the embrace. Breasts heaving, choking, with the force of smothered sobs.

"If I could just be *sure*—of what I'm doing!"

I held her with one arm, and smoothed the other hand over her hair. I did not say, How many of us ever had such surety? I did not babble easy comfort, that he would understand, come back, change his mind. Who was I to know that? I drew her close, and held her; and foresaw another night that would end with her comfort, and my body aching, as so often in the Tower. And remembered those were the good times, and did not complain.

AND IN THE GRAY first light I said, "Let me go to him."

She stared at me, gummy-lashed, red-eyed. Weighing it again, like a general. A Head.

Then with a funny jerk of the mouth, reached for the belt-purse hung at the bed-head. Shook out a silver darrin, flipped it in the air. Said, "Ship, you go. Face, me."

Reduced to such unreasoned, such sheer chance decision. She lifted her hand. And the ship-shape badge of Cataract glittered on the fur.

Outside it was weirdly still. With no work for the day, all the teams were home abed. The stock-tenders had dallied too. In the great curve of hillside Iskarda slept, faded paint, grainy brown timbers pure-etched in the icy mountain dawn. Below me, the fallow-brown patchwork of River plain was just gilded, here and there, with unhindered light. Cocks crowed. Bouncing down the stony path, the feed bucket banged my leg.

He flung back the byre door almost in my face, I grabbed by reflex and he jumped the same way, clear into the wall.

"Get away from me!"

Probably I was lucky not to get killed. He froze there, the broken arm shielded behind the good. He has the rib bandages off now; the crouch was ready to strike. The face was something else.

Inch by inch, I eased the bucket down. Think, I swore at myself, what you're doing. This is not a boy in a Tower in Amberlight.

I said, "Is your arm all right?"

The eyes focused. Black as space, but no longer lost.

"Did you shick her instead?"

River-word. Meaning, to mate with beasts.

"If you were good for anything else—"

Once in a life, perhaps, the Mother gives such vision, without the qherrique.

But I had it, in the second he pushed himself off the wall. Such loathing, such hatred. Such a violence of bitterness. But not aimed at me.

I said, "That happened my first night."

And despite it all, he was listening too. His mouth came open. His foot landed short.

"With Tellurith. Telluir House Head. My first time with a woman. My first wife."

The pose fixed. Not so much stunned as thunderstruck.

"You were raised a soldier. To give orders. To fight. I was bred to tend, to please a woman. It was my whole life."

The eyes were glazed, black as midwinter ice. How thick, I did not have time to wonder, was its shell?

"She said, It doesn't matter. We can try again."

"So goddamn *kind*."

The flick of a whip-cut. He is not one to forgive mistakes.

Nor am I one to avoid them. I glanced from him to the byre door and back and raised my brows.

You could have gone. You had the horse here. You had all night.

He uncoiled off the wall in one long lunge and spat, "You *bastard*!" and slapped my face.

A year passed in a heartbeat's amber-drop. Time to feel the blow's weight and have muscles plunge for recoil and check at impotence's rage and still find space to think before the sting began. Before the impact recoiled on him.

He had jerked his hand back. Shrunk back, the eyes enormous. All the rage was gone.

My nose stung. My fists dug nails through my flesh. My brain was one white glare that lit his waiting like a qherrique flame.

We both knew I could not fight with hands: that the blow's real shame was his. And he knew I could strike back, three times harder. With my tongue.

So he was waiting. To make expiation. To be hurt.

To dissolve his guilt.

I shoved the bucket toward him and said, "Feed your horse."

When Hafas House blew up its mine, the hillside fell like that. Slowly, irretrievably, crumbling, a House, a world collapsing, before my eyes.

Mother pity me, I am far crueler than I ever guessed.

Because I let it go another twenty heartbeats, before I took the bucket in one hand and the man in the other and kicked open the byre door.

Inside it was still dusk. Left-hand, the bulk of bullock-pens, topped by flicking horns, ears, heads; right-hand, the horse's stall. Slatted dark of rails, liquid eye. He sagged against the stall-side, head bowed in the good arm. A fighter, a soldier wounded mortally.

The bullocks shifted, smelling feed, the horse stretched and slobbered and blew on me. I tipped oats in the manger. Then I touched his shoulder, and said, "Come home, before you freeze."

I thought he would refuse. But then he gathered himself. Pivoted drunkenly against the rail. It came hoarsely, no more than a whisper.

"Why?"

Why come home? But he knew that. He had not left. It was, by default, surrender. Admission was only a matter of time.

The kindness?

And the cruelty. Both from the same source.

I said, "I learnt in a different school."

Half-frozen, and shaking, and wracked by hurts and hatred as a crippled scorpion, he kept his wits. I saw him work it out, as I had. A shared skill. A different school. Fighting. With tongue or sword. So what I had said— each thing I said—had not been kindness, but a blow. Deliberate.

He lifted his face, an effort deliberate as mine. He was trembling so hard his very lips shook. But he met my eyes.

Settling. Week 5.

Meditations. Alkhes-Assandar

I COULD HAVE borne it, if he'd flayed me. Everything would have cancelled out. But to have him kind . . .

Gods, give thanks I'm married to him. What would he be as an enemy?

I was so cold my gut shook, and the feelings—the first sensation, after a bad wound. The madness. Like a crippled scorpion. But in the end, I understood.

That his school was the harder. No honor, no surrender, no mercy. Even when you win.

I managed to look up at him. At the very worst, I've looked losing in the eye.

He's so beautiful. Curse that word, but it's the only one. In a dirty stable-coat and his hair tangled everywhere. He deserves her. That perfect face, those honey-gold lion's eyes. Looking down at me, like some sad, stern, incorruptible hanging judge.

Then he grabbed me by both shoulders and burst out, "Ah, don't, Alkhes!"

As if *I* was hurting *him*.

Somehow, to have him touch me this time didn't matter. "Don't what?" I said. Be hung, I think I was almost in tears.

"Don't . . ." He let go. Pushed his hair back. The light was better. Damn him too. Beautiful. And so tired.

"Alkhes. Could you try to—explain?"

Explain. When everything that made you a man—command, war, unarmed combat—is gone. When the one thing left is a woman. And then you fall apart with her.

"Did I jar your arm?"

He had hold of me again. As if I was an eggshell. Yet his hands felt strong. And I had the weirdest—the maddest—urge to lean on him, to let him hold me . . . As if I was a baby. A mewling woman. Gods . . .

Does he hold her like that?

You can lean, if you're a woman. And hold, I saw Iatha do it, with Tellurith. Have seen Tellurith do it, with Zariah, when her daughter slipped and the cutter sliced her arm. Why not men?

"It's understood, in the Tower. That women may want—expect—to share." He took a little breath. "Just as it's understood that—there's more than coupling to sex."

He was doing it again. Explaining himself to understand me. And perhaps it was in kindness this time, but when you prick a lamed horse, he kicks.

I said, "Like they understood sons?"

How *could* I have said that? When I knew, I *knew* about his children. I did do the grabbing that time. "Damn," I said, "I'm sorry, I'm sorry, forget that, I'm sorry, Sarth . . ."

I had a handful of coat. He looked down, I let go in a hurry. For a moment he looked . . . I don't know. I did know what I had to do.

I said, "For men out here—coupling *is* sex. And sex—"it was like a bone in the throat "—winning—succeeding—doing sex properly is . . . If you fail—you're not a man."

I read it plain this time. Bewilderment. Absolute disbelief.

"Being a man. The whole of being a man—depends on that?"

Curse that face of his. How do you resent pity from a god?

"But . . ." He gave his head a jerk. "You're trained troublecrew. You have war-skills and River lore; you had the courage to come here, you can change and learn and—" he turned his face away. I could barely hear.

"And you have wits."

And he was a bed-toy, good for nothing but sex.

I don't think I ever saw our blindnesses so clear. Both of us thinking, in our own ways, that what we were, all we were, was sex. Both of us thinking she valued the other for what we weren't. Both of us—in that case—wrong.

It costs—it hurts—to shuck out of a life. I thought resigning a command was hard. Leaving Amberlight. This will mean rebuilding myself. Tearing up what you build on, without ever having to think what it is.

But I had a place to start.

I took a handful of coat. He twitched.

"You learnt in a different school." It surprises me that it came out so clear. "But you did learn."

The first time I had managed his code. There was surprise. And then the grayness lightened in his face.

Not just that I had said, You are a man too. You are as good as me. You think yourself stupid, but you're not. But also: I've heard what you said. I'll come back. I'll try.

I got a step away from the stall. My legs were like water. I saw him put a hand out. Pull it back. Then he put the whole arm round me. And said—said . . .

The bastard. I swear he uses witchery?

"In my school," he said, "men can lean."

Settling. Week 5.
Tellurith's Diary

MOTHER, DO YOU arrange reality so that no times ever fall convenient? Or is that your special gift to Heads? To have my husbands reappear just when I chew off my last fingernail; and when I rush to anticipate Shia in the kitchen, have Hanni and Desis arrive precisely as I manage to wake the fire? And then hurry me off to the dormitories, because Hayras' daughter has woken with a fever that Caitha thinks could be strangle-cough. In which case we may be confronting a plague.

Which with no qherrique to consult means quarantine, fret and sweat it out, unholy reshufflings of half the House into new quarters. So when I did get home, Alkhes had gone.

While Sarth, looking wan and transparent as any mother after a hard birthing, would say only, "He wanted to think. No, he ate. He drank. He put warm clothes on. He's all right."

So the furor re-closed round me, with no chance to cry, Is he going, is he staying? What did you say, what did he say? Think about what?

Where he went, I found all too soon. Up to the outcrop above the quarry, the area's lookout post.

For a soldier, natural enough. The place is a magnet for anyone wanting perspective and privacy. Right atop the crest, a bastion of creamy gray rock, a cluster of low-growing, pure white snow-helliens behind its parapet. You can sit in natural hollows or on backside-polished boulders, and gaze through the silver-green hellien foliage across the width of the River-world, sunk in fathoms of empty air, while you let a morning, a day, a sun-cycle roll away.

Where Iskarda's women have gone from time immemorial, for ceremonies, or meditation, or mere solitude in the Dark. Where my husband, Mother help me, homed in his own necessity. Straight into Darthis.

"Tel, I didn't see her. I swear, I didn't know she was there!"

"Caissyl, of course not." I put my arms around him and got him to sit at last, on the stool beside the hearth. Iatha, Caitha, Zuri, Quetho, Hanni made a silent chorus of catastrophe behind me. And at my shoulder, Sarth.

"You couldn't have known, nobody could." Somebody took the filthy, chilly cloak away. Somebody else began, very quietly, to build up the fire. "As the Mother sees me, nobody blames you. Can you just tell me what she said?"

He drew a great breath and straightened, scrubbing at his eyes like a wept-out child. Then he dropped the hand, and there was no child in that stare.

"She wouldn't let me go."

My back went stiff as Zuri's. If she thinks she can take the old ways so far as man-theft, I wanted to squawk, she can think again!

"I knew it was a special place the minute I—she had her back to me. On a rock. I thought she *was* a rock. I nearly jumped out of my skin. Started to apologize. She said, 'Stay.'"

Like, his eyes told me, a Head to an underling. Or a dog.

"She asked where I came from. What I . . . was. How I . . . married you."

He stuck. An arm came over my shoulder, holding a hot mug of tea. He nursed it, but his eyes never left me. Even when the blood rose in his face.

"She asked—what I was doing out of a tower."

And, I thought resignedly, you told her to go to—

"I said, 'Telluir's Head told you. She has pulled them down.'"

Mercifully, Iatha kept quiet.

"She said, 'Why?'"

Seeking truth from the mouths of babes. Mother blast her, I thought.

"What did you say?"

He scowled into the cup. The wing of dark hair, drying now, frayed into his eyes. "I—uh—" He set the cup down. That look signaled urgently: Not here. Not now.

"This is a House matter, Alkhes."

I could not make it clearer without gross insult. The others were also on trial. I had no right to shut them out.

He twisted where he sat. Then he gritted his teeth, and looked past me. With more than apology. With dread.

"I tried to explain. That it was unjust. Cruel. Unnatural." He braced himself. "And . . . I told her about your sons."

I swiveled. All the women's eyes followed mine. Sarth had backed a step across the fireplace, but he was not looking at us.

"I meant it for an example. A defense." He had not moved, but the tone was urgent as a leap. "I never meant—!"

I got up and took two strides away. Put my hand on Sarth, as if to run off the lightning bolt. He was rigid. Locked in tower discipline, face a mask only lightning would break.

"What did she say?"

Tel, his eyes begged. But it was too late for mercy now.

"She . . . said: *Of course, they lifted the curse.*"

If Sarth did not know the backwoods, he knew what sort of thing I expected. But I was the one who flinched.

"I didn't know what she was talking about!" Alkhes came off the stool, half across the fireplace. "I didn't—"

The feel of Sarth's side told me why he stopped.

I could have halted it there; could have saved Sarth the worst. I knew there was to be a worst. But to shield him was also to degrade him, to count his courage, his endurance less than a woman's. Again, to shut him out.

I said, "Go on."

For an instant that black stare cried, Betrayer! Then he drew himself up.

"I said, 'What ?' I didn't understand. And she . . . said, *Three times a misbegetting. A curse. It endangers the House. You must wipe out the—sire.*"

His voice wobbled, all the women winced. Only Sarth did not move, and looking up at him I could have cried. Because he had gone away as he had the day Alkhes came, into some fastness, invulnerable, impenetrable, that left us a block of breathing wood.

"Tel, she didn't mean it, did she? She couldn't—gods!"

"This is the backwoods, Alkhes." I shoved a hand under Sarth's jacket as if I could physically detain him, grasp his flesh, the being's shell. "You have to expect that sort of—!"

"You think I didn't? They expose hare-lipped babies in Verrain. But this!"

"What did you say to her?" Warm muscle under my hand, solid, familiar bone. But not Sarth. I had to talk or else break down. "Did you argue? You didn't try to—"

"I was knocked silly, I just wanted to get away. But, Tel," he reached out, pure panic. "She said when I was going, *I have a duty to the House-head too.*"

"Sweet Work-mother!" Iatha's consternation answered mine. A man disintegrating in front of us, a sick child across hill, a possible plague ahead, and now, the worst of all pending confrontations. Not merely revolution, but blasphemy. Could it have found a better time?

BUT IT WAS A HOUSE CRISIS, waking reflexes from other days. I shot Zuri off to arrange lookouts, Quetho to warn Hayras, Iatha to muzzle everyone else. Hanni was already spilling slates across the only writing surface, the kitchen table's wide scrubbed planks. The others would return to make my court. Shia would manage the hearth—

Shia had taken the day off too, with a niece who wanted to walk the hills.

I turned on Sarth and gave him a quick shove; as if protocol was the only trouble, and nothing—nothing!—else was wrong.

"Put the kettle back on. Get that peppermint tea. See if there's wine left. The good cups . . ."

It was like pushing a cliff. I snapped, "Sarth?"

"You heard." The voice came out of that fastness. Remote, alien. "I am more than a provocation. I'm a curse. I'll contaminate the House."

My splendid, beloved man, regained, reclaimed. And now reduced to this.

The anger shot up in me like a veritable qherrique blast. "*Rot* the House!" I bawled. "The House fell with Amberlight! This is blighted archaic nonsense—now find those cups!"

He opened his mouth. Then tower discipline itself cracked, the ice-face disintegrated, and the living man looked out at me, shaken, scandalized, laughing, through those startled topaz eyes.

"Oh . . . Tellurith!" he said quakily.

And went after the cups.

SHE MADE US WAIT, of course, with malice certainly aforethought, until mid-afternoon, time of work-lulls and courtesy calls. She brought an entourage of elders, predictably. I had time to relish their coming discomposure while I wrestled Sarth in the kitchen doorway, hissing, "Get back in there!"

He gave me one desperate look: Don't risk it, don't insult them, I'll bungle it, don't lay the House's honor on me. Alkhes would have raged and raved; when I growled, "Don't you drop a thing!" Sarth went without a word.

Sure enough, the first bristle among the elders told me his mere presence was less insult than tactical point; they had not thought to damn my blasphemy to its face. When Iatha had settled them, and I said, "Sarth, will you bring tea?" for one delirious moment I thought they would all walk out.

Darthis was of sterner forging. When he set a cup at her very elbow, it never touched her monumental calm. So finally, with Sarth back at the hearth-side, I had to open the dance.

"To what do I owe this honor, Ruand?"

She sipped the tea. Inclined her head, stately, decorous compliment; she would not cede him even that much spite.

"Ruand," she answered, "I have a duty to Telluir House."

Settling. Week 5.

Meditations. Alkhes-Assandar

LIVING WITH HER, watching her use those maddening passive tactics, you forget that Tellurith's a strategist first. A political strategist. All I could think, while that woman planted herself like a rock settling was, Here it comes. Disaster. And there's nothing I can do.

When she spoke, Tellurith just inclined her head and looked polite. Second nature. House-heads did it with everyone from apprentice Crafters to visiting kinglets. Fifty times a day.

"For a vassal, my door is always open. Especially to Iskarda's Ruand."

I knew enough to know they were tossing obligations. And that the skirmish had gone to Tellurith.

Darthis drank her tea. "It has come to me," masterly, I have to admit, you'd get no better sidestep from a courtier, "that Telluir House has suffered an—affliction. Blossoms lost in the bud."

She must have known I would spring the ambush. She must have trusted I'd tell truth, knowing the thing's own weight. And I had to feel Sarth go away beside me, the way he had when I told them. *Why* did I never learn to hold my tongue!

"The Mother waxes." Tellurith never flinched. "The Mother wanes."

"The Mother is not wont to have her omens lost."

"I am the Head of Telluir House. It was I who spoke—and listened—to the qherrique."

Turn looks like that to sword-blades, you'd drop an army at a slash.

Darthis folded her arms. A rock, poised to roll.

"I am Telluir House's vassal. I am Iskarda's Ruand." Tellurith inclined her head. The jaw's tension said it was a flanking maneuver. "I ask, What befell Amberlight?"

This code takes unraveling too: as vassal, she had right to query her protector. As Iskarda's Ruand, she had right to protect her folk. On those credentials, she was challenging: if you read the qherrique, the voice of the Mother, and three sons were truly not a pestilence—why did your city fall?

"It was the will of the Mother," Tellurith said.

You'll get as pretty a bromide out of any River-lord's priest when a flood takes your cow. Trying not to let my lip curl, I remembered: Darthis is a traditionalist. The one riposte she couldn't block.

"Assuredly." Head bent, meek as a temple neophyte. "I am a village Ruand. But one who heard the qherrique can tell us: *why* was it the Mother's will?"

All the Iskardan faces said, Get out of *that*. Sarth nearly disappeared into the hearthstones. And Tellurith, bless her, the lovely bitch didn't crack a smirk.

"We abused the qherrique. We sold it to those who abused it. Who used it for blood-sorcery, for battles, to murder and enslave. So the River rose against us. And the qherrique used them for its own salvation. *It destroyed Amberlight.*"

How, after her opening gambit, could Darthis retort, You're a liar?

Give her this, she's a veteran. Presently, she said, "Will my House-head enlighten me wholly? How—could this be?"

And Tellurith, the damned woman, said, "Alkhes, will you come here?"

Even Iatha thought she'd ruined it. All those five strides across eternity, I was thinking, they'll get up and go.

They sat. I stood by Tellurith's shoulder. Man's place. I had to remember it was a revolution I was there at all.

"The River," Tellurith said, "sent Alkhes to Amberlight. As agitator, as spy. A River-quarter gang ambushed him. We saved him. Because the qherrique told me, *It matters, if he dies.*"

No one had to wonder if she was telling the truth.

"He had lost his memory. He had lost his name. When he asked for one, the qherrique told me: *Call him, Alkhes.*"

All the faces changed. Maybe, it was awe, after the shock.

"But when a Cataract assassin aimed for me at Diaman House-head's funeral," sacrilege, all the Iskardans gasped, "he saved my life. And then, I think—the qherrique told him who he was."

Darthis was not blinking. But her eyes had a certain glaze.

"So he went back to Dhasdein. Having—obligations. And knowing the River was fixed on destroying us—he tried to save what he could of Amberlight."

Damn, it's worse than a punishment parade to have your life hung out like washing. I thought of sentry duty in Riversend, out-of-town brats giggling, trying to look up your corselet. I hope I kept my face.

"So we lost the city. And the Houses. Until at the last, the qherrique bade me surrender. And I did as it said."

Now even Darthis stared. Tellurith looked back at her. A consummate orator, playing her pauses as exquisitely as her audience.

"But when Alkhes asked, Shall I go to the mother-face? Can men cut qherrique? It answered, *Yes*."

Darthis was too controlled. It was the second at her elbow who burst out, "Answer? Pigwash! Men can't hear qherrique!"

Tellurith gave them a stare to kneecap an imperial dekarch. "*I* have seen this man bespeak the qherrique. And it heard."

They were vassals, peasants, traditionalists. They sat and goggled. Trying to re-frame the world.

Tellurith turned to me. When she put a hand on me I nearly jumped a spearlength myself.

"For its own plan, the qherrique used us both. But at the end . . ."

She stopped.

"At the end—when the hill—it saved him. It told him, *Run*." A tiny pause. As if she braced herself. "And at the very end—it spoke to me. It said: *Daughter, be blessed*."

And the break in her voice nobody could ever counterfeit.

"That is why," looking back at Darthis, "I am sure the Mother's omens were no curse. And that it was the Mother's will which brought the fall of Amberlight."

Her hand was still planted firmly on my hip. Clearer than a battle fanfare, her stare said: And it is the Mother's will I have two husbands, and I flaunt them here before you. Because the one beyond doubt bears Her blessing. And the other, as manifestly, is not cursed.

I swear, only Tellurith could pull a double victory from a losing fight. When Darthis took her cohorts off, they still looked as if they had been hit over their collective heads. But gods defend me: some of the looks I got across those shoulders said more than, Foreigner. God-touched. Freak.

Some were reverent.

III

Settling. Week 8.
Tellurith's Diary

SHAMEFUL TO SQUANDER such a leverage so easily, but with an epidemic
in the offing, what could I do? Had Darthis guessed at that . . . And it was
thrifty, at least, to bring off my two men under the one shield. I only hope
that Darthis, when she recovers, will not devise some hill-felling counter-
stroke.

Because we cannot truly alienate her. When our daughters are grown,
when, I dream, we no longer marry House fashion, so far more men will
be needed—when, in any case, the blood wants widening—then Iskarda
must provide their mates.

MEANWHILE WE HAVE an epidemic, if not strangle-cough; some sort of
mountain fever, Caitha says, which brings us outsiders down in sneezing,
aching heaps. The medicine store is stripped; they are down to boiled willow-
tea for the joints and hellien-leaf steam for the chest. The children are the
worst. Yet every woman who takes to her bed is another empty worker's
place, another house delayed. And we are nearer winter by another day.

Which has thrown most of the nursing onto the men; so I would
hardly have seen my husbands this last half-moon, even had I not been
ears under in housing plans.

The houses have been the most long-drawn change of all. Women from
Downhill, women from Uphill, shattered clan affiliations to somehow
merge, old-style Iskardan houses to adapt. And men to fit as well. "Not
a tower, no," said Ahio, rubbing her ruin of an ear; memento from the
shaper's shop. "But Mother, how's a woman to bed her husband when he's
running all over the house? What if he's married out of the house? Give
'em a place of their own and let us go to them."

So the new houses are usually cluster-shape: suites of rooms for work,
for men, women, children, sub-sets of clan or kin, about a central kitchen-

hall, store-rooms outermost, to chill perishables. Stone outer walls, mostly: with arrow-slit windows, and the sort of vantage point where you can use a light gun, as well as a bow.

This house, though, is Iskardan built. Meant for a single two or three generation family, and hence segregated except for the kitchen. Which is useless to me, who needs a workplace and meeting-room, and cannot make it among the looms.

Nor, when the time came, would my household disperse. So Charras, who has become our architect, has designed outliers and wings, and what looks alarmingly like a perimeter wall, with storehouses and a couple of byres inside. And now it will be a household, if not a House. My troublecrew and their kin in the uphill wing, and Iatha's folk across the hall, Shia and Hanni's suites where the old weaving-room was; my own work-room next the kitchen, for warmth, and the old dining chamber for a council place. My—our—sleeping quarters, just behind that, will be the only thing unchanged; since, as Charras said, "I'd uproot the hill before I tried to shift that bed of yours."

This afternoon has shifted almost everything else.

CHARRAS HALED me from pay tallies at Zariah's house, amid a roomful of hacking, coughing toddlers and filthy, harried men. They had half the house gutted, on a dour, overcast autumn day; no light weather, up here in Iskarda. We had just settled an underground store-room entrance; after all, the cave is there; and were on to heating pipes when Verrith came striding through the stone-dust, calling, "Ruand! There's a new one in!"

The Korite youngsters' influx has masked a steady dribble of other strangers; fugitives, afterthoughts, slipping away from our old world. The River, Amberlight. And of course their news must be sifted, though their expectation, if not need, to see Telluir's Head in person was growing near ritual. I opened my mouth to say, Iatha can handle this. Verrith said, too blank-faced, "Desis said, Get you."

I shut my mouth and moved.

Desis had taken the incomer to Quetho's house, the only place out of quarantine. She was hunched over the makeshift hearth, a fiery silhouette; elbows, Crafter's plait, Dhasdein soldier's cloak. Then she rose and turned and time ran widdershins.

"You," I said, like the veriest numbskull. "You're dead."

"Ruand." Not a House or Craft greeting; a Navy salute. Everything else, the sharp nose, the tawny eyes, the crinkled Amberlight hair, a perfect duplicate. Except the face, drawn with exhaustion; sharpening, as I looked, with something else.

"That was my sister, Ruand."

"But—!"

"My mother went with *Wasp*. Yes."

I opened my eyes in time to see her within a hairsbreadth of breaking Navy stance and springing to hold me up. "Ah, Ruand . . ."

I had grieved, of course I grieved, as we all had for *Wasp*, most gallant of Navy craft, lost in the last battle against the massed galleys of Dhasdein. And the family with her, mother, sisters, all the precious command chain; except the youngest daughter, who had potential to be a cutter, who had come into the House the season before.

Who died in my arms, during the city's fall.

"But how did *you*—"

She had been wounded all but mortally in the ship's loss. Dragged ashore by Dhasdein marines among their own casualties, still lying, when the city fell, in a hospital tent. Struggling back to convalescence in a world from which her world had gone.

"They want to keep the Houses up; Terraqa and Jerrish. But without the pearl-rock . . ."

The curl of her nostrils said the rest. Would she putter about a wharf or vie for copper fiels in a rowing boat amid the ragged longshoremen of a city that no longer tithed, and graced, and centered the River's world?

And she had another, closer reason for coming after us.

They had been a well-to-do Telluir clan, already with their own modest men's tower just down the hill. As a cutter, her sister might have been their foothold inside the House itself. Mother knows, they paid a bankruptcy price, for Khira to marry there. To share marriage-ties with the very Head.

In the long run, it was probably all that saved Sarth from the cataclysm of divorce.

My household had gathered already: Iatha to deputize, Hanni with the slate for notes; Zuri, more granite-like than usual. Of course, they knew. When does a House-head expect privacy?

I said, "Your father's here."

"M-my—"

This one had known too. Yet for all she had gone through, a Navy officer, she stuttered on the word.

"You needn't see him yet. I thought you might like to know he was safe." How scurrilously easy it is, in possession, to be generous. "Sit down, first, and get warm. And give me the Riverword, while they make you something to eat."

I could feel Charras' scowl on my back. Neglect the house for a Head to play secretary? Zuri's too: Usurp troublecrew's place? But the incomer, Navy by skill and blood, turned to business with relief.

Damas and Eutharie, the chief surviving House-heads, were bent on preserving the forms without the substance of Amberlight, from tithes on the Kora grain to rebuilt towers. There was no real resistance. The sack had decimated River Quarter; the Downhill clan folk who chose to stay had fallen in, willy-nilly. It was, and again the faint curl of the lip spoke her opinion, their only choice.

However paltry, there was trade to offer tolls; there were soldiers, deserters, wounded straggling home, who needed quarters and food. There was a trickle of caravan commerce upriver from Verrain, and another of Heartland exotics, mahogany, ivory, coming down from Cataract.

"Assassination, faction battles, civil war up there." Had she been a River Quarter stevedore, she would have smacked her lips. "Seems Dinda was worse than most."

Dinda being Cataract's half-crazy military tyrant, who had died among the first in the fall of Amberlight. And being from a line of military tyrants, had left the city to settle his successor in a more than usually bloody way.

"Shuya's got her hands full with an Oasis uprising; they say she's lost another five caravans."

President of Verrain, our downstream neighbor; whose wealth comes cross-desert from the Oases, gold freighted in on the endless camel caravans, to sustain the forty Families, over whom she ruled by uneasy consent. And, as with the Oases, by plentiful coercion. For which she had used qherrique. Before I recalled we used to supply her, I had almost answered, Good.

"And Dhasdein?"

She frowned. The impersonal talk had relaxed her; it was the shrewd, informed judgment of a politics-reader, a report such as any officer might give her Head.

"No trouble in the colonies. No word that the Emperor wanted to hang his general, or crucify the officers, or even fell down and foamed. He's got his busted army back. There's trade, or at least, they're buying some timber. But . . ."

But Dhasdein was the River's strongest state, whose army and navy had been the mainspring of our overthrow. Whose might had been hurled down in turn. Whose general had absconded with the enemy. Surely, one might expect more action from Dhasdein?

Such worries are for House-heads, to gnaw the vitals in some sleepless morning watch. I said, "Your news is precious." With a Navy officer, no call for more. "Iatha, will you see to Tez here?" Find what she needed, what she had brought—some came with what they stood in, some lacked shoes to stand—where she could be quartered, what she was good for now. Despite everything, I could not withhold a smile.

"I'm so glad to know you're safe. To have someone here from *Wasp*."

To keep the honor, and the memory, and the family alive.

We had both risen. The smile came back to me, but with constraint. "Ah—Ruand—"

"Your father. Of course. I think they're in Zariah's house." Hanni nodded. "Then let's find him now."

Settling. Week 8.
Journal kept by Sarth

ONE COULD WISH, at times, that House-heads were less—god-like in their resolutions. I see quite clearly why Tellurith spoke as she did with Darthis: balancing consecration against sacrilege, saving the House. Shielding us both. I understand I had no more right to cry, *I want to save myself*! than he to protest his breached privacy. But—!

There has been no time for nursing wounds or grudges since. The epidemic has left us no time for nursing anything. Except the sick, where and whenever Caitha sends us. Heat hellien-steam, boil willow-tea. Wash faces, wipe noses, wipe bottoms; boil nose-wipes, boil bottom-wipes, mop up vomit, carry, wipe, clean ... And I must admit, Alkhes has amazed me. I thought he would jib, or turn up his general's nose, and the perverse creature has kept with me in the thick of it. With his arm healed he has even learnt, after a fashion, to rock a fractious toddler to sleep.

I asked him how, once, in a house-nursery's bedlam: fifteen children from one to ten bellowing, weeping, coughing, choking, throwing up ... He gave me one of those looks, all eyes and dagger-points, and said, "Nobody's bleeding here."

Meaning, I think, that it is worse in a field hospital. Astonishing that one who kills so proficiently should be at all concerned about patching the debris. Let alone confronting his victories' price.

I was the more astounded when he shot into the dispensary this morning squeaking, "Sarth, what am I supposed to—Sarth!"

The dispensary is the storeroom of Zariah's barrack-half: shelves for medical supplies, filthy clothes and gear in heaps, stairs to the wash-tub and boiling cauldron. Huis and I had just heaved another load of water home. Unsighted indoors, I read only the body-stance. But experience, let be Tower skills, forbade, *What's wrong?*

I grabbed the newest basket of foul linen and said, "Help me get these on."

"I can't, I need—"

A fresh child began crying. Huis rubbed his head and hurried off, I hissed, "We can't talk now!"

Down in the washing bay I tipped water in the big cauldron: four trips, and half of it gone. Automatically he shoved wood underneath, and while I sorted fouled blankets from used nose-wipes I demanded, "What's wrong?"

"Sarth, I can't—!" He burst up from the wood-pile looking wild enough to bolt. "I've done everything else but I—"

"What is it?" I did manage to soften the tone.

"Asaskian." Suddenly he was red to the ears. "She wants—she needs—and I—"

"Asaskian!" Laundry went every way. With mother and eldest sister among the rare cutter-wielders, vital to the stone-work, Zariah's second daughter had become the pillar of her house. Just fifteen, she had carried us all, calm, unflustered, resources never failing, until she fell ill herself. "You haven't let her out of bed?"

"Gods, of course not!" She had gone from fever to chest chokeage. Caitha said it was worry atop exhaustion and dosed her with as much sleep-syrup as she dared. "But she—she—"

Asaskian was a daughter to dream of: slim and lithe and elegant as a walking palm, perfect honey-gold skin and great amber eyes and clouds of copper-auburn hair. There were times I wondered if my heart would break, just looking at her.

And when the complications began . . . I tore up the stairs, snapping back at him, "Then what is it, for the Mother's sake?"

"Sarth . . . !"

The tone swung me round. If he had been scarlet before he was crimson now. "She's all right, she just—I just—oh, gods!"

All too clearly, the crisis was here.

I came back down. Threw the last nose-wipes in. Got flint and tinder. When I thought he could suffer it, asked quietly, "What is it, Alkhes?"

His ears were still scarlet. He was so like some Tower adolescent netted in disaster: it was all I could do not to push his hair back as on that first day. At last he muttered it, to the distant floor.

"She needs a—uh—a bed ..."

A bed-pan. When he had been emptying chamber-pots and wiping bottoms for a solid three-quarter moon.

"And I—Sarth, I can't go in there and do that, she's a grown *girl!*"

Mother, the Outland notion of modesty is something I will never plumb. I managed to swallow that too. To say, almost reasonably, "You've done it for all the rest. You'd do it," a stroke of genius, "for Tellurith."

"I'm married to Tellurith! I'm not even related to this one!"

"Oh." It was modesty, decorum, however convolute. Meanwhile, the girl was probably bursting. "Watch the cauldron," I said, and shot upstairs.

Asaskian shared her mother's room, halfway down the corridor. Having been all but embraced for my rescue, having listened for a renewed whisper in her chest; having once again sheathed in my own flesh the thought that said, These speaking eyes, this daybreak smile, the bones under this peaked skin and the delicately wasted shape under this coverlet, these could, these should have been yours; having kicked up the brazier, I hurried for the slops buckets inside the front entry; and ran straight into Tellurith.

With Iatha, and Zuri, and another pocketful of luminaries, some House progress. And—

My very bones solidified. Sharp nose, amber eyes, Navy stance. Thick-crinkled, Amberlight hair.

"There you are, Sarth," said Tellurith. She smiled. "We've been so lucky. Do you remember Tez?"

Trust a House-head at once to find and bridge the gap between a father and a daughter seen once, a baby, in her twenty years. A daughter the image of the mother that I lost, ten years before she died.

And she spoke so calmly. Too calmly. It steadied me, to smother the gulp. To manage, "This is a blessing unlooked-for. The Mother has smiled on us."

It seemed enough for Tez. Her stance unlocked. She even managed the beginnings of a smile. "Father ..."

Father. The elision, the absence in her life. The unmentionable scandal. The loss, the bleeding lacuna, that I had blanked out of mine.

"I—uh—uh—"

"Tez is quartered in our house," said Tellurith. This smile would have thawed the Iskans. "We can talk properly when we all finish work."

When the River runs back to Cataract. She meant it was temporary lodging until Tez was provisioned and chose work, and she—or I—made it her living place. And a graceful solution to the clash of clutching a full bedpan and greeting—or Mother avert, trying to embrace—a daughter. While still feeling hit over the head.

Settling. Week 8.

Meditations. Alkhes-Assandar

I WILL NEVER, never, *never* understand these people. In or out of Amberlight.

Do Sarth justice, he's run this hospital like a veteran orderly, never flinched, not with three brats puking on him at once. To have him come back down those stairs looking like—like—

I dropped the cauldron-stick in the muck and grabbed him and said, "Sit down."

An earthquake, that Sarth should show so much. A cataclysm, that he sat down, plump on the wood-heap. That he did what I said.

In seven weeks I've learnt a little. If they show it, and you have to notice, you never, ever ask these men what's wrong.

I stirred splashes out of the cauldron and muttered, "Sorry about that."

That got a jerk. A blink. I never thought I'd be sorry to see him so, so ... That he's beautiful makes it worse. If you can call beautiful a nursing orderly at shift end, with his week-worn gear stinking like a latrine and circles under his eyes and his hair in witch-knots all over his face.

He shook his head. Shook it again. I forgot all about tower manners and blurted, "Sarth, what's wrong?"

He looked at me then. Those eyes ... I dropped the stick and put both hands on *him*.

"Nothing's wrong." It was still wobbling like an over-galloped horse. "I just—she just—my daughter just arrived."

That time, *I* nearly sat down.

And did bite my tongue on, What daughter? She said that was the tragedy. Tellurith said you had only sons!

I can bottle it up, but I still can't ask politely. The best I could manage was, "Uh—Sarth?"

If you lean, it steadies him. He only wobbles when you try to prop him up.

"Khira's daughter. My third wife. She was," a deep breath, "captain on the *Wasp*."

Forget that name? When she and her hell-hounds cost me three good war-galleys, not to mention the men? And what in the River-lord's hell did that matter now?

"Sarth . . . I'm sorry, but I *don't* understand!"

It got his attention back. It even, can you believe it, produced a breath of a laugh.

"I beg your pardon." Who else, here, would say that? Or omit, Of course, you're outlander. "She. Khira. Children go to—the mother. They belong to—her house."

"But you sired her! You had a goddamn daughter, why didn't that count—oh," I said, and grabbed him. "Oh, damn. Oh, gods."

In a minute he had breath enough to move. To manage, "It's all right."

It was not all right. It never would be all right. But there comes a time when it's kinder to cut an arrowhead out.

"If you had a daughter," I said deliberately, "Tellurith's children don't matter. You can't be cursed."

"Not in the House!"

Time was, if he'd spoken like that, I'd have kicked in his throat.

"I'm sorry. I'm sorry. But surely, wherever she was—"

He shook his head. Got up. Found the stirring stick. Prodding clothes, said quietly—oh, how quietly—"The only children that matter are those by your first wife. The children of her own House."

I had the wit—gods be thanked, I did have the wit not to say, Well at least she's here, alive, we can be grateful something survived. I levered the stick away from him and said, "They probably need you upstairs. I'll see to this."

How can a man get a child and lose her? Have her taken out of his life, neat as a haircut, for twenty living years? How can she not *count* as his daughter, just because she lives in another house? In another part of the *same* House?

I never had a daughter. A son by a—camp-follower. Back in Verrain, working the caravans, I was still a boy myself. She swore it was mine, it had black hair. I gave her two fistfuls of pay tokens—unminted gold—and said, "All right, he's mine, goodbye." She was a camp-follower, she understood.

I wonder, did he die of fever or strangle-cough or all the other multitudinous children's ills I've seen in Iskarda?

With Cherisa, the question never arose.

The River-lord witness, she was beautiful. And well-dowered, a fine Dhasdeini merchant's daughter, a trader to the colonies, climbing the noble ladder faster than I was myself. Antastes' newest corps commander, risen from guard officer, surely going higher, heavens, sir, marry my daughter, I'll be proud.

For the ceremony, even the Emperor came.

So I settled her in a corps commander's house, and went blithely off to campaign in Quetzistan, all set to dream of white fingers and pearl-painted toenails and nubile breasts and hair like a black waterfall, just waiting for me to come home.

While she never waited at all.

Kuris and I had a duel over it. I put the point in his shoulder and disabled him for a season. He was a valued officer.

And she divorced me within the year.

Not for Kuris. Or any of the others, for all I know. Sir, her father said, at the settling up, it's not what she expected. A husband who's never home.

I thought, It's the price of war. It can be paid. What war leaves a mess like this?

By some mercy, this evening our off-duty shift matched a gap in House business. So when I reached the kitchen, leg-weary and brain-wrecked but clean of stench and filth for once, the person stirring the supper pot was Tellurith.

"Tel!" I pounced. "Quick, explain about Sarth . . ."

And knew better before I finished. And had no time to groan, before she took me by the wrist and tugged.

I had the wit not to let *I'm sorry* off my tongue.

She pushed back my hair. Not looking. But she likes to do that, and at least, this time, it was clean. I leant against the hearth-stool and side-eyed her profile, and kept quiet.

"I tried not to hate her," she said.

From a thousand miles away. From a world I would never, ever enter. Never know.

I got up on my knees and put both arms around her. With Tellurith, I know where I am. With Tellurith, we can both lean.

She laid her head against mine. Grief, her muscles brought me, long-festered, long-fought grief. And jealousy. And hate.

"Four daughters. The only ones he ever sired. After my first two—the others—" a sharp breath, "avoided him. And I—"

Had been House-head. Daughterless. Unable to acknowledge his. Unable to forget them, unable to share them. Small wonder she had hated. I would have cut Khira's throat.

"Ah, caissyl . . ."

My muscles too had translated things. She buried her face in my hair.

"And now . . . all the rest are dead."

The rest of Khira's brood. The daughters she had envied, and hungered for, and feared she had wished, if not sent, to their deaths.

Of a surety a god gave me the rest. I gathered her face up, and kissed her, more than carefully, on the lips.

"But she's here," I said. "Alive. And he's out of the tower. He can live in the same house with her. Talk to her. Be with her. Whatever else you did, you've given them that."

When you can convince her—can save her from herself—Tellurith has the loveliest smile.

So as soon as we were in bed, she destroyed *my* night's rest.

There is no way Antastes will sit still for a lost army, a wrecked fleet, an absconding general. The mere cost would cripple him. The loss of face, the threat to the empire from emboldened enemies, is worse.

"Um," said Tellurith. "The River has other news."

The word on Verrain and Cataract did make me breathe easier. Plenty there to distract Antastes. We lay as we had in her House-head's quarters: discussing the River, discussing policy, her head on my arm, her hair across my shoulder, the qherrique a whisper of light on the marbled walls. Trust, safety, warmth. Communion. Two minds matched, shared.

As here, amid the bleakness beyond the dying brazier, the furs, Sarth's breathing, the waxing moonshine on unpolished planks.

A third excluded, because politics was beyond him.

Or so I thought. Until Tellurith took a handful of that hair, as she so often does when he considers it groomed enough, and said, "Sarth, what do you think?"

I thought the quiet was shock. Surely, she had never sought advice in the tower?

But in a minute or two he said, "There *is* a very good road from here."

"And we're north of Marbleport."

The pair of them were thirty strides ahead. He meant the leveled, surveyed, double-wagon width by which the marble goes straight to the Riverside. A good road for messengers. She meant, advance warning from downRiver of incursion by land or water, possibly a spy-ring's base for news earlier still. It was out on my own thought. "A marble factor would be perfect cover. Could you spare a light gun or so for signaling?"

Quite clearly I felt Tellurith gasp. The little startled laugh. Before the tousle of my hair that was a caress, which other times have taught me was compliment. To the speed of my own wits.

She said, "We need a marble factor anyhow, and well before winter's end. We can't spare light guns. But perhaps signal fires."

"Signal posts?" Sarth sounded dubious.

"Once the houses are done, some convalescents might winter down there. Must see Iatha . . ."

The rest came on a mighty yawn. She turned on her side, sleep-time's signal. And, as she did scrupulously, laid her head on one or other of our shoulders. This time, the turn was Sarth's.

I still wonder what she would have done if it were not.

Settling. Week 8.
Journal kept by Sarth

BLESSINGS ON TELLURITH, that after the unseaming awkwardness of that supper, she talked politics in bed, and did not try to ease or clarify other things for either of us. Not in front of Alkhes.

So there was a night to absorb it: a daughter, again, still, after all. A presence to learn and share, flesh and blood.

And exhumed ghosts.

Better, perhaps, that Alkhes was there. All those years between us, and the words never spoken. Four daughters. But what could I say? Tellurith, I would cut my heart out if it gave you a girl?

While she, the Mother knows what she suffered, not to avenge herself on Khira, who had her heart's desire. And now, to welcome Khira's child. What was I to tell her now?

Tellurith, forgive me. I need—I want—you both?

Bless the Mother for mundanity that turned us all out before daylight, and had me emptying bedpans before breakfast, with the length of a shift until we met again. Or so I thought, until the hands across Pheroka's clean sheet grew an owner. Tez.

"I learnt quite a bit," she said, "in the hospital."

As a prisoner-of-war. Mother bless, that there were sheets to pick up, a face to wash, hair to brush.

"I can do that."

In the last resort, a door.

And with it, a message: I don't want you. Go away.

I waited with the sheets. Walked with her. We kept stealing glances, silly as a pair of brats. With Alkhes I would have said, Do this, Can you fetch that? But she was a woman, as well as my daughter. The clash disabled me.

"Father?"

Sorting laundry. More deftly, that morning, than I. The last pile went down, the eyes rose. "I can go away."

Sharp-boned, controlled, her mother's mirror; down to those masked bronze eyes. The face that had left me, in the Tower.

But we were not in the Tower.

I had time to bless Tellurith, and feel the smile blossom even as I thanked Sethar and his antecedent generations who taught me to read and tender a woman, and shape fitting words round my own joy.

"Tez, you're a Navy officer; a woman grown. And you must go where your duty is. I would bless the Mother to have you here. To know you. But whatever you do, you are my daughter. And I know—I've known this long time—you will make me—I am—so proud."

One would not say such a thing to a woman, in the Tower. Nor had I ever touched a woman outside marriage. But I mustered the nerve to kiss her cheek. And to accept—the Mother knows, how well I've learnt acceptance—her embrace.

She was smiling when she looked up. Wet-eyed, radiant. It was "duty" did it. I have not husbanded a Navy captain for nothing. She patted me like a child with a new toy.

"The Ruand wants a factor down at Marbleport. And somebody to run an information net. Iatha said troublecrew, but they don't know ships, and we can't afford to get cheated over freight. And on *Wasp* I gathered the intelligence-reports."

Here, and gone. "Duty" cuts both ways.

"But I wondered. I was worried—"

About her father. Her mother's relict. Her responsibility. She feared Tellurith might have borne a grudge. After the way I treated her, who would be surprised?

She laughed out loud. "But it's all right. It's better than I ever thought. I can come back and see you. And you're doing all this, you're just as good as a woman—"

The eyes flickered, a glint that once had tweaked my heart.

"Except," it became a wicked grin, "*so* much prettier."

Then she patted my rump and grabbed a water jar on her way to the outer door.

Settling. Week 9.
Tellurith's Diary

THANK THE MOTHER, the epidemic has eased at last; we never had more need, for autumn is dwindling too. We have already lost two days to the first storm, and the weather is chilling fast. Mother bless that we still have supplies coming to pack the new storerooms; and six houses done; and thanks to our scavengers, a supply of semi-winter clothes. At times I swear the whole village walks about in those lined double-worsted Dhasdein officers' cloaks, or quilted jackets that still stink of cameleer.

But it is a time to walk, and not just to the workshops or the market-place. Outside the houses the air is beautiful, cutting, but sharp as wine. We finished here yesterday: sealed the roof, set the threshold step, burnt the incense sticks. I gave the workcrew the rest of the day off, and on impulse told my household, "Let's spend tomorrow in the hills."

A cold, austere beauty they have now, the shedding trees stripped, skeletal between the viridian or snow-silver of pine and hellien, the grass a tawny silk that plays like cat fur under the slicing winds. Their eddies sketch out the range front, contour after contour, crest, valley, spur beyond. Drawing your eyes to the horizon, where already the peaks are blanched with snow.

By now troublecrew know the mountain like their hands. Zuri and Azo and Verrith and Desis, they all came; and Hanni, and Shia, and her sisters, and Iatha, and her mother, and the house's children. And the men. And Tez.

I will never know what Sarth said to her; but from the early sunlight as we climbed, crystal-sharp under that pale autumn sky, to the stride back in twilight, the vast bowl of River plain darkening eastward under the jewel-drop of a rising star, in a day clear-cut as a fine intaglio, their commerce has been the purest line. Walking, talking, just sitting together; sometimes with no more than a smile. Until she swatted his rump, as we separated to our sleeping quarters, and called, "Night, Father!" before she whistled off down the passageway.

Alkhes grinned. Zuri gave her an eye. Sarth . . .

Indubitably, unmistakably. Sarth smirked.

Blessings on the Mother. Alkhes was right. Whatever else falls, wherever else we fail, I, we, have given him his daughter. At last.

Settling. Week 9.
Meditations. Alkhes-Assandar

IF THERE WAS just some warning of these things!

I knew damn well Tellurith would try it again. With the sickness, we've been too blind tired to think, let alone sleep at the same time in the same bed. But I should have thought, when yesterday was so easy—so different—

We shave and clean up every night we're home. How else, sleeping with Tellurith? And at any chance Sarth will wash that hair of his. Thick as a rope, sheeny as burnished bronze, halfway down his back. If there's rosemary, he rinses with it. I even helped comb it, before supper, I never thought anything different.

Until Tellurith rolled over. And started kissing him.

What could I do? Climb out and run? I knew how far I'd get. Lie there like a brothel spy?

Join in?

I've been in battles and less terrified. Probably I twitched—who could help it? She let him go, and rolled back over to me.

And I nearly tore the furs clean off the bed.

"Caissyl . . ."

So soft. So quiet. I almost choked. I did manage, "I can't, Tel! You *know* I can't!"

"No demands, caissyl." Her fingers in my hair, running up behind my ear. She knows what *that* does to me. "Nothing you don't want. But you could at least hold me—touch me—"

While he ... I practically squawked, "I *can't!*"

She kept quiet. Of course that was worse. What could I do? What could I say? I swear, they'll *never* understand!

I was still trying to find words when the lamp took light.

He had found the flint, rekindled the wick, before I felt him move. When it caught he leant up over her. A statue moving, all those gilded muscle curves, the hair a bronze flood across his shoulder, the light dark as distilled amber on his eyes.

"Touch *me*, then." It was weird to hear Sarth talk through his teeth. "If she's too much for you, touch me. Or is your manhood too fragile? Does it rub off like face-paint? Can you only say, I'm a man because I do what a man's supposed to? Do you dare say, Being a man is whatever I do?"

I never . . . never thought he could sound like that. But even before breath returned, I understood.

It wasn't anger. Or jealousy. It was a challenge.

And if I ran out, I'd never look him in the face again.

I got out of bed. Tellurith never moved. I stamped round the bed foot, and yanked the covers back, and said through my own teeth, "Move over and see."

He slid across without a word. That hair was everywhere. All over the pillows, mixed in the furs, tawny, gold-streaked, skeins of black-bronze silk. I leant over and dug both hands full of it.

IT HAS TAKEN a long time to write this.

I'm still not sure I *can* write it. How in the gods' name can you think—can you admit—can you feel something like this and still *be* a man?

Hang him. That's just where he challenged me. Are you a man because you only do what's allowed for a man? Or can you say, Being a man is whatever I do?

Before I came to Amberlight, I never thought about it. I was a man, and being a man was what I did, and what I did was right; because that was what men did.

Only, which men?

Is Sarth less of a man, because he was raised a woman's plaything? Because he spent his life in a tower, and lost his sons, and never killed?

When he can carry water till I drop, and coax a child I'd strangle, and read Tellurith ten times better than I. When he has manners, and control, and endurance—

When he doesn't need a weapon. Beyond his tongue.

When he can dare me to—that—and probably feel, know, face already what I still can't bear to write.

That when I took hold of his hair—it was because I wanted to.

Had long wanted to.

How does a man cope with that?

It was so thick. And soft. And warm. Finer than silk. Smoother than Tellurith's. Hers is full of kinks. I wanted to fill my hands with it and smell it and wallow in it. I wanted—

So I put both elbows on it. And slid right down on top of him. And kissed the bastard. Full on the mouth.

That was—something else.

To start with, a man's skin is different. Smoother than a woman's and harder, both at once. But so is the—the bone, the musculature. Harder, more pronounced, more . . . the only word is, masculine. Not in size, even shape. Proportions, perhaps. The shaping under the flesh.

And his response . . . Women—some women wait for your lead. Some women open their mouths like a trap. Some women sit like a lump of meat. Men—I don't know about any other men. Sarth left me the lead and hardly moved his lips, and it was a dozen nuances of reply. Aware. Alive. Answering.

Does he kiss a woman like that?

It was something to wonder while I was asking: What in the River-lord's hell do I do next?

Till he put his free arm round my neck and slid his fingers up into my hair.

With Tellurith, that's one thing. With Sarth . . .

The weight, the heft of well-developed man's muscle in that position almost panicked me. Too much unarmed combat, I was too vulnerable. I half pulled back. He laughed into my mouth. Just the slightest breath.

So I kept still, of course. And his fingers slid . . .

Maybe he learnt it with women. But damn, he has a touch.

My backbone went to bubbling air. And whatever Tellurith was doing came through him to me. Twitch, locked-up muscles. Catching breath. It's the weirdest experience, to respond to someone who's responding to somebody else.

If she hadn't, I doubt I could have gone on with it.

THIS IS HARD to admit too. I learnt—we all learnt, I realize—a long time ago. As a boy, when I saw someone put a hand on someone else in a barrack-yard and have his face smashed in. As a man, with a squadron commander cashiered because he loved—showed he loved—another man. "They gave me a crown," he said, "for killing five men. Then they threw me out for loving one." Nobody ever had to explain it: if you're a real man you never want, never love, never look at, never touch other men.

I'm a man. Until now, I've never known what that means.

Lying there, my hands on him, my weight on him, his hair, his body under me, physically *there*—I understood what *I* was. How "man" isn't "woman." What we truly are.

And then—

I felt it happen. Rules broke. Ties—bonds broke. A wall opened. Something said: You can want to do this now. And if you want it, you can do.

As much as Sarth, I have been inside a Tower.

Worse than Sarth, because I didn't—wouldn't—know.

I TOUCHED his face. You do it with a woman. Learning who they are, how they're different. But this was more than women's differences. Skin, bone, body structure.

And—

I have to be honest. If anywhere, here. Ever since I saw the bastard I've—over and over, I've thought, he's beautiful.

Touching him wasn't just exploration. It was pleasure. It was possession.

Be hung, but it *was* desire.

Except—not like with a woman. Because a woman—You want to have her, yes, to join with her, to be more than human, for a minute, a moment, one time out of time, losing your whole self. But a man—a man is—

You.

And if he's beautiful, the pleasure, the possession, even desire is different. Because wanting him, touching, just accepting that you want him—is to want, to accept—yourself.

I THINK, maybe, I can do that. Will do it. Have done it, or why am I writing this?

Or how could I have gone on with it? Once Tellurith drew his attention back, first to kiss, then embrace, then touching him. Jaw, throat, chest. Nipples. And when Tellurith does that . . .

I knew what he felt from both sides. Enough to disorient anyone. But when he rolled over, I could have let be. Could have lain there like a lump. Like the ones who watch for pay.

Even then I would have learnt enough to put me out of the bed. How *I* ever thought I had technique with a woman—Tel's taught me everything I know.

And everything she knows, I know now, came from him.

But I didn't lie there. And at some stage . . . touching him stopped being for my pleasure. And moved to making his.

Probably I was a perfect irritant. An amateur flute-player in a trio, out of time, out of tune. Tellurith has a better feel for the other's feelings, a better sense of mutual pleasures, of give and take between the two.

I don't think I did a good job of making it three. But I tried.

And River-lord witness, I *will* run if they try that on me!

Settling. Week 9.
Journal kept by Sarth

How can a man become a general—one supposes this is at least the equivalent of Sethar's reputation—and be all but ignorant of love? What *do* they teach Outlanders?

And, the Mother defend me, what has he inflicted on Tellurith?

To be sure, it had a certain—poignance. Like the shy, the clumsy ardor of a very young boy, when he first tries to repay what he has learned. The Mother knows, it was the last thing I expected when he stalked round that bed. I thought I had gone too far at last. That he meant, at least, to murder me.

Who was the more surprised, when he kissed me instead?

It does seem to have eased something. Too subtle to call change, too slight to show in speech, almost too little to read in a glance. One cannot even say he looks me in the eye more often. But he does look. And even without looks, when we meet, or are together now, his stance, all his body language says, All right. Yes. You can be near me.

Going for water this morning, it made me notice the Iskardans more than usual.

Tellurith says that when we finally finish building, the next project will be water pipes. The Mother knows, of the myriad lost joys I yearn for, running water in the house—oh, inconceivable delight, hot running water in the house!—is among the first. During the epidemic, to have had even the Tower hallway fountain, where visitors used to wash their shoes …

It would be churlish to complain. There are plenty of other austerities, from miserly heating to the foul-burning fat-lamps, from soldiers' hand-me-downs to the mere lack of once taken-for-granted delicacies. Oh, for something beyond corn bread and salted meat and rationed honey or dried fruit!

Until we have a trade balance, that must be foregone too. Meanwhile, we chop wood and carry water, and try not to think that, because they are all among the work-crews, the women shirk.

So we were tramping yet again to the fountain. Since his arm healed, Alkhes insists on taking a yoke. We climbed the five stone steps from the washing bay; tucked hoods down against the wind. Thanked our gods it had not begun to rain, and started through the mud, trying not to let the empty buckets bang our knees.

More Iskardans were abroad than usual, it being what passes for a market-day: folk up from the Kora, some hunters from the upper valleys, where fur-trapping has begun. Threading the street, we kept our eyes down. Though it is only sensible, a token appeasement, in different ways it chafes us both. But since I am far better at glancing under lashes, it was I who noticed how they looked at him.

In his own way, Alkhes is worth a look. Over-small by Tower standards, but well-cut features, and the eyes and hair … pools blacker than ebony, sentient midnight sea. Falls of silken mahogany, fine and straight and forever tumbling in his face. It goes up under a helmet, he says. And for all his size, well-proportioned. Subtle, lithe, exquisitely resilient; in heavy coat and infantry boots, he still has a killer's grace.

So they look, if it is only one in ten, with something more than censure. Since the confrontation with Darthis, there has been a spice of awe. But this morning …

Recognition? Acknowledgement? Anticipation? Too slight, too enigmatic for analysis. But there is something—

Something they know, and we do not.

Should I mention it to Tellurith? But what would I say? I can hear Zuri now: a presentiment, some man's fancy. And is it anything more?

IV

Iskarda. Week 10.
Tellurith's Diary

WHAT IN THE WORLD is Darthis up to now?

And why in the world could she not have found a better time?

I swear, the woman *feels* vexation's chink: this morning, after the first snowfall tried our handiwork, a blocked heating pipe in this house, a leaky store-room in Ahio's; half a side of beef spoilt in a night. Just when it would have been pleasant to try my new fur-lined coat; walk out to survey the Iskans, dappled fallow and cloud-cream with snow; to smell that bitter, earthy wind of winter, and pretend we do not miss the sanctuary of the qherrique.

Or to savor that other oasis, waiting under the furs in bed.

Instead I have had a crisis warning before breakfast, and with *that* to help my digestion, a visit from Darthis.

A CEREMONIOUS ENTRY, heralded by messenger, escorted by troublecrew. Ushered into the new council-chamber, where, with a brazier among our feet under the table, we lowlanders had some hope of lasting her out.

When Shia had brought an exotic venture into mulling wine with the last cloves, we finished the preamble: cold weather at last, yes, we may winter some convalescents downland while we set up our factor in Marbleport, do you feel winter traffic would damage the road, no, certainly, we never cut in winter, but then, we were vassals. Both of us understanding, the quarry must work much harder if it is to support the entire House; even such a diminished House as this.

No necessity to mention we still have holdings in the Kora. But then she set her cup aside and folded her forearms on the table and said, "Ruand?"

Formal notice; serious business. I inclined my head.

She fidgeted the cup. "Iskarda asks . . ."

When she stuck, I said, "Telluir hears."

I thought she would balk again. But after a moment, it came.

"There is a matter of the Mother's favor. Whose like we have never heard."

I kept my face still. Alkhes. The qherrique.

"I myself . . . my elders . . . Zdana, who is the Mother's Ear. We have sought counsel. But even in the highest place . . . the sky is dark."

She meant they had called on the Mother, sought auspices, meditated. And nothing had come.

"Therefore," she looked down. Shifted the cup.

It had taken me all that time to see she was discomforted. One does not look for fidgets in a rock.

"Therefore, we ask—as vassals, with no thought to doubt our House-head, only for our own understanding. We ask—"

At the last, she was Darthis after all. She lifted her head and gave it to me face to face.

"We would ask for proof."

No point in affront. It was as humble as she would ever be. And after all, what I had claimed was beyond precedent.

"One would wish," I said, "to hear the Mother truly. With one's own ears." It was amazing to see her so relieved. "But . . . All our qherrique is dedicated."

What spoke to Alkhes had been House-rock, the great veins that grew down from the mother-face, time out of mind. It was common to the House, we used it to test neophytes. To Iskarda we had brought cutters, light-guns; portable tools. Tools only the user could wield.

Darthis pushed her cup a little aside. "Some, I am told, to the Ruand."

The effrontery! She knew I used a cutter. Anyone could have seen it, a dozen times a day. What she meant was that as my husband, its dedication should make it answer Alkhes too.

One must give her credit, at least, for nerve. And for putting both risk and onus of proof on me.

"It's never been done," I said. "Such 'use' comes close to frivolous. If not to blasphemous." I felt her shrink. For once, orthodoxy was with me. "It may prove nothing." She knew quite well that with a dedicated tool failure would be merely dubious. "But I will not deny my vassals their peace of mind."

Putting the onus of trouble back on her.

Then I said to Hanni, "Can someone find Alkhes?"

HE CAME IN SMOOTHLY, if bearing signs of a rapid spruce-up, and a faint dung-stink that said they had been mucking out the byres. He had experience enough, at sight of Darthis, to keep his face still. And to read what he could from mine.

Which made him straighten to military attention and inquire, "Ruand?"

"Iskarda's folk," I said, "find themselves perplexed by the Mother's favor. They ask, respectfully, to see for themselves."

Of course he knew what I meant. And picked up the 'respectfully': I expect you to comply. He understood, from the mere proposal, that I had some hope he would not fail. A moment's thought told him what the test must be. And another, those black eyes flaring minutely, the cause.

He inclined his head. I had seldom remembered, so clearly, Assandar. "Here?"

I reached for my cutter. Like every other, nowadays it never left my belt. The control box clicked, gleaming faintly in the winter light, as it met the roughly polished table. I said, "Now."

When he first bespoke the qherrique, I had woken it beforehand. This was not merely dedicated, but fast asleep. He looked at me again. Then he turned back to the cutter, and moistened his lips.

And there was no concealing the hope, the naked yearning. If anyone doubted, who ever worked qherrique around that table, they had their answer then. Only one who had shared that impossible, that unforgettable rapport could so long for the bare chance of feeling it again.

He took a deep breath; straightening, centering himself. And then relaxed, as troublecrew do for unarmed combat. Emptying life from his features, and all thought, all emotion, from his mind.

Through the house women talked, men answered. Steps passed, children laughed. A bullock bellowed, and crows cawed, harsh and remote as a military trumpet, in the snow-silence outside.

He eased his shoulders, and eerily, uncannily like a Crafter, hummed a couple of notes under his breath. Then he stepped forward. And slowly, slowly, drew one hand through the air, fingers just above my cutter's small block of qherrique.

It spoke beneath his fingertips, slow, sure, brightening, in the gray winter room a small moonlight fire.

The mask cracked, releasing awe, incredulity, a boy's sheer delight. He said something quite inaudible. Then he eased his fingers down.

And the qherrique glistened under their touch.

Delight became aching joy. Moving as if it were broken egg-shell, he gathered the cutter up. Nursed it, in both hands, against his heart.

"Oh, Tel—"

The smile was beatific.

"Tel. It *remembers* me."

Darthis was a Ruand, with face to save. It held her as mute as the rest of us, who knew the danger of startling a novice in actual contact, but it was all inscribed, in letters a mile high, on Iatha's face.

I am eternally thankful that I could keep my voice quiet. That I did not scream, You're not supposed to say that, it's not supposed to do that, it never remembers *anybody*, we don't need more anomalies and omens, we've got trouble enough! That I could say, quite placidly, "Good." And to Darthis, "Has Iskarda seen enough?"

Something is wrong there; something I have not fathomed yet. She should have been bawling and beating the air about freaks and blasphemy. If she was too naive to recognize that, she should have been stunned mute, at the barest least. But she inclined her head and answered immediately, "Iskarda thanks the Ruand's grace."

And made her farewells, and got herself out of the chair, and out of my council-room, as smoothly as a fish.

Only now have I deciphered that expression. Not surprise. Not chagrin. Not even relief, however bizarre that would be.

The blighted woman was satisfied.

WHEREAS I HAVE HAD to spend the rest of the day rounding up Hayras and Quetho and Ahio and Charras together, and pinning down Alkhes in the council-room.

"What do you mean, it remembers you?"

Alone, or in bed, he probably would have burst out, gods, Tel, what's it matter? Being dragged from troublecrew training into what equals a Craft-Head consultation, he took time to think.

"I felt . . ." An uncertain glance around the faces. "I don't know much about this, you know that. But didn't—doesn't this happen—usually?"

It did not take Hayras' black-browed, tight-lipped glower to answer, No.

I could not restrain a touch on his arm. "No one disbelieves you, I promise that. But, no. Usually—no."

Charras leant over the table and asked temperately, "How, exactly, did it feel?"

He knew she was a power-shop expert. He turned with relief.

"I don't know how it works for you. For me—the first time, it was just—there. Not words. Not a touch. I was just—aware of it. And it was aware of me."

Charras nodded. "Waking the mother-face. And this?"

He tugged desperately at his hair. "Words are so useless . . . But—when I asked about—cutting—" that falter was not awkwardness—"it was a definite—a—a feeling. Like trying to find your way in the dark and there's a shape, or a star-bearing, and you—know. This is right."

Charras looked at me.

Though I did my best to be calm, most of the others looked away. Communion, trust, harmony, certainty. Asking and answer, from the House's core. The link I would never share again.

"That," I sounded almost cool, "is how it feels."

"But what do you mean," Quetho asked mildly, precisely, "that it 'remembers' you?"

"I don't—" the look around was half wild, half defiant. "I can't prove it. I can't explain it any better than—it was just—like the questions. I *knew*."

Presently Ahio sat back, and spoke for all of us.

"Talk to a man. Remember him. Hells!"

As MY MOTHER used to say, let troubles hatch alone. After all, what can we do? Anomaly upon anomaly, all of them fit only to disturb House-heads and alarm traditionalists; and who is there to consult now, beyond ourselves?

It still feels like idling atop a block of overcharged qherrique. But however enigmatically, Darthis has kept quiet; for there has been no uproar in Iskarda. And the snowfall has ceased. The pipes are cleared, building has resumed; and heaving stores through the proliferating mud, in the piercing mountain winds. In the intoxicating mountain air, under the pure, distant, ice-blue mountain sky.

A good sight to leave at dusk, physically weary, work done, plans fulfilled, as you seek the kitchen glow. Despite heating pipes and private quarters, the household seems to congregate here at night; I too find myself writing this journal on a corner of the table Shia and her minions have cleared, with a crowd of troublecrew relatives one side the hearth, Iatha's husband-kin on the other, and Hanni totting up trade figures by my side. In the hush, the rustle of expectation, as the children wait for Hanni's sister Esrafal to pick up her drum.

In Amberlight her troupe played for all the Uphill occasions. We have lost the two lute-players and the piper; but she has acquired the hand-drum somewhere in Iskarda. She will pick it up while dishes clatter in the scullery; rattle fingers, tighten a rim-peg. The children all breathe in, a bobbing wall of fire-lit eyes. A pattern of finger-snaps, then she will look about vaguely, and ask, almost a ritual now, "Sarth, do you know . . .?"

And he will materialize from the passageway, a tall shadow taking features, the flute's glitter in his hand. Polished mahogany, with ivory mouthpiece and solid silver stops; an heirloom, inherited by Head's husbands in Telluir House. The Mother knows how or why he got it out of Amberlight, but he is a skilled player, like all tower-bred men. He will meet the buzz amid the children with that slight, correct smile; settle by Esrafal. Bend his head, and answer, "I think so. Does it go like this?"

Tonight they started, "Fire-wings," the old catch about courting dragonflies. The first bar brings it all back: fiery darts of gauze and crimson, flying needles, iridescent sparks. And the river, somnolent silver-shot viridian, a rippled plain below them, beneath that turquoise summer sky.

> "Hear me whisper our desire,
> River's daughter, Goddess-fire,
> Wake me with the burning day,
> Fly a pearl-wing to our play,
> From the sun's eye all the light,
> Dance we in the day's delight.
> Where the sapphire lilies grow,
> And the green runs bright below."

Even lacking the pure white qherrique glow, the kitchen is very warm and secure. The center of the household; the House. The ring of known faces and shapes around me, smiling, singing, beating time on knee or chair, the smell, grown familiar, of new-washed women, stew, wood-smoke, the mountain taints of ox-grease and hellien resin and deep-frozen earth; the easy, familiar jests.

And Sarth by the fireplace, the light splashed on dancing fingers, the long bronze-mahogany sheen of loose-tied hair. Turning sometimes for the fire to etch that profile, distant, beautiful as some old mountain king.

I was thinking that when Alkhes trooped out of the scullery with Shia and Azo's husband, ever-dandy Herar; whispered some jest, and came, still smiling, to hunker on the big shaggy Verrain desert-rug, shoulders settling between my knees. A slight, solid, living resilience. Peace built, assured safety. A sudden rising rill of joy.

Which is why, walking down the passage to bed, I slid an arm around his waist.

Just as Sarth put an arm around his shoulders as well.

All the air went out of him, one strangled gasp. He tried to back; made a frantic shoving motion with both hands. Sarth let go, I caught a forearm. And he jerked out of reach.

"Tel, I'm sorry, I didn't mean—I just—just—"

"No." It had all shattered, the warmth, the joy and magic firelight. "I didn't mean to upset you, either. Let's go to bed."

We walked into the House-head's sleeping room. Beyond the brazier, warmth ebbed to freezing; outside the little fat-lamp's radius was desolate dark. Shedding coats, trousers, indoor moccasins, we all dived under the furs, the usual night ritual. A mockery of itself.

"Tel—"

"It doesn't matter."

"Tel, I have to explain—"

"Alkhes, it doesn't matter! Let it go."

How rarely have I used a Head's voice on him? Never, in our bed.

Let alone rolled over and given him my back.

Silence. Rigid, fulminating, too enraged to draw in breath. Then an explosive snort. Jerk of bedclothes, swirl of garments; reverberatingly slammed door.

Sarth was out the other side so fast I had no time to grab, let alone shout. Sometimes I wonder if "Ruand" means anything at all.

Iskarda. Week 10.
Journal kept by Sarth

TELLURITH, thank the Mother, had the wits to stay in bed. I waved the night-guard back in mid-swoop: he was headed for the kitchen, not the outer door. He heard me coming and spun round, half across the room, as I reached the passage end.

Recognition checked him. I said, "Come here."

He stiffened, pure defiance. Like a weapon, I threw it at him.

"Are you afraid?"

That fetched him in a heartbeat. Not stalking, not stamping. The fluid slide of a killer enraged.

"Of you?"

He was close enough for real blows, and I was too angry for sense. I reached out and caught him, hard, under the chin.

He yelled and tore away. And pulled the kick, I saw that. Another time I was lucky not to get killed.

"It's pride, then? You can touch me, but that's the end of it? I'm not good enough for touching you?"

He jerked as if I had hit him in the wind.

"And neither is Tellurith?"

The sound came, too, as if I had kicked it out of him. The good arm cradled his ribs.

"What happened to, We let her make the choices? And, Whatever she wants, she gets?"

He had both hands to his belly, as if I had stabbed him in good truth.

"Or were you never serious about the marriage at all?"

That one, or its injustice, cut too deep. He made a noise between a choke and a scream. Half-struck at me, and reeled away across the room. The fireplace brought him up, head bowed in shoulders, hands outthrust against the keystones above the hearth, coughing as in a wound-pain's paroxysm.

I had time, then, to feel ashamed.

I walked up beside him; loud enough to be heard coming, near enough for a strike; put a hand on his shoulder, and muttered, "I'm sorry, Alkhes."

He did not lash out at me. He did, like an animal too well-beaten, cringe.

A fine achievement, to break such a spirit. Outlander, killer, barbarian, surely. But with his own pride, his own courage, as worthy as any of mine.

Not deserving to be smashed from jealousy.

It is not easy to admit it; that under my insult, and her righteous anger, the jealousy still burned. That she had preferred him in Amberlight, that afterward she had not been content with me.

"I was thinking of Tellurith."

And *that* was outright hypocrisy, whatever its truth. As I should have known, before he cried out.

This time I knew better than to touch. After a while I said, as sincerely as I knew how, "Can you just explain?"

He was still braced against the stone. The words came up, like loads heaved off a well-bottom, from invisibility.

"Told you. It's not our way—"

I put a hand on his back, unable to help myself. "But it was all right. The other night, we all—"

He let the stones go and jammed both hands over his face. I could barely understand.

"All right—with *you*. But if she asks—"

A convulsion in his chest.

"I'll—I'll *fail*—"

The Mother and the Tower be praised, I had the wit not to rush in; not to offer some stupid hasty condolence, not to put encouragement first. The Mother knows what it had cost him to give me that; to let me at the core of his fear, his humiliation, his self. What sort of courage does it take, to offer such truth to a stranger, a possible enemy?

So I drew five long breaths, before I took his shoulders and turned him about against the wall, and spoke.

"Alkhes—it's not a war."

HE WAS SO WHITE the welling ember-glow turned his face to red-tinged milk. And those eyes: wells, bruises, wounds.

But he did not look away from me. If nothing else, his courage is intact.

I pushed the hair out of his eyes and left the hand to cup his cheek. Even at that, he did not flinch.

But he did begin to think.

"I've been doing it wrong."

The faintest nuance of question, that let me answer easily.

"Not doing. Seeing."

Those eyes were depthless now; no sparkle, sheer drowning black. He opened his mouth. Shut it. Then he took a very deep breath, and plunged.

"Outside . . . We don't just own women. We're nervous about other men. A man never looks—never admits he might want to look—at them. If anyone did—"

An even more vertiginous pause.

"It's a war too. And the worst—the worst thing imaginable—is to lose."

My head reeled. He meant love—desire—coupling—between men. He meant even that was a contest to them. And to be the one who played the woman was to be conquered. Degraded. Scorned.

Never before have I seriously thought this marriage, this enterprise, might fail. But how do you open gates, how do you understand, let alone change the understanding of a man like that?

He had been able to make a third, I understood, only so long as he did not have to "prove" himself with Tellurith in front of me. And only so long, with me, as he was playing the man. So he could see it as a war; and win.

And we had thought he was simply getting used to things.

"Sarth?"

His fingers were ice-cold and sweat-clammy and clamped around my wrist. He understood too. He knew what a gulf was between us, and he did not think he could get across. Not alone. Perhaps not at all.

I took his face in both hands and said, "Alkhes, I'm sorry. I'm so sorry. We didn't understand."

His hand clenched. "Understand what?"

"That you can't change yourself overnight, just by wanting to. Even if—"

Foolish vanity, that in pride of my Tower skills had run me precisely into the ultimatum I wanted to avoid.

The hand trembled, and relaxed. But the eyes widened. Then he licked his lips.

"I—" huskily. A pause. "I do want to. I'm—trying." The eyes came up, engulfing, overwhelming mine. "And I think—I am." If nothing else, his body language said he was taking what, to him, was a madder plunge than before. A leap across an abyss. A step into infinity. "To you—I should have seen it—the woman comes first."

I nodded, mystified.

"To you, the man is—lucky. Chosen. It's the woman who—who—wins." The lashes flickered, slightest signal of embarrassment. "So if it was between men. It wouldn't be war—and losing—any more than it is for her."

If he could not accept it with his body, he could construct it, blessings on the Mother, with his mind. I nodded. I could feel myself, against all odds and caution, beginning to smile.

But for him a last, dizzying step remained.

"And I—" suddenly there was more than fire color on his face. "I've looked at you—I couldn't help looking at you, always. And I have to tell you. It wasn't war—it wasn't winning, the other night."

Not from Sethar, from any boy I ever taught, not from Tellurith herself have I had an avowal so costly, so cherished, so precious to me. An avowal paid in courage beyond imagination. What would it take, for me to equal that?

Less stupidity, perhaps, than I used in that moment. I was too moved for caution. I was too moved to think. I put both arms around him, and kissed him on the forehead as if he were in truth a just-schooled, well-performed, beloved boy.

"Well done," I said, "Alkhes." He was too startled to pull away. I hugged him again and said, "We can do it. We need time and patience, and we must all speak out our problems. But it can—it will work."

Iskarda. Week 10.
Meditations. Alkhes-Assandar

IT WILL WORK, he says. Beaming like sun on a snowy morning. I never realized how much he doubted it.

Disconcerting. As disconcerting as that kiss, that—hang it—embrace. If less terrifying than having to—take your armor off and open your ribs and bare your goddamn heart.

I think he thought it was brave.

At any rate, it was better than sleep-syrup for a belly-wound, to have him—kind. To have him speak to Tellurith, and Tel, blessing on her, not make a fuss. She just hugged me too and let me sleep. So if I felt, next morning, like Zuri had been tuning my ribs with a paving-stone, at least it didn't show in the flesh.

Iskarda. Week 11.
Tellurith's Diary

WHATEVER THEY said to each other, to have a truce of sorts is enough. At least, thank the Mother, it was settled before *this* crisis report.

Also arriving before breakfast, but this time, from troublecrew positively pale around the gills.

Azo has struck a friendship with one of the upland hunters; outliers, hut-dwellers, isolated in winter, they treat their men with even less ceremony than we. What is a tower or a pair of husbands to them? So Azo has given her a Dhasdeini cross-bow, and she has taught Azo to hunt, hill-fashion, with trap and snare for meat, not spears for glory and death. There is plenty of food up here smaller than sour old mountain boars.

Or whatever it is that has torn up and carried away, bodily, Azo's prey.

"Ripped the snare out by the butt." She squatted over the kitchen fire, clutching her tea. With the heating pipes off, the early morning house is bleak. "Three of them. Probably a rabbit or two. But . . ."

"Tracks?"

That was Zuri, materialized, magically, at my back.

"Snow-tracks. All mud and blur."

"Size?"

Azo wiped her mouth and looked up at her trouble-Head. And paused a moment before she replied.

"Big."

TROUBLECREW HAVE searched, beaten bounds, round the house, the village itself. They lost the tracks up the hillside. We have doubled the watch, the last three nights, until they were driven in by the snowfall. There was no sign of anything. No more pillaged traps.

So now, I only—only!—have to worry about the silence from Darthis.

Iskarda. Week 12.
Meditations. Alkhes-Assandar

TELLURITH SAID she wants men out of the towers. Now . . . I'm not so sure about this. It was weather and house-pattern that put troublecrew in the council-chamber over the snow; the only place we can work out indoors. It was chance and house-pattern that brought Sarth to help unroll rugs and manhandle the big table. It was chance and impulse that made me ask, "Have you ever done any of this?"

He stopped in the door and stared. Flicked his eyes to Verrith, rolling shin-guards up her well-bowed legs. Raised one of those eyebrows, and said, "Not in a tower."

Sarth can say more with an eyebrow than a Dhasdeini minister's speech. Thin, bronze-mahogany, perfectly arched. Mannered, ironic, elegant as a court-satirist's curse.

"Do you want to try?"

The brow went straight.

"You worked in a gymnasium, didn't you?"

The mask became doubt.

"So you know the most important thing. How to fall."

He looked from me to the women and back. I said, "This isn't the tower."

For an instant the lion's eyes flared. Something I could read at last. Longing. A man's hunger to compete. Then he started to shake his head.

Under my breath, I said, "Are you afraid?"

Both brows came down, hard. Just as quietly, he said, "No."

"Zuri," I called, "how'd you feel about a recruit?"

Her face is a trouble-Head's, about as expressive as a block of Iskardan stone. No flicker in the eyes, the gray of winter water, no shift in the stocky shoulders, the ready-to-skirmish stance. But I have learnt to read that file at the nose.

"C'mon, Zuri. They do gymnasium work, you know that. And if you bend him, Tel won't mind."

I might have groped them both. Even Azo gasped.

"I'm a man, you know."

Any other time I'd have got a laugh with that, for all it was dead serious: You took me, so why not him?

"Well," I said, "show them you're fit, anyhow." And when he stared at me, "Get out of your shirt."

And undershirt, and woolen indoor jerkin. The first place a trainer checks is at the skin.

I might have committed blasphemy. Sarth, Zuri, Verrith, Desis. They all choked.

"In the River-lord's name, what is—"

Sarth took one step forward, got my arm, and brought me, quiet but inexorable as a landslide, outside.

"Alkhes." He seemed somewhere between hysterics and outrage. "I'm husband to the Head."

"So?"

"So nobody—nobody!—sees my clothes off. Not outside the Tower."

"We *are* outside the tower—!"

"Except in bed, then. Except her."

With anything else, anyone else, I would have let it go. But I kept remembering that look. The longing. The fire.

"Well, we're not in bed, and not in Amberlight, and there's no reason why you can't try out for troublecrew, and they *will* see you stripped sometime. So it might as well be now." I forestalled the expression. "Or do *you* want to let it go?"

He looked back through the door. Challenges so seldom move Sarth. But the longing . . . that was real.

He braced his shoulders. Started undoing the jerkin as he went inside.

"Now is there," I demanded, "anything wrong with that?"

Zuri still seemed to be considering a faint, but she flicked an eye over him and gestured, and I said, "Get dressed." He had hardly gone to gooseflesh. But they can build muscle in the tower, if they do nothing else.

"So, Alkhes." Surrender. "He's your partner." And revenge.

IN A WAY, to work with a man again was a coming home. Even in simple stuff like showing him the warm-ups, sharing the partnered exercises. The real thing was something else.

However stubborn and opinionated, I'm not a fool. The third time we messed up a simple step in and contact, I stopped.

"Zuri?" She was there instantly. Like all good trouble-Heads she has eyes in the back of her neck. I said, "I can't teach."

She did react this time. Tongue click, eyes cast up. Open censure, therefore spurious: how did I deserve this? I fluttered lashes and looked helpless. And as always, got that smothered spurt of a laugh.

"Troublecrew? Trouble's *worth*." She stepped past me, and her voice changed. "Watch this."

Partnering Azo, I caught only the rare glimpses. But he did have a gymnast's balance, and he could learn, from someone who could teach.

"Back leg. Brace. Side. Step. Duck." When we finished our routine they were circling; at the learner's slower, thought-out pace. Zuri wore her practice expression. Blank as all the rest. He was stern, concentrating. But already there was resilience, discipline. A temple statue, learning to fight.

"You know how to fall?" He nodded. "Come in on me." With a learner, Zuri's explanations are meticulous. "It'll be over my arm. Off your own weight."

And the fall was neat as a professional's. Over her arm, head tucked, rolling, a true gymnast, to his feet.

"Keep guard." Zuri's praise is to go on.

When we finished in earnest she had him working on a hip-throw. I could tell the trouble was not fatigue. She had reached his limit. The third time he bungled it she clicked her tongue and said, "To me."

He took breath and launched himself. It went the way all clashes do, brief tangle of limbs and muscle-thrust, chaos swiftly, masterfully resolved.

"Like *that*."

The hip throw is very close contact, both your arms around them, bodies passing all but chest to chest. She looked down where her hands had left him, sprawled on the mat. A winded god. As usual, she was barely breathing hard. But there was something odd about her stance.

"That'll do."

Even for Zuri, it was brusque. And there was something close to violence in the way she pulled him up.

Iskarda. Week 13.
Tellurith's Diary

WILL THERE EVER be a time, I wonder, when my second husband is not setting my House by the ears? Bad enough the business with the qherrique; then he had to put Sarth among the troublecrew, a bagful of foxes with a pigeon; and two men instead of one nursing bruises every night.

Granted, it is a challenge I might never have coaxed Sarth to take. Something to fill this lull, as the rough work shrinks to nothing, so while we work up weaving and sewing and carving and all the other crafts, he has more to do than play us flute-songs. Something to straighten his shoulders. To give pride—as well as blackening—to his eyes.

Mother, I should have foreseen this. All of it. Should have realized it would not stop at snares on that side or training on this. Now a fool Head must squat here keeping the House core safe, while her folk run off to risk their necks.

Blight and blast new customs as well, that can set those two fool dangles running with them, hell-bent to prove their stupid man-selves— when they should, in Amberlight they *would* both be safely locked inside the tower.

THE ALARM was deep midnight, by what moon I saw. I know I was sleeping, because the world switched back on me like a qherrique-strike, hoisting me half to the roof. And Alkhes with me; or over me, both of us with the spinal jerk of a war-alarm, catapulted for weapons and the door.

I got the cutter on the bed-post, he must have torn down the stone-mallet in the passageway. We hit the steps in the heart of it, crash-crash against the byre-walls, the bawl of mortally terrified beasts, in scent of a death-giver and no way to flight. And one cry that turned my bowels to water: a woman's battle, wound, alarm shriek.

Three stone steps from threshold to yard. Alkhes took them in a bound, Zuri overran me, light-gun a slash of white. My cutter beam ripped the sky, Zuri bawled, Alkhes bellowed. Something else bawled back, an alien, coughing roar.

By the Mother's own mercy it was already running; if he had caught it . . . The moon and cutter beams hit instead, too far off to hurt: a striped rush of whiteness flowing up the palisade. The spring of a big cat, but no cat shape. A four-legged beast-gait; but the arms, the shoulders, something inchoate in the sloppy, rolling fur-heap, that said: Human. Man.

And it was gone, the four of us in the yard panting, babbling in paroxysms of more than cold, the cold moon staring; human uproar overflowing the steps, across the hill, a stretching chain of lights. Iatha and a double torch-flare at my shoulder, rapping, "In the Mother's name—Tellurith!"

And Desis, an all but moveless bundle at our feet.

It has claws. Probably not retractable, says Caitha, from the mud and muck in the wound. On the big council table Desis was still half-conscious, eyes rolled back; Caitha, run across-hill with troublecrew escort, cutting away undershirt, jerkin, big outer coat; from a shoulder slashed to the bone.

"Mother's own luck it missed the arteries. And the joint."

Caitha has seen war-wounds. Has salved the wreckage of the great light-guns, legs, arms seared off. Her hands were quite steady, swabbing; Roskeran, handing instruments, was wavering on his feet.

And Zuri, teeth clenched, trying to interrogate a scout who, the instant healers finished, would be under sleep-syrup and out.

"Did you get a look?"

"Came round the back—third patrol." Desis' teeth were shut tight too. Her jaw kept jerking, but that was shock; and wound-shock atop. "Cattle upset . . . Saw something move." A hard-fought gulp. "Blasted *white*— Mother, I thought, 's that some idiot playing ghost-games? But—too big. Primed the light-gun . . . Hell of a s-snarl—Came at me, like that—! Got a shot in—must've slashed—knocked the gun away. Cattle went mad. Thought I was g-gone—"

And Alkhes, at Zuri's elbow, not trembling; vibrating, a killer hair-triggered to charge.

Zuri must have felt it. She glanced about. Those eyes were lightning in a starless sky.

"Can I . . . ?" still aware it was not his command. He read the half-nod. "Desis, did you get a hit?"

"Th-think so." Her jaw clenched tighter, as Caitha set the first dressing and nodded to Roskeran to press the wound-lips firm. Despite the size, they would not stitch it. "I want," Caitha had said grimly, "to be sure first." That it would not go poisoned, she meant. "It bawled—"

"So there might be blood. We can track . . ."

Zuri turned and stared at him. He met her eyes, a look solid as a bar. In a minute or two her shoulders set, infinitesimally, and she turned to me.

"Ruand," very evenly, "if the tracks match, we don't have a choice. If this is what cleaned out Azo's snares, it's moving in. It got over the fence. It probably came for the cattle. If it wasn't hit badly, and we don't get it, it'll come back."

I DID MANAGE delay, till daylight, then for a message to Darthis, who outstripped the sun to my step. The only wonder is she waited so long; all Iskarda must have been roused by the fuss.

And none of Iskarda knows a predator man-height and higher, four-footed, leaving tracks that look like nothing, in the freezing mud, so much as monstrous fang-tipped hands.

They were willing, for once, to help. They counted off winter perils, bandits, lynxes strayed down from the Heartlands, a wolf-pack one famine year. They offered to call the outliers, who might know more. When Zuri was sure of the blood, they brought not only a brace of scent hounds but four of the village's defense-line, the great hunting mastiffs, and five more women to swell the hunt.

They were greatly relieved to see troublecrew with their light-guns, the cutters wielded by Pheroka and Zariah. When Zuri gently confiscated my cutter, and proved, by irrefutable logic, that it was risk enough to hazard the others, they were delighted to agree.

And I will dream of their faces, when Alkhes slid out of the crowd behind us. Put a hand on my wrist. And said, almost under his breath, "Tel? I know hunting. I've done it all my life." He did not let me get it out. "I can help Zuri. Tracks. Advice." And she was the one Head who might listen. "One more spear. It might make all the difference."

To my folk. To who came home, whole or wounded, and who did not.

Except it was not a spear he meant.

I looked at Zuri. My trouble-Head is not expressive. But I could not mistake the look for anything but assent. Relief.

I looked at the Iskardans.

There should have been scandal, outrage. There was certainly worry. There was also, weirdly, something close to hope.

I said, "Ruand, will your hunters accept . . . ?"

At my elbow, Darthis hesitated. Then produced a stiff, short nod. "The Mother," she said, "will be his shield."

All the Iskardans looked as if such a thing were literal. Gods—now I even sound like him—if I could think it might be truth!

I took the cutter off my belt. "Zuri checks this," I said, "before you leave this yard."

"Tel . . ."

A whisper. Gratitude. More than gratitude. It was his very manhood, I realized, at stake.

And he knew how much I would stake. He went down on one knee to take the cutter, and with it in his hand, kissed my wrist.

Alive, breathing, flesh and blood, so close. Murmuring, for my ears alone, with utmost sincerity, as he sprang up. "I give you my word. I'll take care."

I could sit still, perhaps, were that all—all! I had at risk. But Mother blast the little demon, when he had proved he could wake the thing, and use it, and even, chagrin of chagrins, hit something, when they had gathered their dogs and weapons and mustered, twenty coated, booted, anonymous shapes, moving, dark and ponderous, toward the ice-blue sky beyond the gate—

He looked round, to someone at my back.

And stopped.

And said to Zuri, who had already marked him as her shield-point, and swung with him, "He's troublecrew too."

Mother, why was I ever seduced into revolutionary lunacy? Why did I let the pair of them start this stupid *manhood* contest? Why am I sitting here now, tearing my heart out, with both my imbecilic husbands out there, risking each other, and Sarth as war-skilled as a babe in arms!

Iskarda. Week 13.
Meditations. Alkhes-Assandar

IT WAS a beautiful morning. Sun, clear sky, every shadow clean as a blade. Wind to scythe your ears off. Bright air, crisp scent and crackle under the silvery helliens. Intoxicating. Even before the nerve-twisting smell of dogs, pad of boots, tension, expectation. Mortal fear.

The scent-hounds found easily. We had the mastiffs in the van, rotating light-guns near them so some were always primed. The bigger women had boar-spears, and the other two Iskardans carried bows. A good spread of weapon-choice.

I gave the last boar-spear to Sarth.

Gods know what made me claim him. Gods know, I will die of it, if he—gods know, I'll do it before I see Tellurith. All the way up the hill, that was all I could think.

But how could I see that look in his eyes, and let him stay?

Stupidity, what stupidity it is, to be a man.

The women had no such concerns. How did we ever think women couldn't fight? They were solid as phalanx-leaders. No bravado, no doubts. Something had come to ravage their hearth-place. They did not want revenge or glory. They just meant to get rid of it.

High up the hill another joined us, a slender bowlegged woman in a fur-lined hood, slipping from the trees to wave a weapon at Azo. A cross-bow. And with it, word of the quarry at last.

"Snow-walker," Zuri said, dropping back from the colloquy. I had more wits than to push into that. "The legend says they were created before women. From ice and the Mother's spit. They were," a mouth-corner twitched, "a mistake."

I think it's the similarity that's worst. Seven—eight feet tall, the thing was, when it fell down out of the tree where the scent-hounds were roaring and scratching and standing on their back legs. Eight feet if a cursed inch and all of it sloppy great wads of this white—flapping—fur.

It must have laired in the tree. And its wound was light enough to let it sleep. When the dogs first bayed, there was no answer at all. The hunter told us some long story of a snow-walker hunt that boiled down to, only one way to get them out.

Fire.

It was a hellien, after all. Leaves, bark, rich in oil. We kindled the trunk. Waste, savagery, that beautiful great silver-spatched double-forked ancient, propped like a cloud in the coign of the hill. But when the smoke started coming out the trunk-holes—it worked.

Snarl first. Then cough. Then bawl. The dogs went crazy. We had the ring set by then. Alternate spears and light-weapons, backed by bows. I had Zuri at my elbow, and Sarth my other side. What would I have given to put him at my back?

It fell out of the tree like an avalanche, and bounced like a bale of springs. Three arrows were standing in it before it hit the ground and all they did was make it bawl. Kind gods, but the thing was—grotesque.

Man-height, man shape. Running four-legged, yet with feet and hands. And fangs, and a breath like a gut-heap.

And claws. Yellow-tipped like horn. No mistaking that. It went past my face so close.

Zuri slashed with the light gun and took the whole hand off at the wrist. Battle-memory worked my legs without me, I cleared its jump and managed to get the cutter fired. I think my shot was the one in the flank. Then it was rolling like a furry—human-not-human—boulder, with women at it everywhere and a wasp-swarm of dogs.

I have been hunting often. Everything from River ducks to Heartland boars. I know the nerve-fire, the terror, the bloody little chaos and the mad exhilaration. Like a tiny war. It's over. I'm not dead. But with that—

Human. Not human. When the dogs got it down and disemboweled it, the noise . . .

We lost one mastiff. Pheroka burned her knuckles on Zariah's cutter and the boar-spear carriers were bruised. Three of them held it, together, on their blades. One Iskardan had a slash down her forearm, the opposite circle-side from ours.

Sarth and I were quite intact.

Azo patted us down while Zuri oversaw the—trophy-work. They had it pulled out straight while the hunter measured it. The women were chattering then, right enough. Not boasting. More like, "Oh, I was so scared, it's over, what a relief." I think I was patting Sarth myself. The worst of terrors, to be scared for someone else.

And when I looked round, the Iskardans were there.

One of them had been making some sort of sign. The other had a—paw. It had been cut with a blade, not a light-gun, there was still blood. She said, "Stheir, will you honor us?"

I don't know the hill-patois, but the root was clear enough: Goddess something-or-other. But she wasn't blooding a novice. And there was no scandal, nothing like resentment—

If I didn't know better, I'd have said it was awe.

"The Mother has looked on you," she said. "Will you take us under Her shield?"

Be hung if I know what she meant, even now. But there was no time and probably risk in saying, What is all this? As for the blood—whatever the thing was, it was dead. I made a sort of bow. She put her fingers in the blood. And drew this sign on my face. Right on my forehead. Some sort of double-spiral. And nobody in the House knows, and nobody in Iskarda will say what it is.

They wanted me to take the paw too, but I swore the trophy should be theirs.

Iskarda. Week 13.
Journal kept by Sarth

IF THAT IS "hunting," and that is what Outland men do, I give fervent thanks I was born inside a Tower.

War, now; that is another matter. In the siege of Amberlight, when we Tower men went downstairs that last day, in our silks and lovelocks, none of us fit to heave a paving-stone, let alone fight hand-to-hand or wield a knife . . . but I knew that I would try, and die trying, before I saw an Outlander lay hands on Tellurith. No revulsion, no fear, no doubt at all.

Hunting? Terror, peril, waiting's torment. Mess, blood, excrement. People do this for pleasure?

And have their necks wrung by irate wives at the end?

The one thing I am grateful for, after threats of incarceration and bondage if I ever dare such lunacy again . . .

The one thing I am *not* grateful for . . .

Is to know when it will be, whatever they are expecting, up in Iskarda. Mid-winter's Day.

THE SOLSTICE is not really a Mother's festival. It is a sun-mark, no part of the thirteen linked moon-patterns but an ebb-point in the four-fold procession of the year.

None of the women would tell him.

Perhaps, just perhaps, none of the women up that mountain knew. Perhaps, just perhaps, Tellurith does not know either. Because her face did not change when he shoved back his hair and asked her, half shamefaced, half laughing, "Tel, what does this thing mean?"

And she looked at the double-spiral, puzzled, and asked quite calmly, "Where did you get that?"

So he told her. She frowned again, then turned her hands out. "Some backwoods hunting ritual? I'm sorry, caissyl. I'm not sure."

While I stood there with the blood gone to ice down my backbone; wanting to scream, Don't you remember, don't you know?

It's a double helix. It's a Solstice dedication.

In the old days, that we heard of in Tower legends when Sethar wanted to cow us, it was the mark of the king.

Who was sacrificed, as Sethar would threaten us for our wickedness, to bring the sun back, on Mid-winter's Day.

PART II

ISKARDA

V

Spring. Iskarda.
Tellurith's Diary

THE SNOW-FLOWERS have opened. Just this morning. Sheltered in the angle of the stairs, a tiny, indomitable, pure-white sheaf. Immaculate in the mud.

Presages. Omens. Spring. Not here, yet, but promised. The world—something—is going to live . . .

Again.

I NEVER THOUGHT I could write this. How long is it? Two, three months? I have been numb, number than the snow-bulbs, frozen. Just to begin thawing is torment. I am not sure I can write. Not now. Not yet!

Because it means going back. Remembering. Writing what I have been saying in my mind, in my dreams, over and over, in my nightmares. Mother, pity me. Mother, spare me. Mother, forgive me.

Because I didn't know.

Least of all that day, the holy Third-day before Mid-winter feast. With the building finally over, the stores filled, all the hirelings discharged, and a heavy snowfall to cut both roads. Isolating us to run about the hills after festival saplings to set in pots before the hearth, and whisper and giggle over fermenting jokes, and gifts half-made; and hear, through the rising tide of exhilaration, the musicians practicing their part for the day.

We had planned it by the old ways; midnight watch, House and Craft-heads to officiate over the most sacred part, the dousing and renewal of the fires. We meant to do it in my house cellar, with Zariah's cutter, the first to touch Iskardan stone; then the torches would run to children at every other threshold, and every household would keep the vigil before we met, in my courtyard, to sing the dawn hymn. As we always had. As a House.

No matter that last time we did this thirteen Houses strong, kindling the sacred flame on the topmost turret of Amberlight's citadel. No matter that this time we had no idea what the rest of the village intended. Iskarda's blockade endured.

Until Darthis called.

We were in the council chamber: Quetho, Hayras, Iatha, Charras, Hanni, mixing festival tag-ends with plans for after the year turned. Azo brought warning; but I did not look for Darthis to be dressed—more than dressed, garbed.

As a Mother's Voice, with the tall crescent gold-leafed horns of the headdress, and the somber splendor of the wine-dark, blood-dark officiant's robes.

We had leapt up before she entered; Azo's face said: Move. Darthis paused on the threshold, her two proper attendants behind. We arranged our raggle-taggle selves in postures of respect. She planted the staff, gold-tipped with its gilded sacred acorn. We waited. Nor does one anticipate a Voice.

I had just time to recognize a wonder, Darthis uneasy twice over. Before she cleared her throat and spoke.

"We trust your preparations—fare well."

"Assuredly." I almost managed to suppress the irony. Not the smallest boy-child had bothered to enquire. "I trust Iskarda's have also been blessed."

Whatever I had said, both her attendants—gray-haired, council veterans—twitched.

Darthis' lips moved. It might almost have been: Blessed.

Then with a mighty effort she heaved her shoulders up and brought out the words.

"Iskarda wishes—to share."

I all but fell in the brazier. Fool that I was, I felt my face spread, the flash-fire of the smile.

"Nothing—" I even bowed to her! "—could make Telluir House happier. We would be honored." Had she really put on a Voice's robes for this? Well, I thought blithely, perhaps it really was so momentous to her. "Perhaps we could discuss details. The Kindling? Of course you have a sacred place . . ."

She darted me a look that could only have been exasperation. I had the wits to stop.

"Telluir agrees, then." She pronounced it formally. It was binding, a Voice making treaty between folk. "That Telluir and Iskarda will share."

I donned my own Head's voice. "Telluir agrees."

She brought the staff upright. There was something—more than officialdom—in her stance.

"In Iskarda," she said, "we do things our own way."

When did we need telling that?

"The kindling is for Houses. For Iskarda—the Mother's Chosen pays the blood-debt. For us all."

Oh, Mother! A counter-stroke beyond hill-fellings. No wonder she had waited after the first clash. No wonder, after that last visit, she had been satisfied. All, it was all to be returned to her, a thousand-fold. And I, blind, cretinous imbecile, I had drawn the bolt on my own head.

Chosen. What other could there be, what other had I made inevitable? Chosen of the Mother, in Amberlight, in Iskarda, over and over. The only man who ever heard, who ever woke the qherrique. By her own eyes' proof. And who had claimed, sworn, forced it down her throat?

At the hunt she had set it back in the Mother's hands. And had her reply. Even when they sealed it, I did not notice. *Mother*, where were my wits?

Now she sprang the ambush. Revenge's crown. I had agreed; I could not renege. Neither Iskarda's nor Telluir's honor would sanction it. It would be a slap in the Mother's own face.

So I had condemned him. To make, to cement our alliance, the new House we had struggled for. To make Telluir and Iskarda one.

To purge the monstrosity, the abomination. If she could not get at Sarth, she would have his bed-mate. I would expiate my sins with my own—with my heart's own heart-blood.

I hope—I pray—some of it stayed out of my face.

Hers was blank, needless to say. In the consummation of revenge, she remained Darthis. But I saw, at her shoulder, Iatha's look.

Then, I think, I nearly did lose everything. Because it said what filled my own ears so clearly. Even with the pain of it, we will live; we will have bought, however shamefully, the House's reconciliation. But for him?

My eyes began to sting. Not the worst yet, no, not yet; not even that he was going to die; that I was going to lose him.

I would have to tell him so.

Someone brushed past me. Someone—too harshly to recognize—said, "Telluir will arrange matters. Word will come." Sheer blasphemy so to pre-empt, to dismiss a Voice, to make molten threat of ceremonial arrangement. The turn, if not the tone, was Iatha. Then, if ever, I could have kissed her feet.

My vision was going, lost in blackness as if I were dying too. Through it I heard Darthis; not yet, even yet, vindictive. Just coldly, monumentally, smug.

"The Mother's hands prepare the Chosen. Beginning on the Third-day."

They wanted him now.

I RECALL IATHA with me. Holding me. In my own bedroom, a vast silence running out beyond us, a paralysis' baneful tide. Saying, "No. No. I'll do it. It's my fault."

And the moment when they had all gone. When I waited, alone, as I was not even in the fall of Amberlight; listening for the sound of feet.

Light, quick, familiar, beloved as breath; far too quick, he knew, he could not help but know it was calamity, and flew to stem it as only troublecrew could, round the door-jamb like a small human catapult bolt, "Tel, what is it? Tel!"

So there was no time, after all, for the protracted anguish of watching him understand. I was already in his arms, clenched against that hard muscle-warmth, that racing heart, as he went stiff, and very still; then, too softly, he said, "Tel?"

I don't remember the words. Or how I commanded my voice. Only his features, congealing, as the blood drained until his whole face was wax.

My voice stopped. He stood there. Both of us frozen to the floor. He had thrown up honor, glory, a life; begun over, in a strange land, with humiliation and struggle and difficulty harsh as pain.

And now must lose it all.

So briefly I had won him back. Mother, I wanted to scream, if this is how gods joke, better no gods, even You.

He took breath. His eyes, those great eyes that were the life of his face, were the blind black of space. His lips moved, clumsily, as if frozen too.

Then he said, "Well." As if he could not get his breath. "Well . . ." And then, still looking over me. "It's something—if you have to go—to know . . . it won't be a waste."

I did weep then. It burst out of me like the River breaking a wall. He shook me till my neck snapped and his hands were iron claws.

"Don't, Tel. Stop it! If you start, I will . . ." His voice quaked. "And I'll *hang* before I let her win this now . . . !"

So he knew he had no grace-time. He knew we would have to walk out and confront Darthis. And he would not give her that last triumph; to see that either of us had wept.

I did stop. He was still staring over me. White, yes, but something had changed. His eyes were alive; unseeing still, and huge, but something had woken in them. A visionary, a martyr's look. A kind of exaltation, a curse in the teeth of death.

Not a waste. He had been a soldier, and a life-pledge is soldiers' trade. He had always, I understood, had death at his elbow. However tragic, however grievous and unjust it would be to die now, it would not be unbearable. So long as it was not waste.

So I could walk beside him, steadily, down the passage. And somehow, keep my voice steady, as I told Darthis, "Here is the Chosen of Telluir House."

I had not known I would say that. Watching her face, I was glad.

There was silence from my House-mates. The silence of devastation, death. In the bedroom I had managed to let him out of my arms. Even, at the door, to disengage our hands. Now take him, I thought frenziedly, before I grab him back and never let go.

She said, "Does the Chosen consent?"

So much for control and ceremony. Somebody said, "What?"

No impatience. She had known, I understood, that I did not know. This was to be the final twist.

"The Mother's Chosen must also choose. Is there consent?"

The Mother blast you, I wanted to scream. Oh, to be in Amberlight! I would rouse the qherrique and blast you from the world!

But it was not, after all, my choice.

Her eyes had moved. Beside me, I felt him grow taller as he stood. When I looked, it was not the face of a soldier, even of a general. His two worlds had come together, the readiness to trade a life, that life's ransom. Me. My folk. His folk. Telluir House. When he spoke, it was the voice of the old, the royal sacrifice.

He said, "Yes."

And it was truth. He could have smiled, I think, in that moment. Even when they brought out the hood, crimson leather lined with black silk, the Mother's death colors, and the twisted crimson and ebony cords. And blindfolded, and bound him. And took him away.

No doubt I spoke, gave orders, shored things up. I recall Ahio shouting while the tears ran down her cheeks, "Mother *blast* her, she won't ruin it all! Blight and blast her, we'll have the feast. She shan't—"

Destroy what he had won for us. Waste his death.

I do remember the aftershock. Iatha back from the village: a minor miracle, Iatha, too enraged to curse.

"We can't go." Across the council table, quieter than very death. "Nobody goes. Nobody but the servers. And the priestess."

I tried not to let myself think who that would be, because I knew all too well. Would she forego the ultimate avengement, putting the knife in his throat?

Iatha was holding me, for some reason. We were out of the council room. My eyes were dry. It was she who cried, cursing, weeping, a perfect paroxysm, clinging to me tighter than I clung to her, whispering, "'Rith, oh, 'Rith. Mother blast you, cry!"

And I could not. Even in bed, even with Sarth.

Looking back, I recall the numbness in his eyes, but we all looked like that. All shattered, all splinted by resolution; that we would take the gift being bought for us; that broken or not, we would keep our festival.

We did learn the time. Midnight, of course. Mid-winter night. When else?

A cold night, clear, and perfectly still, under a great flowering field of stars. As if the earth, like its small inhabitants, had brought all its affairs to a dead, listening halt. As if he would restart the dayspring, not just for a village, but for the Mother's whole life-woven world.

It was blessed distraction to fettle the ceremony. To put on, bitterest defiance, the white robes that in Amberlight symbolize the risen sun, to go down to the cellar, with the House about me; taking, a greater defiance, all the men. And when word came from Hayras, best of mathematicians, posted on the roof, to give Iatha the looted silver ceremonial snuffer. And try not to think, as darkness swallowed us, what else was being quenched.

Only to vow, as my mouth pronounced the ritual words and the great gout of moon-fire blossomed under Zariah's fingers: this is the gift you bought us.

This will be our life.

THAT CRUEL PRIDE, that bitter comfort upheld me through the long, long watch to dawn itself. So the grief was still sealed over when I came out, the Craft-heads around me, on my own house-steps.

It had frosted in the windless night. All the house-eaves, the wall-rims, the thatch-fringes, the untrampled places in the yard were gray as unwoken qherrique. The great bay of Iskarda valley and the plain beyond spread shadowless but lucid; the snowline was purest moonglow, primed to blaze when the sun lit an ice-turquoise, icily green-rimmed sky.

The world waited like the faces turned up to me: my House, ranked decorously, hollow-eyed but immaculate, down to the youngest child. With the men among them. And the musicians, Sarth at Esrafal's side, breath already taken to welcome the dawn.

I went down into their midst, the Head's place. The air was at its bitterest, the fulcrum point of returning day. I fixed my glance on Iatha, poised above me on the step, to signal the moment the sun's limb topped the peaks.

She was concentrated, slightly frowning; an expression more familiar than breath. Then her eyes' focus changed.

I spun round. Heads blocked my view. Zuri was gone already, crowd furrowed in her wake. Iatha gasped. Then she hurled herself off the step, caught and towed me gateward, grabbed my shoulders and spun me about.

A bier was coming down the path.

Just time to think, Mother rot her, she means to wreck this as well. No time to think, we never asked about the corpse. One avalanche of shock and razed determination. Even now, they should not see us break.

Whatever I said, Zuri enforced it. She and Iatha flanked me in the gateway. Behind us, there was not a sound.

The bier was crimson-worked on wood of polished black. Men carried it. Hooded and robed in black and crimson, but their body shapes were unmistakable. The form on it was draped in a great crimson pall. A treasure. An heirloom. But not so precious as the red it hid.

The priestess led them, anonymous in the night-black sacrificial robes, the death-mask, with the Eater's huge owl eyes and beak. Behind them someone played an ancient mountain pipe, the same five thready, breathless notes.

They passed Quetho's house. The track swung toward our gate. The sun reached the skyline, and every frost crystal exploded, a quilt of prismed light.

And their burden moved.

MOTHER BLESS HER, Zuri caught me. Pinned me, a mouse in hawk's claws, or I would have run screaming and sobbing like a lunatic and wrecked it all.

They lowered the bier. The priestess spoke. Zuri's fingers bit clear to my elbow bone. I must have made an answer. The grip unleashed.

The pall was lined, fire-scarlet silk. Mottled and spatched with darkness, black and crusted, sagging freshly, dark and wet.

The blood was everywhere. Streams drying like a drought-shrunk river on his throat, up into his hair. Blood daubed the double spiral on his forehead, his mouth, his nipples, his navel—naked, of course. Copiously bruised, slashes round his ribs, probably he had been scourged. Oh, Mother, somebody squalled, is every purging ritual the same? And his legs, his foot-soles rasped to blood—had they run him through a field of thorns? Time whirled over time, the road to Iskarda, the first time I ever saw him, battered, bleeding, unconscious, on Amberlight's stones—But alive, oh, Mother's bliss, I'll strangle Darthis, I was thinking, she knew this, alive, alive, alive . . .

I put a hand to the pulse in his throat. The other went without volition to smooth back the matted, bloody hair, another instant and I would have thrown myself atop him, hysterical as any River Quarter husband with a crippled wife.

His eyes opened. Black, blacker than death itself, drowning pits in that drowned bloody face. I got out, "Caissyl," and choked.

The eyes dilated. There was time to see he saw, and know he did not know me. Before he started to scream.

Spring. Iskarda.
Journal kept by Sarth

It is bad, and dangerous, what they have done. Tellurith, who freed me from the Tower. Zuri, who taught me how to kill. Darthis, who gave me cause, and, Mother defend me, more than bloody impulse. Who tore away both wife and husband—

Alkhes.

Husband. Rival. Mentor.

Friend.

Better to sit here and write about it. Even if I have already broken a second pen.

Better than to go up there and stab, slash, disembowel, kick in Darthis' face.

Not enough to write, never enough to write, when this sits in the mind like an amputation, a never-easing burn. To live with Tellurith as with the walking dead. A zombie, these last two months.

Oh, she speaks, and hears, and gives orders. And goes up to the quarry where they have built make-shift shelters over the face. And between snowfalls, has seen the first two pack-trains off on the River-road. And reads the word that comes up from Marbleport, and gives me news of Tez. And lies beside me at night, a breathing, absent death.

The first time, in Amberlight, I was in the Tower. Caitha says he nearly died then. Blood loss. Hemorrhage. Amnesia, afterward. The second time the bleeding was less, but for a few minutes, he did go out of his head.

There was blood enough this time. The carotid artery, Caitha says. Just a nick. The greatest skill, or the greatest luck. Then they must have held him head down and painted it all over him, all over the altar, all over themselves.

The Chosen bleeds for us all.

I have seen the marks over the doors. I saw—before the snow's lustration—the altar stone. Serious, Caitha says, but not mortal. Not the worst.

They did rape him. I know that. Caitha—Tellurith knows that. We all saw the blood. I saw Tellurith see it, and stop, as if shot in her own heart. The Mother knows who, or how many times, but I can guess. Next day, I caught Krestyr at the well.

Son to Zdana, the village seer, bonded to Eria, Darthis' daughter. A good enough boy, as village creatures go. When I walked up behind and took him by the neck, I thought he would swallow the buckets, yoke and all.

"Tell me," I said. I never had such a struggle to keep manners, Tower-discipline. My very fingers had a life of their own, they wanted to arch and drive into the larynx as Zuri had shown . . . "Tell me how it's done."

He choked and gabbled. I shook him. Whatever my face said, he let the buckets fall and went back against the well, all eyes and mouth.

In Iskarda Mid-winter is not only a sun-mark but a purgation. The Mother's Chosen bleeds for our sins as well as our life. So it is a ritual for men. Eight servers for the priestess, to prepare, to maneuver the victim. To perform the last part of the rite. To purge the folk by shedding seed as well as blood.

The Mother knows if the physical reality was worse than Amberlight. But for the mind, to have it happen again . . .

We could not stop him screaming. Nothing stopped it, till we had him inside and pinned down, at gods know what other risk, and Caitha got sleep-syrup down his throat. And Tellurith looked shattered then ... But we got him clean, into bed, both of us stayed with him. The festival went to the fire, of course. A clear, icily pure sunlit morning, a mockery of the house's hush; of Tellurith sitting there, her arms around him, the tears still running. Saying, over and over, "It'll be all right. When he wakes, it'll be all right."

But it was not.

Caitha says it is not impossible. That we should still not despair. The damage is in his soul, it is not physical. The mind simply found reality unbearable, and it has run away.

If it chooses, it could come back.

The first time he woke, he went berserk. More sleep-syrup, then restraints. Waking, another paroxysm, until Caitha, herself distraught, fixed the dose to keep him perpetually drugged.

He still did not know us. Every time we touched him, it was a fresh struggle, to master a frantic, untamed beast. And the first time we left him alone, he tried to run away.

Mother, if I *could* forget that, having to hunt him like a hare, and then the capture, the struggles—the screams—

In the end there was only one other alternative. One that none of us will—can—face.

So we have cleared a storeroom, and set up a lamp, a watch-place, braziers. Restraints. Padded cuffs. Endless care, and still he rubs raw under them. The hideous process goes on, muscles wasting, hair and beard gone mad; no one dares go near him with a blade. Feeding is a brawl. He will not—does not—understand cleanliness. Caitha has designed a hospital shift, that can be tied on over the restraints. Whoever has the round cleans him, changes it, swabs the floor ... The stench is worse than beasts'.

And every soul in the House who is capable has joined the roster for tending him, from Zuri to Roskeran, from Iatha's redoubtable mother to Asaskian. Seeing her there, I had to flinch. But she looked at me, those pure eyes, that delicate face. And said, "He did it for us."

Things do go on: that is the kindest or the cruelest thing. That after that first terrible month, the House is accepting it. He is there, and they look after him. Impossible atrocity. Part of life.

There has been the quarry work. And Zuri, hauling me out, remorselessly, to train. And the Mother knows, I will do that, because it was the last thing that he—

Gods damn, he would say. Now I have blotted half the page. And still I cannot—

Spring. Iskarda.
Tellurith's Diary

I WONDER, is there justice after all?

Stranger, if there is, than this thaw, this week of unbelievably—timely—soft weather that has the hills weeping, ripple and trickle of water, all day and most of the night. That will have the earth ready, they are saying, in the most hushed of voices, exactly when the Plough-star rises, to break the ground for spring.

When for a ten-year cycle it has been capriciously late, or maliciously early, but never with earth and sun in perfect chime. It will be, Azo says the outliers are saying, a most auspicious year.

So I have been busy the last two days setting our new plough-bounds. I remember my father told me once, a mere child, visiting in the Tower, perched on his knee: in the old, the very old days, to break the first fields for a city would require the greatest sacrifice. That they would mark the sacred limits with the blood of the king.

How thankfully—how gladly!—I would do that now.

But the fields must be marked. The snow-flowers have bloomed, the dayspring has woken. The thaw has come. And yesterday, as I set out with the surveying party, the message came from Darthis.

Eria brought it, her daughter. Like most Iskardans, when we see them, unwontedly subdued. Iskarda's Ruand wished to see me, of my mercy; Eria would show me the place.

Mercy? Well, it was nothing so great, after all. I think, now, I have almost worn out the hate. Not to forgiveness; never that. But to write it—and the snow-flowers—somehow, it does not matter so any more.

Eria led me up the quarry side. The track is never well-trodden, and was still deep in snow; only one other had gone that way.

Darthis was in the holy place. Bundled, like me, in winter coat and furs. Planted on a boulder. A rock-woman in a rock-sanctuary, hands flat on knees, staring out over the plain.

I could not rise to enquiries and salutations. I sat on another rock and stared myself.

The little snow-wind drew and died. The torpid earth breathed round us, still cold as a veritable tomb. The last of the wretched winter leaves clacked on the helliens.

She said, "Does it ever seem to you, that our Mother is a cast-iron bitch?"

Such a question, in such a tone, from Darthis.

She turned about on her rock. Put back her hood. Her features were rigid as ever, but she had lost flesh; and there was no rock in her eyes.

"I asked Her a question. A plain question. Is this thing with the men good or bad? Are we dealing with change or blasphemy? Yes or no?"

I could only stare.

Her mouth twisted. Far too bitter to call a smile.

"They do die. It lies on the knife-blade: the server's hand—the Chosen's nerve. My brother . . ." her shoulder lifted. "My mother's man. With the question—with your man—it seemed Her own choice."

She twisted away again. And back. Her voice changed.

"And She has destroyed him. Shamed Iskarda. Filled my mouth with dirt."

The Mother Herself knows, two moons—a quarter moon ago—I would have seen her suffer twice over; would have taken remorse as rage's fuel, would with joy and benison have torn her bowels out and watched her die.

But to know it was not wholly malice; that it had been honest doubt, not impregnable rancor; that she had planned as much for omens as revenge; truly had not meant him simply to die.

That if she had not lost—him—yet she—her folk, all of what she was—had been grievously distressed. And shamed.

And had the courage to admit it so.

I sat a long while, thinking how to answer. In the end, however bitter-brewed, the old words seemed best.

I said, "She is the Sower and Winnower both."

Her eyes jerked up. I saw her swallow. In double—triple?—shock.

She looked down. And said very quietly, "How is your man?"

I did not ask, Don't you listen to men's gossip? Does your whole village not creep about, hearing, with its tail between its legs?

I looked away across the plains, and answered, "Much as before."

Her movement was sharp as pain. "The healers?"

"Caitha says there is hope. There is still hope."

I heard her breath. The indrawn prelude to speech; three times let go.

Before she set her hand on the rock between us, and spoke as Ruand, as Voice; if only for a human will.

"We could find workers for another quarry-shift. If it is the will of the House."

All that I, all that—he—could have wanted. If only he could have bought it as he intended; with his life.

She had begun to withdraw, misreading my face. I wiped the tears off. Then I said, "The House can decide. All the House." And watched her face change back, before I went on, "Today noon. In my council-room?"

We both rose. It is something, to have the sense of occasion that marks a Head, of village or House. But as we moved off she said, "Iskarda would wish—to share the Sowing-rite as well."

Sacred. Even in Amberlight, for women alone. What demon of perversity made me answer, "With us? Or with the men?"

We crunched and clumped down another dozen feet of glistening, half-thawed rock. From behind my shoulder came her reply.

"If Telluir chooses—with both."

WHEN THE SNOWFLOWERS bloom, the ploughs are fettled in Iskarda, then every evening they watch the northern horizon; and the day after Qhastyr shows, the great white flower of the plough-star, they hold the Sowing-rite. The village Ruand, her Mother's Ear, and whoever is that month's presiding officiant, put on their newest set of work-clothes—except the priestess, who wears the brilliant azure and white fur-lined robe of the Mother Rising—hitch a team, and go down to the fields.

This year Iatha, and Zuri, and Hayras, and Quetho and I went as well. With the obligatory bucket of water, and the little bag of meal, and a pair of our future plough oxen, to be blessed.

And with us came Zdana's son Krestyr. And Sarth.

I think Krestyr may be the new Chosen; it would have been impolitic to ask. Sarth was my deliberate flaunting: my husband, the proxy of our Chosen, once Mother-cursed. Somebody I can rely on to cope with ceremony. Somebody to rub salt in Iskardan memory, to keep as well as take Alkhes' place.

The officiant spoke the prayer, then poured our water over the icy dirt. Darthis and I marshaled our teams, the rest leant on plough-frames or handles; the ground is still barely soft enough to break. Zdana's creaky contralto started the Sowing Song; everybody sang it with her as the teams started forward.

Including the men.

While the officiant walked behind us, casting meal broadside into the furrows, earth's symbolic first-food, to be returned a thousand-fold. Of course it is far too early to sprout; it is a kind as well as fitting symbol that we also feed the hungry birds.

This time, thanks to my machinations, the Telluir basket was carried by a man.

He coped impeccably, as I expected. As I had relied on. Unlike Krestyr, he even sang in tune. And all with that exquisitely sealed face, that grace, that perfected composure, which is the tower's bequest. At the worst, he has never surrendered that.

I WROTE THAT too soon. Last night, in the weary, the still dreary, half-healed quiet about the fire, round the kitchen table, where there has been no singing since Third-day. I could not help thinking, as my pen scratched the silence, and I smelt the cold, fresh, body odor of the snow-flowers someone had set on the work-bench: if it were right, by now the pain would have changed. There would have been sorrow and anger, and mourning, and now the natural movement toward healing. Toward going on. Not a loss of loss, but a permutation of grief.

I put up the journal, and said to Sarth, who sat, as always now, silent at my elbow, "It's time for bed."

We shed our clothes. I blew out the lamp. He drew the furs up round us. Then he began to weep.

A man's tears are a cataclysm. An upheaval, an earthquake in his body, the bedclothes, the entire bed, I thought it was a seizure, I leapt on him and screamed, "Sarth! Sarth, what is—" Then I flew up to shriek for the night-guard, Iatha, send for Caitha—he grabbed my wrist and choked out, "No."

"What then? What!"

His body was still heaving, I swarmed over it like a boulder and grabbed for his wrist, his chest, his face. But the pulse was there. He heaved again. There was wetness—there was water on his cheeks.

I stopped thrashing about and slid down and held him, tight as my muscles would clutch, his face against my neck. The sobs still came, tearing, uncontrollable as childbirth, while I hung on, offering the only solace I had left.

Finally it passed. He lay wept out, his body, his breathing quiet; the tears still ran, a freshet, a thaw-rivulet. I tidied his hair out from between us, and rubbed his back; and wondered why I had not been able to cry myself.

At last I whispered, "What is it, clythx?"

Before the City fell, it was the cutters' secret word for the mother-face. In the old language of Amberlight, it means, heart.

Another upheaval took him. Then he stretched out like a dying man in the last spasm and whispered, "Oh, Tellurith—it was my fault."

"Fault? What was your fault?"

The brazier spat and snapped. Out in the pure, icy moonlight, some bullock called. I waited, holding him tightly, stroking his hair. And eventually he whispered, "Alkhes."

Even now it can go through me—the mere name—like a lightning's cleaver-stroke. It took a while to whisper, "How—your fault?"

"I knew. I understood, and I said nothing. I was afraid to be stupid . . . I thought Zuri would—" He twisted his head against me. "Oh, Tellurith . . . !"

"You knew? I don't understand. You knew what?"

"The sun-sign. The double helix. I knew it was a Solstice sign, a sacrifice . . . !"

"*You* knew?" I was too stunned for tact.

"We all knew. Sethar used to threaten us. It was men's business, it was remembered."

In the tower.

"I saw the way they looked at him, but I never spoke. Even after the hunt. It was my fault—all my fault!"

He wept again, quietly now, while I held him, and felt the daggers turn in my own breast. And thought about the myriad chances I had had to turn the sweep of things, and lost.

How can one small human think to control destiny?

When he would listen I turned him on his back, and leant over him, stroking back hair, caressing that beloved, that beautiful, that—last, precious face.

"Beloved," I said. "Whatever we knew, there was nothing any of us could have done." He made a small, strangled motion, and I put my hand over his mouth. "If we had—if we had tried to change it—we would have risked— thrown in jeopardy—everything"—the name blocked my throat—"he— has won. It wasn't your doing. It wasn't even mine. Iskarda and Telluir wove it between them, on the Mother's—on the Mother's own loom."

I thought of Darthis, sitting on that mountain, colder than the unthawed ice.

"If you had something to do with it," I heard my words go out into the listening dark, "that is only what was ordained."

He was quiet. Presently he drew a slow, recovered but not easing breath. So I could go on, to bare what was in my own heart.

"I was far more to blame."

———

WE WEPT a great while, in the bed that is too wide now, and so achingly cold. In the morning, he went to the—sick-room. I was headed for the quarry, when Azo scuttered in the door. "Ruand! Signal from Marbleport!"

A bitter consolation that the signal-line we three planned together actually works. Three relay stations, with sun-reflectors rather than light-guns, spanning the fifty miles of road, manned by weaker convalescents from the epidemic. Far down across the plain, the last of them was blinking now, as Azo and I stared out from the vantage of the front-step.

"Packet follows," she read, her troublecrew hawk-eyes easily outpacing mine. "Must be something big."

The packet came this evening, couriered up from the last station by a wildly intrepid youngster who dared the spring freshets and quags on a saddled mule. Dhanissa, last seen thin as a thread and coughing her lungs out in Ahio's house. It did not need the big red code-seal that was Navy for Open Alone, to tell me the matter was both risky and delicate.

I opened it in the work-room, bleak late sunlight on Tez's sharp, Navy-style printed script, on the delicate azure petals of Hanni's potted hyacinth. The message, Mother knows, was simple enough.

Cataract has settled its succession wars. The new tyrant has sent a winter embassy. Downstream to Verrain.

"Nothing we can do, till we know which way he'll jump."

Iatha is as shrewd a politicker as I, and more ruthless at need. It is true enough. If he goes for Amberlight, what can we do in any case? But we will have to try. If, on the other hand, he means to try Dhasdein . . .

Either is feasible. Amberlight is too weak to resist. Dhasdein is powerful beyond Cataract's scope; but not, perhaps, if he can involve Verrain. Especially now that, with the qherrique gone, the River's most valuable trading stock is gold.

Whose source is controlled by Verrain.

Certainly, if I were Dhasdein's emperor, I would not sleep easily. And certainly, if we have to risk our necks for Amberlight, there is another consolation: Antastes will have even less time for a schismatic Amberlight settlement, too small to weigh in the River's scales, and a renegade general.

I said that to Iatha. And knew very well what that expression meant, before she looked away. Whatever we say, neither of us will be sleeping well.

In the meantime, we have a third miracle. Rising from the House meet, Darthis hung back a moment with me.

"Ruand," staring steadfastly at the table. "Iskarda wishes to share—the other shift as well."

The sick-room watch. My breath went in on, No. But he does not know me, he does not know Sarth. What can another stranger matter now?

Spring. Iskarda.
Journal kept by Sarth

IT IS NOT ENOUGH.

Not a three-quarter moon since that unthinkable moment: when the ice broke in Iskarda. When Darthis and Tellurith walked into this house together, and Tellurith called a joint council-meet.

Our Craft-heads and Iskarda's, at the one table. I would have thought to see the Iskans fall before another such miracle.

Such as Darthis offering—volunteering—her folk for the sick-room roster.

I did resist that. Let them help plan the water-supply and speed up the quarrying and add mules to the pack-train, let Darthis eat at our table and Tellurith dine in Iskarda. Or let Darthis—I thought, supreme hypocrisy—try to express some remorse. Not the sickroom. I talked to Caitha. I went so far as to question Tellurith.

Who looked at me as she had those last two months, and said, "What's the difference?"

But I am not sorry, however rancorously, that when Darthis was the first volunteer, I maneuvered to take her down myself.

It was a fourth miracle that she accepted such a guide—say rather, one more thing bought with his blood. But she followed me without demur: to the kitchen, for Shia's barley gruel, to the house dispensary, for the nose-clips and feeding tube. To the linen stores, for a clean shift, to the washing bay, for mop and bucket. Since I had the food, the last shift would have taken fuel. Then down into the cellar gloom, past the furnace, to the door.

Azo's husband Herar opened to my tap, murmuring, "Been pretty quiet." Nightshifts were not always so. He bulged his eyes at Darthis. I muttered, "A new volunteer."

His eyes got wider, but he sidled past us. I nodded her inside.

Going in was always the worst. And most heart-breaking, that sometimes he would be so quiet, you would swear he was mending; and next time, climb the wall as if he had never seen you before.

She balked. Five minutes would erase the stench from consciousness, but it was more than revulsion in her face.

Horror? Grief? Memory of what he had been, so proud, so lithe and deadly and beautiful, so human. More than human, perhaps, when he chose the sacrifice?

I set the things down. He was a heap of hair and unclad limbs sprawled, as ever, indecently, against the further wall. The padded restraint chains, the cuff on one galled ankle stared blackly to the overhead lamp. But he had not started up and tried to run, or screamed or thrown himself into the wall, I had not had to overpower and talk him down, while he fought me like a panicking beast. The shift was filthy, the floor reeking, he had probably got dung, yet again, in his hair. Cleaning always came first.

I took the warm water bucket and three steps forward, saying, "Alkhes."

We had tried all sorts of tones. We had tried other names, endearments. Whatever ruled him saw no difference.

He jerked his head up. I heard Darthis catch her breath. He thrashed in the chains and untangled as always, trying to run.

It did help to have a second person control him. And to do her justice, wrestling the filthy shift off, swabbing him down, getting salve on the galls, she did not flinch. She even took the mop from me. And hung onto his head while I fitted the nose-clips, and as I got soup down the feeding tube, she looked but did not comment on his staring ribs.

Only when I had the new shift on, and he was back against the wall, sobbing in that terrible way as if we had broken his heart all over again, did she ask, "Is it always—like this?"

I ought to have been cruel; but more cruelty I could not bear. I said, "Pretty much."

"He hasn't improved?"

"Sometimes it's easier. And then you think—"

I have never forgiven myself that I could not go on.

She shot me one look. A Ruand, she understood too much. About hope, and disappointed hope, that is the greatest grief of all.

"And he's never known you?"

"He never knows anyone."

She wore the strangest expression, a rage, a bitterness I never thought to recognize outside myself. She muttered something under her breath. Then she turned to the wall and said far too clearly, "Alkhes?"

He jerked back and cringed. I opened my mouth to shout, Stop, you'll set him off! But she was going on.

"It is my doing that brought you here. That it was not for malice, you have only my word. I called on the Mother, and She has denied us both. If She feels, there is no knowing. But be sure, I do."

Halfway through he was in paroxysm. By the finish I was trying frantically not to tear a gall or break a bone before he battered himself senseless. I yelled at her, rage and hatred over-mastering me, "Forget it, just get out!"

She offered to come back, and I refused. To quiet him took the rest of my shift, and extra sleep-syrup as well. I will not let her tear up his beast's quietude again.

Spring. Iskarda.
Tellurith's Diary

WHY IS IT that the smallest things, the truly trivial things, should break the back of grief? I can—I have come to bear the day-span without him; with no embrace, no speech, no glimpse, in a door or round a bullock-cart, of that lissom grace, that silken black darting head. I—can forget— the strength, the wits, the spear and buckler of his soldier's experience. I can do without the laughter. Someday, I may do without the love.

I can even bear the aching gap, the never-healing emptiness in the place he should have been, inside our bed. I can not-think of him in my arms, the smell, the touch, the dear living weight and warmth of him, the moments that our bodies shared the joining of our minds.

But when I walked past the troublecrew at workout this morning and Verrith, with a most unwonted timidity, intercepted me, saying, "Ruand, we wondered . . ."

And held out the sheathed blade, and the dagger belt. And the tattered, filthy pair of workmen's boots.

The boots—he—wore out of Amberlight.

THE LITTLE, pointless debris of a life. The Mother aid me, what is there in that to make me hide a half-morning under the bed-clothes like the stupidest widower, and weep?

IATHA WOULD answer me. It's the giving up, Yath would say, who has buried a sister already, and a daughter as well. It's admitting they're gone, it's putting their shells away, it's making the—the—losing—true.

Oh, Mother, how am I to bear a losing worse than death?

Iatha would have answered that too. I have seen it in her own eyes, so often, when we shared the losses of Amberlight. My mother, her daughter. My sons.

We go on, those eyes say. We go on.

Spring. Iskarda.
Journal kept by Sarth

THE SNOW-FLOWERS are done. The ploughing is under way at last; we have lost half a quarry shift. Our women still struggle against the unaccustomed weight and weather, blistered feet, hands raw with chilblains, hunting our surly mules and oxen up and down the rows. I have gone out, more than a time or two, to keep a team straight myself.

It is something, to work a while in fresh air. To get the underground smells and sights out of my nostrils.

To forget.

And there are the crocuses.

We never had them in Amberlight. Flowers we had in plenty, roses, and foamflower, white and delicate and sweeter-scented than incense, that a man preparing for the night would twine into his hair. Irises and clove-pinks, that smell like Heartland spice. The great globes of peonies, that blaze thunder-blue and scarlet, the glory of summer's height.

Snow-flowers are white, immaculately pure: cold as winter itself. Crocuses are heart's-blood purple, sun's-blood gold, they incendiarize winter, they kindle the very earth. In Iskarda they grow wild, especially along the ploughing lines. They have weathered the thaw. They will live until true spring comes. They are earth's promise, the vow of returning life.

When I watch them come up, those small wideflung clouds of color out there in the bleak spring sunshine, I am quite sure my heart will break.

Spring. Iskarda.
Tellurith's Diary

THERE IS THE PLOUGHING, after all. And the quarry. The marble-orders. The latest River news.

Our first divorce.

Zariah's brother-in-law. A quiet man, not tower-raised, from a Downhill sub-clan, tied with her sister and a cousin of Charras. The sister is dead.

Another casualty of the assault that opened Amberlight. The cousin is devastated.

Because the man wants to go.

Wants to break the marriage, wants to leave the house, wants to leave Iskarda. Wants to go down to Marbleport. Wants a job, he says, on the waterside. Where he is without memories.

Where he can make his own way.

Divorce.

In the Houses, it was nothing less than a cataclysm. The sundering of House-ties, all woven stronger than the great anchor cables, the shattering of reputations, the unspeakable loss of face. There has never been a divorce, that I can remember, over anything so simple as adultery. The only thing that ever did it was House politics.

Or sons.

This case is simple, after all. Kuira knows what she contracted by coming here: that this is not Amberlight. We have pulled down the towers. We cannot constrain them any more.

That it is not supposed to be a shame.

We will have a ceremony. That is the easiest way, turn the whole thing on its head. Not the termination of a marriage but the opening of a new life's hope, not disgrace and silence but vision, willing secession.

Joy.

WHEN IT CAME to the last, Kuira and I both broke down and wept. And held each other, and sniveled on each other's shoulders, and shared the temporary ease of grief that is no healing at all, in the end. And the admission that, for her, one day, I pray, will be true comfort and release.

That there are times when love is not enough. When you simply have to let them go.

So we have given Theraz a pack and clothes and ten silver darrin, and a note for Tez at Marbleport; and with a little prodding, Darthis arranged for Zdana, this month's officiant, to burn some incense on the altar for him. And we have stood at the quarry gate, and watched his figure dwindle, slowly, so slowly, down the receding road.

Now all I have to worry about—and I pray it will cover many a night-watch—is how many others follow in his wake.

It was Sarth, of all people, who set that specter to rest. When I got round to hinting it, last night. With my head, so carefully, on his shoulder, and both our backs to that empty side of the bed. Who heard me out, and took one long, surprised breath.

Before he said, "Ruand—Tellurith."

His voice is always so composed. I caught the flaw with more than shock.

"Haven't you looked around the House? There are three—four—Korite boys hanging round Zariah's door." The minute tensing of his pectorals added what he did not say. Asaskian. "There are two—three village lads courting Ahio. Not for Fira." Her second daughter lost a husband in Amberlight. "For the Craft." He touched my hair. Again, it was less tenderness than surprise. "And I can't count how many have sidled up to me asking about—troublecrew." The break, the catch of still-strained tendons. I know it so well myself. The troublecrew is his place now; but who put him there, he can never forget. "Lose men . . . !"

Trying, so uncharacteristically, so unmannerly, to laugh. As he never would at me, his Ruand. As he might at me, his—fellow lover. Trying, with gaucherie that tells me just how deep the wound has gone, to cover what we cannot bear to bring to light.

Because it will happen. No matter how it hurts to feel us doing it, it will happen. The great sore in the House's bowels will skin over. We cannot ever forget—not while—but we will get used to it. Obliterate it. In a while it will be only a momentary twinge, an eddy in the current's flow. Losing memory. Losing the past.

Losing men.

Spring. Iskarda.
Journal kept by Sarth

MOTHER OF CRAFTS, of all times and seasons, forgive me.

Because I can no longer fall down with the others who are weeping and laughing and blessing your bounty, cannot vow you heirlooms and hecatombs, cannot even career about outside cheering and flourishing arms in the air.

Because whatever you have returned to us, it does not obliterate the taking. That, I cannot forgive.

And because of that, I can no longer pray.

————

ANY GOD KNOWS, I ought to be in ecstasy. Any god knows, my head reels, and my heart keeps jumping out my chest, and I have to—

Write more sanely. It is three days, after all. Three whole insane, delirious days. And all of it—let me be wholly lunatic, all of it!—was due to me.

Or perhaps it was the beauty after all. The crocuses that budded, untended, undaunted, by the wash-bay door.

I had come back from the quarry near noon; bleak still, but with a diamond edge of sunlight between showers. The air stung the skin, but for the first time it was a goad rather than a scourge. And as I walked round to the back-door they were at my feet. Crocuses, imperial purple, brilliantly golden, tossing their heads up to the woken gale.

Starting my shift, I went back out there. Picked a bowlful. And took them to set, forlorn insistence on that resurrection, among the paraphernalia in his room.

They glowed in the stifling lamplight, a fanfare of color, of the outer, waking world. In my mind I saw the wind, the crow-flocks whirled above the ploughing, wild as wing-born leaves on the gusty air. Stupidly, as I walked back with yet another dirty shift, my eyes were full of tears.

Behind me, someone said, weakly, breathily, "Sarth?"

HE WAS SITTING up amid the chains; lifting, staring at each cuffed wrist. When I got my body round, from what felt the River's length away, he looked up and said it with blank bewilderment.

"What am I doing here?"

The room was frozen, brilliant. The heart-point of a lightning flash. I could not shout, scream, weep. There was no breath.

"Sarth . . ."

I went to him, tiptoe, ridiculously, as if he would shatter at the smallest noise. He watched me come. Sanity, awareness, in those eyes that had been madness' windows, a frown edging the thicket of hair. As I knelt before him he plucked at the hospital shift. Eyed the floor, recognition becoming shock and then disgust. "Ye gods, the stink! What—What in the world . . . ?"

"You've been sick."

It came out like breaking a board. But I could not control the hand that reached out, pushed the filthy mane aside, ran down his jaw . . . He looked puzzled. But he did not, oh, may I never lose the memory—he did not pull away.

"Sick? Since when is the infirmary a pig-pen? Sarth—"

"Let me get Caitha." It came smooth and swift even as terror throttled me, what if I said it wrong, woke the wrong memory, threw him back in the pit? "And," but if there is delight above all delights it is to bring others' joy, "Tellurith."

SHE AND I were too crazy to be let in again. We had to hover—dancing, weeping, jubilating like genuine lunatics—listening outside the door.

"Yes, you've been sick. Look at this. Almost three months. No, watch the light. Mm. Open your mouth. No, not wounds or fighting. Probably, your outland physicians would call it extreme mental trauma. Move your head. Mm. We would say you lost your wits. Whichever way, you didn't know yourself. You had to be restrained."

All the things I could not, would not have dared to say. Recounted so calmly, so baldly, in Caitha's imperturbable, unstoppable, examination voice.

"Give me your wrist. Now, please, keep quiet."

And breaking the silence—oh, gods, breaking the silence! "Let me see those ribs. When are we? It's the second moon of spring. Mm. When did it happen?" A pause, then. A real pause, using her eyes, now, as a probe.

"It happened," yet more steadily, "on Mid-winter Day."

Only Caitha, I think, would have dared bring it out so uncompromisingly. Only Caitha *could* have done it, building a bridge on the sheer expectation that planks would hold, doing it all in that matter-of-fact physician's way.

And they did hold. Because in a few eternities more she let us in. And he still knew us. Even when Tellurith, fiercely forbidden to so much as raise his heartbeat, managed to stifle all but a few tears, a few cries, and an absolute inability to let him go, it never even shook—

Gods damn, as he does say. Another blotted page.

Well, then, he stayed coherent. Is still coherent. Weak, of course, as a starved calf, and bandaged everywhere, and confined, by Caitha's decree, to bed. But it is our bed, now. We can run in and out with the others who cannot bear to miss the sight and touch and sound of him—including a House-head whose business has been conducted from her pillow these last two days—we can share the nurse-work. Best of all, at night we have him to ourselves.

In the middle, as on the road from Amberlight; how bizarre that I could have resented that, when now all I can feel is thankfulness wilder than a spring flood. That he is alive, sane, flesh and blood and breathing reality, safe, back in my grasp.

At present, it is also dire necessity. Though his memory stops, he says, sometime around when they reached the altar-stone, and his waking mind may not remember those last three months, it is all buried somewhere. And night-time is when it walks.

Caitha offered poppy-syrup this morning, after she saw Tellurith's spectacular black eye. There are times when I am terrified that arms and love's restraint will not be enough. But neither of us could bear it otherwise. Let him scream, and blacken our eyes, and sweat the sheets in pools. So long as the House can stand it, I will second Tellurith; who thinks, and Caitha calls it feasible, that this is the last of the mind's poison, and it is far better to let it work itself out.

I did ease my own mind this morning. It has nagged me the entire three days. But we were so peaceful; so happy, in that blissful oasis before Tellurith and I had to get up, with the cold thwarted beyond our citadel, under the first morning sounds. Shia's step, troublecrew talking, smell of fresh-kindled wood. Frost-webs across the window, silver fronds on a stainless, most delicately blue sky.

With his head on my shoulder, the way he will so easily put it now, and my chest, as of habit, supporting his right, the originally broken arm. Drowsy, but fully conscious, his breathing told me. So I asked, quite easily, "Do you remember anything about—when you woke?"

His eyes puckered. I felt the lashes flick my skin; long as any boy's. Tellurith stirred; a warning, possibly. He shifted his arm a little, and I felt the frown.

"Somebody spoke to me. I don't know who. I don't know what they said. I don't have the—the memory. Just the—tracks. That say where it went."

"Someone," said Tellurith very quietly, "you knew?"

"Mm-m."

Doubt. More nerves, now, than bafflement. He, too, feared what monsters might rise from the abyss. Tellurith's breathing warned me, Enough. But before I could deflect the talk he frowned again, moved his head—washed, clipped, his hair is still like black silk—and lifted it, staring full into my eyes.

"I did see something. It's like the last piece you remember of a dream. A—potsherd—left behind. I suppose the rest is sleep. Well, there's—" a small swallow "—there's being here, in the council room. With Darthis. I do remember—other things." Tellurith put a hand on his back. He moved a fraction: yes, I hear, it's all right. "But the first thing now is—color. Bright.

In the dark, but bright as a sun coming up. Sun-color, yes. And I didn't know what it was, but I knew—I knew it was—alive."

The flowers. The crocuses, heart's-blood purple, sun's-blood gold. The bowl I had set on the table, a last cry to the year's returning light.

So I did it, as much as anyone, or all that he did not do himself. Or that was not done by the "one who spoke." Ha! When all of us spoke to him all the time. So maybe Darthis began it; but mine was the final touch.

And I cannot give thanks for that, even yet.

Spring. Iskarda.
Tellurith's Diary

GREAT MOTHER, Craft-head, Shaper of all things, holy Giver and Receiver, once you said to me: *Daughter, be blessed.*

No matter that it was your other creature, my other blessing, the qherrique, speaking through another woman's face; let me give the thanksgiving back to you, thrice over:

Mother, be blessed, blessed, blessed.

VI

Spring. Iskarda.
Journal kept by Sarth

Is THIS YOUR MALICE, that I who would not rejoice with others shall suffer with them instead? Do You think it will force me back to You? After You make my craft a laughing-stock, my Craft-head a monstrosity, my wife—

Oh, Tellurith. Had I known it would come to this—

I would have slit my wrists and left my shame to decent oblivion in the Tower.

At a feast above all: when everything had reached harmony. When we were so happy. Not only because spring had come, or Tez sent the price from our first good marble-sale. Best of all, we had our Chosen back, sane, alive.

So Tellurith, being Tellurith, founded a brand-new festival. "Call it Spring-thanks; like Spring-water, back in Amberlight. Turn out the storage jars! Let's see if there's pickle to liven that horrible dried beef. Can anyone get up the hill, maybe catch a brace of hares? And Sarth, you and Esrafal know some dance-tunes, surely? Let's turn the whole House—let's turn the village out, let's dance in the market-place. Let their blighted sacrifice stone feel some pleasure for once! Now, Shia, you know the wine's done, we absolutely have to have some beer—"

Naturally we had beer. Half the House was making it, after Zdana, of all people, donated the first yeast. And it was all the ideal project for Alkhes, when he was on his feet. Tellurith—do I curse or worship her?—actually made him negotiate with Darthis. "You're their blighted Chosen," she could say it almost without a shudder, now. "Tell her *you* want all the men to come. Pout, scowl, throw a tantrum ... she'll buckle, just you see!"

At least, she knew better than to say, Tell her it's the Mother's will.

Is THAT MORE painful to remember than the night itself? A crisp spring night, the young moon aloft, a slice of qherrique silver with a star for diadem, lustrous as dew in a huge cloudless lavender-rimmed sky. Snow gone, all the earth soft as flesh again; and that smell, that delirious smell of freshly broken soil breathing after the plough.

Nobody was out that day, though, in Iskarda's small, angular fields, before the lugging of tables and barrels began, and the concocting of stores'-end delicacies; before we gathered the House and started, singing behind Esrafal, up the village street.

Ah, it *was* beautiful: the torches in the dusk, sheaves of crocus fire; the glitter of ear-studs and coat-bosses, our motley splendor of festival gear: everything from crimson Dhasdein officer's cloaks to brocaded robes lifted from some Heartland potentate. And the glisten, oh, the glisten of teeth and lips and laughing eyes, in that long, long serpent dancing up into the market-place, and the poppy garden that waited in its light.

Let me record the good parts: Darthis and Telluir meeting at the altar stone, to pour beer, to lay flowers. Alkhes, wicked shyster, who inched his way into the crowning role. He—he!—was to blow the festival horn, three feet of age-polished, scintillating bronze, with a cry like the heavens' rending, to launch the feast.

After which Esrafal and I and a whole consort of village pipers, a fiddle and even a hand-harp player, struck up the dance.

Was there a night so blissful, in my life's length? To have the House whole, to see joy everywhere. To look, just to look at Tellurith. To play, with delight to tune my fingers; later, to be praised and greeted, and welcomed like a woman, a Crafter, into the core of the feast.

Bile canker You, who in my most felicity struck me down.

It was so simple, it could not have been more innocent: well into the drinking, a barrel run dry. All the kitchen folk elsewhere or busy or taking a well-earned mouthful themselves. Hanni who caught me, lathered and red as the rest of us. "The Mother blast it, the spare barrel's still down at the house!" I who answered blithely, glorying for once in manhood, "I'll get it, just ask someone to give a hand."

Who more likely to help? Who better, more skilled than any mason or slab-carrier; a Craft-fellow, a Head, reputable, about as sober as me?

THE BARREL was naturally in the cellar: they were manhandled out over the easy three steps of the washing bay. We clattered upstairs for a lamp; set the hauling straps; heaved, grunted, to maneuver it onto the little wheeled trolley for shifting marble-blocks. Breathless, sweaty, I knelt to yank the last strap home, Zuri's thigh braced against my shoulder, her panting blithely winded as mine.

I stood up. Turned to the trolley-bars. She kicked me, right on the flange of the knee.

Right into the muscle point, with all the skill and strength and accuracy of troublecrew, who can make it a crippling blow.

I went down like a felled tree. The pain—the pain itself was blocked. To be hit like that, by my own Craft-head, with the force she would give an enemy, in the midst of a festival. I was beyond shock.

She took one long step—so smooth, so precise, so deadly—grabbed my hair and hove me on my knees.

Zuri is strong. Stronger than half the quarry-crew, before you add fighter's skill. I came up like a marble-block and stayed there, stunned.

Her hand clenched on my hair. That bit through everything. I squirmed, and she hit me across the face.

Full force again, a battle-blow. Never, at the hottest moment on the training floor, had she struck me like that.

With anyone else, I could have reacted. But against Zuri? My Craft-head, my House's ward. My House-head's right hand?

I knelt there, choking on the shock. My head rang, my eyes ran, my nose ran too. Blood. I put up a hand, blind reaction, and she back-handed me across the mouth.

My neck jarred, my lip split. I did not try to move. I could not. I could not find the wits, let alone the words, to plead, to defend myself. Even to cry out, Why?

Her hand twisted in my hair. She leant down and bit me, jamming her mouth on mine.

Then I understood.

That too we trained for. I learned it, as I learnt everything else, from Sethar. "You are there for the woman." That gentle, precise voice, me on my knees, while he gently, precisely twisted my arm another excruciating notch up my back. "Whatever the woman wants. And some of them want their pleasure mixed with pain. And some of them find it in ours."

I spent a whole three days learning it. So when the split lip opened, I gasped, but I did not cry out.

"There is no pleasure for such a woman," Sethar, calmly, precisely, "if she sees no pain. All the same," as his nails drew blood and I squealed like a pup, "we are Tower-born. We give the woman what she wants. But with control. With," implacably, "grace."

She bent my head back and I gasped again. Her free hand, its fingers parting, slid down my throat, and I did not have to feign the flinch. She herself had taught me all the lethal targets there; I needed no schooling to feel the open, the trembling blood-lust in her touch.

Those fingers, short-nailed, iron-hard, clawed and arched. Oh, Mother, I said—blight You, that in my extremity I forgot myself—not now. Not like this.

She yanked my hair again. The other hand grabbed my belt. I came up like a puppet-man, the knee collapsed, and she manhandled me like the barrel, teetering backward onto the duty-guard's bunk.

It is a pallet at the back of the washing bay. I landed across it sloppily as a half-filled carter's sack, and she like a coil of steel, her free hand whipping down my nearer wrist.

When she bent my little finger back I nearly yelled in earnest. It is a woman's grip, designed to restrain a stronger opponent. Done right, it makes the strongest man follow like a dog on a leash. She hit me in the mouth again—which I read as a finer form of, Shut up—and drew the arm over my head.

There are apertures in the stone at the pallet's top; blocks left out to pass the heating pipes. She got a knee on my hair, undid something with the freed hand, then slid a bond round my wrist and fastened it, tight up against the wall. Before she used what was probably her dagger belt to tie the other one.

Wiping her mouth, she straightened up. Kneeling over me, one knee still anchoring my hair. Her face, profiled by the imbecilically tranquil lamp-light, was half Zuri: stone-featured, unflappable trouble-Head. Half some mountain madwoman, fleshed in and bred to and thirsting for blood.

My belly rolled. Instead of pain and pain's comprehension and expectation, there was terror, as blind and rudderless as what looked out of her face.

I must have moved, must somehow have shown it. Her eyes fixed on mine.

There was a moment long enough to catalogue every scrape and bruise and wrench and bleeding graze. No doubt my look held panic's eloquence.

She leant over me. I knew better than to turn away, when her mouth came down on mine.

And the kiss was gentler than any of Tellurith's, so tender it never hurt my broken lip. She slid down beside me on an elbow, her other arm across me, the hand cradling my bruised cheek.

Making love like that, too, I had learnt. For a Tower man, trained to give women the initiative, it comes readily, if frustratingly enough. One of my wives was rougher, though she never tied me up. But nor did she ever raise me to such a trembling sensitivity, to answer, to leap to anticipate the woman's every touch. If there is no pleasure in pain for me, the gods know, Zuri showed me how pain can tighten every nerve end, until what pleasure comes is nearer ecstasy, step-sister if not pain's child itself.

She did not hurt me again. Perhaps there was no need. She was a skilful lover. It may be usual with troublecrew, but I never found a woman with such muscle-control. One would think her Tower-trained. She let me finish, too, when she was finally satisfied, which is more than some women bother with. And put my clothes in order, and smoothed my hair back, that she had torn, at some point, out of its band. Before she undid my wrists, and took her dagger belt. And walked out, without a word, into the dark.

The barrel was loaded. The door was open. When I could move, I could have wrestled it up the path. I could have washed my face, made some story. Any woman would have swallowed it, and buried it, had I even said it was a quarrel with Tellurith.

But the first person I walked into had to be Alkhes.

In the washing bay, with the lantern, before I could shift it, full on my face.

Spring. Iskarda.
Meditations. Alkhes-Assandar

IT IS—disconcerting—to lose a piece of your life. More than disconcerting to do it twice.

The first time it came back. Eventually. This is different. Because I don't think—I know—it isn't lost.

Not when I wake up screaming from the memory. And burn thanksgiving to the god of sleep when it falls back out of the waking mind.

There is a hole, then. No grasping the breadth and volume of it. Just a discontinuity. The past stops *there* and resumes *here*. *There* with the feel of the altar stone, cold on my naked back. *Here* with darkness opening to the blurry, colored patch of light that coalesces into flowers.

It has taken me all this time to write again.

Too weak at first. Too cursed sore, with chain galls and bruises from ear to heelbone, with muscles gone to wet string and a pot of porridge for brains. Too busy coming to life. Finding people again. Being—

Being with those I love.

So, the brave man's finally admitted it. Both.

Tellurith, yes. Less need to say that than to breathe. Sarth . . .

How can you miss someone you never knew was gone?

I feel it, though. In the hole, the discontinuity, like the pull of an unhealed wound. When I think back it twinges, like a strained muscle in the chest. The great lunk, on his knees in front of me, me with chains in knots and that stupid shift thing round my ears, shit everywhere, wondering what hell soldier's luck had dropped me in— The look on his face. Large as life and just as—beautiful. Trying to be nurse-ish and blank, and looking like a temple sculpture that's seen a god come down. Like if you touched him, he'd crack open and cry.

Now I can even sleep with him. *Sleep* with him, yes—thank the gods, I've been too wobbly to let Tellurith think of more. But sleep with him, and be thankful . . .

More than that. Like it was on the road, yes, to know yourself safe. To be— Home.

More than that. Be hung, but I hate honesty. I do—I do love the bastard. Maybe I can't make love to him, but it would kill me to see him hurt.

So of course I had to walk in, hunting beer Hanni wanted half an hour ago. Of course I had to find him sitting on that pallet, looking like the back end of a guardsmen's liberty brawl. And of *course* I ran amok.

It's not just how I feel. Gods damn it, how could anybody bear to damage that? And there he was, mouth smashed, nose puffed, eyes black, blood all over his jaw.

"Gods above!" I squawked. "What's this?"

He tried to get up fast. I grabbed his shoulder and then his chin. He turned his head away from the lamp, muttering. "It's nothing, the dark, I missed the door . . ."

"Missed the door!" Anybody that ever heard a brawling charge knows fist-work from a wall's. Oh, I was so shocked, I was so—so—

Upset, and hurting for him, and furious with whoever'd done it, I never stopped to think. And I *know* these men hate admitting such a thing, for him it was worse than being hit. "Who did this?" I yelled. "Gods blast her, I'll have her guts!"

"It was nothing, it was no one—" He tried to get up, and the knee gave, and that really set me off. "One of the men—"

"Men be shicked!" I *knew* it wasn't a man, I've learnt that much, not a man in Telluir or Iskarda would dare lay hands on him, unless it was me. "Don't you try to—"

"It was dark, I didn't see!"

"With a lantern here?" I saw the barrel then. "Who helped with this?"

I should have known then. The way he moved, his face's change. But he knew too, he knows far too much about me, he knew I wouldn't leave it and I could find out, with a couple of words. He put out his hand.

"Alkhes," he said. "Alkhes . . ."

How could I *not* have known then? With him still only wanting to hide, to cover the whole thing in decency—or what they consider decency. Too proud, too shame-fast—too modest—to confess to me. Let alone beg. A battered Dhasdein lord's wife would have less modesty. I know that now.

If I'd thought, I'd have known it then.

"Well, I'll put a crimp in this!" Ha, the River-lord's avenger in the flesh. So I got him by the wrist and towed him out in the yard, and yelled to the first person I saw, "Fetch Tellurith!"

Gods pardon me, she came.

I AM NO MORE than just irretrievably stupid. The instant she saw his face—all his face—and I saw hers, I understood.

Out in the yard, half the House around us. Lights, a perfect blaze. Desis, and Verrith, and Azo, and Iatha, and every line of them saying it, louder than he was. Calamity. Catastrophe. But mystery, no.

I had the wit to shut up, then.

Tellurith looked at Iatha. Not at Sarth. No, not at Sarth, who was trying to melt into the ground. And Iatha started off in her steward's voice, All right, it was all over, nothing to worry about, let's get back to the dance . . .

Because they were still dancing, up the hill. I could hear the pipers, half a world away.

Tellurith said to us, "Let's go inside."

Not to the kitchen, nor the council-room. To her work-room, inner fastness of crisis time. She, and Sarth, and I. Even Iatha, trouble's bulwark, pulled up at the door.

She watched him across the work-table, loaded with Telluir business, as she had once looked at me. She said it almost below hearing, "Who went for the barrel, Sarth?"

With her he did not try to prevaricate. Just turned away his head.

I saw her face shift. She came round the table, very quietly. Put an arm around his waist.

Said, like sliding a stiletto in. "It was Zuri, wasn't it?"

He jerked. She turned him about. Held him close. To me she said, more quietly, "Iatha." As I went out I heard her go on, in the voice that is for no one else.

"It wasn't your fault."

Someone tell me, why *didn't* Darthis cut my throat?

Spring. Iskarda.
Tellurith's Diary

A BLIND WOMAN could deduce it. Who was missing, who would never be missing at such a crisis? Unless she was the cause?

She went up the mountain. Where else would—could she go? A Craft-head—my troublecrew head—off in the dark and the cold like an outlawed wolf.

Leaving Sarth to the sort of spectacle and scandal that burns a Tower-bred man to the soul. My beautiful beloved man, made a shame, a gossip-word. To mark him like that; to have it exhibited publicly. The minute I saw him in that yard I knew he would sooner have died.

Sweet Mother, Zuri, whatever madness took you, did it have to end like this?

I will give her a day. I hope—I pray—she will come back. Her honor, her integrity; either it will drive her back, to face me, or it will drive her away forever. Oh, Mother, spare me from yet another loss. From having to face Darthis. From having to fill another hole that I will feel clean to the heart.

From having to go on, with something lethal perhaps loose amongst us, and still unknown.

THANK THE MOTHER, who heard me. Thank Zuri, whose courage, whose honor prevailed. Even if she has left me torn between rage and rage.

She walked in on us at breakfast, or what passed for breakfast, after what must have been an unbearable night. I know I found it so, and if either of my husbands slept a breath . . . So we only reached the kitchen when Iatha, bless her, had everyone else out tidying up.

And Azo, who had guard-watch, why would she forbid the woman who was her Head?

She came straight in with that cat's troublecrew tread. A night in festival gear, up the mountain; she looked no more changed than rock by a snow-fall, four-square, imperturbable, unshakable Zuri. In disgrace or not.

"Ruand," she said. "I've come to resign."

Vintage Zuri. Face her fault, admit and pay for it. No compromise.

"Zuri," I said. Knowing she would hear the rest: I understand your reasons. Now understand mine. "Could you—for the House's sake—explain?"

She was still wearing her troublecrew gear; dagger-belt, light gun. She gripped the belt in both her hands.

"Ruand." No filing the nose this time, Zuri's signal for perplexity. "It's my problem. The Mother knows, I tried . . ."

She did stop. And took a breath, before she went on.

"What you're doing . . . it's right."

I kept my face still. Already, I was beginning to know.

"The men need to be here. They need to live among us. They need new things. Work. Trades. Darthis sees it too."

She stopped again. Then said it straight in my face.

"I've always admired your husband. When they came to help us fight, in Amberlight. On the way here, when he worked so hard. In the epidemic. I've always thought he was . . . remarkable. But that was all right."

She swallowed again. The two men were nailed to the floor.

"I could handle that. I could handle him around the House. But—"

I managed to hold her eyes. I knew what was coming next.

"Ruand, I tried." Now her voice did shake. "But to have a man like that in front of your eyes, in your hands, working out with you, day after day—"

She took a hand from her belt and wiped it, lightly, unconsciously, across her face.

"It was spring. It was a—the festival. We had—Alkhes back. Desis was on duty, I thought, it's all right. I drank . . . not all that much. But down there—alone, in the dark, feeling like— It all let go."

She looked away into the fire.

"I've shamed you," she spoke so quietly, so tiredly. "I've shamed the House. I've shamed myself. And the Mother knows, it was the last thing I ever wanted. But I've shamed him worst of all."

Sarth never made a sound. But I felt Alkhes flinch.

Sweet Work-mother, I wanted to scream, it was my fault, I let Alkhes inveigle him in there, I didn't notice what it was doing to you, I've spent the last three months in coma, I brought us all here and set the men free to start landslides like this, the fault is mine!

To count the dead stops no more deaths.

"Zuri—where will you go?"

"Oh . . ." Somewhere, the tilt of the shoulder said. The voice, the eyes, answered, Nowhere.

Up the hill. To some secluded corner. To fall on her blade.

I took my elbows off the kitchen-table, and set by the cup.

"I have to consider this. To decide the appropriate action." What is there to consider, said her eyes? "Zuri, you are my trouble-Head. I must ask you to delay your resignation. For the sake of the House."

Her mouth set like winter-old ice.

"Have you forgotten," she said, "why I never married again?"

"Zuri—"

She stood up. Her shoulders flexed for mayhem and I got in first.

"You're under detention. Azo!"

Spring. Iskarda.
Meditations. Alkhes-Assandar

THEY TRAMPED OFF, Azo and Verrith, hauling their Craft-head to another store-room, trying to look imperturbable while their city burned. Zuri, hang her, almost looked at peace. But I caught Iatha taking flight.

She doesn't care for me. I understand that. She's Tel's best friend. Her shield arm. I'm her lover. And I cost her Amberlight, and her House, and a River's depth of grief, and worst of all, the qherrique. But when I hissed, Iatha did hesitate.

"Iatha, before I mess it up again—for Tel's sake, explain!"

A frosty snort. A glower. But Iatha could not be stupid if she tried. She beckoned me after her, a jerk of the head. Down through the washing bay, out where a misty sun tried to smoke fog out of the yard.

"In Amberlight. Uphill Amberlight. To mark up a man—it's disgrace." It came by patches, jerkily. "No decent woman would dream of it."

She glowered outward, at a skewbald vista of fog and trampled mud. "Or if she did—she'd never let it show."

I kept quiet. She turned and glared.

"But if it did, the man—never admitted it. Any man wearing marks like that. It would rebound on the woman. No decent woman could do it. So she'd have to be—shameless. And just being married to her—would be his shame."

She yanked her plait and glared into the fog. A jaw granite-hard as Zuri's own.

If I misuse them, I do have wits. When I thought I had it straight, I said, "And with somebody else's man?"

She all but swung on me. "Blast your soul!"

Worse, then. Infinitely worse.

"And you had to bellow it at everyone! Sometimes—"

She bit it off. I could end it all too well. Sometimes I can't tell what she sees in you.

"I—was thinking of him."

You're supposed, returned her hot, brandy-brown eye, to think first of her.

No answer to that. But questions remained.

"Iatha . . . nobody was surprised."

She spun clear away from me. Spun back, and spat it in my face.

"Zuri wasn't there and Zuri should have been. 'Rith's never hit a man in her life. But Zuri was married in Amberlight. A young man, second wife. Six months from the wedding day, he jumped off the tower roof. Nobody *had* to be surprised!"

She stamped past with a shove that all but set me on my backside and stormed into the house.

FOR A MAN in Iskarda, there is no private place. At least, not in our house. I have had to go down into the store-rooms myself, with pen and ink and lamp. And sickness in my belly. Zuri. That anyone, man or woman, could treat him so . . . Be honest, it's known, in Cataract, in Dhasdein, but it's not praised. Gods know, what she said, I can understand that. Can feel for her, as if she were a man.

Gods know, I've—wanted him—too.

But Zuri? Trouble-Head, House-bulwark, more trusted than Iatha herself?

The one to fall, if anyone did, for that very cause. That she lives with violence, that fighting's in her bones.

But I trusted her. I trusted her as much as Tellurith.

And it was my fool arrogant stupidity, that put him in her way.

It was I who scarred his soul, and broke her integrity. And then had to expose it all. To shout it out beyond mending. Will he ever speak to me again?

And what will happen to her? Troublecrew, a Trouble-head, compromised beyond recall. Who could trust her? In Amberlight, it could never have happened. But in this new way of things, who could risk it happening again?

Gods. What will—what *can* Tellurith do?

Spring. Iskarda.
Tellurith's Diary

I CAN'T SPARE ZURI. Not the Head of my troublecrew. Not the one I need above all others, in moments of pure danger, when it matters most. As when the ice-walker came, as when the hill fell in Amberlight. With a life half-built, a House half-established, I can't do without that.

Neither can I keep her, after such a breach of faith. To me, to Sarth. To herself. Even if men were not to join things like the troublecrew, how could I ever trust her again?

Nor can I let her go. Zuri, my comrade, my war-mate. Turn her out, let her crawl off into the hills and in some meager corner, end her life. Whatever she has done, that would put a stain on me, and my House, that nothing would erase.

There has to be a way.

"TAKE 'EM OUT of the troublecrew. Settle all the problems, no risk it'll crack again."

Ahio's verdict. Brisk, radical, untenable. Let be the wound to Sarth's self-respect, there is Alkhes, for whom the troublecrew is very life. Beyond that, spreading far beyond that, are the repercussions: take men from the troublecrew, and how often will the precedent be applied in other trades?

"Send her down to Marbleport. Good head, plenty of experience. Reinforcement won't hurt. Especially now."

Hayras' suggestion, canny, forward-thinking, politically astute. No question, we could reinforce a spy-net that must now carry the weight of early warning in deadly earnest; especially if things on the River go to open war.

Except that Zuri is a Head; and Marbleport has a Head. Leave Tez in charge, affront Zuri beyond efficiency. Set her in charge, insult Tez. Oh, yes, in a crisis she would be invaluable; but what message would that send our watchers? How much value does Telluir place on this lowly shipping agency?

And what does Zuri know of ships?

"Mount a mission to Amberlight."

That, the Mother knows, is most tempting of all. A covert group, led by a woman I could trust with my own back; sure intelligence, advance warning if Damas and Eutharie do something stupid, if things blow up with Cataract. Even, if necessary, advance remedies, of the hardest sort, administered by a woman who would not have to delay a week, seeking permission from me. Zuri as my eyes, my dagger-hand. Iatha has always thought as far, and as carefully, as I.

Except who, here in Iskarda, do I put in Zuri's place?

Quetho, Zariah, Charras are Craft-folk; shrewd in their trade, lacking the initiative in politics. Hanni or Shia, impossible. Azo, as acting troublecrew Head, cannot be asked. Any more than Sarth.

Alkhes? Alkhes might have ideas none of us would find. But . . .

But Alkhes is my husband. Sarth's husband. However subtle or skilled his solution might be, he is implicated deeper than Azo.

Mother blast, I am an idiot.

Spring. Iskarda.
Meditations. Alkhes-Assandar

I CAN NOT believe this. I *will* not believe it! How could she? How can she! Do this to herself—to us—to me!

Gods rot and ruin it, that's where it really galls. Would I give a tinker's spit who she asked, if she'd only asked me first?

Am I so far beyond forgiveness she can't even ask my help?

That she had to ask it there instead!

As it was, Verrith's eyes popped when she took the message, and Iatha blew rivets like a demoted chiliarch. Ten minutes she must have yelled in there before I lost my own head and yanked open the work-room door.

They both whipped round. Hot topaz Amberlight eyes, high Amberlight cheekbones, crinkly Amberlight plaits. Decrepit leggings, dingy brown workers' shirts. Iatha glaring across the table, Tellurith backed against

Hanni's desk. Iatha yelled, "What the—" Tellurith slapped the table like a bullock-driver's whip.

"Alkhes," she said, "what do you want?"

I HAVE BEEN—I *am* a soldier. I have been an officer. A commander. A general.

I *am* her husband. Her lover. I'm supposed to matter.

Is it wits or raving soft-headed stupidity that took that signal? That made me, instead of knocking them both down, back out the door?

Or is it—

A man isn't supposed to admit this. Isn't supposed to feel it. Am I changing? Am I improving?

Or am I coming apart?

Because I am so. Goddamn. Hurt.

So IT'S BEEN a day up the mountain, with Azo's hunting bow. To the fire with the chance of ice-walkers, spring-starved wolves, waking bears. A man's answer to wounds, I suppose, is to go out and kill something else.

Not that there's much glory, if cursed hard stalking, in a brace of skinny, spring-twitchy hares.

But there is peace among rock and mud and half-peeled helliens. Wind, distance, the River-world fading below you on a gusty, sunlit spring day. Iskarda looks so small up there, a knot of roofs and street threads. The quarry's gore, the patchwork of half-ploughed fields. The marble-crews, the plough-teams, the people walking are shrunk to puppets, moving dots.

Even, coming home over the shoulder above the quarry, Darthis and Tellurith.

They had just left the high place. They walked out, abreast, onto the mountainside. The body language spoke consort, if not amity. Tellurith's held an unexpected ease.

How could she bring herself to blurt all this out to Darthis? Who must have taken the greatest pleasure in thinking, in yet more heroically not saying, I told you so?

What in the Adversary's own pits could *she* give as counsel for a thing like this?

———————

Spring. Iskarda.
Tellurith's Diary

LET BE the uproar in the Household, what will it take to win back Alkhes? But what could I have done, at that moment, with Iatha already screaming my nerves raw with objections I knew too well myself? It was ignominy, it was humiliation, it would lose all we had won, it would give Darthis most sweet revenge, what lunacy would she offer, what possible use could she be?

What else would he have said?

In Amberlight I could have called on Averion, on Jura; above all, on Zhee. Here there is no other Head. No one with such a backload of experience, who has shared another community's life.

The Mother blast her, if she is to make me problems, let her help me solve them as well.

THE SNOW has gone in the high place. Small grasses infiltrated the boulders, there were little pink snow-peas and purple-blue clusters of grape hyacinths, brilliant as Dhasdein glass. Even the helliens wore new, iridescent leaves.

While I gathered my wits, Darthis waited; while I drew on the high place's ease. If the qherrique is gone, the Mother remains.

Then I said, "Has Iskarda known troubles like this?"

She knew what I meant, of course. After that—spectacle—in the yard, all the House knew, and after that, nothing could have kept it from Iskarda. Men at the well, gossiping children, it would have traveled on the very air. No doubt she had enjoyed my quittance with the rest.

She grunted. Then she said, "Happens up here too."

Frankness. More kindness, to be honest, than I had expected.

"How do you settle it?"

She paused; not demurral, but a Head shuffling the past. Then she cited me five different cases and five separate solutions, running back over sixty years. The last was in, "m'grand-mother's third year."

"Um," I said.

No umbrage showed. She said, "Not the same."

"Not with Zuri. No."

She understood that too. How could she not? She is no fool, she knows the House. As she already knew I could not take the first of her solutions, to send away the man. Or the second, to pay a barter-debt. Or the third, a simple divorce. Or the fourth, to give the woman new land. Or the fifth, a revenge and compensation duel.

She sat back on her boulder, rubbing her chin. There was a long pause, filled with hellien whisper, a buzz of hunting bees.

Then she said, "Marry 'em."

I am a House-Head of Amberlight. I could not control the yelp.

"You can't lose either one. Or split 'em. Have to risk it, then. That when she has what she couldn't have, it won't happen again."

"But she's *killed* one boy—!"

We sat there while the sun wheeled over. Anatomized Zuri's first marriage, dissected what we knew of the incident. The chances that, freely offered what had driven her to madness, she would override her own honor and accept. That it would be safe. That it could be done at all.

Not to mention Sarth's part in it.

Darthis grunted at that. "You mayn't want to push him into such a thing," she said. "And he will know the risk. Probably better than we do. But he's tower-bred." She stared off at the horizon, toward invisible Amberlight. "Ruand, we've never been there, but we know the stories; we know how it works. He's a proper tower-bred man. What you say, Do, he'll do."

"Mother blast it, Darthis!"

We re-lubricated our throats at the little freshet up the hill. The sun was falling toward the quarry-ridge when she finally conceded, "Don't order him, then. Put it to him. Both sides. Let him choose." She got off her boulder with a grunt and stood rubbing her loins. There was a glint in her eye. "But I'll lay you a foal from that bay mare of yours against my year's first heifer-calf, that he says yes."

It was lewd, it was indecent, it was an insult to my husband. I did not know Iskarda gambles as much as Amberlight. As it would have with Iatha, my mouth said, "Done!"

Spring. Iskarda.
Journal kept by Sarth

I SHOULD HAVE DONE what blood and schooling bade me. I should have gone up the mountain that night, and slit my wrists.

Except I could not bear to think what it would do to them. To him. To her. Above all, to Tellurith.

Is it worse to shame her with my living, after such—infamy? Or to die, purify my reputation—and break her heart? What decent man could settle such a choice? So I have slunk round this three days, a pariah in my own house. If there were somewhere to go—if there were a Tower!

What am I thinking, to wish that back again?

But however hard, it would be so much easier. The way would be clear, the rules settled. Do this, or, Do that. Not this riving pain, this struggling to build a new thing, to construct not only the choice but the grounds for making choice.

One should be grateful, no doubt, that Tellurith has given me that.

And that she did have the—temerity? kindness? respect? to show me the proposal first.

I have no idea what my face said, but clearly, it was far more than it ought; she started gabbling, catching my hands as I stood up. I actually knocked over the work-room chair. "Sarth!" she said. Shouted. "Stop!"

I am Tower-bred, after all. A woman said, Stop. I stopped.

She came and took hold of me. As on that night Alkhes arrived, she almost looked afraid. I did not think I could frighten Tellurith.

"Don't shut me out, Sarth. You don't have to just agree. I'll just tell you my side. Then you can tell me yours. Then you can decide."

So she told me: things she probably has not told Iatha; about politics, about the House. About how much Zuri matters.

More, I should think, than me.

"*Not* more than you!" At that she forgot to be afraid. "Differently! Mother's eyes, you know how much you matter!" And it is true; I do. "You don't have to do this! The choice is up to you!"

A great choice it is.

I looked at her, flaring up at me, as bright and wicked and determined as ever in Amberlight. If I matter, I wanted to say, then have you considered my self-esteem? My dignity? How I will feel, forced to marry a woman who shamed me to the soul, if I have to live with her, make it a marriage in earnest before the House? Have you thought what they will say of *me*?

That I wanted it. That I asked for it. That I seduced her. That I am a wanton. An adulterer.

With a wife so infatuated, she condones it all.

Against that, what is Zuri, and Iskarda? What is the whole thrice-blasted House?

Spring. Iskarda.
Tellurith's Diary

I SWEAR word in this house travels the ambient air. I had barely worn out Iatha before supper, had just been able, afterward, to snare Sarth. Had but that moment let him stamp off to some private fastness when Alkhes pounced as I set my journal on the kitchen-table and literally dragged me away.

"Tellurith, you can't do this! You're out of your mind!"

He yanked me into the bedroom. He all but shoved me across the bed, all his own umbrage, affront, injury wiped out. "You saw what she did to him—you know he won't fight it! Gods, it's obscene. She'll *kill* him! You can't *sacrifice* him like that!"

"Alkhes," I tried to get in. "Caissyl—"

"I don't care what the House needs or how you feel about her—you can't!"

He was crushing up fistfuls of fur, wild-eyed and deaf as a panicked hawk. It took me five minutes to get a hand on him, and another five to coax him down, beside me on the bed.

"Caissyl, I don't like it either. It's a gamble. It's not a certainty. He may not agree. She may not agree. But—"

He did let me rehearse the reasons, however much he heard. At the end, he swung to stare at me and said bitterly, "He'll do it. What choice does he have?"

It hurt almost as much as one of Sarth's own stabs. "I won't force him! I give you my word."

"You won't have to." Suddenly all the fury was gone. "He's tower-bred. I'm coming to understand that. The House matters. What matters more— it's what a woman wants."

He stared at me. His eyes, big and red-tinged as a foundry-demon's by the light of the brazier, said the rest.

And he loves you. He'll do it, because you ask.

"Oh, caissyl." Suddenly it was too much. I had spent the day battling balky vassals, friends, satellites, lovers, my own choice. No doubt I would now have to fight Zuri as well. "Can we just—leave that roof until it falls?"

For an instant he stared at me, stiff and vivid with affront. Then something must have got through. He made an awkward shuffle along the bedside. Both arms slid round me, gathering me in, his body opening, softening. "Tel," he muttered. It went into the side of my neck. "I'm sorry . . . All right."

Blessed, momentary refuge. Before I had to face the worst.

She has been incarcerated in another storeroom, a troublecrew guard, as much ceremony as ward, on the door. To her, I think, it is almost a relief; a decision taken out of her hands.

They had given her a barrel for table, a pair of stools. We sat facing each other across the lantern top. Her face was shadow-splashed, wavering, more than inscrutable, in that sketchy light. Until she understood what I meant.

She rose off the stool then. Rose? She straightened like a pillar of fire. Then she whipped the supper plate past my temple into smithereens against the wall, I yelled, the guard yelled. Zuri, face congested, yelled loudest of all.

"Get out!"

She must be reluctant too.

Spring. Iskarda.
Meditations. Alkhes-Assandar

WHAT CAN YOU SAY? When she looks at you, with all that will, that fire and conniving manipulation gone to doubt and ember-ash, no high-flying empress of a House-head, but a tired woman worried beyond strength? When you remember that you may be carrying ire and insult. But she's carrying you and Sarth, and Zuri, and all the rest of them; that she's carrying the House, in her two solitary hands?

VII

Spring. Iskarda.
Tellurith's Diary

I OUGHT to have guessed. Here have I been battered by Iatha and Alkhes about the risk, the cruelty, the sheer callousness of sacrificing Sarth; and by Sarth's own outrage, that I should expose him to whispers of infidelity, or being a seducer, a contriver, and I too blind to dissent. In all this, I never wondered about her.

Culpable idiocy; when it is Zuri's own honor, her loyalty, her probity, that weighted half my scales. Yet I never asked what they would mean to her. Even when she threw that plate.

Never thought to go down, this morning, and find her gone.

With Desis holding my eyes flintily across the lowered latch. "I'm the day-watch, Ruand. When I came on, it was like that."

The Mother knows when she went, how she went; a collusion, a compulsion, a request? The cell is empty, the House is undisturbed. From her room, nothing is taken. If I tax Verrith, the night-watch, I will get an equally flinty lie.

After all, she is their Craft-head. A nearer loyalty than mine.

Oh, Zuri, better you had blacked his eyes a hundred times. In the Mother's name, was what I asked such an insult as that?

"TEL? TEL? Will you stop flogging yourself for five minutes and *think*?"

He had the temerity to come in here and interrupt: to pull the journal out of my hands. To haul out a dirty handkerchief and yank up my chin and wipe my face. "Think! If she didn't take her clothes or her money or even her scurvy boot-laces, what else didn't she take?"

It must have taken a good minute to bite. Of course she was disarmed in the cell. Of course all her weapons are here. So of course it cannot be the ultimate honorable lunacy, after all.

Except if she stole something.

Or took something from Verrith.

Or from round the House. Or the quarry. It would need no more than a few feet of rope. Or some other resort, to me unimaginable. Oh, Zuri, please . . .

Or unless—it is altogether something else.

Spring. Iskarda.
Journal kept by Sarth

Is THIS MORE of Your malice, to make me, if not Your puppet, a trouble-spot and a vexation, to my own and others' shame?

Nobody knows where Zuri has gone. If she has gone. Useless to in-terrogate troublecrew, who have stated their loyalties. Useless to gossip and guess, as everybody else is doing. As useless to send out searchers or proclaim forgiveness and amnesty across the hills' unresponsive air. Wherever she is, she does not mean to enlighten us.

Useless to say as much to Tellurith. Useless to seek counsel of Alkhes.

It is true, he stalks round as if through his first wife's labor, worrying and fretting, setting his own recovery back by months. But how can I explain what is bred into me, below words, in the bones? How can I convey the—the—shame? Not the blows, even the violation. Modesty, manhood, good name, overthrown. The wormwood of confronting the House, this week now, with infamy branded on my face?

If he could not understand that, then how could he find a way amid the thorn-blocks of this choice?

MAY THE NINE-LIMBED Adversary of Alkhes' River-lord fly away with me, if I am ever so surprised again.

Yesterday was cloudy, gusty, by late afternoon already twilit indoors, just too light for lamps. Half the women were out, Tellurith still in her work-room, the rest of us about supper; a swirl to and fro through doors and passageways, everybody too tired or busy or accustomed to notice anyone else. When Shia asked, "Was there any dried thyme at all left in the store-room?" I said, "I'll see," grateful for another pretext to hide.

So I clattered down the cellar passage without second thought for a lamp, the washing-bay door, troublecrew loyalties, outlaws at large. And a pair of arms slid round my waist.

Round my ribs. Iron-hard fingers poised just under the breastbone, where one stab would punch away my breath.

"So," she said. That low, troublecrew burr, so close the words all but vibrated in my back. "What do *you* think about this 'marriage' stuff?"

I could have resisted. I suppose I could have shouted. I could have done a great many things, had my breath not solidified in my throat.

Not simply the shock of ambush. Of her presence. Of her hands on me, the shock twice over, of memory's doubled threat. Nor the knowledge of what would happen, if I tried to fight.

Nor the astonishment that she had come back.

Nor hearing the anger—that burned—banked, unmistakable—under every word.

Nor the shock of such a question. Of her asking such a question. Of her bothering to ask.

I can be proper. This is my journal, I can do what I like.

Or I can be honest.

I can write down that what I felt, with her hands upon me, and the past week to remember in. That what I felt was . . .

Memory. Printed through blood and flesh and bone. Of how those hands felt when they were not hurting me. Of how that body felt astride me. Of that second, heart-stopping surprise of a kiss.

That what I felt . . . when I should have been well-bred, and modest, a shamefast married man, when I should have yelled my head off for rescue and retribution . . .

How lowering, that at the last it was not virtue that moved me, nor the House. Or even, as gods know it should have been, love of Tellurith. How demeaning, to find myself a bed-toy after all.

Slowly, so very slowly, I lifted my hands; feeling those fingers tense, but no more, before I covered them with my own. Feeling the dryness, though I did not stumble, in my mouth as I spoke.

"Would you have to . . . beat me—every time?"

It felt as if the world stopped. As if the words went on reverberating out into some enormous space. As if we would both be struck dead.

But we were not. Because—gods, how can I write it—because I—someone—went on talking. Because I—he—said—

"Tying up, I can cope with. But . . ."

She moved then. A flex, a breath. Her forehead rested against me, bowed lightly between my shoulderblades, to a long, long exhalation that might have been anything. Even a laugh.

Before she said softly, a note that was all Zuri, yet some new, unknown Zuri, "Let's find out."

She led me one-handed, quick and invisible and impudent as a ghost. Upstairs, I still hardly believe it, past the kitchen, round the corner, into the troublecrew wing, into, mind-boggling audacity, her own room. Without alerting a soul.

Locked, barred the door behind us. Turned around and looked at me, that slit-eyed Zuri stare.

Held out her hand.

And I took it. I went to her, open-eyed and trusting as the most innocent boy.

There were qualms, I grant that. When she drew me down on the bed; when, that moment I have always half-hated, she first opened my clothes. When I tried to put my arms around her, to caress her. Which she bore for all of half a touch, before she rose on an elbow, said under her breath, "Sorry," took my wrists, and pushed them firmly against the sheet.

How can you make love to a woman who bans your every touch?

Only, solely, deliriously as she pleases. With Zuri, that is more than enough.

UNTIL IT FINISHED. And she was still, astride me, a long, long moment, with no movement but our heaving breaths. Before she gathered a leg. Slid off me, and reached for her shirt.

And I knew she meant to walk off again, without a word, this time probably without so much as straightening my hair.

She yanked up her belt. Reached for a boot. I said, "I don't want you to go."

Such license. Such utter shamelessness. When I think what Sethar would have said, my cheeks blaze all over again.

It shocked her too. The dark was near complete, I could see only a blur of solidified shape. Could say nothing; was struck dumb, by my own impudence.

The shape moved. Sparks flew. She said, "I'll fix the lamp."

She came, then, to sit beside me. Hesitated. I felt that hesitation through the marrow of my bones. Before she laid an arm across me, as if I were more fragile than qherrique. Every time she touched me, that night, I felt more than a man, more than a treasure, even an heirloom. More like a sacrament.

Did she say, "I'm sorry"? Not Zuri.

What she said was, "Why not?"

Probably my jaw sagged. Doubtless a charming pose. Who would not be staggered, when he has practiced for a lifetime, supporting, listening, letting the woman lead? When, having done the most outrageously brazen thing of that lifetime, the woman throws the lead to him?

When he realizes that it is not a ploy, not caution.

That it is inadequacy.

It fell on me like a landslide. That Zuri has always been this way. That she can never have been able to speak her feelings—to show any love, any tenderness, except during sex itself. And that only after violence. That this is why her first marriage . . . how could that poor young fool have understood? Have found a remedy? Have seen past the cruelty, let be realized what she needed? When he was not even Tower-born?

In which vertiginous realization I understood what was asked of me.

I said, "That first time . . . I was terrified."

She gave a true Zuri snort. Then leant forward, as if she could not help herself, to draw the hair back from my face.

"*You* weren't terrified." Her hand traced the rim of the black eye's bruise: a feather-touch. "You didn't start squealing like a rabbit. You're Tower-bred."

With that intonation, it was an accolade.

Her hand fell. She looked away, as if to watch me too long, too openly, would be a betrayal. Of me? Of herself? I felt her muscles tense. It would do no good, it might well be precisely the wrong thing, to touch, to try to hold onto her.

I said, "Who thought of the—marriage—anyway?"

Another snort. But the hand came back, smoothing—caressing—down the day's stubble on my jaw.

"Tellurith. Who else? Tricky as a bagful of Heartland hunting-cats and devious as a Cataract tyrant. I should have hit her with that plate."

Touching me so tenderly, so delicately, with ire and soul-deep umbrage in her voice.

I turned my face to her. Sidelong. "Your profile," Sethar told me once, "is your best angle." Tracing it with a connoisseur's pleasure. But not so tenderly as the fingers that dwelt on it now.

Into the pillow I said, "She—they—insulted you."

Her hand stopped. My heart stopped. The lamp ticked. She growled and swept up the tangle of my hair.

"Mother's face! Knock you round, force you, dishonor you before the House. Then make you swallow this—*abomination* . . . insulted *me!*"

There was a lump, a burning in my throat. I turned over, encircling her, so carefully, with the angle of my drawn-up thighs. And shivered, noticeably.

She had been sorting tangles across my shoulder as if in priceless silk. Braiding the length of it, absently, into a Crafter's plait. When I shivered she reached one-handed to yank the outer coverlet up around my ribs.

The lamplight islanded us, secret, isolate. Outside, the lull of supper lapped the House. Inside was the space, the hiatus, of loving's aftermath. The time when Tellurith and I had traded secrets best.

I said, "But you thought to ask—what I felt."

Again she went terrifyingly still. I hid my eyes in the pillow, that smelt of her hair, her flesh.

Her arm slid over me; her body eased into the circle of mine. Under her breath she said, "I should never have come back at all. Should have finished it. Or taken off. With a grain of wit—I'd have done that at the start."

The pillow shielded me; even if I was facing into the lamp.

"And I . . . should have yelled my head off. Saved my reputation, tonight."

There was another eternal pause. When she spoke again, I knew I was no longer playing alone.

"Idiots. Both of us."

She understood. Neither of us had done what we should, in sanity, in genuine refusal. Both of us really wanted to say yes. Tellurith would have made it an avowal, traced out each phase, given me, with exquisite articulateness, everything in her heart. With Zuri, I realized, words would come no plainer. It was her hands that spoke.

Drawing my hair clear, sliding down, under open shirt and coverlet, to turn me about in her own body's curve. Arms embracing me, mouth a feather kiss on the back of my neck.

"Suppose," I whispered into the darkness, "we said, yes."

"Huh!"

"I'm not used to—planning. How would—how could it work?"

"Not used, are you?" Her arm tightened. But the gust of breath against my ear was Zuri's own smothered laugh. "Mother forbid you ever learn!"

"But—"

"Save your innocence, beautiful." From the way that ended, I think she had surprised herself. "Tellurith'll settle it. Probably a gala marriage feast." She kissed my ear. "And you, I can see, will have your say."

"Zuri, I don't mean to—"

"Mother, I don't mind." Suddenly she was shaking against me, not merely a laugh, a whole spasm of merriment. "Those looks, and brains as well. Most likely I'll have to bring you here. Not likely she'd put you in a room alone. I wouldn't. And no way Alkhes could cope with me in there."

Has she listened at the door? But then, our brangles must have traveled—have resounded—all over the house.

"You've shared before. You can settle it. Do I pick you up in the kitchen when I want you, or fix it first with Tellurith?"

What has happened . . . since I left Amberlight and the Tower, what has come over me? How could I have answered, so readily, so brazenly, "What if I want you?"

This time it was more of a fracture than a pause. A winded jerk, as if I had punched away all her breath.

Oh, gods, I thought. She wanted me because I was proper, because I acted like a Tower man. I've lost it, just when I had everything.

Like the merest boy's, my face burnt. I hid its brand desperately under an arm.

She was still absolutely quiet. I thought, with both ears full of heartbeat, Strange deities, save me. No Mother could salvage this.

Carefully, she shifted my arm. Climbed up on an elbow. Turned me, gently but inexorably as Tellurith, on my back. Drew the other arm down from my face.

Silence again. Just before all resolution collapsed, she spoke. The merest whisper. Shakier than my breath.

"If you—do you—Sarth . . .?"

Her hands framed my face. But she had the decency not to pry my eyes open. Instead she kissed me, light as a priestess's blessing. Then she whispered, "If that—if that happens," as if I had just given her the world and eternity with it. "You just have to—say."

Spring. Iskarda.
Meditations. Alkhes-Assandar

MAY THE RIVER-LORD's nine-armed Adversary fly away with me if I was ever so surprised.

After *he* tramps about the house all week like a sacrificial virgin, with a lip stuck out to fetch thunderclouds. After *she* hove a plate at Tellurith.

Then *he* sidles into the kitchen with his shirt cross-buttoned and his hair in rat-tails. Gives Tel a look that bellows, Crisis, and when she flies out after him, *she's* propped up on the passage wall, cool as cellar ice. All ready to say, "Ruand? I've changed my mind."

So now we're abuzz with feast plans and marriage contracts. As if she never put a hand on him, never smashed his lip open and near to broke his kneecap—as if there's every surety she'll never do it again!

I DID MY BEST. When we got in bed, when Tellurith, if you please, is cuddling him like a first-born boy-child. Whatever she said, I think she really was terrified. I do believe, now it's happening, she does have second thoughts. So I got up behind her and took a handful of hair to get some attention. "How in the gods' name," I said, "is this going to *work*?"

Sarth smothered something. Tellurith rolled over and gawped.

"Caissyl," she said at last. Patting me, like some nervous dog. "It's from Amberlight. Women have always shared. You just have to be less—impulsive. Make arrangements. Let people know ahead."

"So you two make up a roster or we all send smoke-signals. Pardon my stupidity: *how*?"

I hadn't blown the lamp out. There was light enough to see Sarth's face, and I will swear I saw his jaw muscles twitch. The bastard was trying not to laugh.

"She—um—Zuri," demure as I ever heard him, oh, I know that tone of voice, "she thought—"

"We'll settle it among us." Tellurith. No doubt at all.

"Who is 'us'?"

She put her arm around my neck.

"Sarth and Zuri and I, caissyl. The marriage-cross doesn't include you."

There are some things still to be grateful for.

And some call to be less thankful. Gods blast, I've just got used to him. I could almost consider—almost contemplate—asking—suggesting to Tellurith—

How can I do that if he's not there?

Anyhow, I'm used to him there. I—

Want him there.

What is this place doing to me?

———

THAT WAS, after all, the least of it. "You may have tried the water," a blind man in a Verrain sand-hood couldn't miss that look, "but how do you know it'll stay warm?"

That sobered him. And Tellurith gave him no help.

"I can't be sure," he said finally. "But we found an—understanding. I think—she'll always try."

"Fine consolation, if some night she comes home in a tantrum and breaks your neck! Sarth, just tell me. Honestly. Not for the House. For yourself. Is this what you want? "

He lifted his lashes and looked at me. Lamplight poured on him like honey, all that gold-glossy shoulder and thick-as-cream hair, those—beautiful—features. The lashes like feathered copper, and those big, solemn, golden-tawny eyes.

And the bastard blushed.

You couldn't mistake it. Dusk-rose, flush-bronze, overlaid with lamp-gilt. Beyond the slightest doubt.

Then he ducked his head down, jammed it in the pillow, Sarth, who knows he can annihilate me with an eyebrow, with a handful of words.

What did Zuri do to *him*?

Spring. Iskarda.
Tellurith's Diary

IT IS A GOOD TIME for a wedding: the days longer, the ploughing done, all the annual trees out, the hills decked in their bright effervescence; and plenty of flowers. I shall send someone down to the Kora. I want irises, the big ones, cream and tiger-spotted and horizon lavender, for the pledging sheaf.

No doubt I should blame myself, should be anxious, if not panicky. Is it wicked, that what I feel is mostly relief?

Probably I should be afraid for Sarth; it is a gamble, after all. I would worry; did not instinct, observation—the way he blushed, the mere way Zuri walks and talks—did not something affirm it. They have made an understanding. Probably I should ferret it out. I will be happy, merely to be proven right.

Even at a first-foal's price.

IT WAS A GOOD NIGHT; not a huge event, like the great House joinings, a Head's cross-marriage, as it would have been in Amberlight, but happy enough. Iskarda and Telluir together, the village musicians, myself as officiant. Wine up from Marbleport, wild extravagance; the last of Iskarda's winter beer, sheaves and sheaves of flowers. Sarth in his best mulberry tunic, Zuri shoveled into a decent shirt. A sufficiency of merriment, and no unfortunate comments afterward, before we drove them off, hand-in-hand, Sarth playing modest, Zuri genuinely tongue-knotted, down the corridor.

And Alkhes and I went off to bed alone.

Curious, how incomplete that felt. When I have slept alone most of my life; when I only had one man in my bed for a bare four months, when there have been two no more than—altogether, it can be no more than five months, if I exclude the time . . .

The Mother be thanked I can remember that, now; a healed wound, a torture past. That I had the memory of it for anodyne last night. For reminder that, in all the time since Mid-winter, if I have shared a bed with Alkhes, we have shared nothing else.

He was already in my arms. When I ran a hand slowly down his ribs, the heartbeat under my ear sped up with a jerk.

"Caissyl." I rubbed my head under his jaw. His arm clenched about my neck. "If you don't want to, it's all right." With Alkhes, there is so much you have to spell out; so much that cannot be said at all. The Mother knows, with Sarth, before Mid-winter, I pushed him hard enough. And She knows, I would understand if he never wanted sex with anyone, ever again.

"No. No." His heart was hammering now. He clutched me all but convulsively. "I do—I do want to." He sounded half out of breath. "Only . . ."

Only I may not be capable. Physically, emotionally. Of invoking the memory, without calling monsters back out of the abyss.

His hand had a tremor as he pushed the hair up off my neck.

"I don't know if I—if I can—"

Thank Her, that I understood, have come to understand, enough to follow that. He did want me, he wanted to make love, desperately, the more that we were alone. But to take the lead, to do it as he thought he must . . .

"Oh, caissyl." I rolled up on my elbows and kissed him, outright. "Why don't you leave that to me?"

I felt his breath release, a long, thankful sigh. Before he turned his head, and kissed my clasping palm; and whispered, miracle of miracles, with something like amusement in it.

"When did I do anything else?"

HE WAS STILL in my arms when we woke this morning: curled tight, as he has slept all this spring, my hands clasped and crossed over his breast. I felt his breathing change, as I listened to the sounds of daybreak: the outer door's open and close, low troublecrew voices, Shia's footstep in the corridor. Then another step, as much yet less familiar; the click of my own latch.

Alkhes sat up with a plunge. Sarth wavered, halfway to the bed.

"I—ah—Tellurith?"

I held out my arms to him. The gray dawn blotted a robe, probably Zuri's, far too short. His hair swathed one shoulder, his feet were bare. He dropped his good clothes from an elbow crook and I pulled him into our midst.

"Sarth!" Alkhes dived on him, a whirlpool of covers and yanked-open robe, hunting bruises behind his very ears. "Are you all right?"

His face on the pillow was translucent. More than dawn pallor, a familiar weariness. He half-smiled at me; then he put an arm up and yanked Alkhes down against him, as you would a lover, a beloved, importunate child. "It's all right," he said, "Aglis."

Aglis. Small. Small One. Has he ever explained *that*?

Without it, three months ago there would still have been mayhem. This time Alkhes gave a strange little snort; and froze; then freed himself, quite quietly, and settled down into the bed.

"Zuri had work," Sarth told me. Something in the inflection said, Of course. Spoke faintly, ephemerally, of reluctance, of loss. "I thought I would come—"

Home? Back? It could have been either, from his eyes. I pulled the spring-lightened coverlets up over us all; lay down myself, taking the scent of Zuri on his skin, recalling, sternly, the times in Amberlight I had been lucky to get near him once in a week. I said, "We needn't get up yet."

"No." He worked one arm under my neck, and the other under Alkhes'. Then he looked from one to the other of us and produced a diffident, wondering smile.

"Now I'm in the middle," he said.

Spring. Iskarda.
Meditations. Alkhes-Assandar

I'M IN THE MIDDLE. When has he been anywhere else? As pattern, as balance, a vital part of our connection. Without him, Tellurith and I, like a mis-fletched arrow, would simply fly apart.

It's the new thing that's beyond my understanding. Not Tellurith's part. I know the impulsions of House-need, of responsibility and River politics; I can understand, with the mind if nothing else, that she was brought up to this. She's always shared. I said it to him once myself.

But Sarth?

Tellurith says I have—says she admires my wits. Gods know, they've failed here. Perhaps I've lost my patience. Perhaps I've learnt fool curiosities. Perhaps I've just got crazy enough, knowing him, knowing the risk it is, that I had to ask.

We had finished the troublecrew morning workout. With Zuri, even my eye sees the difference. No mooning, no besotted softness. No tension and no brusqueness either, and gods be thanked, none of that weird violence. Sometimes, I'd sooner have been knocked down than bear the way she'd pull him up.

So we were on the front steps, a late spring morning, warm enough to seek shade from the new-leafed pepper tree, a pure jade fountain filling the yard, with some Iskardan's leather tools, and a heap of beasts' and human harness to fix. He had the plough-gear, I had a bundle of armor straps. Some Verrain light cavalryman's back and heart-protector plates. The River plain to admire, a great celadon and blue-enameled distance, the day-noises all round us, a cushion for the work. For talking, in confidence.

"Um," I said. "Sarth?"

"You want the punch?"

He was squatted head-down and knees spread like a slum-side tanner; be hung if I know how anyone looks good like that. And as usual, half his mind on what I needed, without so much as a look.

"No."

He shed the palm-guard. Fielded the needle in a half-made stitch. He does know me too well. Straw Korite hat pulled down to keep his nose safe. Those eyes, shadowed to smoke and topaz, far too perceptive underneath. "What is it, Alkhes?"

No point, then, in fooling with neat's-foot oil and leather strips. Or word-fuss. "I'm sorry. I've chewed it six ways from sideways. I still don't understand."

Anyone else would have said, Understand what?

I pulled a buckle free on the harness. "*You* were livid. *She* was mad enough to break arrest. So how in the River-lord's hell . . ."

Every inch of my skin felt the twitch. "I'm sorry, forget it, it's not my affair." Damn, I wanted to shout, I've broken your privacy, and there's nothing else you have left.

"No," he said. Groping, by the note of it, for words himself. "I just don't know—"

He stopped. Picked up the palm-guard. Shoved the needle through, drew up the stitch. I caught on and started another buckle myself.

"I was taught about being hurt—in the Tower."

It came with a lunge that startled me almost as much as the words. He yanked up another stitch. People were calling, gossiping. A bullock-team heaved past in the street. Screek, screek. Screeek.

"You learnt—they *teach* you—how to cope with that?" To be *taught*; to have lessons. In bedroom violence. In something you don't just suffer, but can expect.

His head was down, face buried under the hat brim. He shoved another stitch through, too hard, and did not look up.

I knew, he knew what I thought of that whole life. To shout and scream at some new outrage was superfluous.

Listen, I wanted to say. Wanted to yank him round and shake him and—gods, I'm getting used to this—protect him like a woman, to say, I swear, so long as I've a hand to use, you'll never have to suffer that again.

But he had chosen the risk.

"Tel," I sounded very far away, "would never have made you—"

"It wasn't Tellurith."

This time the needle went completely awry. He yanked it back and dropped the palm-guard; sucked the red freshet on his thumb.

"Here, let me see—"

"It doesn't matter." He held it away and looked full at me. "It wasn't Tellurith. It wasn't the House." Be hung if he hadn't started blushing again. "It was—"

He looked away. I looked away. He took an enormous breath.

"I don't *like*—I don't find pleasure in being hurt. But when someone does it—and then stops. And then," he pressed the unhurt hand against his thumb, and it shook, "and then is gentle . . . It—when you do feel pleasure—it's stronger than you could imagine. Than you could believe."

I had the wit to bite my tongue. Not to bawl, So you'll let her beat you up whenever she pleases for this, this *addiction*? Oh, gods help you, man!

"She didn't hit me again. She hasn't hit me. I doubt she will hit me—do you think it was no shame to her?" That shook worse than his hand. "For me . . . there's no need."

"Hey?"

He took a spasmodic grip on the palm-guard and said it, head down, into his hands.

"It's enough—to know she might."

I hung onto the steps to stop the revolving world. But someone croaked out, "Is it enough for *her*?"

He swung right round and looked full into my eyes.

"It isn't just that with her. But," this time he met my eyes with the force, the assurance of a priest warding some sanctuary, "her side is not for me to tell."

Summer. Iskarda.
Tellurith's Diary

THE FIRST CUTTER died today.

How strange that looks. Yet it might as well be a living creature, a human being; they are mortal now, as we are. When they go, there will be no more.

It was Zeara's blade. Up in the quarry, middle morning shift, one of those cloudless days when every rock-face coruscates like snow on fire. All the Iskans and the River plain beyond us smiling green, six cutters, three handling-teams with sheer-legs and ropes and gloves. A pair of ox-carts, and a tally-maker under the shanty-roof at the road's edge, to record the block number and store-site, to paint them on as it jolts past. That was me.

Such a normal, calmly happy morning, in what has become, unconsciously, routine. Hard work, but work that is productive, familiar. Until the fracture: the pause, break of rhythm at the face. Exclamation. A rising back. A falter that ran the quarry-width, cutters and handlers turning, gathering. From the midst of the group, sudden as a tree-fall, the keening cry of grief.

She will never have another. The last of her own qherrique, the last of her Amberlight. Well may Zeara weep.

BEYOND THE GRIEF it leaves a quandary. Because we have—oh Mother's gift!—an order, a genuine, substantial requisition to fill. Some Dhasdein high priest wants to refurbish the River-lord's temple, Iskan marble is his heart's love; he has bought our last two shiploads and he wants three more.

One shipload we can cover from the store, but the store is spring's laid-up work. Another two loads within two moons? That will ask double, triple shifts, every cutter we have at work.

Which means mine.

I keep it with me, usually. It does not need Zuri's wariness, nor a life in Amberlight, to tell me that the House's head is the most vulnerable, the most precious treasure of the House. Especially this house. That hazards may be like snow-walkers, wholly unpredictable. And even troublecrew may not always be in time.

Nor can I work cutting shifts. A tally-time, a visit or a shift a week, perhaps. There is House business. Above all, at the moment, there is the water-line.

We started surveying after the thaw. It must be strong, and it must be high, for the pressure, for we have no power here but earth's. Then someone knowledgeable had to check each site. That has been faster, since Alkhes recovered, for between troublecrew practice, and house-labor, that he insists on sharing with Sarth, we have had the services of a first-rate engineer, an experienced surveyor, and Charras has not been too proud to learn.

So the spring is chosen, three hills over, high above the quarry site. That has brought us to the line itself.

Iskarda's men have carried waterjars time out of mind. The Amberlight pipelines offer memory and lore, but they too were ancient; we have no working specialists. The pipe-line has ridden every council-meet. We have even, ludicrous marvel, watched Alkhes and Shia construct a miniature range-front from clay and straw, with reed-pipes laid across it and water trickled through a kitchen funnel atop.

Alkhes thinks the gradient is enough. We must build a reservoir, as we had on Arcis, then run the water on down here. In pipes. Clay pipes.

Chasso is Iskarda's potter, but her little backyard furnace will never do. We also need a way to throw the long, narrow pipes. Mother forfend the thought that one day we will have to build a metal-casting furnace, with all the gear for ores, and far higher temperatures . . . There is enough to deal with here.

Far too much to spend my time on quarry-shifts.

AFTER ALL, it is perfectly logical. Iskarda, Darthis herself accepted the evidence; at the hunt, my troublecrew, everyone did. If any House, any Amberlight women could handle it, it would be these. It is well within his scope. He is used to hard work and danger. He is not tower-bred, after all.

It is one thing to convince myself my work-crews will accept a man among them, a man handling a cutter, moreover, once the qherrique's most sacred use. That he will suffer no more than hard labor's heat and fatigue and sweat; that cutting at the mother-face was infinitely more dangerous.

It is another to remember that this is Alkhes, but also Assandar. And it is a far cry from asking a soldier, a military aristocrat, a Dhasdein commander-general to play surveyor, or troublecrew, or even cook and nursing orderly, to run to and fro with children's chamberpots—

To making him, full-time, a dirty, subordinate, manual laborer. With no use for his skill. Or even worse, for his wits.

ALL THIS I should have been able to say beforehand; privately, in our bed, where I could explain, and he could consider, protest, work out his choice.

Except that then it would have come before the council decided; when they have as much right in the matter as he.

So I had to call him to a meeting, in itself unusual; and say it out, with no room for demurral, before them all.

I should have remembered his wits. I did feel those eyes, razor-edged obsidian, as I spoke. I ought to have known he would read the unspoken: that the very fact I did it in public said I trusted him to recognize my motives; to think, as he had before, of the House.

When I finished, it was Zuri who had her eyes screwed in the nearest approach to anguish she can make. While Hayras and Charras and Zariah consulted eye to eye, and picked up Quetho; moved on to Iatha, and then Ahio beyond them grunted in open relief.

"No doubt we need the cutter, Ruand. It would've been sticky," we all knew, an understatement, "to dedicate it anywhere else."

A blade already re-aligned, with no other candidate but Zeara, who might well wreck the bond from sheer grief, or some novice who had never woken qherrique in her life.

"You'll have no problem?"

It was Hayras, the cutting-Head, who I asked. Who, with no doubt of my meaning, took a long look at Alkhes, and enquired, "That arm all fixed?"

"I've carried six water-yokes a day." He was not boasting; he was not, the Mother witness, insulted. It was the rouse of a hunting-hawk.

Hayras nodded. A considering pause. "If the shift's too much at first, you're to let me know."

Hayras had met outland male pride before. When he nodded, she narrowed her coffee-dark eyes.

"No problem working with us?"

Working with women, she meant. No crazed urge to outdo, to risk his or others' necks by being fastest or greatest producer, or first in anything. No repressed humiliation, that would raise quarrels and trouble everywhere.

He laughed outright and gave her an imperial salute. "I've had two seasons with troublecrew, ma'am. What do you think?"

They whipped a glance at Zuri, who still looked like a timber-bargeman's idol with belly-ache. Both of them laughed. "Well, then," said Hayras. "Afternoon shift."

Which meant I could cosset him last night, when he came back caked with sweat and marble-dust, over-worked shoulder muscles trembling, scored with stray flakes and chips, sunburnt even under the hat. That I could scrub his back in the luxury of a bath. That in bed, with Sarth away again, I could explain.

When I finished he worked his scratched, calloused, now roughened hand up to stroke my hair. "Tel . . ." it was half-sigh, half-laugh. "Do you think I give a spit about being an imperial general? Gods' love! I knew you couldn't ask me first. I just wanted—I'm just glad—" It spoke in his voice now, unconcealable, a fierce, hungry pride. "That I can do something for the House."

"You have done something—"

"Something worthwhile, Tel." The gesture was impatience outright. "Something no one else can do."

Perhaps it is outland male pride, after all. But it sounded remarkably close to joy.

Summer. Iskarda.
Journal kept by Sarth

I AM NOT JEALOUS. The—gods bear witness. I am not. Vexed, possibly. Missing him in the daily work-pattern, yes. Irritated, that without the slightest warning I have had to turn the entire house-schedule inside out. Wistful, perhaps. But jealous of daylong labor in sun that would wreck a Heartlander's skin, to ruin what is left of my hands with rock-cuts and tool-blows, and risk life and limb among precariously maneuvered marble-slabs . . . ? No.

Especially not after last night.

Zuri was on edge, the first glance at supper told me that. When she beckoned me down the passage I admit my belly squirmed, Alkhes' prophecies shot through my mind. Yet when it came to the point she was only a little more brusque.

I have coaxed her, now, not to rush off immediately. At least, to leave her patrols until midnight. Lying down by me, usually, she is quiet. Halfway to tense. Last night we had just settled, with her in the crook of my arm, my eyelids sinking. When she sat up.

I made an *Mm?* that meant, *What?* She grunted and lay down again: *Nothing important.* Tower-training insisted, *Something.* I was tired enough, shameful confession, to settle for that.

She shifted. And sat back up.

With Tellurith, I would have asked outright. Here I bit my tongue. Touched her face.

With a jerk, she touched me back. A finger down the jaw. A brush across my lips. A setting back of undone hair, that it is her pleasure to make straight. With another jerk, she spoke.

"You've been training with us—six months."

"Mm."

A nice cross of question and assent. She stared over me, into the dark. I wished yet again she would let me light the lamp.

"You're troublecrew."

Even now, my ear barely caught the nuance: what should have been outright statement, which had jerked my pulse with surprise. With a disbelieving joy. But it was assertion; the slightest fissure of doubt.

"Mm?"

She swung round, feet tucked up, sitting, now, in the angle of my ribs and outstetched arm. I would almost have given that arm to read her face.

"I'm giving you an assignment."

"Zuri . . . !" I sat straight up and grabbed at her.

"Ssh." Great indulgence, all but honor, that those iron-hard fingers should simply clamp my mouth, when shock and truly incredulous joy had broken both Tower and troublecrew rules.

I had sense enough not to fight. To wait. To hear, with opened ears, the more startling nuances, anger, resolution, sour irony, when she spoke again.

"I'm going to make use of you."

She lay down, head settling firmly on my shoulder, leg across my thighs as she likes to sleep, assuring my capture. Growled into my armpit, "Go to sleep."

AND THIS MORNING, she whisked through the kitchen after breakfast to tow me from the washing-up with one brisk tap on the shoulder and a brisker, "Meeting. Council-room. Now."

I have never gone to a House meet. A man, a Tower man, flaunt himself amid the Craft-heads, where decisions are made? Had she not propelled me, I would have turned and run.

She pushed the door to behind us and swung me into the surprise blazoned on every face. Hayras and Quetho, Craft-heads, Charras, project-leader, Hanni, Head's record-keeper. Iatha. House Steward. Every face saying, What is he doing here?

Tellurith's own blank façade that asked, Zuri, is this a mistake?

With Tower training, I did my best to melt into the floor. Zuri stomped past me and planted both hands on the table, staring up it at Tellurith.

"Ruand," she said, "you need a bodyguard."

Iatha goggled. Hayras' jaw dropped. Tellurith folded her hands.

"Is this a troublecrew choice?"

Zuri jerked her chin. Short-code for *yes.*

"We've enough for night patrols. Enough to ward the House-grounds. The quarry's in range. To ward an unarmed House-head, all over Iskarda? No."

They held each other, eye to eye. Even Tower-training could not decode that stare.

Then Tellurith inclined her head. Acknowledgement. Assent, I think. Firstly, that Zuri's judgment of her resources was right. Secondly, that giving away her cutter had tipped the scales.

"Azo?" she said. "Desis?"

Zuri took my wrist and tweaked me forward. "Sarth."

I could read Hayras' face. And Iatha's, before she took Zuri's eye, colder than first spring snow-melt, and brought her jaw up with a snap.

"He's troublecrew." It was all challenge, that stare. "He's trained with us, six months." More than challenge; dare. You claimed to free men, you want them among the trades. Prove it, then.

Tellurith said, "Um."

"I'll teach him the rest. On the job."

Ever so slightly, Tellurith's jaw relaxed. Then she looked at me, and it tightened up again.

Zuri leant forward further, that glare skewering her.

"If you can't carry a weapon worth its while, you need a bodyguard. One that'll do what's needed." She straightened a little, and fired the rest softly as a light-gun, and as lethally. "Like Alkhes."

It was not my being a man she meant. Nor the training. That, I could never match. But I know what she did mean. One who might not be the fastest, or the deadliest, but who would be there when it mattered, as Alkhes was at the Diaman funeral, throwing himself in the way of a Heartland poison-dart. Who would save her if all else failed with his own body, his own life. Not because he was troublecrew.

Because he loved her. The strongest pledge of all.

VIII

Summer. Iskarda.
Tellurith's Diary

BLIGHT AND BLAST that woman! She is as tricky as a bagful of Heartland monkeys and as callous as a tyrant in Cataract. I should have thrown that plate at *her*.

Not just for using Sarth in the best and worst of ways. A job, yes, a trade; the deadliest trade; loading a recruit's, a man's, a tower-bred man's shoulders with the heaviest weight in the House. Nor the callousness. Gambling that, at worst, what saves me will be his love. His blood. His flesh.

Most damnable of all, the cow has shackled *me* into the knot. Knowing, rot and lechery take her, that *I* will be playing troublecrew; that *I* will hunt the dangers, that *I* will limit my risks. That for his sake, I will double-ward us both.

Demon. Trickster. Cow!

Summer. Iskarda.
Journal kept by Sarth

THE GODS DEFEND ME, did I ever think Sethar's schooling hard?

I am bruises all over, body and mind. Every nerve, every reflex scraped. If the light shifts, if someone moves behind me, it all jumps. If nothing happens, every hideous blunder Zuri has recounted, every horrendous possibility runs through my mind, over and over. If this goes on, I will be useless anyway.

Zuri's idea of training; personal; on the job. Knowing very well that if the gymnasium put me far ahead in hand-to-hand work, when it came to real troublecrew skills, street-fighting, tactics, bodyguard lore and practice, knowing where and when to look and what to do about it, I was the veriest child.

So for a week Zuri herself has played guerilla, assassin, street ambush. For a week I have had Tellurith stabbed, abducted, hacked by berserkers or shot with light-guns from a rooftop under my very hands, before my very eyes. Until from being sprung on or yanked away or thrown to earth under me, she is all but bruised solid. And I—

In deepest sleep, if cloth rustles or a night-bird calls, I tear the tendons off my bones and knock my partners clear out of the bed.

Alkhes says it is usual: desirable. All troublecrew, he says, are perpetually half-mad. Living, eternally, on a precipice edge. Eternally overstrung for that one vital, lethal moment which is all that matters. That is what we are for.

Bitter, then, that when it came, I was looking the wrong way.

TELLURITH SAYS, Not my fault. Zuri . . .

Zuri said, when she had me in bed, afterwards, when for once she came back and held me without coaxing, because I could not stop shaking yet—

Kinder, more grateful, even than Tellurith. Because Zuri *knows*.

And *she* said it, quieter than breath, the truest benison.

"You belonged where you were."

Which was at Tellurith's left shoulder, poised, strung, assessing continuously who was where, how near, behaving how; possibilities of weapon-use, further cover and fire-angles and flight or ambush spots; every sense tuned, to everything from body-scents to the turn of pebbles underfoot.

Though it was only an excursion to the reservoir site, Tellurith, Hanni, Charras and Iatha; half the eminences of Telluir House stravaging blithely in the blond summer afternoon, spreading to comment on pipeline points, savor the silken umber cloud-shadows on hayed-off grass. Scattered about the reservoir site, exposed beyond bearing on the highest crest, melted into the digging teams, preserve us, half of them hired labor arrived this spring. How does Zuri manage these events without going insane?

But I did it. I had them headed down, and close gathered enough for hope of warding, however I managed that, when Tower-training made it unnecessary for Zuri to drum into me, You never harass your charges; high persons must never be bullied, or obstructed, or constrained. *Somehow*, they were co-operating.

When we heard the scream.

Iskarda was just downhill, obscured by the quarry cutting, the big rest-break hellien. I was over the edge into the tree's shadow with the guard-duty slashing knife free before she screamed again.

I could have saved the knife. Zariah got there first. Knowing the voice, perhaps, a mother's reflex, that bests any bodyguard's. With the cutter, so craft and mother's reflex wiped the beam across him neat as needle-work and sliced his head clean off.

That one was on top of her, just getting his trousers down. I got the one holding her shoulders when he tried to run. Gods' own luck, Zuri told me, cuffing my head furiously as on the practice floor, that Zariah did not take me too. I never thought about it. By then, I had seen who it was.

On her back in the road-dirt; bruised, the palm-graceful body, the terror of broken innocence in those great amber eyes. A hurt gazelle, a spoilt butterfly.

Asaskian.

Blessings that Zariah was there or I would have disemboweled him on the spot. I think I did break his wrist. Unnecessary yet again. No butterfly, Asaskian. The scream had been for help. She had slowed the dead one with a kick in the gut, when the second pulled her down she used her nails. He was already scratched half blind.

No waste. No loss.

Because he is not Iskardan. Not Korite, not even outlander. He is one of our own. Pheroka's second son.

Summer. Iskarda.
Tellurith's Diary

"WE'RE OUT of the tower. We have the right!"

He said that. When they dragged him in the council-room, knees and elbows bound crippling tight, the kicks and bruises all but doubling him up. Troublecrew justice, troublecrew pre-emption. Fourteen years old. A child—a son—of the House.

Saved from the fall of Amberlight. Brought out of the tower. Trusted to find his way in a new world. Into a new liberty. By women's struggles, women's sacrifice; women's grace.

———

Summer. Iskarda.

Meditations. Alkhes-Assandar

IF THERE WAS a chance, I'd kill the little bastard. But I'd be far down the line. Blast his eyes out. Not just for what he did to his family, to the girl he picked—

Bless the Mother that he got no further. For Zariah. For Sarth. For her own fighting wits. The Mother be thanked . . .

That she will never be dragged back into those memories that come up, later, surfacing like fragments of a corpse. Dark, terror, violence, pain—

The Mother be thanked her body, her mind, the memory below the mind, will never bear my scars.

The River-lord rend his soul, if he were innocent as a baby, I'd still cut his liver out.

For what he did to Tellurith.

Summer. Iskarda.

Tellurith's Diary

I WOULD NOT have let Sarth in the council-room, if he were more than a witness, if he did have the right. When we caught up with them, that look . . . I could hate the fool for that if nothing else. Because he destroyed more than himself. Because I have seen madness, killing madness, on my husband's face.

The boy?

Defiance, stupidity. Incoherent, mostly. Terrified, of course, he literally soiled himself. He knows what he can expect.

But not like this. Not such requital, by such a justiciary. The Craft-heads are rabid; not for Asaskian, but because the thing itself is unimaginable. Not in Amberlight. Men would not dare. The violation of a woman violates reality.

Do they not understand, that order is gone?

Zuri and the troublecrew would be as swift, as summary. Violation is violence, to flesh or privilege. Like me, Asaskian is a trust. Whoever violates a troublecrew trust can expect troublecrew justice; not right or wrong but dead.

Zariah . . . Who would expect mercy there?

Pheroka . . .

He is her flesh and blood. He is also a son. She is from Amberlight, inescapably as all of us. Sons are second-rate. This one has shamed her blood beyond sufferance.

Iatha?

Certainly, she knows the House's hazard as well as I. Let Pheroka hold back too far, or Zariah ask too much recompense—we could lose Telluir, right there.

Does she understand the rest? That I tried to change this; that I wanted men with liberty, with choice, with self-respect. That I wanted an end to tyranny. That—Mother, it is profane to say it—there is worse loss than Asaskian's. There is the loss of vision; the loss of hope.

To condemn this boy out of hand will not remedy it. That he did it is the real indictment. Not, any more, of Amberlight.

Of what I have tried to do instead.

Summer. Iskarda.
Meditations. Alkhes-Assandar

I COULD HAVE born it if she'd cried. If she'd raged, if she'd hit me for being a man too, if she'd blamed me or him or anyone. Anything but that apathy. The silence. The absence, beside me. As if she was sick beyond feeling.

Sick to very death.

I have learnt not to fuss. Even to talk. The body will say it for you, Sarth has taught me that. *You are there for the woman.* Gods know, last night I tried to be. If she had given me one look, one touch, one word . . .

I could have slaughtered him barehanded for her. Could have moved mountains, raised the dead, reversed time and put them all back in that gold-dust sunlight, with the last cut to finish before dark. With Asaskian, up to the quarry carrying her family's break-time honey-cakes, lithe and lovely as an auburn-haired palm-tree amid the rock and the perpetual fog of stone-dust and the spurts of sparks and marble-chip. A momentary god-child, walking away.

IF SHE'D JUST let me tell her that I understood: you thought you were making a new order, you were going to free them, me, all of us. Now you stand beneath a shaken keystone, with nothing to stop the House falling on your head.

Nothing to say, This is not your fault.

Nothing to insist, Men are capable of change. You have not betrayed your comrades, we are not *all* secret beasts.

No way to vow, This is an aberration. A result of long slavery reversed. A single rotten spot.

No chance, no possibility to swear, It will not happen again.

Gods damn it, she may have adjourned the council-meet without verdict or explanation, the House may reverberate with unslaked blood-hate, she may have left them all to froth—

But did she have to go off up the mountain, and refuse to take anyone, even troublecrew, even Sarth? And brood up there till midnight, then come down, a walking zombie, to make me wish I was still eating my heart out in that empty bed?

I would have protested. Iatha grabbed me. I would have followed her. She made Zuri—Zuri!—block me. Literally challenge me. Rot both their eyes, she knows, before I locked blades with a woman Tellurith paid a husband for, I would—

So neither of us had supper. Neither of us slept. But I had to get up and go back to the quarry this morning, while she—

She has gone back up the mountain.

And there is nothing—nothing!—I can do.

Summer. Iskarda.
Tellurith's Diary

IF THERE had been some way to explain. If I could have brought myself to tell him; to soften it for him. Oh, Mother, to be so grievously hurt you cannot ease the hurt of a beloved, cannot even bear to open the wound for sympathy.

I was not thinking, this morning. I wanted only to creep up the mountain, as Zuri must have, as any wounded rabbit would, and seek a sanctuary, a vacuum where I need not think. Need not decide. Need not exist.

She must have tracked me; no doubt all Iskardans have hunter craft. She got up that hillside quieter than a cloud-dark, the first I knew was the pebble clattering past me and the low call threading the helliens.

"Xer's praise."

Xer is the Mother's moon form, mountain style; they say it approaching a stranger's hearth. When I sat up the place finally came into focus: scrubby mountain hellien, thick for summer with creamy tufted blossom-bars, a cynosure of bees; the rock heap in the midst, the little seep of water, glistening out into the fringe of green beyond. Probably I had kept a score of mountain beasts away.

She stooped, for I saw her blue sleeve shift. I said the ritual answer.

"In Xer's name."

She pushed amid the helliens. Found another rock. Slid a tin trail-cup from somewhere, dipped water from the seep. Put it, and the packet of new bread, smelling of mountain honey, by my hand.

How could I have gone near a day's cycle and never thought to eat?

And when she did not speak, finally I could ask.

"Do they have this to deal with, in Iskarda?"

She stirred a little, taking back the cup, sipping herself. Then she said, "Every year or two."

"Every—!"

"Outlanders. The quarry-workers. Always one that can't tell yes from no."

The Mother help us. Every year or two.

She gave her little dour snort. "Up here we learn—we're all taught—to watch for it."

As I had not taught Asaskian. As none of us had thought to teach her. Presuming, in our naivety, that all men would be good-hearted. Never thinking it would not be like Amberlight.

Presently I said, "How do you—deal with it?"

She stared out across the mountain. Her profile was implacable as the rock by which it was framed.

"In Iskarda, we cut the trouble off at the root."

"At the—!"

This time the snort was sour but genuine mirth. "Ah, Ruand, you part a man and his dangle, he'll just use something else. We cut where it starts." She tipped her chin up. "At the head."

After a while I said, "No Mother's mercy."

Her voice was pure stone. "Which matters more? Him or us?"

"No appeal."

"For a man that's got to force?"

She looked around. Then, a marvel for Darthis, reached out and laid a hand, delicate for all its massiveness, on my arm.

"Ruand, put the guilt where it belongs. You couldn't know it would happen. Likely it wasn't the boy's idea. Likely he picked it up from the other, or was pushed into it. He'd know no better. Just a whelp, and out of Amberlight. He wouldn't know—or think—about the price."

"No."

To go on was the hardest thing I ever did; except three. And the least of those was leaving Amberlight.

"Darthis—am I wrong?"

She stared away downhill, turning the cup in her hands. The bees hummed. The wind muttered, bringing me the scent of sweaty woman and acres of sun-warmed grass.

"Six months ago—I would have said yes. But when I asked the Mother," we both winced. "Now ..."

She checked, drawing a long sigh.

"That man of yours runs a kitchen better'n mine, but no man in Iskarda ever had manners like that. Could ever go to a Sowing-rite, then turn round and play troublecrew, and keep tower decent at 'em both. Nor any man in Iskarda could work a cutter in the quarry, Mother aid me, or use a plumb-bob like that lad Herar, or handle bullocks ..." She linked arms around her knees. "I know what you're asking. And as the Mother sees me, Ruand—I don't know."

The bees and the wind hummed. The helliens talked, a tiny, wheezing chatter, olive-green blades laced into the sky.

It was an easing, after all, to hand her back the cup. To get up, and rub a back rigored from long sitting, and offer her a hand. And say, "Then there is one way to find out."

No USE in asking for myself. In any Head's, in any woman's asking. There is only one questioner who might win a reply.

I sent him to Zuri. I could not have solaced him, who was too heart-hurt to salve myself. The Mother knows, I half thought to find him after me up the mountain; Alkhes yelled and fought, when Sarth never said a word, but Sarth—Sarth has his own willfulness; it would have been like him, to walk meekly inside, and straight out the other door.

But only this morning, when I parted from Darthis on the last slope above the village, did the tall shadow in mottled green and brown slide into the corner of my eye.

He wears it now like a second skin. His hands have hardened, the nails clipped short; always immaculately clean, but that exquisite tower manicure is gone, lost with the sleek overlay that tells of muscles polished for show. Now his skin is weather-roughened, his eyes innocent of gold-dust; as hard as his body, with that taut, fined-down look of troublecrew; living on the edge.

And Zuri has made a Crafter's plait of his hair.

———

THAT PRESENCE padded after me into the House. When I had staved off the cries and expostulations, heard the worst business, explained I was already fed, I drew it after me in our bedroom door.

The Mother be thanked, he is still my husband. So he opened his arms and took me, unquestioning, into that haven embrace.

Where, after long enough to block the tears, and quiet my breathing, and assemble wits, I said, "I need you to do something for me."

I felt the laugh's concussion in his chest. The murmur could have been, "When did you not?"

"That boy . . ."

Every muscle went to living rock. I have felt Sarth go away from me before. Never like that.

"Listen, Sarth." I pushed back to look up in his eyes. Oh, Mother, may I never confront a murderer outright. "I can't just condemn him—"

"Just?"

"Sarth." As always, my very ribs stung. "I have to know why!"

He stood away from me. There was more than stone—there was ugliness in the set of that face.

"He won't talk to me; to any woman. You know that! I need someone who can get through to him. Someone who—has the skills that we—" I could not finish, didn't need outside the tower. "Sweet Work-mother, you managed it with Alkhes!"

He stared at me. Even in the moment when he had torn the boy off her body and ripped his arm up his back until the wrist cracked and the brat screamed aloud, even then he had not felt like this.

Under my breath, as if tiptoeing past a lion, I said, "Sarth?"

He did not move. Yet I felt the lion rise.

"If you send me near that animal, Tellurith, I give you fair warning. I may not leave him alive."

It was more than anger. It was terrible. Violent, violating as the very rape.

"Sarth—"

His lips pinched.

"I have to know if it was him—or the other one's idea—or—or—"

"Or . . .?"

"Or—m-my . . . mistake."

His wits are quite as fast as Alkhes'. As the next breath went in his face changed; paling, under the sun-brown, to a chalky bronze.

"So I have to—exonerate—us both."

That old inflection; a dagger made of words.

"Sarth, I—"

He stepped back. "Don't apologize." It came now without any inflection at all. "I understand."

"Sarth!"

I grabbed him then. Never mind expedience, House necessity, House-head's dignity. It was sheer terror, ignominious as a baby's. It was not true, but were it true a hundred times, I could not—I could not! have let him go like that.

His body snapped away from me, where once it would have conceded with trained, schooled grace. Now it was reflex, sharp as I would have found in Alkhes. The impetus threw me forward into him, I hung on like a climber to muscles set as some adamant, brutally rejecting rock.

For a moment my world stopped. Then the blockade broke.

He took me by the elbows, with the oddest mixture of trained delicacy and trained brutality, and let out a breath that cracked like a pot. "Gods, Tellurith. *What* will you want next?"

Summer. Iskarda.
Journal kept by Sarth

SHE CRIED THEN. Wept in my arms as she does in extremity, no concern for her rank or my anxiety, in the abandon of perfect trust. No performance. And no simple relief. I can see that now. Gods, my imbecility. All the rest of us rabid to avenge, to destroy.

None of us thinking past the boy himself.

Relief, then, that I agreed, that, wormwood paradox, he had a chance. And finally, I think—it was grief.

For him. For the rest of us. For the dream she had had, and staked a House's future on.

For herself.

Does Alkhes understand? Very likely, he saw before I did. He was in the same position, once. He would realize this is more than one boy. That we are all, every man of us, on trial.

And so is Tellurith.

Cause enough, the gods know, and no doubt You as well, in Your malice, that I must use every art to uncover truth, when all I ardently desire is to use Zuri's gift and take him apart.

I HAD TO WRITE all that . . .

Had to come down here in the cellar, muster composure, more rigorously than for any Tower test—

Before I could so much as sort the mechanics of it. Tell Zuri, ask to be relieved as bodyguard. Think out the rest. Because of course I cannot take his truth—if I ever get to it—on trust.

At the very least, there is the other one. Who knows him, where did he come from, what manner of man was he? Why was he here?

Where is he now?

Second phase of the mechanics, then. To Hanni, House-memory, to ask where the—body went.

I never saw that. Dust, fallen forms, alive or dead, crying and shouting, hideous stench of cooked meat. Live meat, writhing in my hands. All my intent was to hold him till help came. Not to kill him first.

Zuri and troublecrew came. Tellurith was already there, so the rest would have been fast. We brought the—prisoner—here. Somebody must have—

Succored Asaskian.

Taken the corpse.

After Hanni then, far more horrendously, to Iskarda. To Darthis herself.

Where did I get the nerve to knock on that house door; to demand a meeting from the man who came; to confront *her*, in the big room that must be their council-place, to announce my authority as if I believed in it, and ask: Where? What now?

Give Darthis the due I always have, she took it without a blink, right up to the outrage of some Tower-man proclaiming authority to investigate like a Craft-head. She did not even balk at a man in a Crafters' plait.

Dead outlanders are laid up in the White Fox cellar, the coldest common place in Iskarda, until they go to the pyre. With accidents, there are ends to knit: messages to kin, belongings to bundle up and sell or dispatch.

With killers, there are still ends to knit.

With killers, they add the stuff to the pyre. The ashes—

Iskardan ashes go back to the Mother, to join and rejoin Iskarda, strewn over the fields. Outlanders' go to the hills.

Killers go into the lime pit, to be consumed without return or memorial. Blotted from the earth.

Darthis almost started for me, would have grabbed me, I think, as Iskardan women do a man they think over-taxed. Luckily there was a chair-back. I held on till I could reclaim my voice.

Then I asked for the clothes to be kept. To see the rest. For permission to ask after him, in the camp.

This year everything is upside-down for workers in Iskarda. With no quarry-work, they can dig on the cistern or help to level the pipe-line. The barracks have been absorbed by Telluir House. Some of the usual craftsmen, Darthis says, have gone elsewhere, but others, strangers from the Kora, mostly, have been drawn by news of the silver paid last autumn, or word passed from Tellurith.

All thirty or so camp beyond the quarry edge on the Marbleport road, in our abandoned tents.

Many are veterans of outdoor work; the place has its own kitchen and latrine and a grace-note or two, an ornate lantern, a good Verrain rug outside a tent. Most mean to lay up winter money; all have heard the reputations of Amberlight troublecrew. Even if liquors abounded, I doubt they would get as rowdy as River Quarter stevedores.

First I got the clothes. Say this for qherrique work, there is very little blood. It cauterized even the big veins in the neck.

And we have House-folk who can decode such things. River-work, said Zuri, at a glance. Could be Verrain or Dhasdein, well-worn, by their owner. See the way the shirt's pulled to his shape? Worker's clothes, not hand-me-down lords' stuff. Did you look at his hands?

"Were they worker's hands?" she supplemented. "New to the trade? How long had he been here? Did you—" she stood up. "I'll come to the camp."

By then it was shift's end, evening, the rest coming home. There were hangdog if not outright scared looks when Zuri, stocky, four-square, girded with knife and light-gun, clearly trouble on a hair-trigger, led me in to the kitchen-place and proclaimed, "We're needing news about Hepan."

She has learned his name. Or always knew it, trouble-Heads do. She dropped her eyes and tucked hands in her belt, and in a minute or two, began to get her replies.

He shared a tent with two Korite ditch-diggers, twenty-five, twenty-eight; their own age, but not their experience. His first year in Iskarda. Not given to talk about himself, they thought he might be from Dhasdein. Friendly enough, a good if prudent hand with the dice. Liked to gossip about Iskarda and the new women, but, they vouched, not filthy in the mouth. "Just curious. Never been," with a lofty look, "to Amberlight." Worked on the cistern, was off yesterday with a nasty bruised shin where a shovel bounced on a rock. "Probably," one opined, after grating his chin awhile, "not his proper trade."

What that trade might be, he had no idea.

Zuri said, "He go up the village much?"

He had gone up the village often. A mug of cider, mountain staple, most nights in the Market inn; older than the White Fox, it has no further name. Astakyr, its forthright, broad-beamed ruler, considered the questions with a frown.

"He never drank but the one mug. Out at the fountain was where he spent his time."

Talking to the men.

Zuri left me that part. Taking my temerity in both hands to ask Darthis if I could ask her household men. And Zdana. And Chasso. I came back, at sunset, to where Zuri perched on the Market's step. Nothing but six months training, and bed atop that, showed me cause for worry in her face.

I settled beside her. Before us women and work-teams passed, gold-striped in coppery sunset dust. Telluir and Iskarda: bullock-carts of wood and hunters with a fat summer kill, house-folk and quarry-workers, coming home, tired and dirty and jovial, with the belated summer night.

And the men, with wood-hods and evening waterjars. Congregating at the well, separating, drifting on. Iskardans. Camp-workers. Telluir's adolescents, on the House's unskilled work.

I said, "Du carried water for Zariah's house most nights. He used to idle at the well."

Zuri stared straight ahead of her. Only the minute jerk of her chin said, I'm listening.

"He—the other—used to joke with him a lot. Tease him. About doing women's work. Never having time to talk. Money to dice with. Going for a drink."

Zuri moved, and her face was hard as flint. She said, "Hepan had blistered hands."

Then she gathered up the lumpy bundle under her arm and said, "Need to look through this."

A man's possessions, his life, compassed in a blanket and a carrying strap. Dumped, as gingerly as a half-addled egg, in the corner of our council-room, and the door double-locked.

As Zuri pocketed the key, I said, "You think he wasn't what he looked."

Zuri actually twitched. Then gave a Zuri snort and muttered, "Brought it on myself."

She started down the corridor. Light was ahead, life and bustle and our own evening place. I kept pace, letting silence speak for me. With Zuri silence always functions best.

"Should've remembered I trained you. *After* you had wits."

Hanni's nieces emerged from the cross-corridor. Zuri checked, waving them on. Under cover of their chatter, spoke looking straight ahead, from a corner of her mouth.

"It's not," a pause for emphasis, "a thing I want spread."

"What is it I know?"

She gave another snort. It took an instant to recognize the first-cousin to a laugh. Light as a bee-sting, she tapped my arm. "You do what you're assigned." The mirth vanished. "See to the boy."

One of Shia's helpers came pounding up the cellar stairs; by now they would be getting his food ready too. Prisoner or sick-room, I knew the routine.

Zuri started forward. I swallowed the heart that kept trying to choke me and said, "May I sleep with you tonight?"

Zuri actually broke step. I had one glimpse of feeling in her face before she took breath and said as abruptly, "Yes."

WHEN I finally tapped, light still showed under her door. I opened at her, "Ah?" to find her propped in bed, a slate against her knees. Doing accounts.

When everyone knows Zuri carries troublecrew business, weapons, ciphers and budget, in the back of her head.

She set the slate aside and scrambled out. That I sleep next the wall is not negotiable. Every inch of her demanded: did you come for counsel or sex? And with either, how do I give a man the initiative?

I climbed in. Undid my hair. After five minutes, she settled back against the headboard. Muttered, "Got to do something about this bed." It is narrow enough to make quarrels a nightmare, certainly. The lamp still burnt. I watched her eye turn sideways, wary as on the practice-floor.

Then she slid down beside me on an elbow and asked, "How did you get on?"

To a husband. To her troublecrew. To a man, she must have known, as tried as he was distressed. She would have sinned by asking about someone else's assignment for nothing less.

I had gone down with the food. Planned, arranged for it. The watch was Desis, who let me take the stuff in, and a lantern with it, and locked the door on us, without a dissenting word.

He jumped up when he recognized me. No surprise that he was afraid, but a good deal less personable with it than Alkhes. A stocky, nut-brown boy, with the short new-fashion hair. Well-favored enough, before they—we—added chains, and bruises, a swollen face and a splinted wrist.

I set the food on the timber lengths that served for table and bed. They had not bothered with blankets, any more than padding on the chains, but the meal was out of the common pot. The lantern went on the floor beyond my boots, and I started to eat.

Pheroka had been a cutter, first generation. A Telluir sub-clan, but from well down the Hill. Though decent folk, I doubt they ever had a Tower. Extremity or not, no one with Tower training would have been so gauche.

I kept eating; eyes on my plate. Eventually he edged near and snatched.

Little doubt it was the first he had been able to stomach, if not the first he had seen. I let him dry-clean the plate with the last of Shia's good, solid barley-bread. Let him watch me finish. Gave him time to stare.

Before I said, "Did you dream about her?"

The minute's sheer, unwarded shock, before he went red and spluttered, was truth-pledge enough.

"No!"

"Did you talk to her?"

He scowled then. "Lived in Zariah's house. 'Course I talked to her."

"Did you want her?"

"Huh?"

"Did you want *her*? Or could it have been anyone?"

He got his wind back, and with it his nerve at last. "Why *shouldn't* I want her? We're as good as them—better than them! Stronger, don't get pregnant, tougher—if they won't give, why shouldn't we take?"

I bit my tongue in time. Blinked off visions of this brat with Zuri on a practice-floor. "Some of us are stronger than some of them. Some of them are stronger than a lot of us."

"Huh!" He forgot to cringe. "You old lot're all the same. Brought up to it! You wait till the, the cutters are gone. Then they'll see how things really are. Then we'll take what we want."

After a while I unlocked my teeth. "And what—exactly—do you want?"

"Well, we, ah—freedom, of course! Carry water and chop wood all day. And not get paid for it! Why shouldn't *I* have time to stand around and talk? 'N money—play dice—go for a drink—"

"Instead of women's work?"

The surprise went almost at once. "That's right! Out here, that stuff *is* women's work." He almost pawed at me, I think he had forgotten I broke his wrist. "We need to wake up—act like men—"

I stood up. He almost fell off the planks.

"Of course we should wake up. Forget we are here because women brought us. Bought us, with their bodies and blood, their skill and brains, their fighting craft and their qherrique, out of Amberlight. They never lost their city for us. They have never argued with the Iskardans that we have any rights. They have just left us where Iskardans are: in the men's rooms, barred from House and Crafts. Graciously allowed to sire their daughters, and wipe their sins out once a year by letting them bleed us to death."

I had not been able to control myself. I knew how it sounded. He told me, with his face.

If you're falling, Zuri says, take down the house. "So we should throw away our honor, our decency—if we have such a thing—the first time some fool prates of drink and dice and getting his own back. After no woman of ours would spare him a glance."

At my worst, my very worst, I am quiet. It had been quiet, and got quieter, till by the end I hardly heard myself. And it was the blindest of shots, and the way it flung him clear out of his cowering ball told me it was right into the red.

"Did she snub him, herself?"

"I—I—"

"Or did they just not notice he was there?"

He made some sort of squawk. The look said I was a very witch.

I picked up the lantern; gathered the plates. He cringed like a mongrel dog on the light's edge as I walked away.

"IT WENT," I said to Zuri, "the way you would expect."

She said nothing. I understood that my proper report was to the one who assigned me. Tellurith. But if I needed heart's ease, she was there.

I turned over and put an arm across her before I thought, and said into the cave between us, "I am not meant for this."

Feather-soft, unmistakable, her hand smoothed my hair.

"I am not trained—as troublecrew. I don't know the questions. I lose control. I say—too much."

I had never laid a hand on her before. She had not pulled away. Had not so much as flinched.

"Tellurith says—I have a stiletto tongue."

Her fingers dug in. Softly, gripped and shook.

"She's Ruand," she said. "She uses everybody. Trained or not."

It would have been too demeaning to bleat, Not her husband! Not when the girl is one I loved as a daughter; not when I have to tear myself in two fighting my own thirst for blood!

She said; it came roughly, "*I* used you."

I rolled back to look at her. Dourly, she met my eyes.

"It goes with the trade."

"Troublecrew?"

"Heads."

I understood what she meant. My own experience of power seconded it. I knew that however bleak, it was meant as sympathy. Yet for all my swallowing, the thing still stuck in my neck.

"But Tellurith . . ."

She leant over and swept my hair clear, pressing a finger lightly across my lips.

"Listen, beautiful. There's good and bad both sides of the tower door. I've known men I'd follow to the River bottom, and women I wouldn't give the time of day. But Tellurith's Uphill. She never saw the things we do. And she's made a stake. Can't be, Here and There. Men have to be bad or saveable. Women *have* to be right."

Then she slid her arms around me and pushed her chin into my shoulder and muttered, "Now forget it. Tomorrow, make your report."

BUT FIRST there was Asaskian.

Logic, the method of a house-keeper, demanded that I hear all the stories, be sure they matched. Compunction, remembering Alkhes, protested, Can you force her back through such a horror so soon? Everything that was mine cried, Can you bear this for yourself?

And Tellurith had given me a commission. My duty did not stop with myself and Du.

Once again, I could have saved the concern. She was not abed with a nurse and the vapors, she had Zariah's house-folk out for a late-spring clean. Rugs, furs, bedding reverberated to broom-blows and flying dust. Zariah and Kaina, her elder daughter, were at the quarry; Asaskian's crew were mostly men.

"Speak to you?" she said, when I screwed myself up to thread the carpet maze. "About the other day—oh." For an instant her lips set, her color paled. Then she glanced about; with a Head's decision made it a suitable moment. "Up on the steps."

We sat where she could overlook her cleaning crew, on the barrack-house steps that are now Zariah's entrance-way. I below, not to threaten, she above, where she could escape into domestic concerns at the worst.

"Did I talk to Du? As much as anyone." Her porcelain-clear forehead creased. "He's a water-boy, sometimes he'd go with the wood-cutters. Since the Dhasdein order, he's done kitchen work three nights a quarter moon. I spoke to him like anyone else. Off-time?" The creases deepened. "Well, they do have that . . . Insolent?" The head-shake was unhesitating. "Pheroka keeps discipline. No . . . Did he ever 'approach' me?" The stare was outright amazed. "You mean . . .? Mother, s'hure, no."

S'hure. Male version of Craft-worker, fellow. I tried with all my might not to blush.

"Did I ever give him cause for a grudge?" She thought about that. Scrupulous for honesty; the integrity made a lump in my throat. If only You had ever given me a daughter like this, to keep.

"I can't swear to it. But he was never lazy or slovenly. From my side, no."

"The other one?"

She did stiffen then, her grace made awkward at last. Then looked full at me, those great amber eyes. Manslaughter at a glance. Her mouth set, her whole face spoke the memory, indelible as mine.

"No. No, I'm quite all right." She put my hand away, the tiniest withdrawal, clean through my heart. Then, effortfully, "To the best of my memory . . . I never saw him in my life."

As Du had told me. It was not malice, it was not even lust. Just more than his tiny soul could bear. She had simply never noticed him enough to reject.

———

Summer. Iskarda.
Tellurith's Diary

I AM not jealous. Of course I have speculated: did he find something impossible, did I ask something impossible; did I say too little, did I say too much? Did she ask? How did she know? Has he discussed the job with her? Mother knows, he has the right—

Has he discussed us?

But it was a blessing he did go. I am quite, quite sure Alkhes could not have brought it out in front of anyone else.

I felt it the moment we got into bed. Dropping tired, both of us, each after a sleepless night and a full-length working day, he with the scent of fresh-washed hard physical work still on him, I aching in every muscle from strain. But the withholding, the denial in every scrap of his body, was impossible to ignore.

Lying straight beside him, not touching, I whispered, "What is it, Alkhes?"

Silence. An unmoving retreat.

"Caissyl?"

The breath struggled this time. I rolled over to him, an elbow the far side of his chest, wishing I had not put out the lamp. "Caissyl, what's wrong?"

He turned his head away. I felt him battle within himself.

"I shouldn't—it isn't—it's not *decent*—"

"Is it something I've done?"

"No!" Another jagged pause. "You had—There is a reason, there's always—"

"Is it Sarth?"

This time it was a gasp. His hand caught a handful of hair and clenched. I bit down my own sound.

"You are so damn—"

Quick. As we had always been. Both of us.

I ran my fingers through that silken wing of hair, on across mouth and cheek; love, and reassurance, and as always, pleasure as well.

"Caissyl, I have to be sure—exactly why that boy did what he did. And Sarth; he's from the Tower, he's from Amberlight. He just might be able to understand. Get him to talk."

I expected a jet of protest, acrid with profanity, with outright hate. Not that hesitant, struggling breath.

"Is that not it?"

Under my arm his ribs flinched. I think he came within an inch of lifting me away.

"It . . . No. It's not all. No."

I cupped his cheek and said silently, I'm listening.

"I couldn't have done that. With the boy." He spoke in small, unstressed sentences. The way a woman will speak, not to push broken ribs. "I didn't expect to."

But, the inflection said. But.

"Tel, I wanted to be *some* use. I—I couldn't help the other night, I couldn't help today—I—even when—"

The edge of a sore long festered. After a moment I said softly, "Even when?"

I all but felt him grit his teeth. "It's so *petty*—it's small minded—"

"It isn't petty, caissyl. Not if it can upset you like this."

"Tel—" Then the dam broke. "I couldn't help you this time. I couldn't do anything last time, just shout and fuss and get in the way and—"

He broke off short. Hurled himself. "And then you went and asked *Darthis*—"

"Oh, caissyl, I swear I never meant it like that!" Now, too well, I understood. Sweet Mother, I had thought he knew, had taken it for granted that he knew, never paused to ask if he did not. "It wasn't that you couldn't have helped, I'd have given worlds to have you help. But you're my—you're *his* husband. I couldn't ask you! Any more than I could have asked Azo!"

I hugged him desperately, showering kisses as if they could wipe out time along with the unsalvaged bruise. "Caissyl, do you understand now? Do you know what I mean?"

He put both hands up, holding me away a little; trying, I felt now, for composure himself.

"I understand. Tel, do *you* understand? It's so cursed stupid, but I keep thinking I should be able to give you everything—"

"Everything?" Were my ears inept? "Caissyl, you've given me everything you ever had. Twice over. And saved *my* life as well."

"Huh?"

His life as Assandar, as an imperial general. Alkhes' life, flung between me and a poison-dart. I hugged him furiously, trying to block the tears. "Sweet Mother, what more could anyone ask?"

I felt his breath go in. His whole body enlarged as muscles eased, the soft, wondering sigh; the gladness, wakening, unsure, strengthening; to surety. To joy.

I kissed him. As his body wakened too, I murmured, "Unless there's some other proof you'd like to find?"

HE MADE LOVE to me, that time; with a sweet, shy, awakening confidence more poignant than any passion could ever be. It was in his eyes when we woke this morning: an ease, a gladness that even in Amberlight, I had never seen before. It is as if he finally believes that he belongs here. That this is real.

He had barely gone, swinging the cutter and his midday food-bundle away across Iskarda, when Sarth and Zuri swooped on me.

Whatever they did last night, it was not our sort of unravelment. Sarth looks hollow-eyed, behind that Tower composure. Zuri's dourness signaled, louder than a shout, Beware.

"Ruand, can you come in here?"

"Here" was the council-room. Empty today, a cold, dusty, shadowy space, a jumble across the polished table top. Tight-lipped, Zuri gestured to Sarth.

"Tellurith, this is—the dead one's gear."

Shirts, a jacket, razor, the roll of personal things many itinerants carry. I looked back at Sarth. Whatever the trouble was, and it was serious, it was no longer in the heap.

"Have you ever seen anything like this?"

It was some sort of token: pentagonal, probably brass; unpolished, graven with what looked like script. I looked at Zuri, whose mouth corners drew down like a mastiff's at a stink.

"You have some idea?"

The look said she had a very nasty one. What she said was, "Can you find some reason to get Alkhes?"

WE USED a message about the pipeline; minor hold-up, needing the memory of an engineer. Zuri thought of it. Then we waited, without speaking, since I knew better than to waste questions, for the sound of feet at the council-room door.

"Did you say an *elevation* problem?" A gust of hot sun and stone-dust and vigorous, willing sweat, face a dust-mask, hair matted from the hat-band, the cutter still at his belt. "Tel, what fool—"

His eyes, a soldier's, troublecrew, swept on across me, instinctive as breath. Over Sarth and Zuri and the jumble on the tabletop to where the token sat isolate. Unmistakable.

He stopped dead. Under sweat and stone-dust, I saw his face drain as if he had hemorrhaged.

Then he looked at Zuri and said hoarsely, "It's not mine. It's nothing to do with me."

"Do you," Zuri asked softly, implacably, "know what it is?"

He pushed the back of a hand up under his hair; a sweep of sweat-thickened dust. Inhaled, as if winded. Met her eyes, that held his like the stare of a basilisk. There was an instant's absolute hush; then he looked back to the table and said it flatly, as if accepting a sentence of death.

"It's a passport-sign. For a Dhasdein intelligencer."

Then he all but shouted at her, "You saw how I got here—you know how I left! How in the gods' name could I set up—"

"What does it do?"

"You—they—it's for contact. With another agent—to open doors—to access their news-gatherers . . ."

"What would he want?"

"I don't know! As the gods see me, Zuri. I don't know!"

She just looked at him, and her eyes were deadly as a viper's, and her stance was a viper ready to strike.

Over his temples the dust ran in trickles of sweat. "You know where I stand. At the funeral . . . I saved her life!"

"Then," she answered deliberately, "you ran away."

"Gods, you know why! You know what I did afterwards. What I've done here—" He was breathing like a fever patient. "It's not a lie!"

Silently, she stared.

"Zuri, I'm troublecrew. You've fought with me. You *know*—"

He held both hands out, almost frantically. She looked at them, and looked at him. I am troublecrew, that stare retorted, Yes.

I am made to protect my Head. That comes first.

"I never talked to him. I never *knew* about him. I have no loyalty but here—I have nowhere else to go!"

"Do you," she said, so softly, "have proof?"

His words caught in mid-breath. She watched him, and he stared at her, paralyzed.

Then he licked his lips and said faintly, "I swear—"

Zuri's stare retorted: A traitor already, twice over, to swear?

"Zuri—!"

It came out half a scream. His hand clawed at the cutter-grip and Sarth and Zuri collided on top of me and all but pasted me into the further wall. Squashed under Sarth's impact with his body blocking all view, I screamed, "No!"

Sarth jerked. I shoved him aside so hard a muscle in my shoulder wrenched. They were frozen beyond the table: Alkhes with both hands up, Zuri's knuckles wrapped round her knife. Superfluously, I yelled, "Stop!"

Only their eyes moved, pivoting to me. I could all but hear their hearts. Sarth was trying to get between us again. Tel, Alkhes eyes' said, Help me. Believe me. You'd best know what you're doing, answered Zuri's glare.

I put Sarth aside to reach the table. "Alkhes," I said, "slide the cutter over here."

I saw what he thought, and watched Zuri see; and let her see, as well, that even when he thought himself lost, he did not try to save himself. He did not demur.

The familiar grip slid into my hand; for a moment I was all but sick with relief.

He watched me now without protest. Without hope. He did not say, It was a fumble, a mistake. I would never have harmed you. We both knew how damning the situation was. If I did not believe him, what did he have left?

I said to Zuri, "I know you have to be sure."

She gave a tiny nod. For once, though, those cold gray eyes spoke. Do you, they said, have some way out? For both of us?

"There is a way," my own breath stuck like dust, "of getting proof."

Zuri's very stance said, Tell me. In Alkhes' eyes I saw a last-chance hope.

I shifted the cutter. "They would do it sometimes, in the very old days. With someone already attuned. To test—when there was no other way—somebody's word."

I walked round the table. Zuri and Sarth both twitched. I held the cutter between us, and said to Alkhes, "If I wake the blade; are you prepared to put your hand over it, and swear that you never met, never talked, never saw this man before?"

"Yes!"

It had come without any pause at all. But as I closed my hand on the cutter grip I heard him catch his breath.

"Wait, Tel. I can't swear I haven't seen him. Spoken to him. If he's Telluir—"

Zuri growled, "No."

"Iskarda? Even likelier. If he's from the camp—we run into them every night, coming home. It would be simple, it would be ideal, if I was—was—spying for Dhasdein—"

Zuri grunted under her breath and I knew that had been her nightmare. He looked at me with his eyes alive again, great starlit night-skies in that sweat-daubed face.

"But if I swear I never spied, was never involved with him, that I have no loyalty but to you?"

I looked at Zuri. She gave a brusque nod. I tilted the cutter skyward. Without the slightest hesitation he put his hand—his right hand—full in the white, shearing path of the blade.

Summer. Iskarda.
Journal kept by Sarth

YES, HE SAYS. No fear, no doubt, not the slightest trepidation. White fire plaited through his fingers, dyed by flesh and blood the color of candlelit wine.

And the relief . . .

Even Zuri showed it, the way she came forward, put a hand on him, caught his eyes. And he nodded, answering as wordlessly: I know you had to do it; that I could clear myself is a joy to us both.

Then while Tellurith and I were still putting ourselves back together she said, "What would he have been doing here?"

"Gods, Zuri." He sagged back against the table and dragged dirty fingers through dirtier hair. "In the—when I—was working for Dhasdein . . . I came here once myself." Tellurith's eyes told me she already knew. "It was just routine; checking the other sides' back cupboards. You must have done it often enough."

Zuri's lips compressed. The nod was fairly dredged out of her. He started to straighten and she said, "What would this one say?"

He turned right round and stared at her, and I saw nightmares resurrect in that crossing glance.

After a minute his eyes swung to Tellurith.

"Zuri means," he steeled himself, "that this isn't the worst. Worse is that—we don't know what he wanted. Or what he found.

"Worse again is: we don't know if he'd sent a message. What it was. What—if anything—came back."

He held her look as if confronting another sentence of death.

"Worst of all—is what could happen when he doesn't report back himself."

Zuri stirred, and said it after him, the tolling of a bell. "No. Worst is that: there's nothing we can do."

AFTER THAT, my own report has been an anti-climax—an anti-climax, to deliver the decisive ruling before the assembly of Telluir House. Callow troublecrew, a man, a Tower-bred man, to speak with a Head's authority before Iatha, all the Craft-heads; even Darthis.

To deliver a judgment that will decide the Head's happiness, and the House's future.

And the fate of every man in it. And one stupid brat's very life.

Just a stupid boy. Not bad, not good, simply naïve, and gullible, and weak. Probably quite harmless, before Hepan got at him. There can be no doubt: the words, the very phrases were the same. Maybe a tint of malice or envy, that gave Hepan his leverage.

As to why Hepan did it . . . maybe it was personal, maybe it was politics. The boy thought it was personal. Without word that none of us wants, we may never know.

I said all that. Marvel at me. Before the House, without a stumble, without a fault.

Not at the very worst part. When Tellurith rested a temple on one hand, and looked down the long table at me with those topaz eyes that are knotted in my soul's web, and said, "What do you recommend?"

Then I truly could have run. Because I knew just what she asked.

Sethar would have been proud. Because I kept my wits. My composure. Because I answered steadily as at some elders' test of protocol in the Tower.

"There are near a hundred and fifty men in Iskarda. Hepan talked to every one he could come near. He recruited—one."

I watched the light change, as a jewel changes, in Tellurith's stare.

"Some of the others were from Amberlight. They said to me—" Huis and Roskeran and a half-dozen others, down to twelve years old, "—'Mother, what an idiot.'"

And I saw the jewel-light mist with tears.

So I had some hope of my last, most hopeless point.

"Ruand—s-s'hurre—" how does one commit sacrilege with the most profound respect? I doubt a man had used that title in the last three hundred years. "Du is just a boy. A stupid boy. To execute him will—distress—many other men. It will teach him nothing. And I think—he may be able to learn."

Then I decamped while they were still swelling to explode.

Tellurith let them shout awhile. Alkhes patted my shoulder, in the sanctuary behind her chair. When he muttered, "Well done," I saw something like the sheen of tears on his cheek. When Azo's hand seconded him I nearly shed some myself.

And when the uproar topped out Tellurith brought her hand down, *slam!* on the table-top.

"S'hurre," her Ruand's voice now, into the quiet. "This is the advice of a man who learnt to read men—and women—in the tower. If you don't know already, let me tell you, that means better than any of us."

She swept her eyes across the table's width. "For that reason, I sent him to hear Du. If it has not yet occurred to you that in doing so, I asked him to put himself and all the rest of our men on trial, I urge you to consider it now. Just as I urge you to consider what it means, if you condemn this boy to death."

There was a very long pause. Then she announced a recess.

AND WHEN THEY re-assembled, tea and shouting later, she gestured me back to the table-foot. And then she asked, "What sentence would you give?"

I took the time—I was shaking glad to take the time to think. To gather words. To compose my voice.

"I would suggest, that we consult the one he harmed."

There was a great rustling gasp. But they kept quiet.

"Unless she wants otherwise . . . let him remit her suffering. Twelve strokes with a whip. Let him bear his own shame: shave his head. And for warning—tattoo an R under his eye. So that he can never take a woman unawares again."

I should be proud—now I can collect myself, I *am* proud: not that I saved him, not what it did for us, for Tellurith. But because in the scramble afterward, when Zuri, and Hayras, and Pheroka, and even Iatha were patting my shoulder and shouting compliments and urging emendations and quarreling over who should do which, I came face to face with Darthis.

Who gripped my arm, backed me a step out of the fracas, and said, so quietly I had to bend to catch it, "Tell your Ruand that I am thinking. I am thinking very, very hard."

IX

Summer. Iskarda.
Meditations. Alkhes-Assandar

I WAS SO PROUD.

So stunned, so amazed at feeling pride. And still, so proud.

As no man outside Iskarda could ever be. Because no man outside Iskarda can ever have a—a husband … gods, written down, how does *that* look! Can ever feel—can ever let himself feel—like this about another man.

And no man outside Iskarda could understand what it meant, to stand in that council-room and see any man defend our—our—"honor" will have to do. Defend our—all men's—damn, it's another mismatch—well, then, decency. Defend it with a courage, a composure, that nobody outside Amberlight could believe.

And that he did it, that particular man …

I could only pat his shoulder. It would have been indecent, shamed him, to do more, it was not the time.

But if ever there *was* a time or a man to whom I would have given with greater joy, with bursting pride and total willingness, a hero's crown …

OF COURSE there's no explaining that. He would not understand; would be insulted if he did. But he did come to bed with us. And there, at least, I could put my arms around him, and hug him as I never could a comrade, passionately as I would a woman.

As I do Tellurith.

He gave it back with interest, naturally. He's never had trouble with that. Since the bastard started training he's twice as strong as I am. I swear it bent my ribs.

And being Sarth, he naturally took the next step. The one that's still too much for me.

Held me one-armed, turned my face up as if I was a woman. And kissed me.

Actively. Thoroughly.

When you kiss Sarth, he kisses you back. Expertly, superlatively, but you never doubt the relation. It's an answer. You have the lead.

When Sarth kisses *you* . . .

It wasn't brutal. It wasn't an invasion. It was accomplished, and sensitive, and . . .

And it mastered me, like a willing woman with a loving man. Not just the physical part: lips touching, mouths open, his tongue on mine, filling the mouth's space as you do a woman's, the prelude, the symbol of that other filling, the mutual promise of what you'll give her, how she'll welcome you.

More than that. It was the immaterial reality behind that, the thing that really matters, the mind and soul and intent's passion, the thing that's really speaking when flesh and blood and bodies say in chorus, Yes.

Summer. Iskarda.
Journal kept by Sarth

I WAS OFF-BALANCE. Carried too far outside myself. When he caught hold of me I answered him as whole-heartedly as I wanted, as spontaneously, as completely as I would with one of my own.

Like a brainless, untrained fool, I stopped listening, stopped thinking, and put my own wishes first.

My own desires.

Because I do want him. Have wanted him, from that very first night. And from the very first he has been able to unbalance me. Because he doesn't—still—look like a man. Not a grown man. So I react before I know it; as if he were an untrained boy.

But with a boy I would have remembered his background, his past, his experience. Would never have let him feel what I felt.

And felt him answer back.

Felt sleeping will and ambushed mind and supple, resilient body melt. For that one delirious moment before he froze solid in my arms.

The gods witness my imbecility. Not enough that he is outland, with all their fenced and fearful man-training. Or that the fear of men's passion has been carved into him by the cruelest experience, in mind as well as flesh. Could I not have thought—have imagined—what it would do to him?

Not to lead, but to follow. Not to awake, but to respond.

To him, beyond all doubt, not to conquer, but to submit.

Willingly, where he has already, repeatedly, been forced.

Gods, imagine the shock—the terror—of feeling passion for a man.

From what he would think of as the woman's side.

Summer. Iskarda.
Tellurith's Diary

BLIGHT IT, blast it, three times over, by every god in the Outlanders' pantheon, blast!

What in the Mother's name did they do? What did they think—feel—the Mother knows, it was nothing either of them said! When everything was going so well, everything; when I was happy, for all of that two hours from when the hearing finished till I got them off to bed.

To have it break in a dozen heartbeats, the durance of an embrace. Just when I had hoped ...

That it might be whole between us, the three of us, at last.

Instead of Alkhes tearing free; and the pair of them—Mother succor me, the pair of them going into killer mode so for a flash I really thought I might die trying to keep them apart. And Alkhes trying to apologize; to tell, who is all but a cripple with words, how he felt that afternoon; and Sarth blank and courteous as an ice-face. And both of them trying to solace *me*.

Before a night in bed formal as a stranger's banquet, with no consolation but that they did not kill each other outright!

MAY THE MOTHER hear me, that was an idle word; a moment's spleen. It was never willed. It was never intended to bite. At the most it wished for a minor problem, a vexation.

May the Mother forgive me, it was not intended as a curse.

If this had not come so pat ... This very morning, when I stalked out, leaving Alkhes without a kiss and glowering at Sarth; the pair of them know why, they never ventured a word. Alkhes took his quarry gear and left—whose heart is the sorer? And Sarth ...

I sent Sarth out, when Darthis came.

Dour, redoubtable as ever, redoubtably polite. With, "a thing for Iskarda." The Mother knows, I have used her time, her wisdom. Vassal or not, she has a lien on mine.

We sat in the council-room, agreeably cool now that summer has brought sultry middays even to Iskarda. With full harvest near, the River-plain is rolling silver-beige and sunburnt-gold, and the windows were shut to keep out wasps. Because there were ripe plums on the table. The smell that marks a summer's high-water, sure as the scent of cut hay and garnered corn. Before she began speaking, Darthis weighed one, over and over, between her hands. Round, heavy, black-purple, glistening. The Mother's bounty, in the flesh.

"Ruand," she said, "do you know how we make the Mother's choice?"

I think my blood stopped. I do know I could not say a word. Only incline my head, courteously prodding her on.

"If the Mother blesses him, the Chosen is Hers until next Mid-winter. If the Mother takes him—" she stared down at the fruit, "he must be replaced."

My blood rushed back to my heart and out. Somebody impossibly far away said with impossible coolness, "Forgive the presumption. It seemed—to Telluir House—that the Chosen was now Krestyr."

She jerked her chin and said, "The Ruand sees," and looked up with open relief. "Back then, seemed like we had no choice. But now . . ."

Now they had both a substitute, and the original.

I said cautiously, "At the spring-festival, Alkhes sounded the horn."

She nodded at once. "He had the right."

How I detest it when my folk expect me to play oracle. Especially when there is nothing but terror in my own head.

"But now you need something—something—"

I could not go on. But she leant forward as if I had fulfilled her every expectation, and grasped my hands.

"Did you get my message, Tellurith? I told your man to tell you I was thinking: about what you asked. We have all thought. Yesterday capped it. There was a meet called, when I went home last night. Zdana's summons. The Mother's Ear has heard. Now she wants—Iskarda wants—to know what the Mother says."

And there could only be one question they would ask.

Mother, I had time to think, did You, of malice aforethought, maneuver me into this? That my revolutionary fever dreams should always rebound on the very ones I try to help?

"Darthis." I sounded quite cool, and calm. Absolutely someone else. "What—precisely—do you want him to do?"

She sat back and sighed, and it really was relief.

"Ruand, in Iskarda, high questions, questions the Ear can't answer—the Chosen does. You'll forgive me, I can't tell you how."

Turning the dirty work off, again, onto the men.

"But," I could just restrain the sourness, "you can't settle which one to use."

Her look wiped the gall from my mouth. "We would take your man and be honored, Ruand. If we thought he could bear the choice."

"No," she said hastily, and grabbed for me. "Nothing like Mid-winter, I promise you. At least —not for anyone else."

Darkness and terror then, at the very least. What goddess would ask less? Probably, my wits extrapolated from the River-lands, some kind of drugs, some kind of trance. What oracle would need less? And ungratefully, that they were in a fix not least through kindness and courtesy. Wishing to honor him as Mother-blessed, even if it meant as much peril as pride, not wishing to deny what was his earned, his rightful role; yet all too aware of his fragility.

And I, did I have the right to put him through such a thing again?

I did not even have the right to make the choice.

"I'll send someone to the quarry," I said. "This is not an answer for anyone but the Chosen himself."

Summer. Iskarda.
Meditations. Alkhes-Assandar

THEY WERE GENTLE. Gods help me, I think that was the worst of it, far worse than the—The—

Than all the rest.

I can't write it. I have a pledge, however it was forced on me. I gave my assent.

If it is secret to them, then it must be secret to me.

Even in this journal. Even from myself.

BUT THEY WERE GENTLE. Darthis herself, explaining in the council-room, with my heart already past beating to quarters and breakfast coming up my throat. Even without the look, oh, gods, the look on Tellurith's face.

I think I almost did throw up. The worst of the hole—the discontinuity—is that you get the physical reactions without knowing why. Blind terror, vomit, panic-sweat, everything going black . . . And you pray it stays that way, because otherwise you'll see what the blackness hides.

I did stay on my feet. I did not throw up. Darthis actually put her hand on me, heavy as a boulder, yet with the greatest gentleness. "Stheir," she said, "you may decline this with all honor. You have cause."

I know what it means now. Stheir. Not Crafter or Woman, but Chosen. The Mother's choice.

I looked at Tellurith. She was probably whiter than my own face. I saw quite clearly that she would have said *no* without a second thought, had she not counted that dishonor. Had she not felt that the right to choose, however cruel, was mine.

And no power on earth or off it would make her tell me, with or without words: Refuse.

No matter that I did not understand. Did not ask for it. Was not made for it. Almost died for it. They know, and I know, why, when it came to that day before Mid-Winter, I said yes.

Because I have made a commitment, sealed, over and over, in my own and others' blood. To her dream, and her intention. To Telluir and Iskarda.

To every soul—woman and man—in Telluir House.

Belonging cuts both ways. To belong, you have to give as well as take.

Which is why I could almost command my voice, and my face—I think—when I looked back to Darthis and said, "Yes."

They were both gentle then. No gushing, no hysterics. As the women were gentle, when they came to blindfold and take me away.

It was—I think it was—different. Certainly from Amberlight. And from Mid-winter. I remember—I do remember scraps of that. The women preparing me, who were impersonal, but not kind. And later—

Even—even at the worst—when I went—when I was going—out of my mind.

I remember—I remember, one of them had my arm pinned. And even while the others—he kept patting my wrist.

This time the hands were the hands of—

Friends.

I kept thinking that, while I could still think. At the worst, the cold, the dark, the—rest of it.

Whenever they asked—whatever they asked.

When I said—whatever I said.

I DID SAY SOMETHING. I know the—ceremony—was for a question. I knew, when I came round, by the mere way they handled me, it had worked. I'm stiff all over and bruised from the cold, the smoke's left my throat like the back-trail of a camel-train; but it worked. They had a reply.

Gods damn it, if somebody would tell me what!

Summer. Iskarda.
Journal kept by Sarth

MAY ALL THE OUTLAND gods have pity on me. I did not know. I did not know!

I never dreamt what Darthis was talking about. "Thinking" about. All my pride—my cursed foolishness. I never, in my wildest nightmares, dreamt it would come to this!

I will ask Zuri what Outlanders do as suppliants. What they say, to which one they pray. If it comes to the worst, I will offer sacrifice, fruit, flowers, corn, flesh and blood. If it comes to that, I will offer my own.

ANOTHER HALF-PAGE RUINED. I never knew you could wreak such havoc with tears.

But tears of thankfulness. Because he is back; hollow-eyed, and hoarse as a crow after a hill-fire, with livid marks on wrists and ankles and ribs, and a stink of dirt and strange, stagnant damp in his hair. But alive.

Sane.

At least we had him to ourselves last night, with all of us so shaken that we clung like children, so I could hold on to him as tightly as I—as he—as we all needed. Without the slightest desire for anything else.

Except that he, of course, damnable creature that he is—am I laughing or crying here? He is moving heaven and earth to find out what he said.

Darthis has the aplomb of a mountain boulder. The other officiants ... I have my sources, better than Zuri's own. Iskarda may withhold its secrets, officially. But I can talk to the men.

So I know the officiants, because the men know who was out all night and came home next evening hollow as an unwatered cow. And if none of us know the ritual, we all know the reason. And I have a very fair idea what they asked.

But what he—She—answered ...

That it was unexpected I can read for myself. In the bodies more than faces, at passing, greeting, meeting, commerce with Tellurith. There *was* an answer, it was not denied. Nor was it bad.

A plague take Darthis, who says, and such is her skill that I myself cannot read the body-talk, that the Mother's word will be told to everyone.

On Mid-summer's Day.

Summer. Iskarda.
Tellurith's Diary

WHAT DO I CARE if Darthis chooses to be mysterious? I cannot even bring myself to care what the answer was. Not though it will seal, one way or another, the fate of my wildest hopes.

That Iskarda will accept us. That it will try to deal with its own men as we are trying to deal with ours.

I cannot so much as care about the sword that overhangs us. Let Dasdein's poxed intelligencers draw what conclusions and take what measures they like. All I care about right now is here.

In the bed behind me, drowsing off, with the lightest dose of poppy-syrup in him, and Sarth's arms tight around him as if he fears the captive will tear loose and run away. Bronze hair on the pillows, mingled with glistening black. Both my heart's desired, hazarded, recovered, safe.

Let Darthis do her damnedest. On or off Mid-summer's Day.

OF COURSE that was mostly bravado; there is less than a week till the festival, which has hardly crossed my horizon yet, between the marble-order and the reservoir and intelligencers and rape. We got the last of the order off just this morning; it will be a fortnight or so late into Dhasdein, but what is a fortnight to River-bargemen? If the priest expects better, let him carry it himself. Meanwhile I have cut the quarry shifts and taken Charras back to the water-line.

And left a shift, and the cutter, to Alkhes.

With the order gone, there is really no call for him in the quarry, either. After Mid-summer, I will take the cutter back. But let him, for the time being, retain the work; and the pride; and the place.

There will be a place for him without doubt at the festival. For again, it is less a Mother's than her consorts' day. I have turned most of the planning over to Iatha, so poor Sarth is torn between watching house-routine go to the fire under Roskeran, and his duty to protect me.

The upland harvest is slow; their year's high festival, I gather, is Harvest-home. But there is plenty of beer from last season's hops and money, for once, to ship up wine; how many barrels has Iatha ordered back with the marble trains? Mother, I doubt I want to know. But there is fruit aplenty; and the high summer flowers.

Above all, it is the roses' season. Iskarda is smothered with them. Tamed, they pour up house-fronts, over doors, wreathe about the wide verandas' posts, waves of white and cream and blood-dark bloom; there are some juveniles bravely clambering the walls of my own house. Untamed, they riot about the fountain culvert, the stock byres. Cut, their fierce ephemeral perfume fills and refills every house. Shia is inundated with rose petals for potpourri, for clothes-wards, for sugared candy and spirits of rose-in-wine and rosewater and rose ointment, made with purified lard and beeswax, for any tender skin. Mother help us, I caught her gifting some to Sarth!

He is tower-bred, after all. Tower standards die hard. Why should he not try to restore that superbly cared-for skin, the crown of that beautiful face?

Even if it is as ephemeral as a rose's life, that passes, on or off the bush, within three days?

That will be poured out at their most extravagant, rumor tells me, when they heap roses to hide the altar, the afternoon of Mid-summer's day.

All Iskarda's men have been heaving wood for days; all the women, on the day, will go to gather the flowers. There is a huge bonfire set outside the Market's door. There will be dancing, I am sure. Of a ceremony, I am less sure. Nothing, I am assured, to distress Alkhes. Telluir has been politely but kindly banished from the preparations. We are to bring, we are informed, only our provender and our flowers and our chattels. That is, our men and ourselves.

Summer. Iskarda.
Journal kept by Sarth

How ASTOUNDING. How truly alarming. How aweful in the truest sense— to find that the women . . . to find that for once, even Tellurith . . . does not know as much as she thinks.

That it is a festival, yes. And different, and less a Mother's festival than most of those in Amberlight. And close, this year, to a frenzy, because everyone is waiting to hear the Mother's word.

Especially the men.

Except that Tellurith does not know: this is the one festival in Iskarda that has always included the men. Not by her changes, as with the Sowing-rite. Nor one man alone, as at Mid-winter, and he a sacrifice.

All the men. No wonder poor Du thought I was a witch when I said it to him: "They let us sire their daughters, and shed our blood."

We will—they will, all of them—be siring daughters tonight.

Mid-summer festival. The night when everybody dances. Everybody drinks, everybody lies down, with whoever they have desired and lusted after, whoever the—gods—bring them—whoever the night and the wildness and the festival likes.

It is the—Goddess's wisdom. A festival to balance the sin-bleeding of Mid-winter, to lead off summer madness, and keep mixing the blood. And to judge from the glances, more than a few in Iskarda mean to mix blood across the new bounds tonight.

More than a few of them, with Alkhes.

I did my best to warn him. When we were preparing for bed last night, down in the washing bay, helping to sluice off quarry-dust, his head in a bucket, the enthusiasm spattering my own hair. "Um," I said. "Have you heard about this festival?"

A last plunge, a last wild splash and snort. Rinse water flew off the walls. I stood back and proffered the towel. When his head came clear he said, "Heard what?"

It could have been the washing upside down, or the chancy lantern-light. His slight, wiry torso glistened, his eyes were black as the outer night. But all too clearly the damp skin and eyes' dilation spoke something else.

"Nothing dangerous." I put my hands on him, that look left me no choice. "Nothing to worry you, Alkhes, I know that. It's just . . ."

He let the tension go, a long, slow breath. Leant, ever so slightly against me. How that little constraint can hurt. Ever since the night of the hearing. Trust, yet without absolute release.

"Just?"

"It's a fertility festival."

The towel came down, his eyes came up. Dilation, sparkle, springing to almost hilarious life. "Ye *gods*! You mean—?"

I could not control my own grin. "This time, I think, we enjoy earning our keep."

A laugh. Something more than a laugh. The eyes flaring again as he worked out what it might mean, all it might mean. I squeezed his shoulders and said, "It's all of us."

For the flicker of a lash he stared. Then he dropped the towel about me and swung me round, neat as a captive in a noose, and the laughter broke out, wild and wicked as a boy's. "Well, then, make Iskarda's year, will you? Save me the problem. *You* surprise Darthis."

UPSTAIRS I CAN HEAR them dressing. The buzz, the rustle, the tramp of excited feet. Esrafal rattling a practice-riff. A leap, a plunge in the pulse. Time to put my own best clothes on. Perhaps, time to forget.

That I am Tower-bred, and troublecrew trained, and a House-head's bodyguard. Esrafal says, Let be the flute. Zuri says, I'll keep an eye on Tellurith. Neither has said, You are a man. You will have other affairs.

So I can be free. Can be something else than what I have been taught. Can be whatever this man's form was born for, for one wild, wholly reckless night.

Can even, perhaps, surprise Darthis.

PART III

DHASDEIN

X

Autumn. Dhasdein.
Journal kept by Sarth

SURPRISES. Oh, there have been surprises. Gods, how many rivers have washed the pier-feet since I finished writing that?

They say it a lot here. It is a River superstition that the river is new each morning, and the pier is the hub of life. 'Kiss the pier': get falling-down drunk. 'Tell the piers': an imperial blabber-mouth. 'Pier-wedding': common-law liaison, not worth the barley-beer in which it was pledged. You hear it daylong across these bobbing, nudging acres of deck and fender and rickety gang-planks, amid the children and clay fire-places and fowls crammed under some tattered awning in the rain. Or through the traffic of women with market-stuff or road-maker's gear, amid the knots of ragged, long-winded, constantly drunken men. A city within the city. Sagging on its ropes like patch-work membranes between the great stone ribs that jut into the waterway: shaped, mortared masonry, a hundred yards long and fifty feet wide, chaining the river for its last five miles. The flood-bastions of Riversend.

I can be nonchalant now, about a city big enough to swallow ten Amberlights. I, who when we set out had no more idea of the River, let be Riversend, than a hen of the world beyond the fowl-yard gate.

Less. For the youngest chicken knows the shadow of a hawk.

How LITTLE and long ago and far away it seems. Yet I wanted it to go forever that evening, walking up into the last colors of sunset, mouth dry, pulse fast, good clothes a sensuous, cumbering shell. All my senses bent upon the curve of hillside, with blossoms heaped about the altar and the bonfire's great leaping rose of light.

In truth that came after we arrived, when a dozen young men and unwed women whipped Alkhes away before Darthis' greetings ended, in a whirl of best but briefest summer festival gear and rose-garlands everywhere they would stick. And before Tellurith got her mouth shut they had him, flint in hand, beside the bonfire's heap.

The flint spat. The spark bloomed. He stood up. Somebody all but extinguished him under a garland fit for the River-lord, two enthusiastic girls finished the job. It is the best of good luck to get the Chosen's first Mid-summer kiss. The village musicians struck up. Krestyr, of all people, threw a rose-loop around Tellurith. And Asaskian touched my elbow, asking, just clear amid the tumult, "S'hure, would you care to dance?"

I did not dance. My feet never touched the cobblestones. I never heard the music. I had no need of wine.

At first there is just the dance, rounds, rings and line, change-partners, sets and single pairs. The musicians play their elbows off, until they finish their first wind. Then comes the eating. And the wine.

I lost track of everyone long before that. Even Asaskian was the partner of a moment, instantly whirled away. At one time or another, I think I must have danced with every woman in Telluir House, let be Iskarda. At some time I do remember staring up into the cool, huge, bland eye of the Mid-summer moon. Breathing, we must have been, at the top of the square, by the fountain side. I remember I dipped a bucketful for my partner to lave her face, and made some comment about the bonfire's unquenched fountain of fire.

And I remember the moment when Darthis, with a Head's timing, cut in on the tail of the food, just when everyone was full enough to listen, well-oiled enough to feel enthusiastic, the fulcrum moment before the real festival began.

She had clambered up on the Market's step, solid and anomalous as a rose-garlanded boulder in the wildly splashed rose-colored light. A little breeze swirled the bonfire and made the torches lean sideways as she spoke.

"May the folk hear me," she said. "All the folk of Telluir House."

The plunge of silence said everyone knew what she meant. Tellurith, with another Head's timing, was close below the step. Alkhes was out of sight, but I saw Iatha, and Hanni, and Zdana, and Charras, and a dozen other veterans materialize out of the crowd. And I saw, clearer than the print of moonlight, the look on every man's face.

Darthis lifted her hands to the blandly sailing moon. "May the Mother bless us," she said. "This season. This festival."

It was orthodox prayer. Murmurs of assent ran across the crowd.

"Iskarda has asked the Mother a question." Darthis paused again. Sheer show-play now. "And her Chosen has brought us the reply."

She took her hands down, and looked at Tellurith. Who wore the decorous attention of a House-head. What if, on the next words, hung the future of her little world?

"We asked—"

In that whole square, only the fire stirred. Darthis drew a long, bracing breath.

Across it a torch cracked like a whip. Everyone spun about and Zuri leapt on the fountain rim and brandished flame like a very war-demon, yelling, "Traffic on the road!"

Maybe we were all struck mute. It came like drumbeats through the gap, like a racing heart, like a signaler's panic cry. The tattoo of hoofbeats, at full gallop over stone.

Troublecrew flew by instinct to the square's edge, the road-mouth, light-guns, throwing-knives sprouting from festival-garb sleeves. Trust Zuri, Mid-summer or not, to hedge her bets. Tellurith was beside her, Azo, Desis. And I was there too, hefting a yard-long baulk of fire-wood, pulling garlands off as Alkhes, with a pair of unsheathed carving-knives, slid in on Tellurith's other side.

Zuri stood four-square, light-gun charged. Desis, most hawk-eyed of all, said, "Single beast."

Zuri grunted, "Clear back." Azo evaporated. Dimly I heard the rattle of orders; shifting non-combatants from lines of fire. Zuri growled, "Ruand?" Tellurith, with the snap of our common tension, retorted, "No." Zuri threw one eloquent glance behind her as the shadows yielded Darthis.

There was no time for more. It was past the quarry, I heard the echoes yammer on hollowed rock. Thundering up the last rise, a sudden moonlit blur footed in sparks as Zuri brought the light-gun up and shouted, "Halt!"

More sparks: a clattering, plunging, sidling stop, rider and mount panting in chorus. Then a frantic young woman's voice shouted, "Is everybody up here drunk?"

And Tellurith shouted, overriding Zuri's, "Who's that?"

"Dhanissa!"

A surge of moonlight, crackle of hooves, sudden presence of wildly rolling eyes and lathered shoulders and they were among us, Dhanissa perched atop a heaving mule, a face of moon angles and kaleidoscope shadows spouting words. "Got the message at sun-drop, we've been signaling ever since! We couldn't make anyone *hear*!"

Tellurith was at the mule before anyone could react. A grip on the bridle, another on the girl's leg. A Head's voice, impellingly cool.

"You've done it. Well done. What did the signal say?"

"Marbleport—soldiers!" She flung an arm out, more than half a sob. "Dhasdein soldiers. Coming here!"

I recall the sound behind us: one great surge of noise, and hush. Through which Tellurith and Alkhes rapped together, "How far behind?"—"What do they want?"

"Half a day—maybe less—they marched before dark, the second post said they camped . . ."

Instinctively she had answered Tellurith. As she stopped to pant Alkhes grabbed the bridle and shouted this time. "What do they want!"

Her face came round, black moon-pits for eyes. Her lip trembled. She shot a glance back at Tellurith, and answered some more silent response.

"They want you, Alkhes."

He let the bridle drop. Tellurith grabbed his arm and rapped at Zuri, "Get your people. Sentry-posts!" Her eyes raked the crowd, Iatha was there, inevitable as her right arm, Tellurith snapped, "Fix the stuff! Enough for a week!"

Iatha did not ask, What stuff, for whom? She spun on her heel, grabbed Shia and Hanni in mid-stride and was gone.

"We'll send you up the mountain." Tellurith rapped it in his face. "The hunters will help. Gear. Blankets. The cutter. A bow. Zuri, we need a guard—Desis? Darthis, I need someone who knows the bolt-holes, down to the House with me, *now*—" She was dragging them all forward, the speed of a long-prepared scenario; how long had she foreseen, how many months had she been dreading this? "Come on, Alkhes—!"

He yanked his arm away. Yelled across her, "Tel, no!"

She whipped round. Undone by the dance, tangled with roses, her hair bristled her face. He grabbed her shoulders. She was strong and frantic as Dhanissa and he held her like a child. "Tel, it's no use!"

"Use—!"

She bit it off. Jerked her head. Zuri was moving on the twitch and with her like a living boulder came Darthis.

"NO!" He hurled Tellurith away and flung himself back under the mule's nose, the beast reared and whipped around, Tellurith and Darthis collided, Alkhes bawled, "Will you *listen to me!*"

Thank the gods, Darthis at least had the sense to grab and anchor Tellurith.

"Tel—wait." He held his hands out. He was breathing harder than the mule. "If Dhasdein wants me they'll get me, there's nothing you can do. *Listen to me!* They know I'm in Iskarda! If they miss me they'll go through the village, they'll turn out every house, if that fails they won't just go home! And they won't bother to chase me, gods, Tel, this is Dhasdein! They'll torture—they'll kill somebody!"

He jabbed a carving-knife at Zuri. Tellurith barked something. Zuri's advance stopped. Alkhes shouted at them, frantic as the gyrating mule.

"Will you run the whole House up in the hills? Let them burn the village out? Are you going to defend it? Against *Dhasdein?*"

The echoes crashed back off the mountainside. The mule's breath, Alkhes' breath. The snore of forgotten fire. Smell of sweat and roses, and silence, a festival shattered like the wake of an avalanche.

"I won't let it happen, Tel!" There were tears now, running, down his face. "I'm your husband. I'm Telluir troublecrew—"

He stopped short. His eyes went past her. Suddenly, he drew himself up.

"And I'm Chosen for Iskarda."

The crowd had surged back by then. And the Iskardans, at least, understood fully what he meant.

The sound said it for them, a great, soft, groaning breath. Clearer than the look, terrible as stone's rending, on Darthis' face.

He stared at her. Perhaps he could not bear to look at Tellurith. And at whatever his eyes said, her expression changed.

Then she too looked at Tellurith.

Who stood speechless, there at the heart of the struggle; the festival; the House. Before she rounded on Dhanissa, mute atop her quelled beast, demanding, "How many? What are they?"

"The—s-signal s-said—a hundred." Suddenly tears silvered Dhanissa's own cheeks. "A century." Alkhes spoke quite quietly now. "That means it's phalanx troops." He turned to Dhanissa. "They're marching? On foot?" At her nod, he glanced back to Tellurith. "Heavy-armed."

Enough to tear down everything we had built. Enough to smash any attempt at defense. Enough to massacre Telluir and Iskarda both. The merest nail on the smallest finger of the military power that is Dhasdein.

I saw Tellurith's mouth shake. Before she jerked her eyes back to Dhanissa and said as if words clogged her throat, "What do they plan? Did anyone say . . ."

"Marbleport." Dhanissa was just audible. "When they came ashore. Proclamation, the signal said. That they had," she stopped, with a signaler's precision drawing back the exact words, "an imperial summons. For . . . Assandar."

Tellurith's eyes dilated, full into the moon. She took one quick step and grabbed Dhanissa's foot. "A summons? Not a warrant? Not an arrest order? What did they *say*?"

"Not a warrant." Tears flew to the shake of Dhanissa's head. "I don't know what they said, but not a warrant—"

My own heart jumped to the hope that flared in Tellurith's face. She rounded on Zuri faster than a qherrique flash. "Stop Iatha! Signal the relay-station! Description, exact report. What happened in Marbleport, what the proclamation said. Word for word. Who's in charge, what they told Tez, anything we should know—!" Zuri snapped round in turn, Azo was already off. Tellurith spun back to Darthis.

Whose face spoke the same doubt, fear, hope. Who jerked her head in a quick, heavy nod. And looked at Alkhes.

Who was watching Tellurith. Quiet now. Having carried his point, and saved his folk. And on the ebb of that victory, that sacrifice's exultation, was confronting its price.

Tellurith's face replied. But she firmed her jaw, and spoke almost calmly. "If it really is a summons, it's not—" She could not go on. She did not have to. "And—"

And whatever its expedience, its sacrifice, your course may have some hope.

She held out her hands. He came to her then, breath, resistance, fire going out on one long sigh before he was clenched in her arms. And Tellurith looked past him at Darthis.

Before all else, she is a Head. Before all else, comes the House.

"Ruand," she said, "we appear to be somewhat—unlucky—in our festivals."

Darthis inclined her head. Now they were players, the leaders of the community, acting its purpose out.

"Telluir," she said, "Iskarda—wishes their Chosen well."

We all knew what it meant. But in the hush, Alkhes suddenly turned about.

"No," he said. He freed himself from Tellurith's arms, backing away, ablaze like a living fire. "Gods damn it, no."

Darthis stared. Tellurith said, "Caissyl?"

"We won't have it, Tel." His jaw set. "*I* won't have it. It's not just going to finish like a—I *want* this festival."

Because it is the one resistance we have left. The one way we can thwart Dhasdein. Because it may be the last festival I ever have.

Tellurith's face changed then. And then she straightened. Put back the coils of rose-entangled hair, and glanced to Darthis. Who gave a small, assenting nod.

Alkhes understood too. He lifted his chin and addressed Darthis, throwing his voice to fill the square, as Heads can. As soldiers can.

"Ruand," he said, for the whole assembly, "the Mother had given us Her word?"

So we all trooped back, and somebody fed the fire, somebody saw to Dhanissa and her mule, somebody fired off the signal to the relay posts. The flames blazed up, the musicians re-tuned. The wine-cups were found. As after a winding fall on the mat, the audience reassembled about the Market door, with Darthis ensconced above.

This time she looked at Alkhes instead of Tellurith. For a long time, before she spoke.

He stood directly before her, in the forefront of the crowd. Slight, vivid and resilient as a flame in his best white festival shirt, the nearest torches catching the abyss of his eyes, the glistening crow's-wing fall of hair; the line of his profile, sharp-cut, tense as a tempered edge. The roses flung over his shoulder, re-hung about his neck.

And Tellurith, like a girl with her first lover, pressed into his side.

Darthis cleared her throat. Took a great breath. Looked up at the moon. Said, "Iskarda asked the Mother: Shall we follow in Telluir's steps?"

She brought her eyes down to his face.

"And the Mother said, no. And, yes."

I have never felt a crowd so torn. Never seen such graven blankness in Tellurith's—in Alkhes' face.

Darthis nodded to him, a small, ironic shift, and looked back over the crowd.

"We will not oppose Telluir's way. In Iskarda, we will be one House."

I felt my own ribs undo. I saw the light fountain, as if the fire had leapt, on Tellurith's face, in Alkhes' eyes. Space fired with stars.

Darthis had watched it too. On anyone else, it might have been a smile.

"In our own houses," she said precisely, "we will keep the men's and women's sides."

Yes, the Mother said. And no.

The familiar glint in Tellurith's eye retorted, *The seam has opened. I can wait.* A glint answered, *I will swear that,* as Darthis looked back.

"But in Iskarda," she said, "we will admit men, men who can pass the lore-tests, to the Crafts."

It was Tellurith who broke their gaze at last. Not a smile now, but a glance about the crowd.

"It will be some time, yet, before we dance." She too pitched her voice for hearing's edge. "But we are beginning to learn the steps."

Official approval, official pledge. Charras and Ahio led the applause, the great, sanctioning laugh.

The crowd broke apart, the musicians made a triumph of sorts. Noise began, Darthis stepped back to earth, a single person again. Her eyes met Tellurith's, tracked on across Alkhes.

And came to mine.

I had been at his shoulder. Where else would I be? It was my life at stake, too. Our mutual hope.

But it was I to whom Darthis said, "S'hure, will you drink with me?"

That moment in the washing-bay. That too-accurate jest.

I never had time to prevaricate. I never had time to think. Alkhes had already acted. Had lunged across Tellurith and grabbed my wrist.

"Ruand," he said. "My husband must beg to be excused."

Darthis' brows went up. The equivalent of a dropped jaw on anyone else. I tried to keep my face still, Alkhes ignored us both. Keeping hold of me, with his other hand he snatched Tellurith. Then he hauled us both into motion, and as we passed Darthis, told her with the most adamant courtesy, "We must *all* beg to be excused."

It was high moon by then, clear and brilliant as a noon of qherrique, pouring down over the ranges in a silver, dreaming flood. The sounds receded, the pipe and drum, the voices and laughter, the smell of food and sweat and expiring rose petals, the piecemeal glow of human lights. Before us was only that luminous immensity, where mountain birds sang like woken water under the enormous sky.

It was Alkhes who chose the place: round the hill's curve toward the reservoir. Higher up the mountain, a little cup sheltered from the wind's draw, nested in thick summer grass. Concealed, shielded from the dew, by the fringes of a young hellien clump, whose boughs netted the molten silver light.

It was I who raided the house for blankets, cups, a fresh skin of wine, my own flute. As we settled into the shadows that dappled us like some great Crafter's damascene, Alkhes said, a disembodied determined voice among the silver patterns, "This time I want to get it right."

But it was I who answered, "No, beloved. This time *I* want to get it right."

So we sorted the blankets; took off no more clothes than we needed; passed cups, poured wine; and I played, as I have so often played, as prelude, scene-setting, focus; but also for tranquility.

But first, I gave Alkhes the other thing from the House.

"It's from the dispensary," I said, as I put the cup in his hand. "It's all right."

He stared at me: a splatter of moon-caught black silk, a corner of tight-drawn mouth, a huge, light-drinking eye. I shut the cup stem in his fingers and said it for him alone.

"It's a muscle-relaxer. And a mild aphrodisiac."

I know the ingredients as well as the proportions. I have used it over and over. In the Tower.

The eye got even wider. Something—indecipherable—plucked at the corner of the mouth.

Then he took the cup. Murmured, "Luck on us." And slowly, carefully, drained it dry.

Autumn. Dhasdein.

Meditations. Alkhes-Assandar

STRANGE THAT at the last, it should have been quick and sure as any battle-choice. Not something you think about. Not something you have time to think about. The sword's coming at you, the fronts are moving. You don't think. You know.

Perhaps, that night, it *was* a battle-choice. But when Darthis looked at him, I knew.

That if I have to lose them both, I was going to have them first.

Going up the mountain left no time to be afraid. Battle's not like that. You're possessed, yes, but fear doesn't go away. Going up there ... maybe it was the festival. Being Chosen. To half a thousand people who all know what they want. All know where they're going.

It was far better with Sarth in charge. He could have been a general, he has that perfect sense of time. Letting us settle, listen; think; but with the flute, not talk. So when he put it down, and started threading the roses out of Tellurith's hair, there was no panic; and no doubt.

I daresay whatever he gave me had its effect as well. I do know it was easy—gods, it was so easy. He made love to her, I held her in my arms. I made love to her, while he held me.

Gently, slowly. Sarth's way. Elegant, and skillful, and leisured. As if you had the whole world's space, and all of time.

And can feel more than pleasure. Joy.

I can see them moving, a silver and shadow human tapestry, like some great pillow-artist's drawing come alive. The pattern of woven bodies, the entanglement of shadow-waves, silver skin and muscle under the sinuous veilings of their hair.

I can feel what it was like, to be that living imagery, when she was making love with me.

And how it felt, when Sarth slid down beside me and put those hands on me instead.

He did want me, I know that now. For himself, not just to please Tellurith. I knew it, I suppose, since the night we kissed. But this time I could accept it. Admit it. Admit the rest as well.

That I wanted him.

So I could let go at last. Stop thinking it was a battle, stop wanting to win. And let—

And let him make love to me.

I've refused, I've feared, I've denied the very idea of it, all my life. Have been the leader, the decision-maker, with every woman I ever took to bed.

Well, almost. Looking back, I see that with Tel, the decisions were—are—always shared.

That quite often—hang it —

That *mostly* she has made love to me. But with Tel, that's all right. Because I'm still playing the man at the end.

To forget that; to lose that . . .

To *want* to lose that . . .

It's as well he did drug me. And we had the wine. And it was festival. And ahead, tomorrow, there was Dhasdein.

Otherwise I think I never would have dared.

To lose control, to surrender mastery, to give up everything that's supposed to have made me who I am. To lose, to abandon yourself, in a man's instead of a woman's hands.

If you never lose yourself, how can you ever tell that you've been found?

———

Autumn. Dhasdein.
Tellurith's Diary

I HAVE CARRIED it with me like a talisman, to turn over and over, to re-stamp in memory. Made more intense, more perfect, not only by long waiting; but because we all knew it might be the first and final time.

So I was glad—glad? I was ecstatic that Alkhes made the choice. And glad, grateful thrice over, for Sarth, because I did not have to do everything, after all. I could let Alkhes lead us, and choose a place, and Sarth orchestrate the rest.

I can draw it back in sequence; or I can dwell on some single perfect moment amid the harmony that linked it all. That first kiss with Sarth; the velvet of his mouth, so dear, so familiar, piquant with the flavor of crushed roses, with the new, delicately modulated urgency of his desire. The moonlight on Alkhes' face at the moment of release. The burning of my own body, up, up, into the blind, brilliant emptiness when I was all things and nothing, beyond death; beyond life. The pair of them kissing: Sarth's hands, Alkhes' face, those sculpted fingers shaping the line of a sculpted jaw; and the moon snared, silver turned to bronze, to ebony, entangled in their tangled hair.

A treasure; an heirloom. A life's splendor, in a life that has known not a little splendor. A fire to warm us in this cold, mean city, where we are fighting for more than our lives.

As COLD AS THAT creeping gray before dawn, when I woke with the moon staring, a bone-face, from a drained, windless sky. With the wine drunk, and the grass crushed, and our bodies chilled; and rising ahead of us, the encounter with Dhasdein.

Alkhes woke next; the way he most often does. The rhythm of his breath changed on my neck, the arm wrapped over me found tension. Under my own arm, Sarth still slept, his arm under both our heads, his hair strewn over us all; beautiful as an exhausted god.

Behind the bluff, down the hill, all over the mountain others would be waking; crawling out, breaking apart; slithering home. Nobody questions, next morning, where you came from. But it is cold daylight, the festival over; when you go, you leave the night behind.

I tightened my hand on Alkhes', and felt the troublecrew calluses on his palm. Very softly, all but inside my ear, he said, "I'll meet them on the road."

"Mm." Only sensible, if he was bent on giving himself up, to forestall any contact with Iskarda. "We need to see the signal. Find out who sent it; who's in charge."

"What does it—"

He stopped. His lips twitched against my ear.

"I forgot you know Dhasdein."

So we both knew it mattered desperately who the commanding officer was: a supporter, an enemy, and if so, aligned with which enemy. Above all—

"It may not be the Emperor. No."

That can happen, with such a huge state, with palace factions and favorites and interests from provincial kinglets to Army generals, not to mention the independent armies of government scribes. Antastes might not even know the summons had been sent.

He twitched against me, one quick, uncontrollable flinch. "It'll be from Antastes. He couldn't afford otherwise." But there was a flaw in the note; a divided nuance that said, terrible as Antastes' decree might be, it might not be the worst.

"And there's a lot to settle before we go."

His heart stopped. I felt it, the halt, the resuming leap, the hand become iron in mine.

"You're not going."

"Of course I am."

"Tellurith!" Sarth jerked, I hissed. Alkhes yanked out of my hands.

"They'll know who you are, the first trouble they'll go for you—they'll cut my heart out! Oh, *gods*, Tel, *no!*"

It ended in a yelp. Sarth's plunge overturned us all. Alkhes yelled, I yelled, Sarth yelled as our weight caught his hair. By the time I had them sorted out Alkhes was past sense.

"Tel, you *can't* come, why do you think I'm giving myself up at all? To keep you out of it! You can't," his voice cracked, "come too!"

I caught his hands as he beat at the air. As he tore free another pair closed over them. He gave one furious heave and fell back as Sarth leant in to pin us both.

"Alkhes," he said, in that voice as calm as when he watched Amberlight falling, "be still."

Black and bronze eyes clashed. Then Alkhes gasped and let his muscles undo. But his hands still clung.

"No, Tel. I won't let you. Iatha—Zuri—the House won't let you! You're the Head. You can't run out on them!"

I yanked on his wrists to bring another gasp.

"And you," I said through my teeth, "are my husband and my troublecrew and under my protection. Part of Telluir House."

"What?"

"I have the money. I have the contacts. I know as much about Dhasdein as you do. What's more, Dhasdein knows me."

His mouth hung like an empty purse.

I pulled their grips apart and sat up under Sarth's lightening weight. Gray dawn limned their bodies, beloved, beautiful, the warmth and touch that had been my sanctuary.

"I," I said, "am Telluir House-head. I have met Antastes. I have met the Crown Prince. And if there's anything that they want more than you, Alkhes, it will be to know my resources and my plans. If anybody tries to cut your heart out, they'll have to get past me."

Sarth undid himself from the pair of us. From inside his shirt he added mildly, "And me."

We both shouted, "No!"

His head emerged. Bronze hair cascaded. He shook it clear. Pulled it back. Calm, bland, those bronze eyes met mine.

"Very well," he said.

We both sighed and relaxed. Eyes hidden beyond those unfairly spectacular lashes, he began to button his shirt.

Watching his mouth, I said, "Sarth."

He looked up. His eyes were quite opaque.

I said, "If I have to get Zuri to lock you up—chain you—personally sit on you—I will."

He bent his head. "Yes, Tellurith."

"Sarth!" I grabbed hair by handfuls, yanked him nose to nose and shook him till his teeth rattled. "Do as you're goddamn told!"

He wiped the corners of his eyes. "Yes, Tellurith."

"Mother *rot* you! If you dare run off and catch the next boat downstream, on your own, without a fiel, with no more idea of the River than—I'll murder you!"

He unearthed his trousers under the blanket. Quite mildly, he said, "Yes, Tellurith."

"Oh, Mother . . ."

Alkhes' arm came round me. With my face buried in my hands I heard him say, just as mildly, "Don't you think she has problems enough?"

More quietly, Sarth answered, "Oh, yes."

The arm flinched. "That's why I want to go alone—!"

Softly, delicately as inserting a stiletto, Sarth said, "Of course."

"Sarth—!"

The yell was more strangled than mine. I took my hands down and we stared at each other. Two of us at screaming point. One of us as calmly, as composedly obdurate as he had been first.

"It's no good," I said to the back of Alkhes' head. "We can yell till we're black in the face. It won't work."

He flung both hands to the sky. "Don't I have enough weak spots already? Do I have to risk you—and now—oh, gods, Tel, do you know what could happen to *him*?"

I looked at that beloved, beautiful face, and remembered the fate of tower men in the fall of Amberlight; and tried not to flinch myself as I whispered, "I know."

Sarth's eyes dilated. A god provoked at last.

"Do you also know," still, it came so gently, "that my Craft-head gave me a commission: as my House-head's bodyguard?"

Alkhes' jaw sagged. Sarth glared at him, a blaze of topaz fire.

"So I will honor that commission," he said, more gently, "or I will die."

Autumn. Dhasdein.
Journal kept by Sarth

AT TIMES one must become quite unmannerly to persuade one, let alone both my spouses to the better course. And Alkhes and Tellurith were naturally nothing to when we reached the house, and Zuri and Iatha pounced on us like a pair of mountain eagle-hawks.

The troops were estimated to reach Iskarda in late afternoon. Darthis and Iatha had already organized an evacuation, chosen posts for those, armed with cutters or light-guns, who would remain. "Too risky to leave everyone here. No chance of stopping them if they do decide to torch the place. But we can't let them have it without a fight."

Iatha growled that across the kitchen table, while we gulped down yesterday's bread and the season's new plum jam. Tellurith and Alkhes both looked pinched, washed out: more than love's fatigue. Tellurith just nodded and grunted something about Marbleport.

"They landed three days ago. Imperial galley, escort ship. They left half a century there."

Tellurith put her bread down with a jerk. Like me, she knew that note in Zuri's voice.

"The first thing they did was to arrest Tez."

Somewhere far, far away, Zuri's voice went on. With Tez removed, the information system had collapsed, no one to ask the right questions, to assemble replies. So we still did not know who had sent the summons. Or the commander's name.

"The escort sailed this morning. Downstream. With Tez on board."

I had stood up. My ears had gone dead. A cold stone tumor filled my chest. Zuri's face shot away from me, darkness swallowed the room, Iatha, even Tellurith. But something had hold of my wrist. Was twisting my wrist, viciously, professionally, a troublecrew pinion grip. As the body's pain drilled through everything Alkhes hissed it in my ear.

"Sit down!"

He yanked me into the chair. Pinned me there, troublecrew fingers dug into the shoulder pressure-points in a grip that exceeds main strength. His face was white as wet linen. I only saw his eyes.

"She'll be all right. She's a hostage. Listen to me, Sarth!"

His eyes held me more fiercely than his hands.

"They know who she is. Dhasdein intelligencers." Softer than a curse. "They won't damage her. I'll get her back."

Before I could find an answer Tellurith moved her plate with precise, ridiculous care and spoke more precisely; a cut-crystal enunciation I never heard before.

"It's just as well the three of us are going, after all."

I DO NOT KNOW what Iatha said. I do know the shouting went for half a watch, in Tellurith's work-room, behind the shut door. Because it was still shut when I fought my way out of Zuri's room.

She marched me there, with my little finger bent double and my arm twisted up my back. Sat me on the bed and slapped me, hard enough to rock my head on my neck.

"I cancel the commission. You're relieved."

"Tez is my daughter," I said.

She hit me again, hard enough to bring tears to my eyes. Only experience told me she had pulled the slap.

"You're a novice. You're ignorant as a baby. You're tower-bred. They'll eat you alive."

I stood up. She slapped me down.

"You don't know the River! There's nothing you can do!"

"No, Zuri," I said.

"You bone-headed dangle, you're her husband! Do you want her to lose everything?"

"No, Zuri."

She took me by the hair and bent my head back, and bared her teeth as if to rip out my throat.

"You're *my* husband," the purr was gravel, "too."

Carefully, I brought my hands up between hers. Took her wrists, drew them down. More carefully, drew her to sit on the bed. It is indecent for a Tower man to speak openly, with Zuri, it is not wise. But I had no choice, and no time.

"I couldn't bring you—last night. I would have given worlds to have you there. I don't know anything about the River. I'm not true troublecrew. But I'm her husband, Zuri. And if the worst comes to the worst, I can be there. Like Alkhes."

Zuri is Zuri. Nothing showed.

Except that she did not speak, when I went on, "Instead of Alkhes."

And she did not stop me, when I kissed her, and undid her hands, and walked out the door.

She just announced that she was coming too.

I KNOW ANOTHER brangle would have finished me. But Tellurith just took her elbows off the council-table and said wearily, "Zuri, I can leave the House, at a pinch, to you and Iatha. And to Darthis. I know all the arguments about what only I can do. But I can't—" her eyes met Zuri's—"I have to ask you—to let me risk myself—and your—our husband—and not tip the odds against the House altogether. Because it can't do without us both."

FROM THE QUARRY the Marbleport road runs down a short slope, across a valley-bed, into the zig-zag of the real descent. The paven way is flanked by ditches and silver-beige summer grasses, amid silver-gray clouds of big, scattered helliens, and clots of low olive-silver mountain scrub. Alkhes planned the encounter for the valley-bottom, making manifest that there was no ambush; no opposition. He would stand alone, at the center of the road, with Tellurith and Quetho and Zdana and me, visibly unarmed, thirty paces behind.

It was a warm, windy, lavishly clouded summer afternoon. The great shadows sailed over us, restless as nervous horses, dark across the rippling grass, the trees tossed and hummed to the gusts, the sun flashed and faded and flashed again, its sting drawn by mountain air. The limpid clarity of the further bluffs presaged rain. It seemed forever before the sentry-post behind us signaled that the troops were turning the valley-foot.

A good mile downhill, they were just a curiously silent trickle of silver, a thick, red-prickled bar. Not the slow string-sequence of a returning mule-train, with its dark beads of unarmed human and plodding beast. This was a scaly, regular glitter: the pattern of marching ranks, the spark of light off helmet and spear-point and shield.

Alkhes was quiet, and very pale. But he kissed Tellurith, and walked away from us, that lithe killer's grace become resolution, but not the shamble of fear. He wore an old pair of trousers, his second decent shirt. No hat: they would need to recognize him, he said. He stood at the road's center, at something I know now was a soldier's parade rest, feet spread, hands clasped behind his back.

When they came in sight, Tellurith and Alkhes grunted together: presently I understood that, firstly, they had not formed attack formation, and secondly, there were no scouts.

Zuri had said, tight-lipped, "They know we've had signals." She did not have to add, they know the value of Tez.

Just out of bow-shot, someone bellowed. The twenty-five ranks stopped as one. Bang. Clash. Heavy round shields shot sun-flashes. Spears wavered, scarlet fringes tied behind the heads. Ceremonial fringes, as I did not know. The rest was just metal: helmets, corselets, heavy knee-high greaves.

There was some military mumbling. Then by some peculiar maneuver the two front ranks made themselves a pair of files four deep, flanking a person with a tall red crest.

Somebody else bellowed. The files advanced.

Around me I felt the women go stiff, I felt the speeding of my own heart. They were in light-gun range now. They were close enough to see the eyes in the helmet frames. Close enough, I know now, to have pressed home a charge.

Almost conversationally, the tall crest spoke. They stopped.

In a public-announcement voice the tall crest—the officer— proclaimed, "Dhasdein requires that all allies or associates shall cede to the Empire, without check or hindrance, the person known on the River as Assandar."

He must have practiced, to get it out on one breath.

Alkhes waited the beat that would assert independence and used his own military voice.

"On whose authority?"

"On the authority of his imperial majesty, Antastes son of Thearkos, Overlord of Shirran, Riversrun, Mel'eth and Quetzistan, High King of the Sealands and Archipelagoes, Emperor of Dhasdein."

Beside me, Tellurith breathed out.

Alkhes said, "And your own?"

He was in his late thirties; young, rising power. I saw his shoulders stiffen. He knew enough to keep his mouth still, but we could see his eyes.

"Nessis, son of Dekos, third legion's chiliarch." A pause. "Nephew to the Brigade-commander Quizir."

Meaning that his troops did belong to the heavy-armed phalanx, the Dhasdein battle-front: he was their second-in-command. Adding, superfluously, his family tie.

Declaring, those icy gray eyes proclaimed it, open war.

Tellurith went rigid as a board. Quizir, I know now, had been Alkhes' own second-in-command, leading the Dhasdein troops at Amberlight. And when the hill fell, Quizir died.

Alkhes said, "The imperial commission is in your hands?"

Zdana and Quetho both gasped. The troops' eyes had widened. I made ready to die.

Nessis thrust his jaw out under the helmet strap. "On what authority," it gritted in his throat, "do you ask?"

For such a commission, a virtual arrest, River mandate demands that outside the Empire Dhasdeini officials shall show their authority first. By rights, he should already have read it out.

Alkhes' voice was armed and armored. Only to us, who knew its every cadence, did it reveal what this throw would cost.

"I," he said, "am the general Assandar."

Beside me Tellurith breathed a tiny, stifled groan.

Because, I understood even then, that this was an enemy, whom he had to override, rather than appealing to a friend. Because he could only do so by invoking his own identity. His own rank. Given by, subject to the Emperor. Demanding loyalty. Admitting treachery, if that loyalty was proven betrayed.

By his own doing, he laid himself open to such charges. Had erased other loyalties.

He could no longer be part Alkhes. He was, irretrievably, Assandar.

Nessis' jaw worked. Alkhes stood quite still. But whatever his eyes said, Nessis slid a hand into his neck-piece, drew out a long creamy-brown shape, and thrust it out.

Alkhes did not move. I all but heard Tellurith's smothered moan. I did read the troops' body-talk, when Nessis took the three steps forward to lay the thing in Alkhes' hand.

Letting my own breath go, smelling sweat, hot wool, Dhasdein weapon oil, I kept my face still, thinking, I know you have to force him. But gods, Alkhes, you know what an enemy you make.

The red of an enormous seal flashed in the sun.

"By the authority of his imperial majesty, Antastes son of Thearkos, Overlord of Shirran, Riversrun, Mel'eth and Quetzistan, High King of the Sealands and Archipelagoes, Emperor of Dhasdein."

It was loud enough for the whole century to hear. He paused to breathe.

"You are commissioned to proceed to the former lands of Amberlight, to the village known as Iskarda. Where you will deliver a summons to present himself, at his best speed, at the court of the Emperor in Riversend. To the person formerly known as the general Assandar."

He let the parchment close. Nessis' eyes were viper-stings.

"I hear the word of the Emperor." Precisely chosen phrasing: not, "command," not, "ruling"; and not, "I will obey." He swung sidelong, gesturing. "These are the delegates from Iskarda. This is Telluir House-head. And her bodyguard. They will accompany me."

Nessis had rank enough and schooling enough to read "delegate" as "witness"; of course, he knew Telluir House. He had knowledge enough of Amberlight to let his jaw sag at "bodyguard." No mite of doubt that he would gladly, gleefully have refused. And with Alkhes' rank declared, no other mite of doubt.

There was nothing he could do.

Autumn. Dhasdein.
Meditations. Alkhes-Assandar

It could have been so much worse. They could have just marched in and sacked Iskarda. It could have been a warrant and Nessis could have tossed me straight in chains. It could have come from someone lower down the hierarchy; from some more lethal enemy.

It made it no easier to go forward among those tall red-kilted ranks that were once invisible as home. To hear the commands, once second-nature. The rhythm, familiar as a heart-beat, of two hundred marching feet.

To know that we were wholly in Dhasdein's grasp.

As for Nessis, he had already declared himself. And whatever the cost, it gave me leverage, at the first village, to order horses hired, to enforce our rank. At Marbleport, to dictate when we embarked.

Not enough to ask about Tez.

When he heard, Sarth's face . . . I would have alienated another Nessis, if it let me throw my rank far enough to yank the escort back that very night.

But I cannot. I still cannot let them know how much she is worth.

WE SAILED the evening we reached Marbleport. No chance to find how we had been so disastrously surprised. Gods know, Tez ought to have heard *something*, is a Dhasdein galley with escort and a pair of troop-transports common as timber-barges in Verrain?

Unless she did hear. What she was deliberately told.

At least I got that word to her second. Turning up haughty with a fuss about cabin equipment on the dock, the double dekarchy that was to board with us stiff as spear-hafts, not sure whether to freeze or laugh. It seems I have a reputation still.

Far too risky to try suborning someone on the way downstream, with Nessis burning the back of my neck. What did I do to that boy in his own right? What uncle could have lit such a hate?

Far too risky to ask. Bad enough to play the fool on that dockside, demanding to see the merchant—thank the gods I was still soldier enough to learn her name, back in Iskarda. Haranguing her about stinking cushion-covers, waving one in her face; hissing, "They've read the spy-net, warn Zuri, cut all the links."

They must have had plenty, beyond the one who cut himself. How otherwise would they know I would surrender? How else would they have understood about Tez?

I still cannot afford to think about what they want.

XI

Autumn. Dhasdein
Tellurith's Diary

How strange to see the River, my life's work, my world's staple, familiar to the last placename, with my own eyes.

Stranger, beyond doubt, to Sarth, who never laid eyes even on Amberlight. Except to pass through the streets, on great House occasions; his marriage. House-head's funerals.

The day they pulled Amberlight down.

Tower-discipline held, of course. When we walked in among the soldiers; when he had to ride a horse, for the first time in his life. When, the Mother knows, close-quarters with a Dhasdein war-galley, the dark-varnished clinker-laid swell of her side, the gill-roses of oarport rising in their three staggered rows, the lofty sway of the imperial ensign at her mast, the deadly ripple over the submerged reef of the ram—for me it was a nightmare in waking day.

On board, too, when Alkhes finished playing general, tossing Nessis to camp with his troops; when he had shown us the layout, soldiers forward, rowers midships, ship officers and guests piled in the hen-coop superstructure; when we had cast off; when the timing pipe began, the great oars slid out; dipped; pulled, and the ship surged like a suddenly spurred horse, while the River revolved about us, a mirror of wide, wide, imperceptibly moving gray, its distant reaches a sheen of clouds, and Marbleport became a heap of white and thatch-yellow blocks receding astern. While I was still absorbing just how wide that water is, there was nothing but polite attention on Sarth's face.

Autumn. Dhasdein.
Journal kept by Sarth

The figures say the River runs seven hundred miles between Amberlight and Riversend: that a well-manned war galley can cover that in a month, averaging, between wind and oars and water, twenty-five miles and better a day. What figures do not tell!

Almost I could praise You, whose malice wrecked another festival. Almost I could give You worship, for the world's diversity. How little I knew, in the Tower's tight little, tense little, immaculately serene little maelstrom, of what enlargements I had lost.

Iskarda accustomed me to space, to lofty prospects, to the width of distant lands. But on the River you wake to a fresh land every morning, have seen a third by the fall of night. The Iskan defile, where the river threads the range narrows, gray and cinnabar scarps that twist among small, enchanting perspectives, the turquoise and celadon of remote Verrain—until the cliff portal opens and the entire panorama bursts upon you, dusty green and dazzle-gold, roof-patched, road-seamed, teeming from horizon to horizon, the tapestry of fields, ox-carts, donkey-loads of domesticities, villages whose arteries throb to laborers with knives and loincloths, squalls of half-clad children, women walking with head-loads of cloth or vegetables or shapely pots. The glimpses down some road's length of jewel-bright clothes and pennons in some high family's retinue; and finally, Assuana itself.

Of course I knew the facts. Verrain's capital. Nerve-center of Amberlight's nearest, most friendly neighbor state. The straitness of their earth, whose riches end barely twenty miles from the River-side. Facts lack that dusty pallor that says, Desert, on the horizon sky. Facts cannot extract the smell, wild, sharp, unforgettable, of heat and implacable sand. Nor will any learning anticipate the explosion of grass-hut suburbs, walled green paradises, labyrinthine whitewashed alleys, splendidly intricate temple fretwork, or the reverberant market at the city's core.

For me Assuana remains the market, emporium for anything from Oasis gold to Heartland hunting cats, Mel'eth amber, Cataract timber, embroidered slippers or Verrain sugar-grass. Embracing the river, thrusting out finger after finger of rickety boat-entangled house-encrusted, gewgaw-and-produce-bedizened piers, besieging you in swarms of peddlers clogging up the oars, clinging to the stern, riding the very ram. Assuana lives by the River-trade. Until then, I never understood what that means.

And beyond Assuana, as the desert withdraws its fringes, the empire. Dhasdein.

The land is less crowded there: richer, spreading up into low, rolling hills where they run cloud-size flocks of sheep. And along the river margin they have not cut the mighty river helliens. Red, they call them, though it is less a color than a tint. Ruddy, dried blood, cinnabar, washed in great swathes across the bark's outer, falling sheaves. I never tired of looking at them. Except to watch the motley of the water-traffic, or the river-side.

I "knew" the River's folk are black, brown, white, brindle, and every shade between. I did not *know* the difference between the blue-black of a truebred Verrainer and the dusty, glossy black-bronze of a Quetzistani skin. I did not *know* the way Shirran eyes roll under their lid-fold, or the curious yellow tinge you find among the farmers of downstream Riversrun. Or the motley multitude of face and body shapes in every marvel-crowded mile.

That is most wonderful of all. That there could be so many folk, each with their own personal ways of walking, talking, carrying water, paying a shop-keeper, pursuing a flirtation. Washing their faces, folding their loincloths or knotting their skirts. I could have sailed on, watching them, forever. Except—

Tellurith understood. "She's Navy," she said, leaning shoulder to shoulder above the din of market boats at Deyiko, the Dhasdein border-post. "She's been a prisoner of war. And badly wounded as well."

Difficult to remember that, moldering under this pestiferous awning, with the brazier, like the page, splattered and spitting at the rain, and the pen, like everything else on this wretched scow, clammy with damp. Painful to remember while we swaggered down-river, cocooned in imperial military might. Difficult to admit, at either time, that my daughter was—is—a Navy officer. Blooded and bloodied in battle. That she has learnt more of fortitude, and martial aplomb in adversity, than I will ever know.

Small comfort, when I must sit here, idle, impotent, wondering what dungeon tries her composure now.

Autumn. Dhasdein.
Tellurith's Diary

THE GALLEY REACHED Riversend around middle-hour of a cold, windy autumn afternoon; gusts of sunlight, under a blotchy, turbulent sky. First the River narrowed into the Gates; old, old cliffs whose beetling citadels lap their feet in dragon coils of blockade chain; their bulwark buoys, solid stone islets, divide the stream. Then shadows cede to an ocean rim's remote, watery sheen of sky.

Once the Delta was probably ducks and swamp and reeds. Now you pass quarries of fetid, stone-sided canal entrances, vanishing amid squalid two and three storey tenements. The city's outer reaches, abandoned to the impoverished on their way down and the laborers who will never rise at all.

Next come the industrial quarter, and the main city wharves. Work-places, factories, stench of smoke and clangor, that the tenements serve. And then the merchant quarter. The factories' lords. Great solid buildings, where they keep the money-marts, granite and marble, gilt pediments, somewhat rimed by smoke. They even gild the barges at the well-kept mooring pontoons.

And down from that lie the flood piers, whose might controls the river, whose ribs sustain the city's scum, the riff-raff of homeless, army flotsam, war refugees, Archipelago emigrants; their backs to the wall of great nobles' estates. The paradox of Riversend, whose sores ooze on its noblest flesh.

The estates open only to their own. From the River, they are back walls, private guard patrols, a glimpse of tower tops and delicate gazebos, gilded column capitals and exotic foliage.

Below them, the Army quarter fills the right bank, its own walls protecting a chain of naval shipyards and galley slips. I could buy the Emperor, if I had a fiel for every ounce of blood and gold that place has cost Amberlight.

And on the left, from the nobles' quarter to the sea, is the Emperor's demesne.

The place is a city in itself. The labyrinth of the scribes. The imperial guard and its quarter. The imperial artisans, entertainers, servants' quarter. The imperial nobles' quarters. The imperial merchants' quarter. The imperial ambassadors' residences. The imperial presence-hall. The Imperial government.

NESSIS' SHIP MOORED at what I now know is the common supplicants' wharf. Well-tended stone, but plain timber bollards, and not a soul concerned. Inshore rose the façade of the demesne: building after building, an arrogant glitter of marble, ornament, gold, an enigmatic tide of passers-by. In Amberlight, I could have read their trades and destinations, their very affiliations, at a glance.

It was much brighter, here. All the River beyond Amberlight is obsessed with color, the poorer the gaudier in Verrain. This was the shine of wealth;

not the clothes but the ornaments, not the color but the texture of the cloth. And not a clue to their meaning to read.

I had seen only imperial embassies and the Crown Prince. Not his lowliest underlings would walk these streets. I did guess, from the flood that poured toward the gate-houses and waiting boatmen, that it was the end of the day's work. It was no guess that something had gone drastically wrong; that took only one look at Alkhes' face.

A galley has no privacy, even within the superstructure's hencoop walls; we had not so much as shared a bed. Alkhes had played soldier; played general; demanding to Nessis, terse with the soldiers; formal, at best, with us. My heart, my arms had ached to hold him, to offer solace, however brief and illusory. I understood very well that I could not. I could imagine the ribaldry, the slum ballads and courtly sniggers Nessis' account would leave of our marriage; let be the deadly damage it might do his case.

Whatever that was, to whomever it must be made.

Playing the general, he could not sink to demand details like, where do we disembark? I, too, had been braced for incarceration at the citadels. I had seen the way, when they slid by, his shoulders finally relaxed. I, too, had then expected the next worst: the Army quarter. When the galley veered palaceward it had been almost an anti-climax. Until we started to moor.

We stood outside the hencoop hatch. Nessis and his usual two escorts tramped along the galley side. Alkhes said, "What is this?" in a voice I had never heard before.

Nessis came to attention. His body was rigid decorum. Revenge, fleshed at last, exulted in his face.

"My orders were to convey you," he even managed to sound unctuous, "to the imperial court."

Leaving us without instructions, without a resting place, marooned.

And with Tez immured somewhere in this labyrinth, no more able to escape than fly.

Alkhes did not move, did not speak. He only seemed to grow more and more compacted, all eyes, like poisoned swords in a killer's face. I had never so clearly seen his double nature. A general who was a killer as well.

It shouted from the troops' stance. I understood, in some side-brain, that the display was partly for them; that he could not afford to be shown at a loss. It shouted clearer from Nessis' stiffening, whitening, furiously determined, appalled face.

When I thought my very sinews would break he said, in the barest whisper, "You have leave to go."

Nessis kept upright. Barked commands. The sweat, running like water under his helmet straps, was betrayal enough. I saw the sidelong glances, the fury in Nessis' back as they stamped away.

We picked up our traps. Descended the gangplank. The galley cast off. However loathed, however alien, it had become familiar. I tried to feel calm and independent, not ignominiously dumped. Alkhes stalked across the wharf and yelled at the nearest boatman, "Hire!"

"Residents, guest-billets, license-holders. Nobody else can stay in the Quarter at night."

He glared out over the stern. The boatman, at first curious, had begun to cringe. The air round us was still incandescent with rage. Then, under his breath, "Have some darrin handy. It'll cost about three."

I stifled the outcry. In Amberlight three darrin would have bought you the boat. Neither of us asked, Where are we going? Neither of us had to say, That we have neither instructions nor reception committee nor imperial billets signals either Nessis' malice, or some greater enmity.

When the boatman deposited us it was almost dark, and we had come clear back across the merchants' quarter. Heaving my gear onto the other shoulder, following Alkhes past some deserted barrack toward a street-mouth, I said, at last, "Where are we going?"

"I hope," he dived into the darkness on a splutter of rain, "to my house."

Of course, I thought, ploughing after. The uptown streets were cobbled, but you could turn an ankle between the stones. Of course he would have a house. Have you forgotten? He had a world here. A whole other life.

Merchants live behind their business quarter, in a modest copy of the nobles next door. Honest folk, or residents, hire torch-bearers. The streets are dark as pits amid blank ten feet outer walls. Alkhes counted corners, to an occasional stifled curse, up to yet another dark, barred gate.

"If Gessa's still here …" He set his gear down. There was a big iron dog's head with a bar in its mouth. He yanked the head, the bar slammed into the resounding rim of the iron-shod door.

Dark and quiet.

Sarth said, "What is this?"

It was fixed to the keystone, three feet overhead. The final twilight caught its salients with a glint of faded, official red. Some sort of badge, I thought; or perhaps a crest. Yet it did not look as if it belonged where it was.

Alkhes stared up at it. I knew, by his face, to expect the worst.

He said, "They've attaindered the house."

I understood. Sarth knew to keep quiet. Alkhes gazed up, very, very still now, but not with the menace of the wharf. Then, carefully, he picked up his gear, turned on his heel, and led us away.

After an eternity of stumbling through the dark, higher walls brought, blessedly, voices; noise; food-smells, however noisome; and lights.

Tenement-dwellers live willy-nilly in community, their stairs shared, their hallways the open street. The quarter rattled with workers headed home, peddlers, cheap wine-sellers, cook-stalls fizzing and smelling over half the street, dogs and indiscriminate chamber-pots perfuming the rest. But there was activity, movement, laughter, however unfamiliar. Food; and, I devoutly hoped, a bed.

"It isn't," said Alkhes curtly, slowing against me, "the best of suburbs; but the inns are cheap."

Only now do I know how desperately important that was.

THE INN was cheap. Its communal dish was something like pork and pickled beans. It had a room, with only two adjoining walls, and sleeping arrangements were our own concern. We dumped our gear. Alkhes set the lamp down. I checked the latch. Sarth's eyes moved around. Then he thumped the wall.

When nobody thumped back, Alkhes let out a long silent sigh. Then we did what we had been aching a month for, and fell in each other's arms.

Eventually we could let go far enough to look at each other. My fingers, for some reason, were entangled in Sarth's undone hair. My other hand would not leave Alkhes' face; and he was holding on to me, tightly, almost desperately, the general's façade crumbling like plaster and too much feeling in its place.

I pushed his hair back, rubbing his cheek, feeling the familiar, beloved burr of bristle against my palm. As once when he had been half-dead, memoryless, a scrap of suffering consciousness, I tried to let that touch say, I'm here. It's all right.

After a minute he sighed again, quite inaudibly. Leant his cheek against my hand and shut his eyes.

Sarth understood. If we two were strangers, adrift and shiftless, Alkhes was a renegade; perhaps already tried and condemned; in mortal peril, having already lost all but his life. Only here could he let the terror show; Sarth put his arms around us both.

When Alkhes' eyes opened I said, "What sort of bribes will it take to reach Antastes?" Sarth added, "Does Nessis' faction have much power?"

His eyes went wider than encircling night. Then, shakily, with a sudden flaw in it, he began to laugh.

"Gods. Gods . . . to have had such a staff!"

I maneuvered him toward the bed, the only sitting place. The mattress, needless to say, was all lumps. "Should I make myself known, or shall you try your own channels first?"

"No! Not yet!" He settled thankfully, eagerly, between the pair of us. "If the house is attaindered, I don't want—it would be safer not to compromise my friends."

"Fair enough." Almost certainly, they would be watched. "Do we try the palace, then?"

He thought about that. Then he rubbed his forehead, a gesture I had hardly seen since the siege negotiations in Amberlight. I knew what outcome he expected, from the tone in which he said, "Why not?"

"THE EMPIRE," Alkhes told me once, "isn't a system or a hierarchy, let alone a command-chain. It's a free-for-all." Now, I understood, we must map the shoals of conflict as we sailed; in a year, every configuration of power would have changed. I could imagine what upheavals would follow his resignation, the disaster at Amberlight. Nor, until we stormed the court, could I do much to help. The old Telluir spy-chains had fallen apart; lacking our funds, Tez's intelligencers never attained our levels. Had I known them, they still could not have reached liaisons and cabals among the heights of power.

"Nessis," Alkhes said carefully, "belongs to Quizir's faction. Which is mostly an old, sizeable, family. But on the army side."

We could track its connections later. What mattered for the moment was that they would have less influence on the government side; so we might, at least, get in the Imperial Quarter gate.

First we had to shop, in the ruinously expensive nobles' quarter. "I can't turn up as a civilian. Not at the palace." As his escort, we had to look our rank. And with each darrin disgorged, all three of us winced.

"If I can find the marble agents," I comforted Sarth, "I can get credit, at least."

He went on inspecting his new coat: high-collared, double-breasted in the latest fashion, a glorious deep yellow silk that woke the highlights in his hair and gave him lion's eyes. I tweaked my silver-embroidered leggings. As he pulled the crimson officer's kilt straight Alkhes said, sounding unwontedly cheerful, "At least you can wear decent clothes."

When we both stared, he slid an arm round my waist. "All that beautiful stuff you had in Amberlight. All thrown away." We gaped like idiots. He smirked. "I used to lie around on the floor at night, just to get a look at your legs."

I slapped his face. It came lightly enough to make him laugh; but as he shooed us down the stairs his eyes held no mirth at all.

THE SUBURB BEYOND the Court's outer guard-house is spectacular, as Alkhes once remembered when he could remember little else: dead flat Delta land, wide, superbly paved streets, full of immaculately shaped trees. Discreetly withdrawn from the imperial wall, there are magnificent dining places full of very expensive whores. At the ornate iron gates a stream of petitioners narrowed, clogged, and swirled, before the imperial blockade.

Not the gorgeously armored guards. The officiating scribes.

There was a suite of them, inspecting, questioning. At the barrage of demands, assertions, pleas, cries of outrage, suffering wails, I felt my heart shrink in my chest.

Sarth was inscrutable. Alkhes wore his general's face. I touched the great Crafter's brooch, the only heirloom I had brought out of Amberlight, and told myself I was a Ruand. I was the Head of Telluir House.

The intake swallowed us. We reached the outpost. Alkhes tucked his helmet under an arm and said, "To see the Emperor. General Assandar."

The scribe was young, dapper, smartly groomed, in his strange narrow Dhasdein trousers and a cleverly cut light winter coat. He ruffled the parchments in his hands and frowned.

"General—Assandar." A long pause. "Ah. Sir."

The pause before the elegantly sketched distress would have been signal enough. But I had seen the preceding flicker in his eyes.

Alkhes raised his brows. The youngster fluttered again. "Ah . . . sir. I don't seem to find the—ah—name."

"Perhaps you should look more closely." Alkhes sounded quite calm. "Or you might let me see."

The eye flicked to Alkhes' left hand, cradled behind the helmet, suggestively cupped. They both looked. The underling grew more elegantly distressed. "Perhaps, sir, my superior . . ."

He cost fifteen darrin. His superior cost twenty-five. The Head cost fifty, when we came to him. He too was destroyed. Desolated. But with no sign of the name on his admission lists, "I am most terribly regretful, sir, but the imperial security . . . is more than I dare breach."

I moved closer, as if to examine the list, and let my shoulder touch Alkhes' arm. As if at the list, he shook his head. "Perhaps the signals were delayed. Another day . . ."

They fawned on him with the sincerest gratitude. He was not going to raise a real furor, force them to inelegance, drag it to their superiors, blast them as he had Nessis. And surely, the accreditations would be here, in just another day.

When we reached the inn, Alkhes sat a good while on the bed, staring blankly before him. Before he took his chin out of his hands and said, "Sarth, can you get me some clothes?"

Autumn. Dhasdein.
Journal kept by Sarth

STRANGE TO REMEMBER, that when I walked out the inn door that day, I had never been at large in a city before.

Of course Tellurith had to come with me. She would have worried herself crazy otherwise; I would have died of fright. A Tower-bred man thrust into the hurly-burly of the tenement markets, brangling with the keepers of old clothes shops, the most brazen cheats of the thieves' bazaar?

I had to go, Alkhes explained, because Tellurith would be pestered silly without me. She had to go to keep my haggling in some control. If she did it herself, he explained more wryly, they would remember her.

And any memory of us was more than we could afford.

Only when he was dressed did I remember his other side: my flesh and blood know, from working out, that he is a trained street-fighter. My mind knows he was a general. Not till he put on the scruffy black pants, the nondescript over-tunic, when a quick dishevelment of hair, a smudge of lamp-black over his upper lip, another in his eye-corners, a hunch and cringe created the seedy, shambling dock-worker, did I recall he had also been a brilliant intelligencer.

"Ai-eh, ly-dee, m'wife's sick o'the croup, I got three little'uns starving, you got a heart, ha'n't you, cancha spare a fiel . . . ?" He crooked his shoulders and cupped a hand and Tellurith, for all the brewing thunderclouds, could not restrain the laugh.

"Get on with you! Shiftless lout!"

He ducked with the perfect motion of the thriftless, much-battered poor, slid oil-wise round the door-jamb and was gone.

AFTER BREWING a further thunderous while, she said, "I had no business taking you out there."

Not what a Tower-bred man would expect, no. Not what he should have had to bear, who had never even met the weight of eyes in the mannerly streets of Amberlight. Let be shoving through a press of laborers who did not know him from the next slop-porter, skirmishing to avoid the kennel-slush among whores' bullies and beggars and petty—or not so petty—criminals. Abused for simply being there. Punched in the ribs in one of the tighter scrambles as I fought to keep her from crushing against the wall.

Not to mention, in a darker alleyway, the hand, ownerless, invisible, that pinched me hard as a lascivious crab on the rump.

Entirely unmentionable, that any decent Amberlight woman should have died of shame before she put me in such jeopardy.

I am a decent Amberlight man. It is more than unmentionable—it is all but impossible, only to write it, even here.

That it was not just shock, bruising, shame to body and mind. That it was also enlargement. Exhilaration. Learning, as with the troublecrew, a new dimension of myself. A new life.

Right down to the pinch.

I sat down beside her. Looking straight ahead, I said, "You needed somebody."

She made a strange little sound and pushed her forehead against my sleeve. Half-crying, half-laughing, she answered, "I need you both."

WHEN THE TIME had crawled to sunset, we went downstairs. Chose something to eat. Watched the dark ooze down into the street-glare like inexorably deepening mist, until we could bear it no longer. We were perched side by side on that lamentable bed, trying to pretend no cockroaches had moved below the candle, when he slipped the latch up on the door.

A long time after, Tellurith asked, "Where did you go?"

He shifted his head on my shoulder; sighed, and untangled his mouth from a coil of her hair. In Riversend autumn comes dank and coldly, especially down in the slums. The clammy chill fingered through to us, even knotted three together under the inn's tatty padded quilt.

"I went," he answered, "to my—father-in-law."

She must have known—he must have known that she must have known—long since. How could a House-head not know? Yet against my side his muscles were wringing tense.

Tellurith put an elbow up on his shoulder and reached to tap the brazier. More wood-dust fell off the inner tongue onto the coals.

"Not a friend, but obliged to help, for his own sake. For his sake, not likely to talk. Not bad," she said.

Alkhes laughed. Surprised out of him, a concussion of breath.

"Gods, Tel . . . !"

"You told me you were married." She cuddled complacently into his back. "*Once*."

"What," I intervened politely, "did he say?"

"He wasn't best pleased to see me, no." It went through his muscles clear as expression on a face: stretch, relax, re-tense. Relief, habitual complacency of a good soldier reporting success. Memory of the report. "But yes, anything to avoid a fuss. I sent a message with his steward from the gate." A different easing now, as his mind turned to analyze as well as recall.

"I moved heaven and earth to get that command; but I was the Emperor's own appointee. Antastes, thank all the gods," he really meant that, "isn't mean-minded. When the crash came, he didn't take it out on everyone else."

Tellurith waited a good while before she murmured, "So your friends . . ."

"Have been very lucky." Bleaker, more bitter, than old mid-winter snow.

We waited, until at last, he went on.

"Kuashir doesn't know the threads. He's a merchant, he just sees results. And of course, he's kept his head down. He's jumpy as a grasshopper, or he'd never have whipped me in like that. But so far, he hasn't been touched."

Very gently, Tellurith laid her cheek against his hair.

"It's not that bad, clythx." He rolled over, gathering her close. "They've been demoted, posted to dead-ends, they've—disappeared, the way people in the Army can. But nobody's been arraigned for treason, nobody's been executed, there hasn't been a witch hunt or a wholesale purge or . . ."

Whatever worse he could imagine, we left in his own mind.

"Of course I don't have a leg to stand on over there." He had steadied his voice. "And anyone in the imperial demesne . . ."

Was beyond the scribes' wall. Out of reach.

Very carefully, Tellurith began, "Did you—ah—"

"Did I have enemies this side? Of course I did, the Army's an enemy. Especially anyone who pushed them around like I did over Amberlight. But . . ."

Something—firecrackers, probably, Riversend poor quarters dote on them—exploded in the street: whamm, pop-pop-pop! All three of us jumped.

When his heart quieted under my arm, I repeated, "But."

His ribs lifted to the sharp, sudden breath.

"But the whole merchant quarter's jumpy. Kuashir kept saying, 'I'll tell you what I know, that's all. No other questions, no upsets, no compromising *my* friends, we've been left alone and we want to be left alone.'"

I knew Tellurith's silence meant she was shuffling her knowledge of Riversend. By his tension, he knew it too.

"So," she said too casually, "it's probably a lord."

Every muscle in his body twitched. Alkhes, who has the iron command of the trained intelligencer.

He caught himself. Drew a long, ragged breath.

"It may very well be—Yes, to upset the entire merchants' quarter it has to be—among the l-lords."

I know more than I am saying, warned that flaw in his voice. More than I can say. Don't try to make me. Don't ask.

Tellurith slid an arm over his back, drawing the pair of us close.

"Then I think it's my turn," she said.

"ANTASTES WAS a Crown Prince. He's been upRiver. If I go to the Emperor as an Amberlight Ruand, I need an entourage."

She announced that over our breakfast hot milk and noxiously sweet rolls. In the slums of Riversend, coffee, that staple of Amberlight, that life's necessity, is unknown. When Alkhes opened his mouth she pointed the cup at him and said, "Women." When I opened my mouth her eye swiveled and I shut it again.

"You," to his address, "are staying indoors. You're too well known. You," to mine, "will be my bodyguard. I," setting the cup down, "am going to the marble agent. Today."

For the first time in my life I took a concealed troublecrew dagger. We wore our traveling clothes, good cover through the tenements, but when we worked our way into merchant country I saw they might be more hindrance than help. When we had been repulsed from the third granite palace's doorway, I began to comprehend the will of a Ruand.

She battered her way into the quay-Head's office by sheer moral threat. By then I was growing used to men in positions of power; and to her doorman-tactics, a mixture of arrogance and scorn. When the bald-headed little snirp behind the polished desk put down his quill to stare, I met her higher grade of bullying.

The priest's order had gone straight to the temple. "And how, madam, am I responsible if it arrives three weeks late? I do not run the River; only the docks." But, he finally admitted, there was an agent for Iskardan marble. "Suri used to do it, years and years. Until—" his lower lip protruded, but he evaded her eye. "Not good enough for the new factor, apparently. He dealt with the Hejjami. Certainly I know, madam. Turn up-river at the corner. Their warehouse is third past the last pier."

It was a Hejjam Tez had dealt with, singular. Her name was painted across the warehouse lintel, as Riversend traders do, above the dirty old blue paint in staring yellow half a hand high. "The Widow Hejjam. Freight and Shipping. Specialty Long Haul Trade." The last words did not quite erase the under-pattern, which had read, "Amberlight."

Nor did any amount of staring erase the locks, their wards already rusting, on the shut, deserted door.

Tellurith did not stare anywhere near so long as Alkhes. Just time for her face to sharpen, before she turned on a heel and made for the shippers next door.

"No, ma'am." He was the warehouse foreman, but she had been subduing male stevedores before she was ten. "Ol' Hejjam died, oh, eighteen months past, the widow just took his half and carried on. Lotta women do, round here. Then three weeks, maybe a moon past, it happened. Apprentices, clerks, porters come to work one day, and phut! Doors closed, locks up. Widow gone."

Tellurith's face got sharper so fast he backed away. Her eyes flicked round again. I saw the knowledge, the expectations of a Head, to which my troublecrew lore was baby talk.

Her eye walked the foreman up and down. She took a couple of silver darrin from the inner purse; dandled them in her fingers; enquired of the River prospect, "Trouble of some sort?"

"No'm." It came too readily for misunderstanding, and too concernedly for a lie. "Nobody saw—nobody heard—a thing."

"And you would have heard."

He held her eyes. "The Widow was well-liked here. We'd've heard."

Tellurith stared at the River: honed, high-cheekboned Amberlight profile, redoubtable, tightened Ruand's mouth. We both watched expectantly. We both recognized what we saw.

"I was looking for the Iskardan marble agent." This time she took out the purse. "I wanted some women who knew what to do with their hands." The purse opened. Her palm cupped the subtle fall of silver coins. "But I reckon men—some men—would do as well."

Autumn. Dhasdein.
Tellurith's Diary

HE WAS the neighbor's foreman; he had announced his House the widow's friend. It was really no greater gamble than shaping a statuette. He did shy a little when he realized I wanted convoying into the palace itself, but only till we chaffered the hire-price. I provided the money. We hired, together, the gear and clothes. He found the men.

So I stalked up to the imperial gate as a Ruand should, with the great brooch at my throat, troublecrew behind me, and a liveried posse of retainers on their heels. And when the scribes' underling had been passed up the hierarchy to Alkhes, who sneered, and Sarth, who gave the impression without moving a muscle of a dead rat under his nose, I announced, "I am a Ruand of Amberlight. I presume you understand what that means?"

He did not. His superior did not. And before admitting it, they would have died.

As we paraded along amid the other fortunates, Alkhes moved up, with the utmost deference, to my elbow. Only my ear could have found the laugh half-choking him as he murmured, "I presume you know where we're going?"

I swept my hand to set the fan on its wrist-band swinging. "Wherever they go."

Naturally I did not mean that wholesale. All too clearly the ranks were multitude, but the stream separated slowly enough to keep the best-dressed in sight. We paced down shady avenues over splendidly smooth flagstones, past statues, pergolas, fountains, along fabulous arcades. In the imperial quarter, they use glass in the very roof. I still see the sun riddling that arbor with shafts of azure and emerald, blazing like opal on the iridescent trains of the peacocks beneath. As for the animals, the exotic trees . . .

The courtiers.

We never met. Down an avenue, across a garden's prospect, we glimpsed some legendary nosegay of wealth and rank, the posture of impossibly lofty breeding, the beauty only power can buy. They do not do business. At least, not as it is understood by the Court.

Our stream held wealthy merchants, scribe department-Heads; lesser lords, visiting potentates. My eye did pick out a Verrain embassy, obviously private, a couple of petty nobles from Quetzistan; that tint of cast-bronze skin, not to mention the brocade robes and tiny caps, is unmistakable. There was even some minor mission from Cataract. At least, if that was not a Heartland cow-hide cloak my eyes are giving out. That alone told me our choice was right.

The hall was, needless to say, sumptuous: clusters of exquisite mahogany furniture, colored glass in tall windows, some kind of flat brocaded covering; not plaster, not tapestries, not—the Mother knows, never again— the marbling of qherrique, on the walls. And gate-keepers, at the door.

"An Amberlight embassy. Ruand, the Emperor is honored beyond reckoning." This one knew the proper level of respect, the correct title; knowing that, he had to know both what an absolute prodigy and what anomalies we were. An Amberlight Ruand, in Riversend; with a train of men. But his control was as perfect as his manicure. He bowed me, without hesitation, without hindrance, with never the most delicate intimation of a bribe, into the hall.

"If the Ruand will be seated?" How did he convey that there was an order, that as a noble of Amberlight I would naturally respect it, without recourse to words? "If the Ruand wishes anything else?"

Anything else included refreshments: wine, if not Wave Island red, a respectable white; tea of a dozen varieties; coffee; a bevy of succulent morning cakes. Had I wanted it, the bearers' attentions explained with equal delicacy, I could have had one of them as well.

And when the audience term ended, it was with more delicate protestations that their master convoyed us out.

"Ruand, I am prostrated. Devastated. The press of business is impossible. But if the Ruand deigns to waste more of her time on us, tomorrow I am sure, I can swear . . ."

AWAY FROM THE GATE, the hired men dismissed, the wide, elegant street empty, Alkhes said, "It's no use."

On such a note that I stopped dead and stared.

He was staring away down the avenue. The muscle of his jaw was clenched; more spasmed than resolute.

I said, "How do you know?"

"I know the Court. He knows who you are, he'll know why you're here. Better than we do. If he was going to let you in, he would have whipped you past the rest of them and into—wherever—today."

I looked at that jawline, white-wealed, and bit my tongue on, Where, if not the Emperor?

Sarth opened his mouth. I jogged his elbow and said, "Three times is fair trial. I don't see that I need the others again. But I'm coming back."

In the taproom, rank with stale beer, deserted on the third mid-afternoon, Alkhes demanded, "How much money's left?"

In the tone I had heard wounded at Amberlight ask, Will I lose my leg? I answered, "Enough."

"Don't be crazy, Tellurith! Just to live's costing us fifty a day. The clothes—the bribes—! You can't get credit . . . my funds are gone . . .!"

The sweat on his forehead glistened in the half-dark. There was something near panic in his voice.

I looked at Sarth. "Will you get me another mug?"

Sour, thin, Dhasdein beer. I cannot bear the stuff. He went without a word. I slid up the stool to touch Alkhes' shoulder and asked softly, "What is it, my dear?"

He flinched as if I had grabbed him on a burn. "What is—gods, Tel, we're destitute in Riversend under an imperial summons that we can't answer and no way to leave—isn't that enough?"

"No."

"Tel—!"

One is not House-head without learning when people as well as qherrique have been pushed too far. Sarth came round the doorjamb. I set my hand to rest between Alkhes' shoulderblades and felt the fine crimson wool sodden as the saddlecloth on a panicked horse. Looked up as Sarth arrived and said, "What chance do we have of finding Tez?"

Autumn. Dhasdein.
Meditations. Alkhes-Assandar

I can't tell her. I can't face it. I can't even write it down.

The gods forfend I have nightmares about it, because then she will ask. And she'll mean to know.

The gods be thanked for Tez, who is distraction, a pretext—*how* can I think that? Who is as much a *necessity* as reaching the emperor.

Even if, without reaching the emperor, we don't have a snowball's chance in a Verrain sandstorm of getting her out.

But it's been something to try. Tellurith's project. How I wish she'd been my chief of staff. She knows I haven't a contact left across-River, but I do know the system. Tez won't be a prisoner of war, she's a political detainee. That means the Citadels.

Out of Riversend. Up the River. Without the proper permits and signatures, impregnable.

But even Riversend citadels are manned by human beings. And they have shifts. And they come into the city, and somewhere they have houses, and families, and places they buy food, or eat.

And drink.

And I know, from scribe-skirmishes over twenty years of Army life, that Citadel people are Army to the rest of Riversend.

So I have been dispatched to the Army taverns this last week. With—gods help us—too much of our money, and another cover: "A veteran, clythx, what else would you be?" A surly mood and my own story as front, to scour the quarter clean.

Easy enough, for any competent intelligencer. I know the argot, I can do the bearing in my sleep. A discharged soldier from a border garrison. Doing spy-work for a merchant family that's offended someone. No need to say who. A relative whipped up, probably, "you know where." I never thought I could make Kuashir's twitchings work for me.

Because there were earthquakes, of course, when I went. Too many big houses had invested too much, too many angry questions were asked further up the line. The waves have washed back down, in the rumors and gossip that the Army passes to and fro and out to its hangers-on. So I know about Tez.

Quartered in the Court-bank Citadel. Unharmed. "Nobody knows what in the River-lord's hell they want her for." Under someone's authority, this one saw the seal on the order to the governor.

But whose seal?

That he did not—would not? say.

And I don't have the money to find out.

BE HONEST HERE, if nowhere else.

I don't have the *courage* to find out.

———————

GIVE ME CREDIT, I've also found this rat-hole. Or Catheor found it for us. When he oozed up by me in the alleyway I damn near did die of the shock, after I near killed him instead.

"Whoa, sir, whoa, damn y'r eyes—!" Yanking his cloak between us, the knife-counter I taught him against Oasis raiders, instinctive as the yelp. He remains a cavalryman.

"Thought it was you, sir," drawling, while I disappeared the dagger and worked my heart back through my teeth. "Remember scouting in t' Hamadryah bazaar?"

Out of uniform and unshaven as I. Born Shirran, as I was. Mercenary, as I had been. Troop-second, my right arm for six long months in the Verrain border-guard.

And if nobody else would know that reference, anyone can be turned. Except, what did we have to hide?

"Less ruffians scoffing imperial rations, huh?" I said. We gripped elbows, Verrain fashion, both starting to grin. "Blast me, it's a wonder the god of lies han't run away with you," he said, laughing; and still laughing, "Sir, what're you doing *here*?"

Grinning, I let my eyes, as in Hamadryah, say, Where?

"Lemme buy you a drink for old times, anyhow." Arm round my back, sweeping us both along crony-style, hand under the tangle of cloaks pinching my biceps, one, two, one, one: danger. Watch out.

Not waiting for the suspicion of an inn and heads together, saying it out casually, an old friend's discussion, as we walked.

"You pulled the wheel off the store-cart when *you* fell out. There's more'n grass-wrens," slang for officers, red-crests, "after you, there's plenty'd ease a grudge for money right down here." We were in my own quarter: the flick of his eyes told me he believed it truth. "I dunno what you want, sir, but you better up-sign," shift ground, uproot the standard, "at the double, if you wanna get out."

I smiled back into his smile and said, "Imperial summons. I can't."

"Do you tell me now? After all this time!" His voice rose, as at some astonishing gossip. Whatever else I taught him, he learnt intelligencing well. "Is that so?"

We walked, I smiled, he, clearly, furiously, thought. I kept quiet. It is neither kindness nor justice to push a man preparing to risk his livelihood as well as his life.

"Tell you what, whyn't you come home with me this evening; see the brats, meet the wife?" He stopped, smile firm, eyes telling me the rest.

"Gods know, we haven't got much, this city don't care for cast-off soldiers, but ... we're down in the boats."

The smile spoke embarrassment. The eyes said, Do it fast. I smiled back and answered with equal embarrassment. "I, um, have some people myself ..."

"Sure! Bring 'em! Bring your stuff! Stay the night!"

Which is how we have withdrawn on this leaky sampan, with an awning over the midships fire-plate and a chicken-house astern for nights. Stacked in the depth of boat-town, where nothing short of an imperial sortie can override a veritable fusillade of alarms, from bawling babies to irate geese, where any attack must thread a maze of boats and gangplanks a child could twitch loose, where a couple of slashes with a guard-knife can have us in mid-stream.

Strange to be welcome in such a place. I have lived in them often enough, but never in good faith. Never known myself welcome, for my own sake; another renegade, disgraced soldier, too familiar for remark but not for acceptance, on the shady side of the law.

At least, the gods be thanked, we have an escort, however ramshackle. Catheor knew, I know, how easy it would have been, back in the merchant quarter. A couple of gold fenn, a posse to the inn, a few bravos in the street. A passing brawl, another murder. Who would remark on it?

And just as well we have backing, considering the madness on which Tellurith has embarked.

Autumn. Dhasdein.
Tellurith's Diary

ARE WE TO SIT twiddling our thumbs till the Emperor lets us rot? To attend the palace only takes the afternoon; with Catheor's crew and a sedan chair I am perfectly safe. The Mother knows, to run an intelligence intrigue atop that would be half an hour's consultation a day in Amberlight, and I have an intelligencer. He fumes and splutters that we can never breach the Citadels, never find a forger, without palace ratification it will never work. Mother's eyes! I have a forger, and I know quite well she will not talk. I have a line into the jail-shifts already. Meanwhile, my other business is not a full morning's work. A little patience will give us citadel routine, and then we can think about a boat. In a little while, I will have the money to set that in motion. In a while more, there may be money for a good deal else.

I must admit, it is Sarth who should have credit for that. After all, it did begin before Alkhes turned up Catheor.

Sarth and I had been to the market, that self-same morning, to eke out the cook-stalls' work with what passes for fresh produce in Riversend. I had already found an old woman who sold black-market apples and late-season beans from some Delta farm. I had also learnt—how quickly—to ignore the stares, the stupid comments, to slap off invasive hands. Amberlight looks, it seems, are most uncommon in the capital; and highly esteemed, and the poor quarter had no scruples about showing it. To us both.

At worst, Sarth would produce his knife; they can read the message of troublecrew training that says he knows its use. So when the bleating and catching at our sleeves began, we simply walked a little faster, heading for the edge of the impromptu market stalls and a place to turn.

"Sir, lady!—sir!" Province idiom; the Delta, like the River, uses "Ma'am." "Just one moment, for the Lord's love, wait!"

He had stopped grabbing; as I swung round it was the tone of that last plea that pulled my slap.

A fair-sized man, bulky shoulders, but not a fighter's grace. Artisan's leather apron. Indoor skin, a well-fed belly, a blacksmith's hands. With an embossed gold ring whose like is marked at a thousand darrin in noble quarter shops. Squinting up at me like a toddler who sees her life's desire and does not dare to grab.

It was that, or the honest confusion, so unlike pimps or the pimps' customers, that made me say, "Can we help you, sir?"

He sucked in a breath that tightened his gut. "Lady—uh—lady, I'm a sculptor. Working down at Nahan's temple, just over there. And uh, I'm aware you're quality, but, um, I saw you in the market and I know it's an impertinence but I thought I'd ask . . ."

His hand waved, the ring spraying gold to the rare autumn sun. The inflection on "sculptor" had said, Unlike everyone else, I don't consider myself scum. Nor was Nahan's temple "just" over there; it was the merchant quarter's shrine to the River-lord, a bedizened edifice with gilded column capitals the length of its nave.

"Ask," I said, "what?"

His shoulders almost relaxed. "Lady, you are a fount of beneficence and I quench my thirst at your spring—it's the god. I'm commissioned to do a new statue. Been commissioned three months. I know the pose, I've got the block, beautiful Heartland porphyry. But I can't—I can't—"

He stuck. We stared at him. He wrung his hands and burst out, "Lady, I can't find the model I want!"

We stared in pure bewilderment while he, with a look as if he had just confessed to the filthiest of vices, stared back.

"Er," I managed. Mother, I thought, if he can't work to the patterns, what does it have to do with us? "Ah?"

"Strethilis, lady, name's Strethilis, I've made stuff for half the nobles' quarter, I've a piece in Lord Tanekhet's country house and I can swear to you, there's no hanky-panky in my establishment even when I use a girl. I treat 'em like daughters and I—ah—" Whatever my eyes said, he began turning crimson. "Lady, I can—I can—pay . . ."

The last was clearly the fundament of obscenity. He stared at the ground. But he did not leave.

I gathered my wits. Took breath. Sarth's hand shut on my arm.

"Ruand," he said, "I think he wants one of us."

I can only suppose I was still thinking Amberlight, where the statuettes' shape had been tradition for six hundred years. I should suppose my eyes bulged. Sculpt divinity from a human form? From the form of an Amberlight Ruand, which no dweller in Riversend should ever have seen?

Sarth's hand tightened. It was a palpable jerk. "I think," he said, "he means me."

Expose my husband, the highest Uphill blood of Amberlight, in some Delta sculptor's work-room? Have his features immortalized under the profane gaze of Riversend blood-suckers begging—or, utter outrage— mooning after their outland god? I took breath to roar, I'll die in a gutter first!

Strethilis had read it all on my face. "Lady I know you've got the say and your men are kept tighter than a Cataract harem and I'm sorry I never meant it to be sacrilege and I'll apologize, I do apologize, I'll burn incense just don't give me a curse . . ." He was backing away, both hands up. And in his eyes the hopeless, the helpless yearning of a craftsman, who confronts in beauty not only its own glamour, but the fleshing of his Craft's desire.

Across me Sarth said in the purest of tower-bred accents, "How much?"

As Strethilis' own jaw dropped he went on, "May I say one word, Ruand?" And gently, inexorably, backed me to the nearest alley wall.

"We need money. He has money. He's working on a wealthy temple. He understands who—what we are. He won't—he wouldn't dare lay a finger on me."

I stared up into his eyes. At that splendid body, the beautiful face, under its crown of tended hair. At my husband, who should never have been exposed to the streets of Amberlight, let alone the slums of Riversend.

"Tellurith, it's one thing I can do!"

Anguish clear as in that lion's stare. I may be just a pretty face and a bed-toy and auxiliary troublecrew, that look said. Let me do what I can.

I turned on my heel, walked back to Strethilis, and said, "How much?"

HIS WORKSHOP was on the margin of the workers' quarter, an old spice-seller's store. He had torn half the roof out, substituting a single sheet of Riversend glass. Beneath was the usual chaos of sketches, tools, models, mud and bronze drippings and stone-chips, torn clothes and meals' debris littered throughout. Strethilis lived, when he remembered, on the workshop floor. His furnace, the store-rooms, block-hoists and other paraphernalia and the house watchmen filled the lower floor. All this we saw as he ushered us, still talking a River fresh, up the stairs.

The going rate for artists' models in Riversend was twenty darrin an hour; for living costs, little enough. "But, lady, I'd pay your man fifty, I've been stuck three whoreson months!" He knew, of course, that I would accompany them; as he yanked back the skylight shutters and whipped the cover off a massive lump of clay and scuttered after shaping tools he found time to scrape up a chair. "It's sound, used it for my seated Justice, just last year." He cast a somewhat bemused glance over gilt arms and legs carven with dragonettes. I could tell, from Sarth's demure look, he was working not to laugh. "Now'm, if you just make yourself comfortable . . ."

The River-lord was to appear stepping from His stream, one leg almost knee-deep. Tilted on one shoulder He would hold an enormous bowl, from which the River would pour back into the water at His feet. "They've asked for a fountain, they know hydraulics is my specialty. Lord, it's no trouble, just pump the water up a pipe behind the arm, plenty of pressure in Riversend plumbing, no trouble at all—um—"

The trouble, it emerged, was with the bowl.

"I can't find a model in the city that can hold the thing ten minutes, let alone hold it the way I want. But your man, lady," he eyed Sarth's shoulders hungrily, "he's got the build for it. Lord, not even those Archipelago athletes're made like that."

The River was a hip-bath which he filled from an upstairs tap; mistaking the looks on our faces at a luxury unknown since Amberlight, he assured us, "I've sent Shen for the braziers, won't be a minute till we have the place warmed up."

Despite the sun-patches it was, to be sure, another mean autumn Delta day, but the building was comfortable enough. At my look of puzzlement Strethilis began reddening again.

Resignedly I said, "What's the rest?"

He forgot the tap and plaited his hands like a temple supplicant. "Uh—uh—"

In Riversend, it seems, it is not enough to portray the gods in human form. That form must also be unclothed.

"Lady, I thought you knew!"

Knowing perfectly well I did not. I tightened my arms to get out of the chair.

Then I looked at Sarth.

He was a little pale, certainly. But he met my eyes squarely. And for all the consternation, the undoubtedly tried modesty, there was determination in the set of his mouth.

Strethilis was not as gauche as he pretended. He gave us a minute or two before he murmured into the floor, "In Riversend—it's an honor, to portray a god."

I looked at Sarth. He looked at me. Strethilis looked at the cubicle in the corner, where a shabby curtain hung. Evidently his models were granted privacy, at least, at the start.

I said, "Are you ready, Sarth?"

Autumn. Dhasdein.
Journal kept by Sarth

NOT SINCE SETHAR finished schooling me, I realize, have I taken my clothes off for a man.

Ridiculous that behind Strethilis' dirty curtain my heart was going pit-a-pat. That only sheer memory moved me, elegantly, deliberately, as in those lamplit Tower rooms, to Sethar's guiding voice. Down to beginning with my boots.

The very Towers of Amberlight had heard about artists. I do not know what I expected. I know I was prepared to put up with much. The moment Strethilis' eyes grabbed me I knew that if he lusted for me it was not as myself.

"The foot a little higher on the block—so. Ah, the thigh muscling—exquisite. The torso flexed—the definement, oh, yes. The shoulder, turn, so. Lord, skin like polished silk. Now the head. Your chin up . . . Lords of the forge, that profile, a carver would die." Lust, yes, and sated. But it was the lust of Craft. "And now—"

The bowl was no counterfeit. It was bronze, a quarter inch thick, big enough to sacrifice a bull over; I could just compass its circumference. But he wanted it held almost vertical, grasped over my right arm and shoulder, level with my head. Even without the load, that pose was bad enough.

I may have managed ten minutes before my biceps began to quake. Strethilis was deep in his mystery, but the minute he realized the spatula went flying.

"Down, yes, I'll take it." For all his sculptor's muscles it made him grunt. "No, no, don't think of apologizing, that's twice anyone else's time, put this on, just sit down, I'll be back—" Tellurith helped me into the dingy, plaster-daubed robe: but for all its age, it was fur-lined.

After two more sessions my muscles would spasm at first grasp. By then he had the armature of the model set up and clay packed about one leg. "Have to sort out load-bearing before I touch the block. Now get that robe on and over to the brazier, I've sent Shen to Argit's, sit down, lad, you're clemmed." I had lost 'lord' before the second session finished. "Where did I put . . ." He stopped patting my shoulders and began to ferret through the mess. "Ah."

Coins poured like the River-lord's own waterfall. At Tellurith's grunt he gave her a defiant stare.

"Fifty an hour I said, but this is worth every fiel, m'lady, now don't argue, here." Cascading, overflowing her hands. "Take it, I can afford it, Lord, I'd pay double, just bring him back."

Fifty, a hundred, a hundred and fifty darrin. Shoveling in rice and water-buffalo steak from the nearest cook-shop, I watched Tellurith count. A week's living, a week's rescue time, a week's hope. For thirty minutes' work.

WHEN CATHEOR ARRIVED that afternoon there was no time to boast. By the time we were established in this mud-float I thought the whole thing would be lost from mind. But when we creaked out to a quayside cook-stall for breakfast, Tellurith measured the distance up-River; swallowed half her mug of milk-sludge, and gave me a nod. "We might be late," she said. "I'll send a message to Strethilis."

We were late, of course, because we had to spend a three-hour shouting match with Alkhes first.

I let Tellurith do it. She is the decision-maker. I am trained, but only as troublecrew; neither of us knows Riversend. But when Tellurith chooses, with or without qherrique, I swear, she does it with the gods.

So by noon I was knee-deep in the water-tub. We had just begun the second session when the courier arrived.

At the knock on the open door Strethilis ground his teeth. Catching Tellurith's eye, his hunted stare changed. "Lord, yes, honor me."

When my biceps gave out, Tellurith brought him the stuff.

He undid the sealed paper one-handed. Riversend uses beaten papyrus. Cracked it out. Scanned the seal, gave a grunt and a jerk to the bag in his other hand. A dark maroon, fist-sized bag of glove-leather, with a weight and clink you cannot mistake.

"Not before time, either. He had the thing a full moon ago." He looked vaguely about him, then tossed bag and paper among the mallets and dirty mugs on the closest bench.

I visibly saw Tellurith catch her breath. Once and always, she is a House-head, to whom accounting upholds the world.

Carefully she said, "Strethilis? What was that?"

"Wood-nymph and panther. For Lord Drusis' inner hall. Life-size. Shirran bronze." He picked up the last hot drink Shen had left and took a hearty gulp. Proprietary reminiscence faded as his eyes went back to the model. "I'm not sure about that right thigh . . ."

"Was that the payment?" He nodded. "Strethilis, can I ask: what will you do with it?"

"Well, I'm not too sure. Shift the knee forward, perhaps—oh. Oh, suppose I'll count it sometime. He will pay in gold . . ."

Tellurith took a bigger breath. Gently, so gently, she said, "Strethilis? Who does your accounts?"

THERE WAS SOMETHING like eight thousand darrin scattered round that workshop, in gold and silver and banker's pledges, in cloak pockets, cupboards, buried under plates. A thousand of them had come in that bag. Tellurith was three days assembling and counting it, before she tackled the question of receipts.

Outlays were recorded, if at all, in a crow's-nest of papers and tallies behind Shen's plates. Getting that straight gave her another week in an apoplectic paradise, where Strethilis joined her when she told him he needed a bank.

"Lady, I don't know a thing about money, I don't need the stuff, I've got my work—! Lad, just hold that a minute more—" He let out a yelp. Muscles tremoring, I let the bowl down. Tellurith had taken the clay from his hand.

"I don't have the *time* for this stuff—!"

Then his mouth shut. He narrowed his eyes. Cocked his head and enquired, with ingratiation that lacked all doubt, "Lady, I don't suppose . . . ?"

Composedly, Tellurith stared back at him. "I don't want to cheat you," she said. "Forty darrin an hour?"

He pays her fifty. Tellurith is scrupulous, she charges only the time she works, and she says that is little more than an hour a day. But after Strethilis began singing her praises in his local tavern, the neighboring spice-agent knocked on his door. And then there was his shipper, and the shipper's brother, and next thing the temple almoner's messenger stopped her in the street.

So the workshop has been augmented by Tellurith's desk and chair, and a scrupulously tidy locked chest that holds accounts, Shen has become Catheor's lieutenant, and every two or three days, Catheor's crew escort Strethilis' takings and our wages to a reputable shipper's bank. Where the wages barely touch before Tellurith sets them to work.

I think she has found a forger. I do know she has sent a message to Tez. Meanwhile we go every day to the palace, to sample tea and cakes and change courtly smiles. Tellurith's patience is monumental as her will.

And the model is finished. Strethilis is ready for the block.

And we have been here—gods, will I ever see Iskarda again?—near another entire moon.

Autumn. Dhasdhein.
Meditations. Alkhes-Assandar

GODS HELP ME. Gods defend me. Can all the gods in heaven tell me: what am I going to do?

XII

Autumn. Dhasdein.
Journal kept by Sarth

~~MOTHER OF~~—
~~Giver and~~—
Curse You, are You going to let me pray?

Autumn. Dhasdein.
Meditations. Alkhes-Assandar

MY HANDS ARE still shaking. If I let myself think I'll throw up again. Oh, gods save me, I ought to be raving. I ought to be ecstatic. In the name of all that rules the universe, why must it happen like this?

She is quite tranquil. Quite matter-of-fact. About everything. Her accounting, her palace siege, prostituting Sarth to some cursed marble-chipper, her damnable machinations over Tez.

Quite calm when she told us this morning. Perched on the boat-side, nursing the cup of tepid milk. Staring across neighbors' backs and brats and flotsam, into the half-broken fog. For Riversend, a clear, almost pure autumn day. She lifted her face to it, letting the sunshine slide like nectar down her throat.

Before she turned to the pair of us and said, "I'm with child."

SHE WAS only sure, she says, this very morning. When the old moon looked into our chicken-coop as we made ready to rise. Making her pause; think; begin to count.

Realize her last cycle was before Mid-summer's Day.

One missed month, Tellurith says, could be anything. Change of climate. Stress. Two is something else. Not everyone, she says, gets sick. And it is, she says, too early to show.

It was Mid-summer night. I am sure of it. We are all, I think, sure of it. I look at them, and see the memory in their eyes.

If it is so, I have no need, no wish to ask: is it his or mine?

Gods, beyond the paralysis, the thunderbolt. The disbelief. The belief. There is the, the, how am I to say it. . . ?

Joy.

And beyond her felicity, his.

I ought to feel the same. I may have done it for her; it may be my seed that has gifted them both.

But, gods of the universe, why must it happen *now*?

Autumn. Dhasdein.
Tellurith's Diary

BLESSED MOTHER, Shaper and Maker.

What am I to say?

Autumn. Dhasdein.
Journal kept by Sarth

I AM STILL ANGRY.

I have gone out and bought fruit for You. Burnt incense, sacrificed flowers. When the moon comes round, I will do as the old wise-woman at the pier-head says, the nearest thing we have to a seer, and give You my blood.

Anything to be sure, this time, that it is all right.

Including, blight upon Your immortal machinations, that I must give in. Bow my head and submit myself back under Your yoke.

Because You have requited me—us.

Even for Mid-winter.

Even for Alkhes.

SHE IS SO HAPPY. Bloomed like some queen of legend, dreaming, glorious. I could weep, looking at her. I could sing her triumph hymns, I could take her, in what passes for a Riversend festival, to some nobles' dining-house, to squander our money on exotic wines all night.

Whatever I do, it will not help Alkhes.

If Tellurith thinks I missed it, her estimate of me has slipped. How could anyone Tower-bred miss it? There is something here, in our fix, in Riversend, that threatens him alone.

His terror. His fault.

How could anyone miss it, who sleeps with him every night?

Tellurith has not spoken. Like me, she knows how much he can bear. That he cannot so much as mention it says more than enough.

No wonder he is torn in half. No wonder this child is the summit of felicity—and terror's abyss. Because if I or Tellurith can be made hostage, can make him vulnerable—what price could be exacted for her child?

And the crisis is approaching inexorably. The moment when he will have to explain it. Meet it, face to face.

Only by doing so can we reach the Emperor. Get Tez. Leave Riversend. As we must leave Riversend.

All in a moment, there is no time left.

Autumn. Dhasdein.
Tellurith's Diary

I WANT ZURI.

I want Iatha, I want Caitha and Hanni and Shia and Quetho and Hayras, Charras, Ahio, Zariah, Verrith, Azo, Desis, oh, sweet work-Mother, I want my whole House around me, down to the men like Huis and Roskeran, the daughters like Asaskian, down to the merest newborn child.

I even want Darthis.

Carrying before, I always had a fortress round me. Telluir, Amberlight. The qherrique. Even after the first time, when anticipation was less hope than dread.

It is my belly now that aches. Wanting to curl tight, to wrap myself around it, to stave off perils with my naked flesh. And the Mother knows, that very flesh can feel them. Ridiculous, when I have gone shieldless two months and more, to become frantic now.

I only know what my body tells me. I need protection, I need succor. I want Iatha. Most of all, I want Zuri. Troublecrew. Women's wards. Guardians I can trust.

Failing that, I want us—Tez, my men, above all, this precious, precious burden—out of here.

Autumn. Dhasdein.
Journal kept by Sarth

I DID NOT KNOW. I swear to all the gods, You included, I did not know!

She must have had directions from Strethilis. I know he knows the Imperial Quarter inside out. I daresay he has actually had audience with the Emperor.

It was so simple: a word to Alkhes at breakfast, "Caissyl, I think there's something different about Exenor," the audience hall gate-keeper. "Could you come along today?" The usual debarkation, chair left with Catheor's ruffians at the outer gate, the usual bland courtesies to the scribe-crew, if I could grind that smile down their throats! The usual promenade into the Quarter's labyrinth—

And blandly off down a colonnade temporarily deserted, round a corner that obliterated the suppliants' stream, under an arbor whose statuary must have been done by Strethilis, into a entry where Alkhes got breath to yelp, "Tellurith!"

"Caissyl." She patted his arm. She did not look round. "Just down here, it's quite all right."

He was in mid-arch before he managed to balk. She slid through his arm and strode out, in her long-skirted bronze coat and rust-gold shirt and chrysanthemum-embroidered leggings, into a sea of emerald and golden fire.

The portal opens on a park of sorts: grass, the deep, deep green of grass turning toward Riversend winter, under deciduous southern trees. In the bleak, misty, low-skied afternoon, she swept like a fire-spirit beneath their fire-clad branches, amid drifts that crackled like flake-fire round her boots. Alkhes is fast on his feet. Sheer shock, or knowledge of the blasphemy, hampered him just long enough.

"My greetings." She had rounded the little marble pergola, white as a snow-ghost against the emerald grass and blazing leaves, cut across the further lawn and confronted the guard at the ornately fretted marble gate. "I am the Ruand of Amberlight."

They were Imperials. What else would they be? Gorgeous in parade cuirasses, hefting a pair of eight-foot ceremonial pikes. I did not have to see Alkhes squeeze shut his eyes.

The senior guard inclined his purple-plumed helmet. I half-thought to see his eyes painted, but the jewel was in his ear. He said, "Ma'am. May I direct you to the audience hall?"

"I am here," said Tellurith, with the autocrat's supreme confidence, "to see the Emperor."

Alkhes gulped. I grabbed his elbow, dug my fingers in to warn us both: Too late.

The senior guard was obviously a veteran. With perfect courtesy he answered, "You would most easily do that, ma'am, in the audience hall."

"Unhappily, sir, my business is an imperial summons. It will not wait."

The bow was courtly too. "Unhappily, ma'am. . ."

She took a step forward. Elegantly, they inclined their pikes from parade rest. The triangle of leveled points met before her breast.

Tellurith took a step back. Folded her hands into her coat sleeves. The senior guard bowed again. "Ma'am," he began, "I am truly sorry to disoblige you. The emperor sees visitors in—"

Tellurith took her hand out of her sleeve.

They had either seen service or knew something about Amberlight. One made a weird gulping sound, the pike-heads jerked like startled snakes. The cutter beam stood straight up in the misty air, white and incandescent as a burning sword, and Alkhes almost tore my arm out at the butt.

"Dekarch, hold rank! Wait!"

The pikes rippled. I nearly yelled aloud, Don't touch her, you'll set it off!

"We have to see the Emperor—it's an imperial summons. We've been trying two whole months!"

Some god be thanked, Tellurith kept the cutter still. Their eyes turned, rolling inside the helmet frames. Then the senior said, "And who would you be—ah—"

I felt Alkhes steel himself before he came to the military posture. "I," he said, "am the general Assandar."

They knew the name. Their eyes said it. They knew more than that. They wished they did not. They even wished to cede. But they were Imperials. As Alkhes must have known, the Emperor was their sacred trust.

"I'm very sorry, sir." The pikes steadied. "But we have standing orders. Nobody—not the Supreme Commander—passes the private gate—"

Tellurith swept the cutter before her. The pike heads fell like lopped lilies, hiss, clangg! Both the guards grunted; shock, panic, fright? Then they leapt together in the gateway with a rasp of drawn blades as Alkhes made one wild lunge and snatched her round the middle, bawling, "NO!"

The cutter beam made a searing white arc, the guards' swords whipped up and it would have been massacre except for the, "Halt!"

Near as nothing to a Craft-head's bellow. I have heard that, and I know. Even Tellurith froze.

The gates swung. The gap filled with a rustling flood of palest turquoise, silver-embossed brocade robes.

She was taller than Alkhes. Taller than Tellurith. She might have looked the guards—she did look me in the eye. Long, long eyes whose huge almonds were widened by kohl under long, long, winged brows, to match the narrow face planed back in an elongated almond from the central keel of nose. Not a pretty face. A magnificent face. Sculpted in solid mahogany, imperial as her height. As the sapphires big as thumbnails on the narrow gold tiara that spanned the multitudinous tiny plaits, studded with seed-pearls, of her thick, black, desert hair.

The guards both went down in a full prostration. Like Alkhes, I dropped on my knees.

Tellurith looked her in the eye. Inclined her head a hairsbreadth. Said, "Your Majesty." The eyes focused. Tellurith said, "I am Tellurith of Telluir House. Formerly of Amberlight."

The eyes said she did not know about the summons, or the conspiracy. She inclined her head and replied formally, "Riversend gives you welcome. May I ask . . . ?"

Tellurith took a step back and gestured. "My husband, who was once the general Assandar, had a summons from the Emperor."

The splendid brows rose. I found myself thinking, profanely, what Strethilis could do with *her*.

Then she moved back from the gateway. "I will listen," she said.

"WITH YOUR OFFICER there will be no problem. The Etheor chatelaine is G*uri."

She had left the Imperials gobbling and used her servants' escort to an actual palace room: an Empress's palace room, from the silver-coffered cedar ceiling to the malachite, sardonyx, topaz and carnelian pavement, the exquisitely carved fireplace and the golden candle-stands. Unlike a normal hostess, she had a chamberlain to seat us, two footmen to make us comfortable, three maids, with the same mahogany skin and queenly bearing, to offer sustenance. When we were warmed and eased, she laid her hands upon her knees, leant back in that delicate silver-wood chair, and commanded, "Begin."

Tellurith told it. Nearly all of it, beginning with the imperial summons. Blaming no one, remembering Tez. The empress heard her through, with hardly a change of that imperial profile. Before she straightened a little and told us what we had to know.

Etheor is the Court-bank citadel, G*uri is the main Quetzistan tribe. She was Quetzistani, unmistakably. So in the imperial free-for-all, she prevailed not by rank but by faction; by the ties of her own blood.

Whatever Tellurith's eyes said, the Empress pushed aside the all but transparent cup from which she had sipped her chocolate, and spoke as if they were alone.

"He married me for Quetzistan. And so he can never be sure I married him."

Quetzistan is the wide, wild, eastern province beyond Riversrun. Nomad country, desert country, its folk kin in color and near in land and too kin in custom to Verrain. He had married her, as some great clan leader, to bind their loyalty. That their loyalty needed such binding ensured he would never trust the bond.

She trusted us enough to speak so. Perhaps she recognized, in Tellurith, a rank to understand hers. Despite what else she had said.

That she could not override our enemy. Could not get us to the Emperor.

Tellurith set her cup down, the grace of a Head's signal, preparing to rise. "Majesty, you have been gracious beyond reckoning. If our poor House had a gift worthy of you, I would offer amends for my intrusion in a way that would not shame us both."

The Empress made a gesture as regal as economic: nothing to forget. "I will write to Dzakas." Her glance round said, I will do it now.

Tellurith sank back. A maid came, read fluid, graceful hand signs, evaporated. I saw a last flash of appalled loyalty in Alkhes' stare, and the Empress, following my glance, grinned like a wicked child.

Yes, that grin said. We are as disloyal as the Emperor fears, and we have a spy system that lets us talk without ever being overheard.

While Alkhes did his best not to splutter the imperial eye moved to Tellurith; and there was sudden yearning in that glance.

"Before I married, I was Jhuir family priestess."

Alkhes' stiffening told me he understood as well as Tellurith and I. Jhuir are the royal family of Quetzistan. Like every other royalty who could afford it, they had bought qherrique. As priestess, she would have tended their statuette.

And she wanted to know if what she had seen at the gate was real.

With the greatest care Tellurith pushed her swinging coat-front back. Neither Alkhes nor I looked round. Beyond doubt, her Quetzistani women would double as troublecrew, primed to protect their blood-kin: Tellurith's gesture was risky enough.

Slowly, she drew the cutter out. The Empress paid us the honor of an indrawn breath.

"It's only a cutter," Tellurith said. With the grief of Telluir House, of Amberlight. "It has perhaps three years left."

The Empress had leant forward. She glanced up, making a hand sign, and the others clustered at her back. The Empress looked up at Tellurith, back to the cutter. And up.

Tellurith held it out. "It won't wake for you. It's dedicated to me. But no, it won't bite."

Because she was a woman. She, at least, could touch.

She nursed it across her palms. An imperial stance that celebrated a gift beyond price. Beyond giving. The grief was in her eyes as she gave it back.

"No," said Tellurith, with the tiniest sigh. "Never again. Never, ever again."

Their eyes met. Then the Empress turned and held her hand out for the embossed imperial paper, gave the reed pen a deft shake, and began to write.

When we reached the park it was late afternoon, the skies opening on a last slit of sunshine before dark. The grass glowed, the trees fountained their living fire, the Imperial escort closed about us with the utmost deference. Its officer walked ahead, making urbane conversation with Tellurith, the season, the latest River news, while Alkhes and I followed meekly as hired bravos at their backs.

We reached the outer arch. The escort eased open a little, preparing for the narrower gate beyond, and some flutter of movement, of color, caught the corner of my eye.

There was a side-street, a long, ornate alley probably leading to noble residences: the sun struck down it like a sword into paradise, gilt columns, carven façades, trailing flower vines and statue fantasies, some glistening marble, some painted in the Archipelago way. From one door came a woman with a maid and a brace of little silky white dogs. Against the black-rose of her skirts their collars shot diamonds' fire. The sun painted them, as it painted the group almost at the alley's gate.

Three men, rich men, by the velvet and brocade, noble, by its extravagance of color and cut, the arrogance of gesture and face. Two were at a stair foot, one leaning on a statue plinth, both looking up where the third lounged on the landing's vantage point.

The stair and plinth were jasper-red Heartland porphyry. The man's carriage did them justice, more justice than his consummately cut Dhasdein trousers, the outrageous embroideries of his peach brocade coat. The sun caught him full face, limning the slight, lithe shape, elegantly resilient as a master swordsman's steel; the chiseled features, the ever so slightly disdainful but perfectly cut mouth. The mockery, the recognition, tinged with irony, in his curiously full-lidded, green-hazel eyes.

Caught in the sun, those eyes glowed like a forest pool. A ring blazed. He had lifted a hand to us. Ever so faintly, smiled.

Alkhes grabbed his belly as if he had been gut-shot, spun round, and fell back in my arms.

I caught him from pure shock. His head dropped on my shoulder, thump. As if he were indeed heart-shot, and the spasm, the dying moments, already past.

I made some noise. The guards jumped, Tellurith and the officer whipped about. Alkhes slid through my hold, every muscle limp, eyes rolling back in his head. I had recognized that symptom before he folded up, a tidy little heap of debris, on the Emperor's immaculate flags.

Tellurith made them fetch Catheor's crew and the sedan chair. She was absolutely coherent, absolutely forceful, and her lips were absolutely blue. When the messenger left, she sank down by Alkhes, opposite me. Took both his hands, and never moved.

"It's a seizure, yes," I told the officer. I sounded as shaken—where was my Tower training? as she. "It happens sometimes. We don't know why." Gods forbid, I was praying, that he should go the whole way with it. That he should panic and fight.

Or start to convulse. He had done that too, after Mid-winter night. Perhaps he did it at Amberlight.

And this time I did, indeed, know why.

WHEN CATHEOR'S FOLK had Alkhes in the chair, still limp as wet silk, and the bearers took the poles, I gripped the nearest guardsman's arm and said under my breath, "Who was that?"

His eyes rolled in a way that said he understood all too well. "Who was what?"

"At the house door. Over there."

His eyes pivoted. He gave a gasp and jerked his arm free. "Get moving. You're supposed to be out of here!"

What power does it take, I wondered, as the chair creaked forward, to make an Imperial guardsman lose his manners with a guest?

Tellurith kept her wits after all. Despite Catheor's efforts, she made them take us first to Strethilis. Only when he arrived gesturing and goggle-eyed at his stair-foot did she let her composure flaw. But when she said, "I need a doctor," her voice cracked. Strethilis took one look and started for the street himself.

I helped get Alkhes upstairs. Shen was about, there were enough others for safety. There would be enough to hold him, I considered, if it came to the worst. Either worst. If guards failed, any trouble would still have to get past the cutter. And Tellurith. I went quickly but softly down the stairs behind the one I wanted, and got his arm at the outer door.

"Man—!" Catheor whipped round with the street-reflex and I all but broke his wrist. Zuri taught me well.

"Gods above—!" he panted. I gripped him harder. "What . . ."

"A lord," I said. "Young. Young-looking, at least. Between Alkhes and my height. Brown—cinnamon-brown hair, worn back off his face. Good-looking. Hazel eyes. Clothes like—an emperor. He waved to us. He knows Alkhes."

He went paler than Alkhes himself. I looked in his eyes and understood.

"He turned you," I said.

Zuri's talk. Tower skills. Whatever my face said, he quailed. But then he got his wind and shoved his hair back and threw it in my teeth.

"They both turned me. Him and—Alkhes."

I stared. He jerked his chin at me.

"I took his money, yeah. I gotta live. But when he—Alkhes come back—I put my standard where it belonged."

"You—"

"I send him word, yeah. Stuff that don't matter. I do," with sudden fierceness, "what matters for you."

For a moment we stuck, eye to eye there in that dirty urine-scented passageway. I do not know what I looked like. I know how it felt, when I said, "Tell me his name."

And how he looked when he whispered it, as if the very walls might stab.

"Tanekhet."

CATHEOR DOES NOT KNOW what grudge is between them, but he knows it is old. I do not need to ask him particulars. The lowest boat-folk's ale-shanty knows of Tanekhet. Regent of the Archipelago. Suzerain of Riversrun. Warden of the Crown Prince, eminence of the nobility, familiar of the Emperor. The greatest power in Riversend.

Perhaps in all Dhasdein.

Strethilis will tell me what else I need. Most of the great nobles keep only a presence house in the imperial quarter. Their true strongholds are outside. Beyond the Emperor's reach. He might have been visiting: a festival, a rendezvous. Or perhaps he came especially for us. Catheor may not know. Strethilis will.

Autumn. Dhasdein.
Tellurith's Diary

THE MOTHER BLIGHT and blind that man and strike him dead with leprosy! The middle of Dhasdein—of Riversend—a child to ward with nothing but a bunch of discharged ruffians—a man to ward—Oh, the Mother succor me.

A man to ward who has had too much. Who has done, I do not need Caitha to tell me, what he did before when confronted with an unbearable reality. Who probably never even chose it. Who has simply fallen out of the world.

I cannot cry. There is no time to cry. I might miss a step, a vital second's warning on stair or floor. I can keep the cutter charged. And Catheor's folk about the entry-way. The doctor is less use than teats on a bull, he can only say it must be a swoon and talk of leeching blood. Barbarian! I could diagnose that myself!

At least he has not come round. Has not failed to recognize me. Has not started screaming—and fighting—and—

I have to stop this. Strangling the pillow, breaking pens, dripping all over him... Strethilis will take care for me—us. Catheor will send the rest into the city—Wenami, the warehouse foreman, might find other folk for me. I could see my way, I could plan something—

If only I knew where that other fool—By the Mother's heart I promise, Sarth, when I lay hands on you I will flay you alive!

Autumn. Dhasdein.

Journal kept by Sarth

I AM GOING to write this down. I need to have it clear—not to remember, but to put behind me—in my own head.

I went out as soon as it was dark enough: nobles are seldom home of a night, but none would think of junketing until late. Strethilis gave me directions with a cringe as from an irate god. I put on my good clothes, hid a trouble-knife, borrowed a fistful of darrin from his last commission. Called a torch-boy, and left.

Ironic, that Riversend should so mix gold and scum. Tanekhet's mansion is hardly any way from us. A veritable stronghold, walls, turrets, parapet, bastions, a double zig-zag entrance and a guard detachment. None of the manners of an imperial chamberlain. I offered my knife at the outer guard-house. My clothes, or my manner, or what I said, got through both gates.

"If the lord Tanekhet misses me," I told them, as serenely, as calmly as if it meant nothing to me, "you will rue the day."

Inside the wall's patrol glacis is something like a park: great trees, a carriage road, with exquisitely wrought iron holders for flambeaux it must take another detachment of lamp-lighters to tend. Then like an entrance to some fairyland, behind the trees' filigree looms the bulk of the house.

Away from the glare and steam of the slums it was moonlight on a fair, cutting, late autumn night. The clouds must have blown away. Looking up, I saw a brilliant spray of stars above the spires and gargoyles that mark the chine of Tanekhet's roofs.

The house is very old and of course magnificent. A façade long as a palace, a terrace, armies of tall, pointed windows lavishing light. It went in my favor that when they halted at the porch for overtures to the house steward, I contemplated the marble paving, the bronze column-nymphs, the scatter of rose-petals and ambergris scent from some wonder's transit, and did not gawk.

I had wondered if there would be negotiations. If I should have taken some token, though You could tell me what. A lock of Alkhes' hair? I had expected to wait half the evening, even to come back. I did not know what I was dealing with.

The messenger reappeared almost at once, with a higher eminence. In the hall they searched me again, with perfect courtesy. I stood flat-footed and did not so much as think of troublecrew. Idiots, I did not have to cry, Zuri trained me. I need no weapon but myself.

I had luck or good timing. A yet higher flunkey and escort led me down a side passage, to a carven mahogany door. And beyond, Tanekhet himself.

He still wore what nobles count as street clothes, less the coat. It was a small room; some sort of reception place, by the furniture, which was wholly decorative, the elegant arrangement of scented lilies, the newly kindled fire. I remember, on the wall behind him, there was a statue of some goddess, jade carved in curves that flowed like rose-shot water, in a small family shrine.

The steward wished to linger. Tanekhet straightened a little and waved him out.

"So," he said, "what will my servants rue to leave unheard?"

By daylight, he looks thirty-five of his forty-five years. By firelight, in his shirt-sleeves, his hair loose and those eyes green as a panther's, he might be some elegant, deadly boy.

I said, "I have a message. From Alkhes."

I had not under-estimated his intelligence work. The lips curved in a smile.

"The little general!" Tanekhet's voice is his supreme asset. Soft, superbly flexible, with a touch of husk that can deepen to a panther's snarl. "How delightful. And what message does he send?"

"I am the message," I said.

He had his hand half-out; a slim hand, manicured as mine was once, hardly larger than Alkhes' own. The jeweled border on his cuff-lace winked. His eyes flew up, wide and luminous green, to my face.

Then he smiled again, and I saw the panther wake.

"So-o-o." This time it came on a musical, falling breath. The gesture said, Over there. It was a lord's command. I went.

He turned a little to scrutinize me, in the intersecting light of lamps and fire. The eyes moved over me, head to toe, as palpably as a hand, and as indecently. With the light in three-quarter profile their glow was bronze-shot celadon, like very new leaves.

"Amberlight," he said.

I inclined my head.

His lips curved. Beautifully cut lips as any girl's. As a boy, he must have been devastating.

"Is it true what they say—about Amberlight men?"

"I don't know," I said, "what they say."

He cocked his head. The curve of the lips replied, Everything you think we say. Everything you are imagining. Everything you think I am imputing, I am.

He took a step away from the mantel. I had a sudden, longing memory of stripping for Strethilis.

"Does he know you're here?"

I shook my head.

His breath came and went, a quick little sigh. He turned to the wall beside him. A catch gave, opening a hidden door. He gestured, with an emperor's graciousness, for me to precede him through.

It was his bedroom, sure enough. Big enough for a House-head's apartment, candles everywhere. Hangings of a tapestry to beggar Verrain Families, a marvelous great forest-work with children, animals, curiosities, ambushed in flecks and flashes amid the reticulations of the myriad leaves. More festooned the canopy above his lake of gold-worked coverlet.

He leaned on the bed-foot. Every motion, like every pose, was conscious, articulated; deadly grace. He said, "I think I should see you're safe. For myself."

After all, it was what I had come for. As slowly, as consciously as he, Sethar's directions in my ears, I went on one knee and began to unbuckle my boots.

Reaching the under-shirt, I flicked a glance up. He looked as graceful as ever. He was certainly not breathing fast. Even his eyes had not widened. But in the fireglow they were almost black.

I slid the shirt onto the convenient chair, atop my coat. Unfastened my belt.

He let me stand a good minute, feeling the full burden of my nakedness, before he made a graceful wrist motion that said, Come here.

As I reached the bed-foot he said, "Is it true you're trained?"

I said, "Yes."

"From childhood?"

I thought of the hours with the schoolmasters. Music, deportment, dancing, the gymnasium. Conversation. Sethar. From the day I was old enough to walk.

At my nod his eyes flickered.

"For both women and men?"

What point was there in trying to explain?

He came round behind me. Everything Sethar ever taught me I used in keeping still. With grace.

His fingers plucked, light and adept as Sethar's own, at the tie of my plait.

As deftly he ran his fingers through my hair, spreading, teasing it out. And behind my eyes I heard Zuri curse, felt her hands, so contradictorily gentle, setting tangles straight; felt Alkhes grab my hair by handfuls as he climbed into bed with me that first time.

Tanekhet said, softly, genuinely, "Beautiful."

He came back round my shoulder, and gestured to the bed.

Remember Alkhes, I told myself, as the linen molded, cold and pristine, to my back. Remember Tellurith. No one else can save them. Not like this.

Tanekhet leant over me. Gently as a mother, he took my right wrist and drew it over my head.

It was a silk-padded strap of antelope hide, with a knotted silk cord. Contrary to belief, silk is stronger than very steel. And the buckle was tempered steel. He had been used, I understood, to dealing with very strong men.

With his hand on my right ankle he paused, contemplatively. His eyes fingered my body. As the crowning savor, they lifted to my face.

And narrowed. He came to the bed-head, a panther stalking now, slid his fingers under my chin with a connoisseur's touch that stabbingly recalled Sethar, and stared into my eyes.

Very, very softly, he said, "You're trained for this too?"

I controlled the wryness. As coolly, as calmly as Sethar could have wanted, I answered, "Yes."

His brows flew up. Rolling his sleeves, he turned quickly away.

The brazier was small and ornamental, but the coals it held were no cooler for that. He set it carefully beside the bed, on a square of naked marble, and grinned impishly. Yes, that grin said, we both know I make a habit of this.

The knife was small too. A jeweled hilt, a slender, glittering blade. I was almost glad that it would be wickedly sharp.

With a long, voluptuous sigh he sank down by me on the bed. "I wonder," he said companionably, "what your little general will appreciate most?" He teased a lock of my hair through his fingers. "Lord, it's almost too beautiful to cut." His eye flicked back to my face. Then he laid the knife point-down along my breastbone, and leant closer, the mouth curling to show the age lines at its corners now, the panther eyes flaring into mine. "So then, beautiful. Where shall I begin?"

He smelt of aniseed and myrrh and freshly laundered cloth. My heart panged as I smelt Zuri's body, hard-worked woman's sweat, as I felt the blood running down my nose, the agonizingly gentle touch of her mouth on my bruised lips.

I will be eternally grateful to Sethar that I managed to force back the tears. But I felt Tanekhet's muscles tense. Before I read how his stare had fixed.

He sat a moment, immobile. Then, on a note less chagrin than wonder, he said, "You're not afraid."

No, I wanted to scream. I am not afraid, I am terrified out of my wits. Not enough that I must remember Zuri, and making this a gift of love. Will I come out of this with my vision? Will I come out alive? Here there will be neither mercy nor gentleness. Whatever happens, you will take my last resort, my best weapon, my life's foundation. When—if—you let me go, I will never be beautiful again.

Cold touched my throat. My eyes opened on the panther's truth.

"*Why*," through his teeth now, the blade against my jugular, "are you not afraid?"

Thirty years a courtier, the Court's master of intrigue. What else would he think?

No, I wanted to say. It is not a trap.

Tensely, delicately as a spring-coiled panther, knife still poised, he scanned every inch of the room. Then the eyes came back to mine. Under the attention, the will, the concentrated analysis of the lord Tanekhet, chief power of Riversend, I felt like a mouse in a hawk's grasp.

I heard his breath. The brazier's rustle. The beat of my own heart.

He took the knife away. Then he leant closer, hands planted either side my face. The eyes were midnight water over leaf-mould. If I had never known Alkhes, I could have lost myself in that stare.

"No weapon." The murmur was almost confiding. He slid a finger up my arm. "No escape." The hand came down. "So." The eyes transfixed me. "*Why*?"

It was not a lord's pre-emptive fright. He had no need for that. He truly wanted to know.

Words clotted in my throat. It was lunatic, it would be pointless. One more useless postponement, a greater imbecility, a degradation of more than myself. He would never understand.

But some shred of pride, of discipline, restored Sethar, whispering behind my eyes: We are Tower-bred. Whatever we do, we do with grace.

I swallowed a gulp and got it out, hardly aware of what I said. "I'm sorry, my lord."

He gave one quick gasp. His hand shot out, a light, stinging kitten blow almost as involuntary as the laugh.

"Lord above, you've got a brain!"

I could only gulp.

Still chuckling, he ruffled my hair. "I didn't think he could be besotted by some village oaf."

I bit my tongue on another, What?

He took hold of me, a hand either side my jaw. His eyes glowed, but the menace was gone.

"Too clever, O exquisite one. You've ruined my pleasure. And you do, don't you, understand why?"

Sunlit forest water, the eyes smiled, merry, predatory, into mine. He understood what he asked all too well.

I said, "The real pleasure is the power."

He laughed softly and tapped my cheek. "Which is not the freedom to hurt. But the raising—the savoring—of fear."

If I really had spoilt his pleasure, how could he have been so urbane? Now I realize that for a lord like Tanekhet, torture victims come by the bushel. He could have mangled me any time. It had been far greater diversion to make me expose my wits.

He nodded at me. Then he dropped the knife on my breastbone and brought those eyes to bear.

"So now we understand each other, perhaps you will tell me. What, precisely, are you doing here?"

I bit my tongue again. With the most subtle of opponents, Sethar used to say, the only practicable weapon is the truth.

"You know what I am doing here."

His brows snapped tight. They were fine and arched, probably penciled, under the artless aureole of hair.

At some moments, perhaps a god does take you. At such moments, with every drop of blood and fiber of brain quickened as excruciatingly as Zuri made them, against such an opponent, one can be inspired.

I said, "My lord, how much do you hate Alkhes?"

He jumped as if I had pinched his rump.

"How much . . . ?"

I kept quiet. My life, all our lives, I understood, turned on the whim of a lord's response.

He put a finger to my jawbone's angle. This time his eyes devoured my face as a duelist would, not a connoisseur.

"You are here to buy me off. You know I know that. So you want to know, how much do you have to pay."

He dropped his hand. I could not read—I dared not try to read—the expression in that green-lit stare.

"Don't you want to ask me, Why?"

"I am honored, my lord. But, 'How much?' will be enough."

"You'll leave me some secrets? But *I* want to know, beautiful. *Why* weren't you afraid?"

Fiel for fiel, as the market-folk say. If I wanted my answer, I would have to give his first.

He gave me another of those looks. Then he disappeared behind the brazier to return with a cup. Pausing to enjoy me, before he sat down and slid an arm under my head.

"Water and wine." With an ironic half-tone. "You've no call to be afraid."

It was white wine and iced water, a desert's bliss. He set the cup down. Sat back, and panther-blandly, stared.

An inspiration near divine, yes. But it would lay me open far deeper than the knife.

"One of my wives—"

"*One* of your—" he caught himself, clearly recalling what he knew of Amberlight. "Go on."

I looked into the hanging's forest depths. A red horned deer, a tree-man with leaves for hands looked back at me. Of them all, she would be the first to understand. To say, Use this.

Quite softly he said, "She likes to be hurt?"

"She likes to hurt."

It was out before I knew. I caught my own breath and tried to take it back. "There isn't—she doesn't know any other way."

He was quiet. Then, the way a collector might cherish a rare, priceless porcelain, he cupped his palm around my cheek.

"I understand it." I had to speak. His sympathy was almost as bad as wrath. "She's troublecrew. She's never done it—she's never needed to do it again."

His body tension gave me bewilderment before he carefully turned my head to meet his gaze. "Never needed?"

He was a lord, and my life, Alkhes' life, all our lives, perhaps Iskarda depended on me. But I had to look away.

"She hurt me, the first time. But then she was gentle. And when someone's kind—"

Zuri's fingers, featherlight on my bruised jaw. Zuri's caresses, an excruciatingly pleasurable fire.

Quite quietly he said, "And you remembered that."

I could not reply. With all the moment's need, all the Tower's discipline behind me, I could not speak.

He sat silent longer than I could bear. I opened my eyes.

I had lost the torturer. The one who sat there, so sober, so silent, was redoubtably the lord. And yet there was something, for an instant far less redoubtable, in those forest-shadow eyes.

Then he gave his head a tiny shake and reached out to fool with the knife laid on my chest.

"I don't," he said abruptly, "hate Assandar."

I waited. Zuri had enforced that lesson well.

"Malice, perhaps. Revenge? Ah, gods, the man irritates me. No sense of humor. All prickles and kicks. It started when I met him, years ago. A raw Imperial recruit. I made some joke, pretended to grab at him. And almost had a spear-butt down my throat."

He swung a little to look me in the face. "I do not," he said wryly, "even when they're pretty, make a habit of debauching the Guard."

And grinned more wryly, and flicked the back of a hand, but lightly, against my cheek. "My silent judge!"

"I would never," I was caught by surprise, "judge where I did not know."

"No?" The connoisseur returned. He traced my collarbone with the jeweled hilt. "Well, perhaps I will confess to you, that I held malice over that. I teased him. Pursued him. Not seriously, just enough to make him twitch. All the way up the ranks." His mouth corners pinched, then curled. "Oh, it sounds petty, but I am so often bored, beautiful. And he always—always! gave me such good sport."

I kept quiet. Tried not to remember, before he collapsed, the look on Alkhes' face.

"Right up to corps commander, he never learnt to cope." He ran his fingers, sensuously, down my hip. "So I can never resist. Lord of waters, before he went to Amberlight—!"

I bit down on my lip, hard. When my voice was in control I managed, "So it's really—just a game?"

He chuckled and dropped the dagger hilt first on my breast. The blade's chill reminded me with what I dealt.

"It's been so amusing to watch him these last couple of months. To work him round and round like a fox in a maze that finds every bolthole stopped. And push him, no matter how he tries to wriggle, the way I mean him to go."

My throat was scalding. I wondered if the wine would burn if I threw up.

"And something about him teases me. I think he's lying to himself. If you could ever break through those scruples—I swear, you'd find a firepit underneath." The eyes glowed, a predator's stare. "Or have you found that for yourself?"

I made myself lie still. Take three long breaths. Before I said, "My lord . . . may I ask something?"

"I thought," he spoke with irony, "that you had."

"Something else, my lord."

He had read my voice, or my face, too well. The eyebrow came down. The eyes were alarmingly acute.

"Do you know—what happened to him, in Amberlight?"

He shook his head.

"When he first arrived, he was caught by a street gang. Robbed. Bashed. Raped."

His brows flew up. It was genuine shock.

"He nearly died. He did lose his memory. And when we went to Iskarda . . ."

I took a deep breath, staring up into the forest lushness of the canopy. You have no business doing this, someone said. Someone else retorted, You do what you must.

"There was a festival. He was the Goddess's chosen. And it—happened again."

When he did not speak, I went on.

"That time, he did lose his mind."

I looked at him then. But he was staring down at his hand, shut on the jeweled hilt, on my chest.

After a moment he said, "The poor crazy . . ." Looked away, and shook his head.

Then, in an odd voice, he said, "He came to me. When he was trying to get the command for Amberlight. He knew there was no other way. So he walked into the residence book-room one morning and said, 'What's your price?'"

He looked down at the knife, and then back into my eyes. "I teased him, and handled him a little, and kissed him a couple of times. I was afraid to do anything more. I had the feeling that he might fly apart in my hands."

I shut my eyes, and heard Alkhes, gruff and furious. "Do you know what I went through to get that command?"

"He walked out the door," murmured Tanekhet. "Got a dozen feet down the hall and threw his belly up."

I was afraid—too afraid of myself—to speak. The silence stretched like wet leather. Until Tanekhet moved, with the decisiveness of a settled choice.

"So," he said lightly, "you came in his place."

At times the gods take us clear out of our sober minds. "I came to sleep with you, or whatever else you wanted, or to kill you," I heard myself say. "I don't know if Alkhes will recover. If he doesn't, I would have killed you anyway."

I shut my eyes. Then I made myself open them. At least, I told myself, the penalty will be quick.

He was watching me with that lord's stare. The fop, the torturer, had entirely gone. I set my teeth and waited to hear all our fates.

"So," he said, "you can lose control. And you do feel. If you had not said that, I never would have believed the rest." Whatever my expression said, he gave me a taut little smile. "My pretty, it's obvious what he means to you. Anyone who had not said that would be either a traitor or a liar."

He looked away, and tossed the knife up and down in his hand. Then he said, very softly, "And I would not want you that."

I was still blinking when he turned back to me. The knife was gone, laid carefully somewhere beyond the bed.

"Go to the palace," he said. "Not tomorrow, the day after. Ask to see Antastes. After that— it's in your hands."

What it is to see a mountain fall, and look up, to realize that another waits beyond. "My lord . . .!"

"Your darling," said Tanekhet evenly, "was a directly appointed imperial general. Don't you think, after all that's happened, Antastes has a right to ask him, Why?"

I gulped. "But the summons—"

"Came from Antastes, yes. I didn't try to provoke it. Or to stop it. I had no hand in Nessis' tricks." His mouth corners quirked. "You really should absolve me of pure pettiness." For a moment the lips went straight. Then he turned on the bed-edge, with a different expression in those greenish-glowing eyes. "And now, my pretty, since you've destroyed my first plan, I shall have to manage your conquest in some other way."

And he did conquer me. Not since Sethar, not on Mid-summer night, have I surrendered so utterly, to woman or to man. Whatever Alkhes learned or failed to learn, it seems there are generals of love somewhere in Dhasdein.

XIII

Autumn. Dhasdein.
Tellurith's Diary

Aм I to laugh or cry? Or, rot and gangrene the pair of them, laugh and curse, or should I simply curse?

Alkhes came round this morning. Praise the Mother for that at least: no convulsion, no loss of wits; not even, bless Her name, a waking-nightmare scream. He just opened his eyes in the mixture of dawn and candle-light, their black the sentience of night itself. Lay there, unsmiling, blank. Then blinked; and recognized me.

I did manage to avoid hysterics, and to strangle more than a few sobs. And I did not ask, What happened? I did not ask anything.

Until he blinked around over the hot milk rushed from a sleepy breakfast seller, and asked, "Where's Sarth?"

And the blood, the very life drained out of his face when I managed to answer—almost calmly—"I don't know."

He does know. Because he got out of the blankets as if they scalded, and he did scald the ears off Catheor. And five minutes later he was tottering downstairs with me hanging on behind like a driver with a bolted mule; not a word of explanation, just a face as gray as risen death.

Till a quarter mile down the Embankment we encountered Sarth.

Strolling out of the raw mist amid the first boatmen and posy-sellers gathering to the lords' pontoons; shaved, hair tied, good coat immaculate; gazing about as if he belonged. With an escort in lord's livery at his back.

One look at us and they evaporated; but I had a look myself. At the livery, then at Alkhes' face.

He could not talk at first. He just grabbed Sarth's arms and shook him like a sawdust-doll. "Sarth," was the best he could manage. "Sarth?"

I never heard such a mixture: fear and rage and absolute self-loathing; a distraction of disbelief. And a crazed, shamed, terrified hope.

Sarth stood there looking tower-inscrutable and never tried to resist; until he looked at me. His face cracked then. I read the record of stress and fear and travail worse than Alkhes'.

He put out a hand. I grabbed Alkhes as well. He spoke to me over Alkhes' head, with victory, and its cost, in his voice.

"Tomorrow," he said, "we can go to the Emperor."

Alkhes let go. When he stepped back only terror was left.

Sarth put both arms around him and hugged, shook him like a child. "Aglis, don't worry. It's all right."

Alkhes tensed away. I could just hear it. "What did you—did you—"

I knew what he had done. I had seen, had helped to produce that translucent look too often to mistake. But whatever Alkhes feared, too clearly it was not that.

Sarth drew him back, quite gently this time. "Aglis," he murmured. "I give you my word. There isn't a mark on me. I used . . ."

He stopped and looked startled. I almost saw the laughter swell in his throat before he swallowed it and went on in that composed voice. "I used my wits."

Alkhes drew in his breath. Then I felt his control go. We both caught at him as he started to shake, and when Sarth pulled him close he went as if every muscle had failed.

"Oh, gods," I heard him whisper as he melted onto Sarth's shoulder, "I have," shaky now, almost laughing, "this time, I have to lean . . ."

PRAISE THE MOTHER whose blessings are sometimes manifold. Because we had hardly got back to the pier, under the mean, dirt-gray Delta sky that I hate so much, with a sea-wind thin and wicked as a Heartland throwing knife, we had not even dropped down in the motley of wicker shanty cabins and makeshift awning huts when Catheor bristled like a guard-mastiff. And we all saw the patch of color amid the hawkers and beggars and road-women and tatty stalls; all read the new green of the surcoats, the lizard sheen of corselets beneath. All froze, for one minute before Sarth's mouth fell open.

Before he was off up the pier, into the midst of them, grabbing her in his arms like the veriest River quarter whore.

Pale, taciturn, head cropped like a fever patient; Navy, and hard usage, in every laconic line. No point, no need to ask. She is here. Safe, whole, signed over by the Citadel lieutenant. Bemused but patient under what I can only call Sarth's ecstasies. Mother, I never thought to see him quite so undone. He cannot look away, cannot go away from her, for five minutes at a time.

Tez bears it, as she probably bore all the rest, coolly, patiently. Along with the embarrassments of finding place for her in a space too small when three of us did sleep together. Bad enough in the daytime. At night, what would we have done?

Still, the Mother knows how grateful I am; for her presence, her silence at my back; the awareness, asleep or awake, of her eye, her stealthy tread. Something of a come-down, from Navy officer and marble factor to troublecrew. But Mother, if I could have asked anything, beyond being safe home, it would be to have a woman like that here, at my side.

Especially now.

I STILL HAVE to finger the table occasionally as I write. To prove it solid, masterly carved mahogany, with a polish of years, to wriggle my toes in the magnificent rugs. To bask in the warmth of a fire—not qherrique, never qherrique, but after all those nights congealing over the wretched little brazier, never knowing when one might capsize and the whole floating crazy-quilt burn to the waterline—oh, the ecstasy, to be on solid earth. Within walls, without drafts. Dry! With more comforts than I have known since Amberlight.

If not—even yet—safe.

It was mid-afternoon, the light drawing in on the day's misery; men on the pier shivering round the chestnut-sellers' fires, women and children on the boats shivering, amid the stinks and susurrus of talk, quarrel, complaint, that never stops . . . There is no color there. I never remember the boat town as anything but gray, and dour shades of dun and dirt green and scummed-over brown.

Which made them stand out worse than the Citadel detachment, coming down the pier in a bow-wave of hawkers and beggars and leaping urchins, from our vantage nothing showed but the fracas. At the boats' rim, a strip of gold braid emerged; a scrap of lace, the blood-velvet flare of coats. And steel, cold amid the turmoil; the drawn swords of a noble's guard.

I did not quite believe it, though I knew where they must be going; knew, I think, who it must be; I sat gaping till the three advance guards filed across the Skethis' gang-plank, crossed their boat, under the little girls' goggling eyes, and with most untoward courtesy, lined its nearer gunwale. And through their gauntlets and wine-red embroidered surcoats came a presence, a whiff of perfume. An exquisitely subtle and resonant voice that remarked, "Hello, the boat?"

Alkhes had already leapt. Sarth was beside him in a jump. Tez could not have understood but she was Navy; one cat-spring had her posted with the heaviest frying pan at my back. I gawped like a dairy-maid, while my two men tried to make me a bastion of their flesh.

The voice repeated, "Hello, the boat?"

After all, I am Ruand. When neither of them moved—except I could feel Alkhes' buried snarl vibrating, like a terrified, cornered dog—I put a hand on each shoulder and pushed.

He confronted me in the gap. Not a lock awry in that aureole of light brown hair, not a mark on the skirts of that perfectly cut forest-green coat. Its shade brought the color out, bright with life, with intelligence, in those curiously lidded eyes.

As our looks met he smiled.

Alkhes and Sarth both jerked. I said, "My lord . . . ah . . . ?"

The smile deepened the merest fraction. I had just given him the best joke of his life. He drew a tiny breath and dropped it, delicately as a snake.

"Tanekhet."

I did not know the name. I did not have to know. But however you have frightened my men, I thought, keeping my face blank as I had learnt in a far harder field, you have not yet dealt with me.

"To what do we owe this honor?"

The mouth corner's curl was an accolade. The pause, the expectant look, a challenge of imperial presumption: You know I know I am not welcome. Will you play into my hands?

I took Alkhes by one wooden biceps and Sarth by the other and said, "The house is unworthy beyond mention. The favor of gracing it must be yours."

Autumn. Dhasdein.

Meditations. Alkhes-Assandar

THE FAVOR, she says. With majestic—with imperial courtesy, with ultimate insolence.

I could not have spoken. Still could not think, had not even come to think what Sarth had done for me—oh, gods, what he has done for me . . . If it would not hurt him worse, I would hang myself for the shame.

He swears there was nothing. Not a mark on him. I can vouch for that, I made him strip and looked. But when I think what might have been . . .

Enough of that. This is not the boat-dock, where nobody cares if you throw up.

But to have . . .

Him.

There. In front of me.

In the flesh.

TANEKHET.

So THIS is what undid me, at Iskarda, in Amberlight. Another man— another of my kind could have borne that, even the gang. But he was there already, in my past, in my mind. A monster, an ogre. An absence carried like an inner wound, another place I could not look. Ever since the day he walked up on me in that palace corridor. Smile, scan, lordly clothes, every line of him saying, If I want you I can have you, your officers will jump to sell you, dare me. Tell me I can't touch.

I don't think he did touch. The words, the look— I never came nearer execution for mutiny. If he had not left it at words . . .

After that he haunted me. I know the craziness that makes lunatics say that. On the River-lord's hand, I swear, it has been the truth. And then, in the Imperial Quarter . . . when he took my eye . . . smiled, waved his hand . . .

It is another discontinuity. *There* and Tanekhet in the sunlight, smiling. *Here* and Tellurith bending over me, her dear face, those beloved Amberlight eyes, and Strethilis' studio full of dawn.

To have him, after all that, come after *us* . . .

TELLURITH COPED. Sarth and I were only good to stand like a pair of guard-dog posts. She brought him aboard, found him, with more magnificent inso-lence, a seat. So superbly careful to remark on the care needed with his coat. Every syllable rubbing in, you are slumming, what a remarkable charity, turn-ing the patronage back on his head, driving the arrogance down his neck . . .

And I adored her when she quashed Darthis.

Tez sent one of the Skethi girls to the pier. Chestnuts, mulled wine. "We have," Tellurith explained—oh, that magnanimity! "plenty of money." And he sat and swallowed it, in five minutes she had him laughing, straight-faced as she was and mentally reduced to hiccups. I could tell it by his eyes.

He has the most remarkable—the most brilliant, most eloquent eyes.

How much too well I know.

Tellurith dispensed wine in our motley clay cups, made it a ritual. Spun it out, even I could see, so he would have to make small-talk. Or announce his purpose, first.

In war, it is called an offensive defense.

He understood that too. I saw the laughter ambushed, demure as Sarth's. He nibbled a chestnut. Sipped, set the cup down on the gunwale. Smiled and said, "I've wanted to meet you for so long."

I think I snarled. I could not help it. Even Sarth twitched.

He understood. The smile he gave me was full of it. I opened my mouth and the gods know what would have come out. Except Tellurith smiled more sweetly and answered, "You could have found us any time."

She plays with truth for swords. Have I not understood that yet?

He nodded. Agreement. Acknowledgement. A hit. Don't, I prayed, duel with him so brilliantly that his pride demands he win.

"I've heard," he said, "so much about Amberlight."

"You never visited?"

Hang it, but she is good. Innuendo foiled, perilous gambit declined, insult beautifully veiled: you never reached the Crown Prince's entourage? Your family was not great enough to buy qherrique itself?

He took his cup back. The smile was a courtier's parry. The tiny tap of a fingernail was applause. The eyes were luminous as forest water.

"I see," he said, "that the reports were true."

Tellurith sipped in turn. Glanced at Sarth, then at me, and gave him a smile whose sword was naked. "All of them."

A Heartland tigress's warning: you may know about Amberlight men from experience. Trust the rumor of its women too.

I know too much about his power. I might have snarled. I could not have dared like that.

Tanekhet is a word-sword master. He let the pause go long enough to make me sweat outright.

And there was something I don't understand in that look, as he set the cup down. Slid his eyes across the pair of us. Not insolence. Not lechery, however provocative. Something . . .

"The Emperor will see you tomorrow." He slanted an eye, at last, to Sarth alone, and his mouth corners curled. "My pledges are good." A pause to bring out the sting. "But . . ."

He looked back to Tellurith. Who raised a brow in quite as noble arrogance: But?

Tanekhet looked at me. "Your chances of seeing him might improve measurably," it came lightly as a crony's invitation to cards, "if you spent the interval—elsewhere."

It was Tellurith who repeated, "Elsewhere?"

"In fact," Tanekhet answered languidly, "with me."

I should think my heart has teeth-marks still. Sarth actually twitched. Tellurith's own face went stiff.

Tanekhet read us, and offered more than a hint of panther-teeth. "There are still plenty of others who would be—happy—to see you never reach the Emperor."

I knew what he meant. It was Tellurith who said, "Nessis?"

The lack of surprise was, I know, a compliment. "And highly as you may estimate your friends' loyalty," his eyes came back to me, "you know it would take no more than a couple of dekarchies . . ."

To cut down Catheor's motley and decimate the boat-folk and have the feud over, our corpses in the river with slashed throats. I knew. I had spent the nights resolutely unknowing it, two whole months.

Tanekhet nodded again. Quite without devilry now. The great lord, the Court-master I have never known. With that something in his eyes still, when he glanced at Tellurith. Before the glint revived, as he said, "I have quite a large house. There are separate guest suites. You will hardly encounter me more than necessary. Even for," the mouth pucked, "discreet guests."

All of us understood: if Nessis' faction came after us we were lost. With Tanekhet we could be far worse lost.

But we had, and he knew we had, no choice.

Tellurith considered him. I know that look. Have seen it across so many council rooms. Across a parley table, across eighteen inches of paving stone, across a blood and war-stained granite step.

She said, "The lord Tanekhet honors us."

Autumn. Dhasdein.
Journal kept by Sarth

I do not understand.

If Tanekhet wanted me, he could have kept me. He had the power. If he wanted Alkhes, he could have taken him. Any time since we came to Riversend.

If he had wanted Tellurith . . .

We would have died first. Both of us.

Perhaps he does want her. He has wits and skill enough to know he will never manage it except by her own choice. And that means, taking us as well.

He did look at her. Would talk to her, I think. Admires her, that much is evident, oh, Mother, the touch of his eyes on her is a sword in the heart.

Yet there is something in that look: the power, yes, the mockery, assuredly, the world-weariness that is the core of Tanekhet. Maybe there is lust. And yet—

He has made good his word with this guest-suite, that opens on an inner courtyard, with a pear tree whose winter shadow is a great artist's charcoal on a whitewashed wall. As contrived and perfect as the bathroom and bedrooms and servants, may You save me, at summons. More than luxury. A stronghold, where no danger can reach.

Except Tanekhet himself.

Autumn. Dhasdein.
Tellurith's Diary

LAST NIGHT, Tanekhet came to me.

Thank the Mother, both my men were abed; safe in the inner room, as I finished the last journal entry, in the luxury of clear lamp-light, a writing table before the fire. There was only Tez to rise, silent and lethal with her impossibly acquired dagger, as shadow checked in the silently swung outer door.

Tez would do the hand-work. That left words to me. If I could have found any, with the heart stuck in my throat.

He shifted weight. A ripple of firelit brocade, dress-sword's glint. Gleam of eyes. Clearer than words, that movement said: I will respect the conventions. These are your rooms. You must acknowledge me.

I said, "Lord Tanekhet."

The shadowy head inclined. "Ruand."

And then, more softly, "Lady Tellurith."

I set the pen down. Got out of my chair. "Did you want," I said, "to speak to me?"

The tilt of the head was more than an acknowledgement. "Yes," he said. The slightest tint of amusement, adding, I know you will not let me near your men, and if I try more than speech with you it will be all our deaths. "I did want to speak to you."

There were plenty of his own servants to set chairs before the hearth, to supply three sorts of late-night wine. There was Tez as my shield. He did not seem inclined to cavil at that either. But when we had sat down, he nursed the winecup, staring into the fire.

Tanekhet is Dhasdein's master-intriguer. In word-war my undoubted better, his sense of battle's rhythm and timing excels Sarth's. But whatever his aim, I had the defensive. I sat and waited, letting him know I understood his testing of my courage, and my vantage; letting him come to me.

Until he turned the cup a little, to admire its chasing in the midsummer-sunset glow. And asked softly, "What is it like: Iskarda?"

Mother blast the man. The baby is far too young, yet I felt it move; a kick under the heart. I saw market-bustle and high wooden gables along an autumn hillside; mud, slush, marble-glare. Blistered hands, tested brain, broken heart. Snow slopes candescent with moonlight, mountain wind running on hillsides of silver-beige summer grass.

And the presences, the faces, the pasts; the women—all the women—of Telluir House.

"Home," I said.

He had leant forward, clasping the cup lightly as he stared into the fire. Tanekhet is too much a master to disregard light; its dangers, its use. Yet there was something in that look . . .

He gave me a little smile. "I see."

Our eyes held. Yes, I know mine answered: I think you do. That you know all that Home means to a Ruand of Amberlight. Not just hearth and hold and resting-place, but House. The center from which my folk live.

For which they, and I, will fight.

The smile sharpened. He straightened, lifting the cup. I felt Tez stiffen behind my chair, as his eyes toasted me.

"And," he said, "all new."

I let my eyebrows riposte: You do have intelligencers.

He nodded: We both know. It was almost absent. His eyes went from the fire to the cup and back to me.

"I wonder, Lady Tellurith: is it going to succeed?"

I did not look around me. Neither of us needed the reminder. If the sense was political, the answer was his to give, not mine.

So he meant something more.

What would survivors of Amberlight matter to a lord of Dhasdein?
We had no more qherrique. That, too, he would know.
What would a bunch of hill-women matter to a lord of Dhasdein?
But it was not the women who were new.

"How much," I said, as I had once said to Alkhes about Amberlight, "do you know about Iskarda?"

Talking to Tanekhet is uncannily similar. He is as fast; as skilled in word-war; with the same redoubtable wits. He put the cup aside and said, "Did you do it for them?"

Oh, more than redoubtable. A lord of Dhasdein might know enough about Dhasdein, and Amberlight, to understand what, for Alkhes' sake, I might change. But to guess about Sarth . . .

He deserved more than word-fence. I said, "I did it for us all."

He went absolutely still. Only the light moved, the fire's play in those eyes like sunlight on a forest stream.

Then he sat back, slowly, carefully, as a duelist does to signal, Disengage. Shot his cuffs, the automatic Dhasdeini lord's gesture, over the priceless lace that overflowed his sleeves. Got out of his chair, the exquisite motion of a schooled panther, and as I rose too, bowed before me. The full Court courtesy, the obeisance only a great lord makes; only before the Emperor.

"Lady Tellurith," he said, as he straightened, "your husband is a very—lucky man."

Autumn. Dhasdein.
Journal kept by Sarth

Blessings on Sethar, on the Tower whose training is branded into me. So I could leave Tanekhet's house, reach the Imperial Quarter, pass the gate where we have gone so often. Find a detachment of Imperial guardsmen waiting, and still veil the terror that blackened my sight and turned my legs to water. And follow them, decorously—Tez vouches that I did it decorously—into the imperial palace itself.

My palate has sickened, like a child over-fed on cake. What I would give for faded timber walls, scuffed floors, that mis-mended window of Tellurith's room in Iskarda.

What I had was a pile that dwarfs Tanekhet's: they gild the finials and gargoyles atop those walls the color of just-flushed apricots, silver-veined

Archipelago stone. There is nothing fortress-like about it. Beautiful, yes. Magnificent. Those halls outshone us, and I do not boast when I say we were superb. Tellurith had been to the nobles' quarter that morning. And first, to Strethilis.

So when we reached the private ante-room, our splendor shone, comet-like, from the polished ebony walls: Tellurith in a coat of bronze velvet brocaded with gold-thread chrysanthemums, I with quilted golden satin, cuffs and collar of sumptuous blond fur. And Alkhes, of course, dressed as an imperial general.

The presence room is not merely magnificent, but in impeccable taste. The simplicity of the very best. He was sitting, to match it, alone in an heirloom chair. There was a guard, a secretary. Nothing more. Except him. Antastes. The Emperor.

He is gray-haired, stooped. A faded gray-brown, from Quetzistani blood, I suspect, and keeping indoors. Not graceful, as is Tanekhet. He has never needed grace. He sat at ease, almost casual. My throat had shut, my ears were deaf. I could feel Tellurith—Tellurith!—struggling to compose herself. And Alkhes . . .

The Imperials parted. Antastes' eyes came straight to him.

His lips were bleached. His eyes were enormities. But he went forward, steadily, halfway to Antastes' chair. Then, alone in the small open space, he went on his knees, his head bent. And said, almost inaudibly, "Sire."

Antastes is far less legible than his Empress. The opacity of power. He looked at that bowed head, and I doubt Tanekhet could have deciphered him. The waiting stretched until I thought it would burst my heart.

Then Antastes shifted. Laid an elbow on the lotus-carved chair arm, sighed and said, "Oh, lad . . . Come here."

He could have had Alkhes executed. Tortured. He could have done it himself, with words. Perhaps he did. I saw Alkhes' shoulders clench, and was glad I could not see his face.

He got up; the Imperial behind the emperor tensed, but he took those last three strides like a sleep-walker. Antastes looked him full in the face and said in that low, gravelly voice, "Do you think you can tell me, Why?"

Perhaps it was worse than abuse. Whatever Alkhes' face said, the Emperor looked away; and his eye fell on me.

Alkhes must have guessed. When Antastes looked back to him he sounded almost steady. "Sire: if I may present . . . ?"

Tellurith stepped forward, I followed. Tellurith is a Ruand of Amberlight. She did not kneel, and I saw reason to follow suit.

"This," said Alkhes, "is Tellurith. Telluir House-head. Ruand of Iskarda. My wife."

Antastes' expression was clearly legible. Recognition; of more than rank or name.

Tellurith nodded. "It has been a long time," she said.

"Before my father died." Antastes spoke as naturally as an old acquaintance on a street corner. "I rejoice to see you in Dhasdein, Ruand. I rejoice to see you in health."

For all I could tell he did remember. Had personally liked her, and was glad she had too.

Tellurith said, "The rejoicing is mutual."

The rulers' moment was over, to extend the personal one unfitting. Antastes looked away.

At me.

I felt Alkhes take breath. I knew, from the way his whole body stiffened, just what he was going to do.

"This is Sarth," he said. "Born of Hafas, wed into Telluir House, now of Iskarda. The Ruand's bodyguard. Her first marriage-tie."

He took a little breath.

"And my husband as well."

I never would have dared. Nowhere else in Riversend, nowhere else in Dhasdein; except, perhaps, before the Empress. I did not dare look around. If one of them sneers, I could not let myself think. If one of them laughs . . .

Antastes is an emperor in truth. He looked from Alkhes to me to Tellurith and back. Then he sighed again, a ruler martyred by a subordinate whose brilliance is only matched by his scapegracery. Gestured to the Imperials, Out. Shook his head at the protest of the secretary. "Now," he said, "you really had best explain."

"I NEVER DID . . . break faith with you . . ."

He had to stop in the middle. But he met Antastes' eyes.

They had found a place for me, a chair for Tellurith. Alkhes stood, as behoves an accused, braced in that military stance; parade rest. In the middle of the floor. Alone.

Holding Antastes' eyes. As he finished, almost on a breath, "Sire."

And for all the stress, the guilt, the knowledge of his peril, there was something that said, We are long acquainted. If I fear you, it is only with justice. Far more deeply, I expect you to understand.

I trust you to understand.

Antastes rested an elbow on a chair-arm, a temple on a palm. There was the same long custom, the same fundamental acceptance in the way he answered, "Go on."

"When I came back from Amberlight—" the look added, You remember, I told you, the loss of memory, all the rest? Antastes' nod answered yes.

"I was—two men. I remembered why you sent me, I understood the whole . . . I was still Assandar." He stopped, frowning, took a deep breath, and plunged.

"And I was Alkhes."

Antastes was listening. Perhaps, to listen like that is the supreme skill of an emperor. He said, "Who is Alkhes?"

I knew how much he had heard as Alkhes' stance loosened; as I saw the gratitude in his eyes.

"Alkhes was . . . a problem. A danger. A prisoner." His eyes flicked, for a moment, to Tellurith. "Then a—house-guest. Then Telluir troublecrew."

Another breath. "Then—the House-Head's favorite."

How well Antastes knew Amberlight spoke in his face.

"When I came back—I'd made a contract here. I knew there was no stopping it. I tried—to be loyal to both sides."

Antastes was still listening. I read a history of listening, to ideas, to arguments, to daring schemes and impassioned defenses, from a man he had trusted, perhaps, as much as any emperor could.

"I wanted to improve the River's balance." The inflection said, You know. "Once I was there—I wanted to change—to improve—" this time the look he sent Tellurith was apologetic, "Amberlight."

As he looked away Tellurith said, "But there was another player in the game."

Antastes' attention swung with the weight and speed of an enormous snake. She met his gaze full on and said, "The qherrique."

Antastes' brows came down. He glanced at Alkhes. Read acceptance, and shifted focus wholly. "The qherrique."

"Which we had abused, and misused, and let the whole River misuse with us." Tellurith spoke quite clearly, and quite coolly, too audible in the silent little room. "Which we had sold for blood-sorcery, and coercion, and nations' power. Which saw no escape from our misdoings—but to die."

Antastes' back stiffened. " 'Saw'?"

Minutely, she smiled. "I don't know how to explain it. Our words don't apply. But it was sentient. It spoke to us: the House-Heads. It laid—its plans."

"*It* laid?" I had not thought it possible to surprise Antastes.

Quite calmly, Tellurith said, "Yes."

Antastes' back straightened. I understood. I was born and bred in Amberlight, I knew the House-heads' intimacy. But that the qherrique itself should plan, manipulate, have consciousness? It had beggared my mind, as, in his turn, it had beggared Alkhes'.

Antastes drew one sharp, harsh breath. His eyes went back to Alkhes. There was more than old tolerance now. Are you my man? that look said. Is this, however incredible, the truth?

All Alkhes said, and those eyes invoked a lifetime's integrity, was, "Yes."

They waited, while he thought it through. Then he shook his head, a man who had thought the world no longer held astonishment. And turned back to Tellurith.

"So there was," he said, "another player in the game."

Tellurith told him what she had told Darthis.

"And when it had used us: you, me, Alkhes, Amberlight, Cataract, Verrain, Dhasdein . . . It had the victory."

Antastes was staring before him, at the exquisitely simple bronze on the corner pedestal. The River-lord, his hands full of invisible water. The divinities gift us as they choose. And when they choose, they take their gifts away.

Then he brought his eyes back to Tellurith. "And now?"

"It's finished. Amberlight is finished." Antastes' brows rose. "Telluir House are marble-cutters. We have a quarry. We want a livelihood. Nothing more."

Antastes was still listening; with an emperor's ear, to the language below words. He said, "Not even the Sahandan?"

Tellurith's mouth corner moved. "By all means. If we can."

If you choose, said that irony. You know who has the say.

Antastes nodded. To her, as Tanekhet did. To the secretary on his tall scrivener's stool, who made a note. Neither of them had to ask if the boundaries would be right.

Then he looked at Alkhes and said quite gently, "There is also a missing intelligencer."

"He was killed," Tellurith announced clearly, "during an attempted rape."

Antastes' look remembered the siege of Amberlight. Tellurith nodded. "The girl's mother was a little—stressed. The cutter took his head clean off."

I heard the secretary's pen stop. Tellurith stared at the Emperor, and in those eyes, topaz hard, pitiless, I saw the judgment of the Mother herself.

Then Antastes sighed silently: ruler to ruler, admitting, It was not wise, but we both know it is done. That it will be done. Adding aloud, with an equal irony, "It won't happen again."

No, Tellurith's look retorted. You will be more careful, with us.

Antastes turned toward her in his chair. "What news do you have of the River, Ruand?"

We all knew his intelligence far outdid ours. Tellurith met his eyes steadily.

"Cataract has a new ruler. My watchers tell me he has been flirting with Verrain." She lifted a shoulder-point; so delicately. "Dinda wanted a new statuette, before he died. As for Verrain . . ."

"Theirs," agreed Antastes, "is four years older than mine."

Then you have your answer, said her eyes. Nobody on the River can compete with you.

"And," he said, watching her, "Amberlight?"

"Amberlight no longer counts."

Amberlight, said her inflection, is a pack of fools dreaming in their ruins.

"Do you?"

Tellurith gave a small, delicate snort. "Who is in whose house, in whose city, at whose command—Emperor?"

Even Alkhes caught his breath. But nobody walks the balance of word-bouts like Tellurith. Antastes' mouth quirked, and then permitted a half-smile. "Are you a seer, Ruand?"

"When I was a House-Head, Emperor, I could ask. And once—once, without asking—I knew."

He waited.

"There will never be peace," she said, "along the Riverside. Peace is not humans' way. But there will be balance. Cataract will not sell its lands or Verrain flog the Oases dry to buy qherrique. Nor, though it may lose a province edge, will making colonies to raise money for qherrique to hold more colonies, bankrupt Dhasdein."

Antastes relaxed. So slightly it was all but invisible. Saying, clearer than words, So my realm is safe.

Then, very quietly, he said, "You are sure."

Her jaw firmed, and she held that gaze.

"It's gone. We have guns and cutters, yes. As long-lived as your statuettes. There are no mother-lodes. And if there were—I would not use them." The silence caught. She dropped her words into it like stones. "I would never see it enslaved again."

Antastes looked at his hands, and curved them in his lap, as if they cupped a statuette. "Never?"

"Not even for that."

Antastes looked up at her, revealing, for once, half the truth of the Emperor. Who had also known qherrique.

Then he turned to Alkhes.

Sighed, and shook his head.

"Well, lad," he said, "I'll miss you. But," the face was straight, "I see you know where you're going."

Alkhes' face said all he felt. Antastes had already turned away.

"Ruand," he asked, "will Telluir House make treaty with Dhasdein?"

He could have made us vassals; could have enslaved us by stretching out a hand. Could have garrisoned troops on us, and what could we say? I saw Tellurith swallow; before she rose from her chair and answered regally, "Emperor, you honor us."

For once, between rulers, it was the truth.

Autumn. Dhasdein.
Tellurith's Diary

WINTER OR NOT, there will be ships. My bones ache to leave this bleak southern weather; my belly aches for safety, for home. Hardly three months on, the child has not yet upset my balance. In the body, at least.

The treaty should be finished in less than a week. The exact wordage of mutual support and aid will take some thinking, but Fais has given me the draft; such speed is only to be expected, from the Emperor's personal secretary. I will look at it tonight.

As soon as I collect my wits.

Sarth has gone back to the studio; as he says, with that demure face, he has a contract to fill. I send Catheor's ruffians with him, or some spruce young fellows of Tanekhet's. We both know it would be the cruelest of possible disasters, to lose one of us now. Tez goes sometimes, when Alkhes is escorting me. But by the Mother's mercy this morning he had gone, as he has once or twice, to talk with Antastes for himself. Old friendship?

A last change of ideas, between two who valued each other's minds? Whichever it is, he was gone.

When Tanekhet walked in on me.

Tez's growl warned me, as I sat late over morning chocolate—even the nobles lack coffee in Dhasdein—with the treaty draft. I yanked the faded old work-shirt round me like a corselet as I said, "Lord Tanekhet."

"Lady Tellurith."

He was sure of his welcome; already he reads my body-talk so well. He came to the fire; nodded to Tez; sent the waiting-man, with a nod, for a fresh cup. I poured, he sat. Glanced at the draft sheets, smiled briefly. Looked, the sun-on-water eyes expectant, back to me.

"The Emperor has been generous," I said.

His mouth-corners pucked. He was immaculate as ever, in new, still more outrageously brocaded cloth-of-gold. Outrageous as our common certainty that I owed the most of it to him. He settled back in the chair, dandling the cup; his sparring weapon, as is a lady's fan. Then he flicked an eye at Tez and asked, "Will you trust me alone?"

My stomach somersaulted. Sarth, Alkhes had already paid for our success. Was there to be a price from me as well?

But what could I say, in his house, in his debt, in his power, except yes?

Tez glowered, but she went. I waited. But he was staring out into the courtyard, where the pear tree laid its exquisitely spare winter geometry on a sunlit wall.

Tanekhet is a conversation-master. I still thought it was mere pose. Until he brought those eyes back to me and said, "It will be a slow voyage, in winter, upstream."

Then I did let my eyebrows say clearly: Spare the feints.

He gave me that kingfisher glint of smile. With a woman he wanted, it could be lethal, that charm. "Tell me," he said, "how is it, in Iskarda, for—Assandar?"

No doubt my eyes boggled. It was sheer reflex, from endless council-meets, that made me retort, "That is something he might wish to answer for himself."

He made an eloquent, elegant grimace: Be serious. Looked down, up, and gave me a genuine, heart-wrenchingly genuine smile. "This is harder than I expected . . . Very well. How is it for foreigners, in Iskarda?"

His intelligencers would have told him. Was there a thing his intelligencers could not have told him, from where we built the privies to how often I combed my hair? I could feel my eyes glaze. Normal assault and intrigue, the Mother knows, I can manage; what do you do when your opponent, the most dangerous opponent you have ever faced, apparently runs mad?

"There—uh—have been quarrymen in Iskarda every summer. There is—uh—trouble sometimes." Darthis' sardonic growl re-echoed: Always some can't tell yes from no. "Over women. Their—our—customs are different."

He knew all this. He could not have been ignorant. Yet he was watching me like some oracle that would explain his life. "And," he said softly, "with Telluir House?"

"Telluir and Iskarda are one."

How grateful I was, to answer that in truth.

He looked back into his cup. His lashes were thick, curled, bronze, and if they were artificial, it was a magnificent fake.

"How is it," a little pause, "for a foreigner—inside Telluir House?"

I opened my mouth and stopped. Foreigner to me had meant husbands, or women linked by marriage-ties. And, I suddenly realized, I had not thought beyond Amberlight.

"No women," I said carefully, "beyond those of Amberlight blood, have joined Telluir House."

He watched me, with those ambushed forest eyes. But, that silence said. But.

"Alkhes was—an exception."

"And," said Tanekhet gently, "how is it for him, now, in Iskarda?"

How to explain the trials, the struggles, the tensions, the manifold adjustments, on both our sides? That we were building a new world together. That he was a part of it, as much as I, as much as Sarth. If I could, would I have unraveled all that to Tanekhet?

"He is," I said, "one of us."

His lashes fell and I caught a release of tension so fine I had never felt it. Then he looked up. I had the strangest sense, as he spoke, that his heart, his very soul was in his voice.

"How would it be," he said, "for someone else?"

Did my jaw fall? I thought my very spine would melt. It literally felt like surfacing from a head blow, in a shower of blur and sparks. I blinked and gulped and probably gasped aloud.

When vision re-assembled he was still watching me. Exquisite, immaculate, deadly as ever. Down to that ironic smile.

Quite gently, he said, "Yes."

I let myself fall back into the chair. What I wanted to do was splutter, swear, bellow at the top of my lungs, Have you truly gone out of your head?

I could have fenced; offered stupidities like, Do you really mean this? I could have bleated such novice crassness as, But, oh, Lord Tanekhet, *why*? I could have blurted crudities like, You, with your fine clothes and pampered body and the lifelong, unconscious possession of power, you, the force behind the throne in the River's greatest dominion, want to be a *man*—in Iskarda!

Some reflexes of Head-ship do remain. When I could speak, I said, "Lord Tanekhet; do you know how it is, for men, in Iskarda?"

He cocked his head.

"They are—were—chattels. Underlings. They have no vote. They don't choose their wives. Even in—Telluir—they don't make decisions or sit in council or use cutters or even—take up Crafts. They carry water. They chop wood and empty bed-pans and they—have you seen Sarth's hands?"

He nodded. He did not so much as blink.

"Once, they looked like yours."

He looked down at them: white, smooth, every nail's polished pink almond perfect. To be sure, he had labored, but as nobles do; I doubt he had pulled up a girth, let alone carried a bucket, in the length of his life.

"Lord Tanekhet—"

He got, with a motion swift and far less graceful than a panther's, out of his chair. Took three strides to the window and a fistful of curtain in that exquisite grasp.

"Lady Tellurith, I am the highest noble in Riversend. In Dhasdein. I have money enough to buy the Emperor, and its use has not challenged me in fifteen years. I inherited my rank at sixteen. At twenty, I ruled the Court. I have never been dethroned. You know," he never had to stress the word, "what that means."

We owed him our interview, Iskarda, our very lives. If Antastes was supreme rank, he was that rank's power.

To his back I said, "I know."

He let go the curtain. Its silk was crushed. He swung round, and for once: in how many years? there was no conscious management in that stare.

"I am forty-five years old. I have had three wives who gave me two daughters, some delusions, and enormous expense. One is dead. Two I have divorced."

The eyes narrowed. The elegant, resilient body went tense.

"I have some nasty personal habits; I've only just understood the worst. Do you know, Lady Tellurith, that I tormented, persecuted—that I very near killed a fine soldier, a loyal Dhasdein mercenary, a possibly great general—just because I was bored?"

I felt the understanding, the rest of it, stick in my throat.

His body relaxed. For an instant his face relaxed too, and I saw, prolonged and open, the expression I had caught the last time we talked.

"Your husband, Lady Tellurith, came to me for his sake. Would have borne," a wave of the hand that said, You know. "He said to me, I came to sleep with you, or to kill you. Whichever will get Alkhes safe. If he dies, I will kill you anyway."

He cocked his head and studied me.

"When I came down to the boats." He smiled suddenly. I had never seen the look before. "You would have died for them both."

I was speechless. But I did manage to nod.

The smile twisted. "What Assandar would do for you—I already know."

Face you, I did not have to answer. In your full power, when he was renegade from Dhasdein as from Amberlight; and do whatever you asked of him to get that command.

Very softly Tanekhet said, "Lady Tellurith, when I saw you three together, I knew you had built a tie—a trust—a—a—fortress—that—I never dreamed about."

I heard an ember crack in the fire. I heard a board creak in the table under my elbow, a switch of wind against the windows on the court. He was still watching me. I understand what it means, now, to say someone's heart is in their eyes.

"That," he said even more softly, "is something—that I do not think could have happened in Amberlight. Something—that I *know* could not happen in Dhasdein."

He straightened a little.

"I don't know if I see it all. I don't even know if you do. But . . . gods, if it succeeds—it will go beyond a feeling between men and women that I," he swallowed, "never reached. It will be—a new world."

He looked down at me, trying to smile.

"I understand your reservations. All your reservations. You know what I have. What I am."

The smile sharpened. Began to twist.

"But this, Lady Tellurith, is something for which I would give it all. Not to be sure of winning. Only for the chance to try."

I MUST HAVE SAID something: Wait, let me think, sit down. He came away from the window. Even his elegant sword-resilience had become simply, plainly, tense.

When I did not speak he leant back in the chair. Drew a long breath and added, on a note that struggled for urbanity, "Lady Tellurith. In Khasterian convents, they accept a dower."

He read my look. Both parts of my look. I had just been offered all the resources Iskarda would ever need.

And all the bribes Iskarda could never take.

"Forget the money! Do you know what I know, about the River, Dhasdein, the Court, the Emperor? Do you know what I could give you, without need for intelligencers? Do you know what my resources ...!"

He checked. Produced a short, ragged laugh.

"I can see, if I go on, it will only dig a deeper pit." He was on his feet. "All I ask is that you consider my proposal." A soft, almost balanced little laugh. "And remember," the look made it clear he was talking beyond money, "you can name your price."

Now I HAVE my wits back ... Now I have had time to adjust, it is not so entirely ... unthinkable. Given a little time, it is not quite entirely ... impossible.

But beyond any doubt, it is not something to be decided alone. It ought to be talked over, pondered, in Iskarda. By all Iskarda. By all of Telluir.

Here ... It is a matter for what passes as my House.

At the very least, it can do no harm to hear what they say.

XIV

Autumn. Dhasdein.
Tellurith's Diary

WHAT ALKHES said was, "NO!"

At the top of his lungs, before the entire guest suite shuddered to the crash of the door.

What Tez said—after a gulp, and three minutes with her head in her hands—was, "Be almost worth it. Change a bed-pan? Tanekhet!"

What Sarth said, shaken beyond all caution, was, "But, Tellurith—who's going to marry *him*?"

Autumn. Dhasdein.
Journal kept by Sarth

I REALIZE NOW, fully, truly. There will *never* be a time when I can guess what Tellurith may do next.

Not the—incredibility—of Tanekhet.

But the way she looked at me, and those eyes went away; and when they came back . . .

"Well," she said: demure, as only Tellurith can be, saying such things, "perhaps, it's time the House had men who are there in their own right."

I think I am so calm because all of this is so entirely impossible. It is a fantasy, a waking dream, a sequel to the fairy tale of meeting the Emperor.

Of course Tanekhet would want to throw away the apex of the River-world to spend the rest of his life hauling pots. Of course the Emperor will say, Go, parcel up your inheritance like a peddler's pack, of course there will be no uproar to make Amberlight's fall a carnival play. Of course he will be accepted, with never a ripple, into Telluir—by Zuri!—

let be Darthis! Of course he will live happily ever after, a noble, a man, a Dhasdeiner—Tanekhet—unmarried—in our House.

Can even You imagine what Tellurith intends to do with *him*?

Autumn. Dhasdein.
Tellurith's Diary

IF THE QHERRIQUE is gone, perhaps the Mother has not deserted me after all.

How else explain that lightning stroke? That vision's blast, cleaving reality, that blinding prospect beyond imagination, on a—

" . . . new world."

How did he know?

Returned Here, There remains inconceivable. I have no idea how to get there. For this at least, precedence remains. Assemble the House. Let the defendant plead his case.

Let Tanekhet do what I can not.

I talked the other two round with no more fuss than you would expect. They are House-folk, of Amberlight, the idea of a House-meet is instinct to them; and they know the necessity. They are realists.

It was dark before Alkhes came home. Past supper, a grating prolongation of luxury, before any of us judged that thundercloud fit to broach. I felt Sarth beside me, tenser than a bowstring in the elegantly fragile chair as I spoke. I prayed there would at least be no man-handling, no more than words of violence.

I did not expect Alkhes to start up; grab my wrist; and yank me, with the street-fighter's lightning expertise, straight into the bedroom as he slammed the door in Tez's face.

The boards rattled. With more than street-fighter's skill he ripped over the lock. The door vibrated. He shouted, "Let be!"

In a tone that would have deterred Zuri herself, before he whipped about on me.

To face that look, amid polished wood and brocaded hangings and perfumed shadows in the tastefully screened firelight. To feel the way his hands shook as he grabbed my shoulders, to hear the note on which it came out . . .

"Tel—*gods*, Tel, you can't go through with this!"

"Caissyl—"

"*No!*"

For an instant, staring in those eyes, I felt the molten surge of physical terror. For an instant, I really did think he was going to savage me.

He was all eyes in the fire-dusk; I could feel his heart race, could see, too clearly, the sweat beaded on his face. The hands spasmed. I bit my lip not to cry out. If I did that, Sarth would take the door down without waiting for Tez.

"Tel, can't you *see* what will happen—if you say yes?"

He had looked no wilder Mid-winter morning. I reached up to grasp his wrists. Slender, wiry, troublecrew wrists, flexing now like the wings of a frantic hawk. I held them, for the faint hope of quieting him, as I replied.

"Caissyl—can't *you* see what will happen—if we say no? . . . Caissyl, don't!" I jerked him by the waist, I really did think he had been going to faint. I could not bear to think past that. I shook him, trying to deny the undeniable for us both.

"We can make demands, we can do it on our terms, it's not as if—" He made a sharp little sound that said, all too clearly, Don't mock. I drew him close, the only comfort I had, and he leant on me as he had that first night in the slum inn-room, as if there was nothing else to hold him up.

Tanekhet; the monster at his nightmares' core; present, accepted, permanent. In Iskarda. In his refuge. In Telluir House.

Tanekhet; the power of Dhasdein. Who might sue as a suppliant; but we had learnt already what subtle, unmanacled captivities he used.

If we said, No, we might never see Iskarda again.

"If we have to, we can run—"

The noise this time made me clench my arms on him. "No, all right, we can't, if we do . . ."

Then Dhasdein's power might reach, in malice, in all too earnest, to Iskarda itself.

He must have felt my terror then, because, crazy as it sounds, it steadied him. An outland man's reaction; where Sarth would have been undone by my undoing, it threw the weight of decision back where Alkhes' life had trained him to expect it; on him.

"We talk then. We delay. Keep stalling, think of new conditions. Send letters to Iskarda. Even if it takes until next spring—"

"No!" He jumped, I jumped myself. Without my knowing, both arms had locked over my belly. "We don't—I don't—we have to get out of here!"

His eyes told me how I looked. What he understood. We stood so still amid that perfumed luxury, understanding the cruelty of its façade.

Then he shivered and reached for me. Over his shoulder, the firelight caught the faces of the statue group in the holy niche opposite the fire. Sweet, bland. Implacable. He let his breath out and whispered it into my hair.

"No—I know what can happen—if we say no."

Autumn. Dhasdein.
Journal kept by Sarth

I THOUGHT Alkhes *understood* what we were about!

When Tellurith got him out of the bedroom, he looked fey, but he seemed sane enough. He agreed we had to meet, he suggested this morning: give Tanekhet a day's leeway, he said, at least pretend it's time to assemble his case. I thought he knew how much hope, how little choice, how infinitely small a time we have. I thought he at least, as I never doubt Tez has, would be thinking ahead. If the Emperor lets us play out this charade, what can be simpler? A man alone in our company, on the winter River, on a boat?

Give me grace!

I still thought it when we gathered, this fine, bright, frosty morning, after the servants tidied and furbished and set out at Tellurith's order the chairs, the writing implements and paper, the refreshment, as for a great House-meet in Amberlight. When she settled at the polished table's head, with Tez for recorder at her elbow, with Alkhes and me to approximate Craft-Heads at either side. When, prompt to his hour, Tanekhet was announced.

As you might expect, it was not an entry but an entrance. No speech-scroll under an arm: Tanekhet would naturally speak free-style. No papers or ledger-evidence either, just a flat carved cedar box, elegant as a fan case. And no escort. Statement, question, arrogance?

Or humility?

The Mother knows, that coat was pure provocation: quilted silk, the most delicate new cherry blossom pink, embroidered hand spans deep with horizon-lavender irises. He bowed to the meeting, as a great lord, as a veteran of lords' assemblies; with the most delicate of inflections, to Tellurith. "Ruand, I am honored," he said.

How many decisions has Tanekhet swayed, for a man, a city, a province, a nation's life? And not upon the crude instrument of a public assembly, but before a lords' counsel; before the Emperor.

He knew to begin with our advantage. He does have all the inner knowledge he promised. For a quarter of what he said about Verrain, let be the word from Cataract, Zuri would sell her soul. And of course he knew better than to squander it all, but I watched Tez's face, and knew what more Zuri would pay.

Till he reached a period, and Alkhes slashed it like a knife. "What's it worth without you?"

Meaning, the staples of intelligencing, the plans, the passwords, the agents, would all change. And in six months the rest would be out of date.

Tanekhet smiled at him. Alkhes held his eyes. He was taut in the chair, every muscle clenched. Every line said, I'm here to fight, to thwart, to shatter you. But at that smile, I saw the lines come out, fine as chisel-work, beside his mouth.

"I beg your pardon," said Tanekhet softly, and unclasped the box that lay before him on the table. "There are also—these."

The sharp winter light caught them as he lifted. Sifted, let fall, trickles, handfuls: crystallized sky, immortal grass. Everlasting blood.

"They are," the inflection said how little they meant to him, "a dowry gift."

Even at black market rates, sold off in haste, they would supply Iskarda's income for a year.

Alkhes flicked a hand. As delicately, the mere direction of the words an insult, he addressed Tellurith. "A bribe?"

Tanekhet's smile widened. I tried not to yell, Every time you respond he knows he has reached you. I tried not to shut my eyes.

"Shall we say, an earnest of the rest?"

Alkhes put his brows up. I have seen him incisive, and enraged, and truly lethal, coiled to immobility. I did not know he could insult as urbanely as Tanekhet himself.

"The Suzerainty," Tanekhet addressed Tellurith, his aplomb unscathed, "will go—doubtless to his utter ecstasy—to my nephew. The lands are entailed."

"Ah." Alkhes folded his hands. "So when your intelligence is out-dated and your—jewels—spent—which may be all of six months—we will be offering . . . charity?"

Tanekhet's smile was absolutely genuine. To have driven you so far, it said. Wonderful.

"The Regency is mostly title. Antastes will probably administer the colonies himself. The Suzerainty includes the family lands in Riversrun and Mel'eth. Quite a large part of Mel'eth, actually. And various possessions, in the colonies. There are also the commercial, ah—ventures. My scribes could give you a full list. Beyond this, however, my mother left me land in Verrain. Just west of Assuana. Quite a fine horse-farm. And there is the mine."

I did it partly to cut the knot between him and Alkhes, partly as proxy for Tellurith. Partly it was uncontrollable. I heard myself repeat, "Mine?"

The forest-light eyes turned: polite, ironic, knowing as ever. "The silver mine was one of my first personal investments. Near the Quetzistani border. At present, it works at half-capacity. I trade the silver for 'exotics.' From Cataract."

Alkhes made a tiny sound, just short of outright derision. Tanekhet smiled at him again and added, "Naturally, in my own ships."

Some southern bird landed on the pear tree, a blur of scarlet, a flurry of water-pure sound. I was glad of the pretext to look. I doubt even I could have controlled my face.

Silver; a shipping line; trade ties with Cataract. Everything we needed, for the future of Iskarda.

It was Tez who tossed away her recorder's role and leant forward to fling at him in her clipped Navy voice, "Then what in the Mother's name do you want with us?"

Tanekhet's eyes flicked from her to Tellurith. He was too great a master to betray reluctance. He did say, "The Ruand knows."

Tez said, "This is the House."

Tanekhet looked at Tellurith. Who answered, too quietly for offense, too steadily for argument, "This is the House."

He took in a breath. Straightened a little, from that posture of orator's grace.

"It's time," he said, "to make my soul."

He surveyed us, with that half-taunting, half-ironic smile that acknowledged the incredibility; and dared us to be so crass as to mock.

"I have been forty-five years a lord—a noble—an eminence in Dhasdein."

He thrust a hand among the gems and turned them over, as a farmer might turn tally-sticks at harvest's end. "I have had my fill—the world's fill—of power. Luxury. Wealth." The gems cascaded. A twist of the wrist that said, more elegantly than any actor, At the last, what is all that worth?

Tez's uprising in her chair retorted, a folk's survival. Alkhes cut across her outrage with two acid claps. "Felicitations," he said.

On the performance, he meant. Tez snorted aloud and cut in after, "And it'll make your soul to catch pneumonia chopping our firewood in the rain?"

Tanekhet's smile applauded them both. I think Alkhes actually ground his teeth.

"If I can make my soul by catching pneumonia," he answered sweetly, "I will chop your firewood and give thanks."

Tez's growl cut off as Tellurith laid a hand on her arm.

"Lord Tanekhet," polite, utterly inscrutable, "what you encounter here is itself a warning. Do you wish to live with it for the rest of your life?"

The way he faced her told me the real battle was opening at last.

"Lady Tellurith, I know no jewels—not a whole silver mine—will buy what I want. I offer that only as—compensation. I know what sort of life it will be." The curl of those mouth-corners was almost gentle. "You've made its drawbacks very clear."

Tez's expression yelled, Are you out of your wits?

Tellurith sighed and leant a temple on her palm. "How," she said, "will you persuade Antastes?"

"Ah." He need not have shown us that the shoe pinched at last, that was calculated as the rest. The turned-up hands, the regretful, charmingly humorous complicity said, You know as well as I that to let his highest noble stroll out of Riversend is the last thing Antastes would allow. In myself I am a vital resource. In an enemy's hands, I am a threat that would be insupportable. I may well be the death of Iskarda.

Alkhes snapped, "Forget it. Your soul is safe."

Tanekhet's eyes turned. I had time to think, Oh, gods.

He did not change stance. Not a lip lifted. Yet the light in that eye changed, and my back crawled, as the panther looked from its forest depths.

Very softly, all but a sigh, he said, "And to whom should that matter most?"

If Alkhes had managed to wait . . . if he could have matched that subtlety. If he had not had to challenge Tanekhet, to imply, too broadly, This is all a pose. If he had not remembered, too clearly, the reality none of us was admitting. If he had not provoked Tanekhet to unveil that reality, in a way he, of us all, best understood.

I saw his face drain: the lips go white, the eyes freeze, gelid and opaque as death.

Before he got out of the chair, with the lurch of a crippled ancient, and walked away.

Autumn. Dhasdein.

Meditations. Alkhes-Assandar

I DON'T KNOW how I found the door. I don't remember where I meant to go. I was past thinking. Just, the way the worst wounded do, needing some hole to crawl into. Somewhere to hide.

Probably I aimed for the house door. But there were people in the way. Something was still thinking for me, something must have said, These are not house-folk, these are wardens. The trap-jaws have begun to close. Oh, gods, the nightmare of a lifetime; because at every occupied door I turned and there was another passage, another door, another blockade, he was hunting me through that house as he had hunted me through Riversend, through the army, through Dhasdein, through every twist and turn and subterfuge of my life.

I do remember the brass latch, the room round as a fighting-ring, a lord's whimsy, with its little round windows on some inner courtyard and its shelves of scrolls and the extravagance of a daily fire in the little tiled fireplace.

And no door but the one I had come in.

WHEN I turned about, I already knew what I would see.

He watched me, framed between the jambs; that expression, impregnable as armor, of polite regret.

"Monster," he murmured. "Nightmare. Ogre. But, I think—I do think—you might have granted me this much. That I would not coerce a guest—in my own house."

He cocked his head a little. Years of nightmares told me what came next. He was going to step forward. Walk up to me. And I had either to stand there and enter waking nightmare—

Or strike like any cornered, over-driven beast.

And if I did, he knew—both of us knew—exactly what would happen to the rest.

What came next . . . It is not the discontinuity, of the palace courtyard, of Iskarda. Not *There* and then *Here*—memory remains, but great sheets and spaces have torn out of it. A sail loose, a ripped curtain, a painted screen disintegrating upon shards, swirls, wave upon wave of black . . .

Before the hands gripping, slapping, shaking me, the voice yelling on a note I never heard in that voice before, "You whoreson, you're not running out again—NO! Gods rot it, NO! Assandar—Alkhes! Come back here—come BACK!"

The ferocity, the furious determination. More terrified than I was myself.

The black swirled down like draining water. The world took on color and vibrating resonance. Someone had slapped my face.

"NO!"

I don't know why it worked. It never worked for Tellurith. Or Caitha, or anyone in Iskarda. Perhaps it was being called a coward. Perhaps it was that I had reached the worst moment of a lifetime. Backed in a corner, in his hands, with no way out. There was, in all truth, nowhere to go.

"Look at me—the River-lord blast your eyes out, look at me. Are you a soldier or a gutter-louse? Look at me!"

I forget what else he said. Because I was looking at him. Looking, working to look, hanging onto looking for dear life. Anything, even facing Tanekhet, to fend off the onset of that black.

"Gods!" he said. And let go, on a great, gusty breath.

The world came back. My shoulders up against a bookcase, scroll-ends jammed into my spine, a coat drenched with sweat. Parquet floor polished, shining dizzily under my feet . . . "No," he said furiously, "look here, curse you. Look up!"

Exquisitely arranged brown hair and forest-green eyes and an absolute absence of mockery or irony or merest self-assurance. Tanekhet's face.

"Damn," he said. Still breathing hard. "Damn, that was—"

I could not answer. I could not fight back. There was nothing left in me at all.

"Assan—" He stopped. Amended, quite shakily, "Alkhes?"

Even then, inexplicable lunacy, I had to look defeat in the face.

Whatever it cost, and it did cost, he did not look away.

What he did was to square his shoulders, and put his chin up, and—I am still not sure I saw this—set his teeth.

"I understand," he said, "what I did to you. You may believe it or not: but I never intended it. Not like that. I don't think about forgiveness. I'm not sure—that I could forget."

My vision went red. No, I wanted to scream at him, I can't forgive and I can't forget! You have been my life's canker, you were nearly my double destruction, everything I ever had as Assandar you blighted, and now I have another life you want to ruin that!

"No." His mouth corners said it all. Penitent, rueful, unsurprised.

I was beyond war-skill; beyond word-war. It came out as if I was a five-year-old. "Why?" I said in his face as if he, the master of intrigue and manipulation, would ever answer openly. "*Why?*"

He looked away. I think—I know now, looking back—that we were quite alone. None of the servants or guards had thundered in after him, none of—us—had followed. He understood I was the greatest obstacle to his desire. He meant to have his say out. He was managing even this.

"When I said, I wanted to make my soul—it was true."

He looked up under his lashes. I could not even sneer.

"You must know what I said. To the Lady Tellurith."

A new world. A fresh beginning. Something never seen anywhere in Dhasdein. With him hauling pots about the foundations. To be sure. Tanekhet.

"It's more than that."

His chin came up in earnest this time. I got the great lord, stripping before a clod.

"I have to go."

No doubt I was staring like the veriest of dolts.

"Not for my own sake."

The chin came down again. He looked past me into the fire and said it almost under his breath.

"Because of what can happen—if I stay."

The eyes came back to me.

"To Dhasdein."

To how many men has the great lord Tanekhet revealed himself? His innermost self, and its secret cancers, laid open, how often, in the length of a life?

My sense came back from somewhere. I was angry then, but no longer for myself.

"And what will make it so much better for Iskarda?"

He flexed his shoulders and shot back almost in his old style. "You keep telling me how much power I'll enjoy there."

Oh, certainly; till he cozened Tellurith or charmed the Craft-heads, or seduced some gullible innocent, until he turned the flank of some bastion like Zuri—

Or Sarth.

"No!"

I had not meant, quite so loudly, to yell.

And still, no one came. He watched me. Standing quietly, hands down, posture quiet; the way I have stood myself, coaxing some half-wild colt.

"Of course," I said it as I had in the meeting; a last resort, "we have so much choice."

His eyes sparked. The color came up this time, brighter than rouge on his cheeks.

"I told you before: I may be a nightmare, an ogre. You might have credited I would not coerce a guest. Not in my own house."

While I gaped, he lifted his right hand, palm outward, and said it softly, ironically, cutting as a rapier slash.

"You have my word."

Half of me wanted to revenge myself; to sneer, And what is that worth, the word of the greatest trickster in Dhasdein? The other half wanted to shout, Prove it. Let me walk out, right now.

I said, feeling my throat tight as if going into a duel, "What if we say no?"

"Then you leave." The hazel-green eyes focused past me. I all but saw his life's meaning, its back turned, walking away.

"But," I said, more stupidly than ever. "You can—"

"Compel you?" The eyes flashed, impatient at true idiocy. "To be sure! I talk my way past Antastes and force myself into your company—you, and that Navy termagant, and your—husband—How far upRiver would one of you put a blade in me, or doctor my wine, or just slip me over the side?"

I think my mouth fell open. I had been too deep enthralled to the past. When his shield would have held far beyond the borders of Dhasdein.

He all but snorted. "What will the Empire care? And if it hasn't crossed your husband's mind by now, then I give you leave to tell him it's crossed mine!"

I heard his sleeve rustle. The tick of the fire. Of a sudden he put his hand out and pushed—gods, almost as Sarth had done—pushed my hair back. The way Sarth did, that very first time.

"Don't look so shattered, little general." There was the strangest quirk at the corner of his mouth. "You won't believe it, but I wouldn't have him otherwise." The voice softened. "Come—Alkhes. If you take me, it has to happen willingly. It can't work anyway else."

My throat was dry. "What if—they know all this. And they still say— no?"

He took a visible breath. "Then—I go in any case. Up the River, down the River. To the archipelago. To Cataract." He flipped a hand. "I told you—Alkhes." He still wanted to use my old name. "Your husband—Sarth—showed me too much."

He meant it. He would do it. It was the truth.

And if he meant it—there was still a choice.

Near twenty-five years, I wanted to say to him, you have terrorized me. I could never forgive you. I cannot forget. I would never do it for your sake. But for others?

I thought of the horse farm, the ships, the silver mine. Just as much resources as Antastes might let him take, just as much as might tip the balance for Iskarda. Of the resources that he might bring, in his own brain.

Of that mind, that presence, loose in Iskarda.

THINKING BACK NOW, I am sure of it. The gods witness: I did this without malice.

I did not do it for myself.

While all that went on, he had waited. I don't think he even looked at me. Tanekhet was a master of so much; not least, of wheedling what he wanted from one with the ultimate mastery. He had practiced it all his life.

I looked away into the fire; that was my one cowardice, that like an officer commanding an execution squad, I could not look at what I wrought.

"If I could do it," I marvel now at how steady I made it sound, "I'd say I forgive you. But —I can't."

Our eyes held. Then he lifted and dropped a hand; the delicate, ritual gesture of a lord conceding victory at dice.

"So be it," he said.

And turned, and walked away.

Two paces, three paces. The doorway. Freedom, safety, friendship lay beyond it. Iskarda, intact.

Forgiveness and forgetfulness. That he had dared to offer.

That I, less magnanimous, could not give myself.

WHEN I SAID, "Stop!" it came out more grunt than cough.

I saw his shoulders jerk. At the last, he could not conceal that.

I leant back on the bookcases and the scrolls dug like scabbard feet into my sodden shirt.

"Rot your soul," I said to that upright, elegant back. "How are you going to get round Antastes?"

———————

Autumn. Dhasdein.
Journal kept by Sarth

So much for sense, and patience, and a quiet solution to this imbroglio. Mother—no, this is nothing to do with You, this is pure outland imbecility—gods, what do Outlanders use for brains?

If he was not my husband I would cheerfully poison him.

I HAVE LOOKED at that five minutes. And now I must renege.

I would not poison him. Whatever he does, I doubt I will ever poison him. Not just because he is my husband.

Because he is, with all that means—

Alkhes.

THIS IS *not* to say I could not joyfully have slaughtered the numbskull, however long it was after he sleep-walked out, and Tanekhet, without a by-your-leave, an abyss of discourtesy, went after him—and Tellurith grabbed me so hard I myself have bruises and shot at me, "No!"

She was white as he was. "No!" she snapped again. And bit her lip till the blood came. "This time—you can't help."

It was an eternity, until we heard the footsteps. Until they came in, the two of them, side by side. Both looking as if they had spent a night as the Mother's Ear in Iskarda; and Alkhes, needless to say, wan and weak as a man back from the River-lord's hell.

Yet somehow, as on that morning in the cell under our house in Iskarda . . . reborn.

But whatever life's nightmare he has exorcised, did he have to give Tanekhet his pledge?

His honor-trothed word. Cut in granite: if Tanekhet does not come to Iskarda, it will not be for want of our attempts—our whole-hearted, completely earnest attempts—to get him there.

Atop that—atop that! He—Alkhes—my husband—my supposed fellow in the House, in everything Tellurith struggles for—*he*—

Has dared to demand a plighted word, a personal vow not to hinder, to resist, to lay a *finger* on Tanekhet.

From ME.

What Dhasdeiners, what soldiers, not to mention intelligencers, can mean by "honor" is beyond my understanding. A man, however bizarre it sounds, well-versed in politics. And ready to throw away Iskarda for the sake of a "personal pledge."

Were he not my husband—were he not Alkhes—I would resort to Zuri's tactics and beat in his head.

Autumn. Dhasdein.
Tellurith's Diary

WHATEVER ELSE we lose here, Mother, I give you witness: this has been worth it all.

To see Alkhes walk through that door, shoulder to shoulder with his demon, and read in his eyes that at last, at long last—Tanekhet is just a man, nothing else.

But I guess why Sarth has spent half the day looking a perfect thundercloud. Like me, he is, at heart, still Amberlight. Like me, like Tez, he would have been ready to nod, and cede, and acquiesce.

And if Antastes failed to solve the matter, on the way upRiver, for ourselves.

Well, that door is shut. I daresay Tanekhet understood, when he went after Alkhes, exactly what lay on the dice-throw. But it is settled now.

Not for the House itself will I overturn my husband's pledge.

Autumn. Dhasdein.
Journal kept by Sarth

TANEKHET WOULD not say how or when he meant to do the thing. Nothing surer than that he would gain instant audience, whenever he chose, but even the Riversrun Suzerain must consider manners, policy. The tidal wave of rumor, the imminent panic if he tore straight off to the Emperor.

So I expected time for lordly revelations, imperial ponderings, diplomatic courtesy. Not an Imperial guard detachment at Tanekhet's door this very afternoon.

Praise the Mother, Alkhes was not abroad: because they broke clean through stewards and chamberlains, bundled us from our midday soup and marched us off, like arrested felons, in what we stood in. Even searched us, like felons, at the arrest point.

No surprise, if some crazy relief, when they stamped and clashed their way straight to the imperial palace. Or when the gate guards admitted us with a glance at the commander's token and not the slightest check. House-folk and dignitaries parted, ushered, opened doors, not a face revealing anything. Some of Antastes' folk are worthy of the Tower.

By the time we arrived I feared to disgrace it myself. My throat was dry, my back running sweat: not least at being haled into the imperial presence in house-clothes, with my hair in a workaday tangle. It was the first time, since we left Amberlight, that I truly wished for a veil.

Antastes was in a small audience hall. With guards, a whole ten ranged behind the Emperor's presence seat, glittering like scaly statues, pike-blades gleaming above their heads. Scribes and scribe-Heads, a small detachment, with the look of those who hold actual power. Our own troops formed a line below Antastes' two-stepped dais, with the Emperor ensconced in his tall, carven chair.

And Tanekhet.

He stood against the side-wall opposite the scribes. Alone. Gorgeous in a gold-laced ivory-and-copper brocade coat, with more rings than I ever saw him wear: both his ears bore pearls. A lord's court-dress. That did not match the bleached, frozen, almost bruised look about his face.

Alkhes looked once. Tellurith never seemed to see him at all. She inclined her head, the tiniest obeisance, to Antastes. A fellow ruler's acknowledgement. A ruler scanted courtesy, a determination to overlook it just so far as her own dignity was not impaired.

Antastes dispensed with flowery greetings too. He sat a little straighter and said, "So Ruand, you want to take my Suzerain as well?"

He did not sound particularly angry. At the tiny burring undertone I felt rather than saw Alkhes flinch.

Tellurith said, "The lord Tanekhet asked to come with us. Yes."

Do not try to browbeat me with what I already owe you, said the under-text. The treaty is another matter. And, it added, do not try to insult your vassal. The lord Tanekhet is not a parcel or an animal, to be "taken" anywhere.

Nor, it continued, will I now eschew any hand in it, to throw the onus back on him.

Antastes frowned. "For what purpose, Ruand?"

"Surely, Emperor, the lord Tanekhet has explained that himself."

Don't, said the under-text this time, try to divide us by humiliating him, speaking as of a nothing, over his head.

"For what purpose," Antastes said very quietly, "on your side?"

Tellurith considered. I have never seen her in combat with the Thirteen, but I know what it means, when her eyes look like that. She is working out, with the speed of thought, some wholly unexpected riposte.

"The Mother sent me a vision," she said.

Then as Antastes blinked, stared, stiffened upright, she shook her head. "No, Emperor. I told you, never again."

"Ruand." Now the weight of Dhasdein was in that frown.

"It came from something," Tellurith answered evenly, "the lord Tanekhet said."

It was a long moment before Antastes leant back, hard, on an elbow. An eagle's curve about its prey, unappeased.

"Ruand?"

Tellurith gave him the face I have seen her show Darthis.

"It is not a matter that need trouble Dhasdein."

Antastes' stare demanded, Do you wish me to prove that for myself?

Tellurith's equally unblinking gaze retorted, I am your treaty ally. Will you sully yourself with violence to me?

All too readily. We all knew the answer to that.

"It is a matter," Tellurith said, "for the House."

She held his eyes, the way you see Heartland lion tamers in the great markets, when they pretend to cow their beasts. As Antastes stared back we could all feel the grains going into the balance: This is a treaty-sharer, ruler of a small but valuable outpost, imperial honor is at stake, there are a considerable number of them to disappear. This is a treaty-sharer, but with no power behind her, imperial honor is a matter of publicity, and how will they make a noise in the imperial dungeons? Or the River itself?

And there is, after all, Tanekhet.

There was, after all, Tanekhet. Too valuable to lose so easily. But too powerful, to make so easily disappear.

"Does this matter require my Suzerain in the flesh?"

My servant, said the under-text. My weapon, my possession. What reason will make me let him go?

"It would be a poor requital," Tellurith answered, "to begin it without the lord Tanekhet."

"My Suzerain."

"Not after he leaves Dhasdein."

Almost—almost—Antastes scowled.

"In six months time the empire will have forgotten the office-bearer. The office remains."

Antastes' brow did furrow. In six months' time, as Alkhes had said, the information Tanekhet carried would be out of date. The sub-contest was not going his way.

"A high price for a treaty."

Especially, said the under-text, growing more unscrupulously truthful, to such a rag-tag ally as Iskarda.

Tellurith spread her hands. She has picked it up in the market, a haggler's gesture she often used when bargaining for Strethilis. "A valued; a priceless boon."

Gracing such an ally with imperial magnanimity. No one turns swords in the hand like Tellurith.

Antastes almost snorted. "There is something on the River beyond the compass of a Ruand of Amberlight?"

"I am Ruand of Iskarda."

"The Empire's valued—friend."

He had drawn a breath that made it deadly, before he threw. Suppose, said that small, wicked hiatus, Iskarda changes its mind?

Tellurith repeated that little snort of hers. "Need I remind you, Emperor? Who is in whose house, at whose command? How would one man change that balance? Even the Riversrun Suzerain?"

There was enough truth in that to silence both of them.

After a moment Antastes folded his hands. "But it would no longer be," he repeated, "the Riversrun Suzerain."

Tellurith smiled at him. The smile of a teacher to encourage a slow but advancing child. "No."

Antastes sank his chin on a fist and stared. "You really expect him to resign his rank? His honors? His wealth?"

"I expect the lord Tanekhet to do nothing he has not proposed himself."

Antastes' eyes moved. Tanekhet did not straighten. It was the merest tensing of muscles that said, I am at your service.

That braced for a trial which had already sapped his strength.

"You did offer to resign the Suzerainty? The Wardship? The—" a pause "—revenues as well?"

"Sire."

Tanekhet has lived a life at Court. The frost was the merest trace in his voice: are you calling me a liar and venial too?

Antastes glanced at Tellurith. "So this matter requires the lord Tanekhet—solely in the flesh?"

"The lord Tanekhet," the faintest steel undertone, "has requested admission to Telluir House. He tells me he has private revenues." Her chin came up. "But if we accept him, we will do so if he comes to us solely in the flesh."

With a hook in the end that asked, Are you so paltry you will strip him bare?

Antastes looked back to Tanekhet.

"And you would be prepared to go: solely in the flesh?"

Tanekhet's jaw did stiffen then. But the control, or the training, or the desire held. Take my lands away from me, that cool stare said. You will not take what I am, in myself.

"Sire."

"The greatest lord of Dhasdein. Setting off to live in an upland village among folk who—I am told—are still close kin to Amberlight?"

That innuendo encompassed all that Tez, all that Tellurith had said: Are you really prepared to live a dog's life among folk who will treat you so?

Tanekhet's cheekbones flushed, but he bowed exquisitely. Exquisitely as Antastes himself had at once galled him and flirted the insult past Tellurith's head.

"To live amid such—austerities. Such simplicity. Such—ah—lack of wealth."

Tanekhet inclined his head. The parody of sanctity was exquisite.

"And what, exactly, do you expect to do?"

"Sire." It came through his teeth, for all its urbanity. "I will do whatever the lady Tellurith," the bow was a miracle of affronted grace, a hairsbreadth from insolence, "requires of me."

Antastes' brows rose.

"The first lord of Dhasdein. Negotiator of the Wave Island Peace, commander-in-chief of the Riversrun War. Out in the mud in a week's worth of beard and bear's grease, scraping pots."

Tanekhet's nostrils had pinched white. The glitter of the brocade across his shoulders marked the rhythm of his breath.

"You insult your allies—sire."

I nearly ducked. I expected the sky to fall. Antastes merely leant a cheek on his palm and shook his head.

"Gods," he said. "Oh, the River-lord bear witness. A scullion. A—"

"Enough!"

The word was a panther cough. The panther eyes shot sparks, he came upright with the spring of the panther ready to charge.

And Antastes looked back to Tellurith.

"Behold my leopard," he said. "How long will he wear your leash, if this is how he honors me?"

Tellurith looked from him to Tanekhet and back and folded her hands into her sleeves. "But in Iskarda," she said, "he will be carrying wood and water; a scullion, in the mud."

Tanekhet's eyes went wide. One tiny second that was almost glee before the mask reformed. He was breathing hard, but his bow to Tellurith was an exquisite dance between noble's courtesy to her, and a double-finger obscenity to his emperor.

Antastes tapped a finger on the chair arm, watched his Suzerain and produced a small, bleak smile.

"So you'll renounce it all. Your silver-lined bath. Your twenty tailors, your shopful of perfumes. Your silk underclothes. Even your manicurist."

Tanekhet managed to look almost blank. Antastes cocked his head.

"I suppose you've already told a steward to fix your clothes?"

Tanekhet did flush then. It flooded from brow to throat, a tide of color, uncontrollable.

"If my Emperor deigns to release me," with a stress on the "deigns" that made it a silk-lash, "I will be happy to go in my shirt."

"And," Antastes said softly, "forsaking your entertainments as well?"

Tanekhet's face drained. From scarlet to bloodless, in a couple of breaths.

Antastes nodded. "I've been happy," he said affably, "to spare you the odd stray from the criminal pens. Slum people. Riff-raff. A couple of foreigners better off—elsewhere."

Did you really think, that half-smile added, I didn't know?

Tanekhet had not known. It was in every breath, in every muscle of that blanched, that rigored face.

Antastes looked back to Tellurith.

"You do know," he spoke politely, the tinge of kind concern, "about the lord Tanekhet's—private tastes?"

And Tellurith, the Mother's blessing on her, looked him straight in the eye and said, "I know."

It winded them both. Tanekhet's chin came down and for a second he literally gaped.

"I also know," Tellurith went on evenly, "why the lord Tanekhet wishes to come to Iskarda."

For one instant, before he put the pieces together, Antastes' look said, So he told you first. And Tellurith's eye responded, All of it.

Antastes looked back to Tanekhet. Who gave him the stare of a cornered panther, before it flings itself on the spears.

"And all," said Antastes softly, "for the sake of a—soul."

Tanekhet said nothing. A goaded panther's rage looked from those eyes.

Antastes leant back in his chair and glanced, quite kindly, back to Tellurith.

"Ruand," he said, "with the greatest regret . . . I could not, in all conscience, loose such a hazard upon you. I think it only prudent, and wise, and kind—to keep my plagues at home."

Tellurith said softly, "We will take the risk."

"Ruand, in all conscience—"

"And if worst comes to worst, you will take two birds with the single stone."

She met his eye then, and it was the topaz glare she had bent, on our sampan, upon Tanekhet himself. I take your challenge, it said, I strip your hypocrisy. I call your bluff. I will, in all truth, dare you to run the risk that is your hope.

The contempt passed any of Antastes' shots. I saw him turn dull red over the cheekbones. Their eyes grappled, and all of us watchers held our breath.

Then Antastes turned his palms up: a graceful gesture that said, So be it. And, I am magnanimous. And, Your fate be on your own head.

Tellurith never shifted a muscle. But I saw the look on Tanekhet's face.

Before Antastes said suavely, "Whatever risk you were prepared to run, Ruand, the lord Tanekhet remains my counselor. The realm's first noble. My right hand, my mainstay, in politics as in wealth. Who, in the empire's width, could possibly replace him?" He shook his head. "Ruand, whatever your probity, whatever his soul's need, I fear for the Empire. I must think of Dhasdein first."

He did not glance at Tanekhet. He had no need. So the stag looks, when, coursed to exhaustion, he sees the forest rise before him—and a fresh band of hunters spurring across his way.

Tellurith's limbs had gone stiff, her eyes dilated, with a wild elation, a Sight more than sight.

Vision returned with a jerk, a glance from side to side, a huge, leaping breath. "Emperor," she said, "will you see me alone?"

"If you do that," she went on, to Antastes' baffled stare, "I will offer you a counselor. A counselor more than fit to replace the lord Tanekhet."

-

Autumn. Dhasdein.
Tellurith's Diary

IT WAS SO obvious it was blinding. Indisputable. I had only to persuade Antastes I had no knife in my sleeve, and reassure Alkhes, and nod the once to Sarth and Tez, whose eyes held more distressing hope, and try not to look at the other . . . the Mother knows, I would not have trespassed on any one's privacy just then.

And when Antastes and I were finally private in his little throne-room, I said what he was waiting for.

"The lord Tanekhet's replacement is obvious. One who would be doubly useful, with even greater power. One who has been in your hand for years."

Spare me, said Antastes' eyebrow, the rodomontade. I nodded and said, "The Empress."

When he had mastered his disappointment he moved his hand for the little bell at his side. "Ruand, I appreciate your thoughtfulness.." He was going to remember his imperial dignity. He would not shout aloud with laughter, let alone disgust. "But a woman as chief counselor—"

"You doubt her abilities?"

He shut his mouth with a snap.

"You married her to keep Quetzistan," I said. "Let her keep it, then."

"Ruand—"

"There's only one way to do that. Let her see you trust her to share the empire too."

"Ru-*and*—"

He had lost patience in earnest. At last. It went up on a note wholly uncontrolled. "Do you have any idea what intelligence networks, what double-agents, what second-payrollers I would have to circumvent? What sort of powers she has in Riversend alone? How do you imagine I could root out—"

"You don't root out." Sometimes, I wonder how these people maintain an empire. "Win the empress and their loyalties come with her. You double your resources. Because they work for you."

He opened his mouth and went to answer. Shut it, and stared as if I had grown another head.

I nodded at him and took my hands out of my sleeves to hint the interview was closed. "Your empress is the second-greatest power in Dhasdein. She has never turned against you, but you have never asked her to act with you. No doubt you found reason. And she has never," it was all clear as crystal, "been able to bear the power you gave Tanekhet. Why waste both of them?"

He opened and shut his mouth a couple more times, but now, I could tell, his brain was engaged. Then he straightened up in his chair, and reached again for the bell.

"I had forgotten," he said to me as we waited, "Amberlight."

"Emperor." Forgotten, indeed. A Council of the Thirteen would eat him alive. But if it pleased him to torment his chief noble like a boy with a lame puppy, to lock up his best asset in a coward's quarantine, what is it to me? I only want to take my men and get out of here.

All my men.

It took much second-thought and stipulation-setting, and then interminable jargon, all intended chiefly to convey, If your prize eats your chickens, kill the fox yourself. But I came out with an official agreement, scribed, sealed, signed, and a leave-pass; and agreement that Tanekhet's private incomes will remain. Before Antastes finally let them release his private scribe, and on the threshold of the main audience hall, at the focus of my folk's all but desperate eyes, turned to me for the actual farewell.

"Travel safely, Ruand." He offered the imperial seal ring. It is a noble amethyst, intaglio cut with the thunderbolt and serpent, darker than imperial blood. I dare say his nobles kiss it. I made do with a quick touch, he with the restraint of a frown. "No doubt we will hear more of each other. Should there be need."

That meant, If word comes downRiver, you had best get us early warning, if you value your hides, of any threat to Dhasdein.

"Emperor, our allies are our sworn friends."

The old pledge of Amberlight. He nodded then; and paused, glancing across the hall.

"I half wish I could see what you make of him." He paused again, and then he sighed. "I do wish you could say that, as you did in the old days."

I touched the cutter at my belt, and glanced the other way, to where,

I know, the Dhasdein statuette stands in the palace's deepest sanctum. Then I said, "You will keep the old days longer than I."

He thought about that. Then his eyes lightened, an emperor to the end. He had the statuette, which would last longer than my cutter. The power, and the glamour, of the qherrique would belong, at the last, to Dhasdein.

TANEKHET HAD TAKEN his own honor guard. As they formed up outside the Imperial Quarter's gate, lapping us in files forty-strong, he turned to me at last; bowing, with the most perfect grace of genuine feeling, as he kissed my hand.

"Lady Tellurith," he said. "Ruand."

On a note that added, all too clearly, You have worked miracles. You have my undying gratitude. You have my loyalty.

For good.

We looked in each other's faces, in that little cell among the shuffle and clash of arms. He was as immaculate, as exquisite, as impregnable as ever. Until you saw his eyes.

I glanced about my own folk and said, "Is there a wine-shop anywhere close? I need a drink."

Tanekhet's eyes went wide. Alkhes let out a snort part disbelieving, part delighted, half hysterical, caught my arm and said, "I'll show you, Tel." Even Sarth's body language seconded, Yes.

"Down that next cross-road, to the fire with troops, we can look after ourselves . . ." Alkhes waved, autocratic as any general, Tanekhet's henchmen parted. I looked at Tanekhet himself.

It would be our last private time before Iskarda. It would be a celebration, a release, a comfort beyond any outside the House.

And it would be cruelty, at this moment, beyond words.

I checked Alkhes, and said to Tanekhet, "Will you come with us?"

He had control enough of his body language. Nothing, except the very absence of expression, had spoken the longing, the abandonment. Now the polite inclination was impeccable. His eyes lightened, on my face, slid past me to Alkhes, whose stiffening spoke unconcealable dismay, and flickered. He would come, if only to vex. His eyes slid on to Sarth.

Who stood as formidably, inimically expressionless as only Sarth can, and let that speak for itself.

"I am honored, Ruand." He would keep that, as he had defied Antastes. "But—"

Alkhes said, "You have to start some day."

Tanekhet stopped short. Their eyes clashed; Alkhes' stare was a challenge, unmistakable. Saying, This is what you've got yourself into. Well?

Sometimes, I could hug my second husband; not just for his courage, his recklessness, his wicked intelligence. But because he reminds me of Averion.

Tanekhet's brows arched. Then he looked back to me and finished the bow, perfectly calculated, a noble now among equals, not an obeisance. Softly, politely, he said, "The Ruand honors me."

As our cumbrous train wheeled he was right beside me. Perhaps to fight so hard for something makes it yours by virtue of the effort; dear even when, like Tanekhet, it may be a scorpion with poison in its tail. It was, I think, a kind of affection that made me set a hand between his shoulderblades, as I might have with Sarth, with Alkhes.

Perhaps he had never been touched so, in public, not of his own volition. He gave the tiniest of jumps, instantly restrained. But not before I felt the priceless brocade under my fingers was sodden as I had once felt Alkhes' tunic, drenched like the saddlecloth of an overgalloped horse.

Autumn. Dhasdein.
Meditations. Alkhes-Assandar

NOBODY ELSE would think of it. Nobody else would have done it. Except Tellurith. Gods!

My legs gave out the instant I knew a chair behind them. No stools in there, of course, it was a noble's toping-spot. We had to leave the bodyguard at the door. We three would have been out with them, but for Tanekhet the proprietor in person bowed himself double, ushering us through silk curtains, upstairs to a private cabinet, with a view to the palace and our own door-watch, and furniture as good as Tanekhet's.

The gods know, despite down cushions and footrests it was not comfortable. Even with the winecups: mulled, spiced, probably Wave Island red, in our hands.

Not with Tez like an on-guard mastiff and Sarth radiating *Go away* as only Sarth can.

But Tellurith was right. If we are to take him, we have to take him completely. And we may as well begin now.

And he had the courage to accept the challenge, when I threw it down.

Maybe he has more. Because when the server finished, and we lifted our cups, and hesitated—what toast could anyone give?—he sank back in his chair. And let his face relax, let us see everything the day had cost him, as he could not have in that whole day's length.

As you would only among equals.

Among friends.

So I said it as I would have to an equal. As I might have to Catheor.

"Is it often as bad as that?"

His skin looked like parchment. Over-dried parchment. His eyes were copper-green in the discreet lamp-light. A newly-leafed forest, the shine on a burnished shield.

Then he took a great swig from the elegant goblet and wiped the back of a hand across his mouth like a workman on a tavern-bench. And answered with a tavern's roughness, "Not since I had to dodge his father's bed."

Tez's mouth fell open. Even Sarth twitched.

He met my eyes, and let that look say, You held out a hand. Can you keep hold of mine?

Very quietly, Tellurith asked, "After your father died?"

Without looking away from me, Tanekhet answered, "No."

And I had thought my side was bad.

"My mother died when I was twelve." For all Tanekhet's control, it held an ache that must have almost shut his throat. "*Why* she died . . ."

I felt my own breath hiss through my teeth.

"But my uncles felt that support would make things—shall we say, difficult?"

I saw Tez's lips shape something. Prayer or curse.

"I grew very adept at—keeping in public. Being indisposed. The number of upset stomachs, not to mention outright swoons . . ." He shrugged lightly, mocking himself. But there was no shield about the twist of his mouth.

Tez burst out, "Your father could have—!"

"My father never knew."

"He never noticed—!"

"I turned myself inside out to be sure he never noticed." He threw back his head and stared at her. "Because if he'd found out—the Emperor would have had," now the mouth's twist was verjuice, "his heart's desire."

Tez's jaw sagged. Very delicately, Tanekhet lifted a shoulder, the way a man will to cover a naked wound, and stared down into his wine.

"So comforting," he murmured, "to know yourself just a pawn in the game."

Not enough for a boy, if not an innocent, to be lusted after, to be hunted by the court's supreme power. Not enough to be denied his father's shelter, he had to know he was courted for the provocation: as an agent for his family's ruin.

Tez let out her breath. I think—I am nearly sure I did not show the pity. The shock. The disgust. I did look at Sarth, and the ice had gone.

It was Tel, of course, who picked us all up. Not with a look, a touch, not the barest open expression of sympathy, that would have burnt deeper than verjuice itself. But spreading our leave-papers on the table, saying, "You might wish to hear the Emperor's terms."

The farm. The mine. We can, he says, look for a ship tomorrow. He says, with his funds and our leave-pass, we can be out of here as soon as his affairs are wound up.

A week. Perhaps, he says, less than a week.

Out of Riversend.

Out of Dhasdein.

Going home.

PART IV

RIVERSEND

XV

Spring. The River
Meditations. Alkhes-Assandar

IF IT HAD just been five days. Or three days. Or even seven. Anyone knows, ten days is little enough. To quit an empire, to set a great noble's affairs to rights, to shuck off a life. If it had not been—

Maybe I am unjust. Would three days, or seven, or any number of days have made a difference? Would anything puny humans do have altered the pattern that had been weaving, six, seven months already, upon chance's loom?

I'm starting to sound like a priestess. Maybe I have to, if I want to write at all.

TEN DAYS' WAIT. When we had a ship in five, and she was solid enough for winter on the River, yet with a fair turn of speed. A light freighter, designed to ply the River's length, carrying Heartland exotics and Dhasdein luxuries, with a couple of cabins that the shrewd owner had added to exploit chance passengers, or to off-set an empty hold.

Predictable enough, given the best chance. That she was Tanekhet's own.

So we had the bonus of a thoroughly safe departure, and a spectacle to erase our marriage's scandal. The owner, aboard, in the flesh, bent on making himself a beggar overnight.

GIVE HIM THIS, the devil is as shrewd as he acts. We were hardly past the Gates, into the first complete interminable day of tack, row, tack, struggling, even with the impetus of that knife-blade winter southerly, against the River's swollen weight. We were all still on deck, when Tanekhet arrived. Took one look at the way Tel moved around the spare cable coil, narrowed his eyes, and murmured, "What is it, Ruand? Six months?"

Even Tez was transfixed.

He and Tel stared at each other—green eyes, amber eyes, I looked to see sparks fly—as if we didn't exist.

Then she let go the forrard hatch rim, and carefully, so carefully, straightened up.

And said, "Six and a half."

His new garb of merchant's dark coat and winter trousers hardly disguises what Tanekhet is—was. Not just the slightly raised eyebrow as he murmured, "You remember, I have had three wives." The slight smile. The considering pause. The soft, "Ruand, I felicitate you. Now with *that* card in my hand . . ." But, in answer to Tellurith's equally wintry smile, retorting, I took good care you never knew, the great noble's bow, acknowledging defeat.

And the way we had barely made fast at the next sizeable town before the captain hired ten extra oarsmen. And, as we cast off, Tanekhet drifted past her elbow, murmuring, "Ah, Ruand, there was something I wished to ask . . ."

He had innumerable questions—that his intelligencers have answered long since—about Iskarda. Innumerable councils on how best to dispose his funds. Innumerable consultations about Cataract. Innumerable times he needed her ideas, her advice. Or just her presence, in the half of the big cabin that was his—there is no word for it but audience hall. With our wake-thresh bisecting the River's slate-gray or flood-brown sea beyond the stern window, the two ship's braziers cracking and spitting in their clay grates, and the bitter light of winter's day, or the amber glow of a ship's lamp, on the counters or the pieces. As Tanekhet presided over his endless games of chance.

Great lords must know waiting as well as soldiers, and be as sternly disciplined. If he felt anything about the future, it ought to have been dread. He never showed it, any more than I would to troops dicing in the interminable lull before an assault. But he knows every gambling game in the army, and he plays them like a depot quartermaster. At castles he could master Sarth.

Doubtless it was two-sided as ever. After all, how can you hate someone you have played at jacks for days on end? Someone who treats your— loved ones—with unfailing courtesy? Who is prepared to do everything money can make humanly possible to get the woman you love home for her child's birth? Who gives her the fruit of skills learnt waiting on emperors, who for her slightest whim will turn the ship inside out?

YET IN THE long run, the canniest shipmaster, the dourest oarsmen, the smartest sailor who can tack and tack and tack forever on that turbulent southerly can gainsay the winter River. Can do better than, at best, fifteen miles a day.

Sarth and Tez are consummate at concealment, tempered by adversity, trained by Amberlight. But even I could tell they were afire with impatience. More than impatience. I felt it myself. Less than a twelve-month, and Iskarda is graven on me, down to the last stone, tree-root, half-nailed board. I wanted to burst out yelling at the ambient air to be there, back where I belong. But none of us were chewing our nails to the bone just for Iskarda.

All those interminable ten days in Dhasdein she never so much as fidgeted. For all Tanekhet could do, she would spend hours on deck, staring upriver, sometimes long into the dark or falling rain. But even then, very little showed.

Except at night, when we would feel her shake between us on the narrow cabin bed, or watch her bend inward, the arms folding, cradling, when she thought herself entirely alone. Or wake to the gasps, the frantic voiceless plunging of her nightmares. When we all but fought each other to hold, to comfort, to give her our vain protection, she still would not make a sound.

She carried high, and in winter clothes, only someone as damnably sharp as Tanekhet could have deciphered the slight backward tilt of her body, only somebody as close as Iatha would have read the new wariness in the way she moved, the constraint.

Only Sarth and I, in bed with her, could feel her belly's swell. Were permitted to lay hand or ear there, hoping, craving a flutter, a motion, something we could construe as a sign. Sarth claimed, once or twice, that he could hear a heart-beat.

I never managed even that.

FROM MID-SUMMER to autumn's end, four and a half moons. Two months of winter, into the third month before we left.

A month on the River, to get out of Dhasdein. Seven and a half months.

True, Dhasdein's River-span is the longest, the one to make your heart burst. It was better after Deyiko. We were in Verrain, two-thirds of the way back; given no bad storms or a heavy flood, granted a late child, Tellurith might still give birth at home.

Given that boon, that small, simple—Ah, gods—

Spring. The River.
Journal kept by Sarth

WHAT MOCKERY of all I have felt. Of all I have so long . . . But if there is anything—if there is ever anything here for which I can, someday, offer something a thanksgiving, it will be for Tanekhet.

Tellurith's lunacy justified. Tellurith's bounty returned a thousand-fold. When I think how close I came to taking things into my own hands . . . A pinch of nerve-poison in the soup, a stroll on the evening deck and a quick lift over the side . . .

And I did go close in those early days, when he passed beyond displaying wounds to work his wiles on Tez. Nothing so crass as compliments for Tanekhet. Questions about the marble-sales, about travel and freight costs, deferral to her knowledge of the Navy, the River. Not even so disingenuous as to ask for yarns. Not Tanekhet. The wine of his approval is from heaven's own vineyard. It is in the never-spoken weight of his rank and experience, that backs the most delicate intimations of interest, of approval, of respect.

Yet more diabolical, it is in his treatment of those for whom you care.

Tez herself, whose heart is locked tighter than any guard-dog's, started to melt under his kindnesses to Tellurith. Ah, he could have been a great waiting lady. He could almost have been trained in the Tower.

Tez melted, rot him, because he worked on me as well.

When he would turn to me, ask questions, convey with every nuance of a word and turn of his eyelids that I mattered, that I was valued, worthy, full of excellence, and I saw that light reflected in Tellurith's or Tez's or Alkhes' own face.

Alkhes I think he won outside the palace that day. Or the first time they fought to the finish in a game of castles, or with the oarsmen he hired. For all his wits and war-skills, my husband is an ingenue. Show him courage, show him gallantry, and all his antagonism fails.

And Tellurith, of course, had already signed over her citadel. Whatever he showed her, that day he talked to her about Iskarda, it is a vision she cherishes, and its harbinger with it. Why else would she have fought so hard to save him from Antastes?

And I?

Now I look into my heart, it is most infuriating to confess it was the loneliness. That it began in that wine-shop, when he showed us a past to make paradise of the Tower. To have been raised like that. To have been defiled like that. Yes, defiled, if there was never a finger laid on him. To have been lonely like that, all his life, in the heart of power.

And to forsake it all for another loneliness, to begin making his way again among people knit in a community he must know he can never truly enter; to endure our mistrust and accept our qualified kindness, like a dog beneath the table of our love.

And never to falter, never to complain.

Curse the man, all the way up River I waited for that, for the day he would turn to me, not for advice but for sympathy, the day he would try to open his heart. Because I knew he knew how I mattered: that with Alkhes mastered, I was the one who had to make his conquest complete.

He waited till we were in Verrain; till we were past Assuana, till we had—

Perhaps I can write this after all. Till we were actually in sight of the Iskan range. On a dour, lightless day when the wind had almost died and the very landscape seemed to hibernate: fields bare, trees pruned or leafless, roads empty, not the merest urchin to caper shrilling on the occasional village quay. I was on deck, waiting for a turn at the sweeps with Dorias, the strongest hire-on. He was the only one who matched my weight. So I had pulled on the big oarsmen's gloves and gone forward to the bankside rail, or what passed for a rail, when I felt a presence at my back.

If he has abandoned his perfumier, he brought a keepsake of his wares. His elbow slid over the rail beside mine. I ducked my head, but did not turn.

After a space long enough to mark my boorishness he murmured, "I suppose I am lucky to be alive."

"It is," I said without turning, "the will of the House."

He let me hear the intake of his breath. As a master swordsman will make much of a student's having clipped his sleeve.

We stared out into the torpid Riverside. With the wind down it was minimally warmer, but the River was proportionally stronger. I could hear them grunting in the forrard rowing space, the sound of a shift closing early. Tired, tiring men.

He said, "Do you want me to leave?"

I was too surprised—rot him!—for control. I half-turned before I could help myself. He ought to have looked triumphant. But there was no sign of a smile.

"I said it to—Alkhes. Upriver. Downriver. Cataract. The Archipelago. It doesn't matter. I can go."

I thought about that. Before I said, "It would matter."

"Bah. Your—Alkhes knows. In six months, what will I be worth to anyone?"

"What might anyone ask for your return?"

He laughed aloud. "Come, you saw it. Antastes would cheerfully tell them to cut my throat."

"Would Tellurith?"

I heard his breath go out, oof. He, too, put a hand to his ribs.

"I keep forgetting," he said, under his breath. Then his chin went up and he stared at me, the River-breath waving the aureole of his hair, the panther eyes dark, but not with rage.

"So," he said bleakly. "No choice for either of us."

I turned full-face to the rail and let the silence answer, No.

Stillness. But not peace. Forrard, the heart-beat of the timing drum kept pace, thud, thud, thud. Beside me, resource and daunting experience and intimidating determination revolved a dozen stratagems. Drew breath, and turned away.

Something about that breath . . . that motion. Praise be that I was raised in the Tower, to cipher the smallest signals given without words.

I turned around and said, "Where are you going?"

Caught in mid-stride, across a shoulder, the eyes were no longer a panther's. They were a startled, more than startled boy's.

"I—uh—" for once the stumble was not artifice. The gesture, jerky, with a touch of clumsiness, indicated the cabin-deck door.

I said, "Why?"

"Ah—" That too, was no part of Tanekhet. He ought to have demolished me with an eyebrow, the merest shoulder-tweak.

Then I remembered where I had seen eyes like that. Zuri, the morning she tried to give Tellurith her resignation. Meaning to go out and fall on her blade.

I said, "Come back here."

His lips parted. For the barest moment I saw the wild-wood adolescent, the untamed, untouchable creature that had enthralled the old Emperor.

Then the brows went up. Coolly, languidly, ice in reserve, he said, "Why?"

I said, "You know."

In so many ways it is like dueling with someone from the Tower. Someone as skilled and twice as astute as I. For an instant longer than a year the pose, the impasse held. Before the chin and the shoulders yielded together. Silently, he took three paces back to the rail.

We stared out at the Riverbank. He swallowed once. Twice. Three times. Then, on a hoarse note that shattered all the worldliness, he whispered, "Why?"

"I do not," I said without looking round, "want your blood on my hands."

"Where else would you like it, then?"

After all, he was incurably Tanekhet. Ignore him, try to freeze him out, obdurately resist his courtship I might. Push him to the limit, and he would not fawn but bite.

I turned about. The panther eyes flared at me, all black centers and sparks. I said in my turn, "Why?"

His fingers clenched on the rail timbers. I heard his breath catch, before he said, almost inaudibly, "Must I do this every—" Then he took a breath and put up his chin.

"Beau—Sarth." He swallowed on it as if my name was a very swordblade. "If I'm here at all—it's because of you."

He held my gaze. If that was any harder than to maintain my own composure, I should be surprised.

"You showed me what I was. I never realized just how I—until I looked through your eyes."

In those forest-depths I saw a great lord become a grotesque, pitiful torturer; mirrored in an unflinching, unjudging, but never innocent topaz stare.

"It was you who made me—go through with this. And I wanted . . . I wanted . . . "

The panther-flare had quenched itself. Instead there was longing, all but hopeless longing. And admiration, impossibly, admiration, and a hunger for respect, for acceptance, understanding in grief and bitterness that it would never be slaked.

He took another great breath, and turned blindly from the rail. Tanekhet, whose address never failed. Not under the provocation of an emperor.

I grabbed his arm. He remains a great lord in the sheer shock the laying on of hands causes him. I swung him round beside me and set my hand, as Tellurith had, between his shoulderblades.

He froze as solid as if he had been Alkhes. I reached higher, to the noble's queue in which he still tied his hair, a wind-ruffled tail on the back of his neck.

The drum thumped, louder than our heart-beats, thud, thud, thud. His heart outran it. As I righted the tangle he looked at me along his shoulder, the stare of a trapped wood creature. A frightened boy.

I put my arm right across his shoulders and hugged him for an instant, as close and kindly as I would a boy. If it was artifice, it won its reward. But if it was artifice, it was worth any reward you could give.

I felt every muscle in his body quake. Before the tension undid like a turned lock. He leant into my grasp for an equally short instant, and then straightened up; the slight, careful straightening after a great weight's release.

All but under his breath, he said, "Sarth . . . "

Staring out at the River, I said as quietly, "Yes."

AND WHO KNOWS to what fatuities we might have descended, without the clip of feet, the sudden third presence at our backs. Tez, breasting the rail at my other shoulder, to stare under the limp leach of the foresail, muttering, "Don't like the look of that."

It was probably with gratitude that we examined a dour sky and a windless River which to me seemed absolutely no different. But Tez was licking her finger; sniffing; frowning, with a tension I had not seen before, at the horizon that had just begun to roughen into hills.

My House habits are, sometimes, unbreakable. It was Tanekhet who asked with commendable aplomb, "What is it, Tez?"

She sniffed again and frowned. Shook her shoulders. Said abruptly, "Cloud's thickened. I don't like the smell of it." She swung from the rail. "Where's Verek?"

As captain, Verek had exercised his prerogative to nap through the afternoon watch. He was surly at being haled from his temporary quarters: being lectured by an Amberlight woman turned him outright sour. When she had the temerity to warn him weather was coming simply because, "I feel it," he opened his mouth to demolish her.

Before he caught, at her shoulder, Tanekhet's stare.

Verek's instant remedy was to haul his wind and run for the nearest wharf. Quite often we had lain at anchor in bays or in the lee of islands for the untrafficable time of darkness, but he insisted that for a real storm, "We gotta have a wharf!" Tez curled her lip like a true Navy termagant. But when Tellurith put in, "They have no qherrique," her scorn collapsed.

Whereupon Verek pushed his vantage too far: when he decreed we dared go no further upstream, Tanekhet said, "What was your plan, Lady Tez?"

She scowled at the title as she always did, but she went to the stern-deck fall and sniffed the air again, and frowned furiously. Then came back to Tellurith and spoke in the flat voice that means extreme distress.

"Ruand—I'm not far south of my home-waters, and I've known that tang all my life. That's the first spring storm headed through."

Tellurith nodded silently. She had grown very quiet of late. Tez read, Go on, from her look.

"The front'll be bad: rough water, and the wind'll swing all over the place. But once it's gone, the River'll make the Narrows impassable. Last spring, we had nothing up from Verrain for a month."

Tanekhet looked at Verek. Who scowled, and chewed his lip. And burst out, "No way we'd be sure to pass the Narrows first! You wanna be quick or dead?"

Tanekhet looked at Tez. Who looked at Tellurith and burst out in turn, "It'll be blighted risky down here!"

On a River driven wild by wind and flood; with no help around us but from Verrain.

With the risk of political detainment, of who knew what wild ideas would burgeon, if a Verrain land-owner found himself harboring the Ruand of Iskarda?

And more than the Ruand.

Tellurith's hand slid over her belly, one slight touch. Alkhes at her shoulder winced.

Tellurith got out of the makeshift chair of freight-sacks with an effort. Since we entered Verrain her body had thickened almost overnight. I can add the times up in my head now: six and a half months to leaving Riversend, six weeks upriver. Eight months.

She leant on me and Alkhes impartially as she looked upRiver. I felt, keenly as in my own heart, her longing, her all but terrified, instinctive need to have the baby in safety.

At home.

She did not, like Tez or Verek, fidget or scowl or bite her lip. She asked Verek, "With this wind, could we make the Narrows by daylight?" And when, despite his squirming, he admitted we could, she said, "Is there anywhere to lie to close by?'

There was. Tez's eye said so. Verek, squirming harder than ever, admitted to an island just where the Narrows spread. "Can lie to behind there, but—!"

Tellurith measured the sky again. "How soon?" she said to Tez.

And when Tez cried, "Ruand, I can't tell that near, I don't have—! I don't even know how high it'll *rise!*" She looked to the sky once more. Then she opened her fingers in the gesture that is a cutter's invocation to the mother-face, and said, "In the Work-mother's hand."

Spring. The River.
Tellurith's Diary

A CHOICE that was no choice. Miss the Narrows and we might as well raise flags and tell Shuya, Here we are, a political windfall; a revenge on both your neighbors, a way to exterminate Iskarda's flea-bites, a royal road into Dhasdein.

And I could not have suffered it, to risk the most precious hostage of all. The child.

AT FIRST it went well enough, with the oarsmen doubled and Sarth, Alkhes, even Tanekhet sharing the load; at least, Tanekhet did it till I saw his hands. Right through the big rowing gloves, his palms were nearly raw. The worst was Tez's edginess. Fidgeting on the stern deck, almost bursting to yell for more speed, riskier tactics—but there was no use at all in beaching ourselves on a sand-point, or holding a tack too long. With what wind there was to tack.

And we did get there. We reached the Narrows foot with an hour, an hour and a half, Verek's navigator calculated, before full dark.

Through the Narrows, on the downstream run, had been the best part of half an hour.

The sky loured worse than ever, the first drops of rain had already needled past. The wind was beginning to gust. In the lee of Verek's island the River stood two feet below the white splash underlined by a stain of flood-wrack: some hardy soul's highwater mark.

I looked at Tez. Tez looked silently back.

I started calculating distances to the nearest substantial moorage; I might dare to risk myself and my child. I had no right to hazard an entire ship-crew's lives.

Tez said as if it had been prised out of her, "Ruand?"

Beckoning me to the far rail, downwind, so far as possible, of the Outlanders, she said it in my ear.

"Ruand—there's a place."

I said, "What?"

"My mother swore me. It was Navy. *Never* tell, she said. Never use it, unless the City's at final risk."

She stared at me through the flicking rain-tips.

"But," she said deliberately, "I reckon the City's here."

It was three-quarters up the Narrows, all but invisible unless you made straight for an eddy that warned any sane soul, keep clear. A pucker in the cliffs, nested under a curve's outside ending, where the eddy's skirts would lift you into dead water, a space just fit for a Navy stinger, like *Hornet* or *Black Widow* or her own mother's *Wasp*. "I reckon we'll make that before dark easily. And from there . . ."

No matter how it rained or blew in the night, from there we could force the rest of the Narrows in early morning, before the main flood came down.

DESPITE VEREK's chatterings and his navigator's outright denial of such a thing's existence, it took a bare three rowing shifts. Before the clouds inflamed to a watery red sunset we had found the bend, picked our way past the eddy, and noted the convenient projections where a ship could cast a cable fore and aft, and lie; our stern, to be sure, was nervily near the eddy rim, but we were snug out of the main current. More wonderfully, the wind-eddies cancelled out, so we could light the galley fire.

And thanks to Tanekhet's instigation, after supper we had gathered in the stern cabin to chew our fingers in urbane company. So we were together for the crash.

THE SHATTERINGLY unexpected crash and more shatteringly irresistible impact that threw us half across the cabin and sent the whole ship backward like a child hit by a bolting horse.

I heard the stern cable go, a fusillade of smashing timber as shackles tore clear out of planks. I dived deckward on the impact with images of a sheared cable decapitating stevedores on an Amberlight wharf and three people landed atop me to the more terrifying plunge and wild backward motion that meant the bow cable had gone too. We were not only cast-off, we were already in the stream.

And over it came the thunderbolt's aftermath. The report of parting timbers, the rattle and rumble of loose debris. The screams.

It is fairly certain now what happened. Beyond our memories, there was the River's testimony. It was a timber-raft. A big one, out of Cataract, full-length cedar-trunks. Headed down-river, trying with more than our recklessness to run the Narrows and overtaken by dark. Probably having clipped a wall, even lost a steersman or both the actual steering oars, and cartwheeling down the current, out of control.

Crashing through the eddy, where no sane, normal traffic would pass. Head-on into us.

It was Tez who saved my life. Who with River skill and Navy experience read the horrible din and was out the cabin door in three bounds and back before I had the men off my shoulders, swamping us in loops of rope.

She had grabbed it from the store-bin behind the mast, just down the passageway. Medium-weight sheet; light enough to pull, flexible enough to knot, strong enough to take the weight, in flood water, of a human being. Forget the ship, already doomed. The bows must have been stove in completely. Forget the crew, even those who had been our comrades, let alone Verek. For her there was only one imperative, and it was in the stern-cabin. The Ruand. The House.

She clove-hitched the doubled rope loosely round my belly, cast herself on within twenty feet of me, bawled at Sarth, "Get the stools! The table! The small one!" Hurled the rest of the rope at Alkhes, roared, "Cast him on! *Move!*"

Alkhes had kicked the stern window out already, he was hauling Sarth toward the gap. We struggled in a madness of haste and terror, feeling the ship flounder, feeling her wounded bows sink, her rudderless side turn, a convulsion of frantic effort in the bucking lamplight, with the cold, the dark, the maelstrom of flooded River waiting, our only chance . . .

The men were secure. Alkhes grabbed a stool with one arm and Sarth with the other, Tez grabbed me and the table, Sarth grabbed another stool and Tanekhet. Tanekhet, cooler than I could have imagined, grabbed the shattered window side and levered himself out onto the sill. Glanced round and bawled at Tez, "Quick!"

The ship had spun as she was flung, dying, out into the current. Already the cliffs were moving walls of darkness above the River's neck. There was a faint glow from the water, there was a ruddy splash forrard where something had overturned the galley brazier. There was hullaballoo amidships where Verek's survivors were fighting with the skiff. There were men—in the brazier glow I saw them—making loops about oar-blades and dropping overside. The hire-ons, who knew they had no better chance. There was a jagged black silhouette against the fire-glow, and a vast perturbance, an unintelligible screaming beyond. We had collided so hard the raft was jammed bows on in the wreck. It would not sink, not that monster, but it was even more wildly out of control. Even as I looked the inevitable happened. There was a tearing, wrenching impact that ricocheted clear back through the ship-frame as the raft stern hit some wall projection, and the two of them tore apart.

Tez gave me one shove in the back and jumped.

IT CAN only have been the Mother's mercy . . . No. Or if so, the mercy was that we had Tez. And so we had rope, and furniture for buoyancy, and her skill to do something like steer. And if the water was an icy maelstrom, the current was so fast, all we had to do was all we could.

Try to keep to mainstream, cling together. Pray we did not snag on some rock, and wait to be flung out into quieter water at the Narrows' end.

The Mother knows why we achieved it. I have no idea how. It is a blurred eternity of snatching madly for bearings and guessing eddy swings and sight of rocks, of praying with my heart fit to suffocate me—if, with the need to follow the River, there had been time—that the men would be all right.

Tez and I had the table. And by the Mother's providence, we were the downstream end of the line.

And by her further providence, we had Alkhes and Tanekhet.

The one raised a River-child, the other tempered in disasters. So neither panicked. And each had some water skill, to hold them and their stool-floats behind us, even in the fastest water, where I thought I must surely choke on spume if I did not actually drown.

So we whirled like thinking flotsam back down the River's road, with the very spate-strength and speed that we had cursed become our one hope for life.

I FELT the current change. Sensed rather than saw the hedging darknesses widen. Caught a sudden single glint of star, saw clearly the yellow beacon of a cottage-light, glimpsed from a momentary wave-top, impossibly far. As the turbulence eased I heard Tez choke, "Starb'd!" We caught our breath together. Grabbed the table as swimmers do with a foundered skiff, and began to kick.

Alkhes heard us. Tanekhet understood. Occasionally, through the River-noise, we caught word-fragments. A splash. The River bore us onward but now, more and more often, we caught the solid rise of dark.

We came in like all flotsam, grounding far out on the snag of a sandy point. Far closer in than we would have in summer, to tell truth. My foot touched just as I heard Sarth, the tallest of us, give a surprised grunt.

The worst came after that, with the great tension gone, but still in hazard of the current, having to struggle through a myriad unknown snags, toward the still distant shore. And predictably enough, it was Tez again who saved us. Because, even in the cabin, at dice, she had worn her knife.

With which she slashed us free to make our own way, no one else's hindrance or drowning point, toward the shore.

She and I kicked along again upon the table. I saw the men sometimes, the froth of turbulence, the black bob of a head. Then my knuckles collided with a tree-root, the smallest, most grievous scathe of the night.

Tez hauled me out. It was some kind of thicket. The water-light silhouetted scrawny branches, a lattice of stems, a fiend's abattis for crawling through the dark. Tez propped me back against a trunk and yelled.

Sharply.

Once.

Because even now she was Navy, troublecrew, intelligencer.

And we were in Verrain.

There was a lull, then. Time to tally the bruises and bashes and the sopping wet winter clothes already glued to me, and the gusty wind, and increasing rain. Time for the heart to slow, for the body's shock to announce itself, in shivering that simply would not stop. Time to take mental stock, to re-confront the nightmare. Time to tally what we had not lost.

Alkhes reached me first. He fell on his knees and threw both arms round me as if I was another stool in a far deeper River. I think he was incapable of speech.

Sarth came next. I knew his footstep, familiar as the beat of my own heart. Felt his arms take us both, heard the strangled breath that controlled whatever Alkhes was doing—sobbing, hiccupping? Trying not to weep? And I felt, too, the way Sarth reached past, the moment the touch of my hair identified me. To Alkhes.

To Tez.

Who had already sat up in our survivors' huddle, head turning as she scanned against the pallor of the sky. Before she coughed, sharply as a hunting cat. Just once.

Tanekhet made a fair job of quietness too. Through the rain splatter, the wind-skirls, I doubt a sound would have carried beyond the copse. I felt his hand patting, closing on my foot. Then the quick low, "Ruand?" and when I made a noise, the long, long released breath.

He knew better than to move into the huddle with us. I felt him settle by my feet. Heard him haul the sopping wet, indoors coat about him; none of us had been foolish enough to shed clothes in the River, we knew, if we lived, what would come next. For a while there was no sound but wind and breathing, as we all got used to being alive.

Before Tanekhet said with shaky but urbane restraint, "Well."

What set me off? The shakiness? The restraint? The utter improbability of squatting in a River-side spinney with a lord of Riversend, who, having lost all but the coat on his back, in deadly peril and among no good friendship, could still sound so bland about it all?

Alkhes gagged me eventually; he was laughing too, I could feel the smothered vibration through his hands, through his chest. When he let go I was still spluttering. I heard him say sharply, "Tel, are you all right?"

That, of course, set me off again. This time Tez caught it, I felt her begin to rock and strangle her whoops. She infected Tanekhet, and Tanekhet's attempts to stop overset Alkhes, whose choking undid Sarth . . .

He crawled to me eventually. I could feel him still gasping for breath as his hand touched my shoulder, slid upward to my cheek; as that dark velvet voice enquired seriously, "Tellurith, *are* you all right?"

And as I gasped, "Oh, caissyl—never better!" I felt the warm flood that was not water down my legs.

Spring. The River.
Meditations. Alkhes-Assandar

I HAVE TO—I have to write this and I . . .
    It has to be purged.
    To write it is unbearable.
    Not to write is unbearable too.

The only thing more terrifying than death
    The only thing
    The only thing more terrifying
    Is birth.

The only thing more terrifying than death or birth
  Is both of them at once.

That's no good either. I sound like a deranged priest. A goddamn—
  Oracle.

I'm doing it again. Start at the beginning then. Behave like a soldier. Make
a report of it.

THE COLLISION must have been less than an hour before midnight. We
seldom made Lights Out before that. An hour, at most, in the water.
Without cloud, I could have read the stars. But we could not have been
ashore a half an hour. So make it morning watch, middle morning watch,
the coldest time, the worst time for the wounded, beyond memory of
evening, before the hope of dawn.

If it had not been middle night. If we had not come ashore drenched
to the skin, with no means of making fire. If it was not the only gods-
forsaken uncultivated patch of shoreline on the River, in the middle of a
rainstorm, if it had not . . .

If it had not been Verrain.

Tez yelled that at us when we panicked, and Sarth and I did that
immediately. When he started babbling about the storm, when I said,
"We've got to have fire," and tried to run, it was Tez slapped me a piledriver,
Tez who yanked Sarth's plait and snarled like a very guard-mastiff.

"We can't get anyone. It's Verrain!"

And Tellurith—between grunts—who gasped out, "Get them tie
trees—hang up coats—rot it, get over here, Tez!"

Tez ran. She knows—knew—as little about birthing as we did, Tellurith
had to organize the whole. No physician, no instruments, no hot water,
not even a bed. Clothes off as cover, coat under her. Our coats, when we
gathered our wits, roped to trees as a windbreak, hung above to break
the rain. Sarth and Tez and I as a living windbreak, a birth-couch. While
she—

No wonder they call it labor. At first she could lean on us, have us rub
her back or belly, help her walk up and down. But then the pains came
so fast she could only brace against whosever turn it was. I never knew
a woman had such strength. Never heard any human being breathe like
that, who was not dying.

Tanekhet—Tez chased him with some pretext about guard duty. Off in solitary misery somewhere at the coppice edge, while the rain gusted, and the wind thumped, and thunder cracked, to seal our misery, overhead. Once Tellurith gasped, "Rot and gangrene, what a time to pick! " Once, at a particularly close crack, she flinched.

There was lightning, so I saw her face as she panted, "Mother, this one's in a rush . . . "

Gods pity us, we never understood what that could mean. It was Tel's fourth, she was our only expert, we thought it was all usual, we even hoped it would be quicker, we prayed . . .

I prayed, when Tellurith started to groan, when she gasped, "Get in here—Tez—feel head . . . ?" When she started heaving so hard I thought she would break open. When Tez vanished beyond all but a sense of movement, when Tellurith literally bucked in our arms, when Sarth started panicking—the worst was, there was nothing I could do but pray. Till there was a convulsion against us, Tellurith grunted, belly deep, Tez made a companion noise and Tellurith choked, "Coming! Feel her . . . ? Uh!"

One enormous heave, one last strangled yell. And Tez's muffled, "Yes!"

Frantic motion then in the dark. Sarth and I hung on, utterly bewildered, only sensing the event from Tellurith's sudden relaxation, the huge, easing gasps. Till she said suddenly, faintly, "Have you got it? Tez?"

And Tez spluttered, "I think—I don't know—"

"Give her here!"

We all jumped. Tez lunged, Tellurith plunged about. We felt her grab something, frantic searchings, sudden breath of panic, a more frantic, "Grab her heels—hold her up! Quick!"

The darkness writhed. Tellurith panted, "Find backside—slap . . . "

Tez slapped. Only with the reports did a shred of birth-bed tradition come to me. Only then did I understand.

Sarth gasped, "Tellurith—wait—" but she had lunged upright, swearing like a Cataract trooper. "Give it here, give it here, gods blast—!"

Slap. Frantic shake and pant, more frantic slap. A great peal of thunder, a flash brilliant enough to have lit the River-lord's deepest pits.

Lighting Tellurith, upright, wild-eyed, hair plastered to her sodden face. Straining up by the heels a naked bloody baby whose jaw hung loose and whose skin, by the lightning flare, was purple-blue.

I think—I *know* none of us wanted to understand. I know Sarth grabbed Tel and I grabbed the baby, shook till my arms ached, slapped till I feared to break its back. We forgot Verrain and babbled, cursing each other to perdition at the top of all our lungs.

Until Tellurith bit Sarth's arm. Tore loose, ripped the baby from me. Slapped Tez off and spat at us, "Look for a pulse!"

She searched.

Tez searched. Sarth—oh, gods help us—

I have to go on.

Sarth and I searched. Ah, to recall the feel of it, that small body, so complete, so perfect, blood of our blood, flesh of our flesh.

With not a whisper of heartbeat. Never a sign of breath.

I THINK we tore our hair. I know we wept. I saw, next day, how Tez literally slashed her breast. The gods know who or what heard our lamentations, the three of us there in the bloody mud and pouring rain, could the gods have shown us no pity at the last—

Except Tanekhet.

The first I knew was a head-rocking slap. He spun me round on the wake of it and shook me fit to break my teeth, then spat a cascade of blasphemy that ended, "What's happened, you clot?"

When I could not answer he literally threw me away and flung himself down by Tellurith, yelling, "Ruand? What is it? What's wrong?"

She looked at him. Open-eyed, empty-eyed, a white tragedy mask turned to the lightning. With the child, naked, unmoving, on her breast.

Tanekhet doubled his profanity. Then took the child up, more delicately than any woman, and held his ear to its breast. Laid it down. If I had had a feeling left, the way he did that would have broken my heart.

The lightning rocked, the rain lashed round us. On the next huge flash, I saw Tanekhet brace himself.

Before he turned to Tez and demanded, "The afterbirth?"

Tez said, "What?"

"The *afterbirth*! Dhe blind you!" In ordinary stress he swears by the River-lord. I think Dhe is a goddess of his childhood. A lost past. "Has anyone kept some sense?"

When Tez gaped he fairly spat at her. Laid the child on Tellurith's breast. And to our utter disbelief, dived under the coats laid on her legs.

Tez snarled and grabbed for him, Sarth snarled and leapt. Tanekhet tore the coat away and Tez shrieked aloud.

It shone purple black in the lightning blaze. The coat, the ground under Tellurith's thighs, was all glittering, sodden wet.

TANEKHET BROUGHT me round as well. Another slap in the face, a wrench at my shirt that all but broke my teeth on his chin as he snarled, "Give me that!"

He was a great lord. He was the one voice of command, of competence we had left. He stripped the pair of us half naked and added his own shirt and demanded Tez's as well, then scrambled between Tellurith's thighs in a way I would have had his tripes for any other time. And yelled at me, face distorted, "Hemorrhage!"

And I had thought there was no feeling left.

It is not like Tanekhet's library. Nor the discontinuities. But there is neither sense nor sequence, no idea of time or of event. I do remember Tanekhet punching Sarth in the jaw. I think he wanted Sarth's trousers. I clearly recall Tez pulling the windbreak down, sobbing and praying as we do in utter extremity, when there is nothing to answer, and no pride left. I can recall Tanekhet's voice in the dark, terror and exhaustion blurring that high-bred Dhasdeini accent.

"A miscarriage can make them bleed that way—we have to slow it down—staunch it. We must!"

With a frenzy that needed no explanation: otherwise we would lose them both.

At some point the rain must have eased. I recall shivering convulsively as I knelt in bloody, clammy mud. But the core of numbness had widened. There was no more fear; just the knowledge, as I have had in so many midnight watches, that if I let her go, if I for one instant relaxed not the body's but the soul's vigilance, she would die.

And at some time, Tanekhet's voice again. Curiously quiet and empty now, as if answering a query that was almost everyday.

"She miscarried. Out hunting. The horse fell. My first wife."

And some knowledge, perhaps something already spoken, that in her case both mother and child had gone. That she had bled to death.

I do know that finally, eventually, eternally, the dark paled. We had light.

May all the gods bear witness, I would rather have lost my eyes. Rather been blind till death than seen my heart's love lying so shrunken, so gray, under that coat. A shell, bled dry. Amid our pack of sodden, shivering, naked scarecrows, faces that the cold and the—rest of it—had turned to deathmasks. Amid the debris of trampled mud and branches and ripped up coats and bloody, stinking shirts.

And the pathetic, the terrible little heap that was—
That should have been our child.

THANK WHATEVER masquerades as providence that Tel, at least, does not have the burial's memory. That like us, she only carries the loss.

Embedded in the heart. Eternal, insoluble. A dying's shard.

Unlike Sarth, I do not even have the consolation of losing a qualified happiness.

Because it was a boy.

Because it was—it would have been—my son.

XVI

Spring. The River.
Journal kept by Sarth

THERE IS NO GOD—there are no gods, to show mercy or anything otherwise. There is only a blind, indifferent universe that crushes hopes and dreams along with terrors under its chariot wheels, and neither knows nor cares.

That is what I would have thought, if I could have thought, that morning, as we squatted watching the first light etch our fellows' spell-corpse faces, and wondered why we ever lived at all.

I did not want to live. I did not want to exist, let be feel or think. No telling how long I would have groveled there: had not Tez made a motion, like an old, half-paralyzed woman, and croaked at us, "Got to get help—get her warm. . ."

Otherwise, said the wave of her arm, it will all be futile. She too will die.

I could not move. Alkhes did not. Tanekhet looked up painfully; squinting, from eyes deep-sunken as ours, amid the elf-locks that snagged another haggard, stubbled face, another scarecrow shivering uncontrollably to the bitter breeze, the diamond-blue sunlit sky.

The light had that too pure, too limpid look that says, more rain ahead. Had I the wits, I would have cursed it for baring us to any watchers it might draw abroad. But I simply crouched in the mud, till Tez stretched a shaking hand to the nearest broken branch and slammed it viciously across Alkhes' back.

"You," she could just whisper it. "Only one that fits."

She hit him again. He gasped, and then stared numbly, while the first welt rose, livid, beaded with blood, across his naked ribs, and Tez snarled at him like a wolf. "*Now!*"

He was the only one who could chance exposure in Verrain. Tanekhet was too risky, we three too clearly Amberlight. And it had to be done. We no longer had a choice.

I do not think she could have moved him. I am very certain I could not have moved him. I watched her arm sag, I saw the terrible expression, as she came where I had come. As she made ready to give up.

Behind us there was a vague sound of rowlocks and parting water. Tanekhet made some pretense to duck. Tez cast one frantic glance about and groped futilely for her knife.

I could not make myself care. I crouched there, not moving, like some over-beaten dog.

Low voices. Women's voices. A curiously familiar nuance and turn of women's voices. Then the grate of timbers against a root.

Tez cast one more wild glance for help. Tanekhet looked at me, at her, over his shoulder. Like Tellurith, Alkhes never stirred.

Tez looked at Tellurith. Too clearly, her face said, I can't fight, I dare not move her. There is nothing we can do.

Cautious, very cautious disembarkation noises. A rustle, just the one, in distant, rain-sodden brush.

Then a woman walked out on the edge of our ramshackle clearing and said, in a voice I knew, "Ruand?"

I did not think I could move. But something stood me up, and someone said, "Zuri?" before I sat down with a thump that emptied my lungs.

So perhaps there are gods, after all. Because it *was* Zuri. And Azo, Verrith, Desis, three more troublecrew, and a patrol-boat from Marbleport, manned by Tez's folk. And I will cherish forever the moment when Tellurith prised her eyes open; whispered, "Zuri?" and as Zuri hunkered beside her, that terse, that familiar, oh, that blessed voice grumbling, "I'm here," Tellurith caught her breath. And began, at last, to weep.

They had spare cloaks and warm River-gear, they had an ex-Navy physician who had injury lore aplenty, if she knew little of births. They had hot soup—paragons of the world, they had coffee, for the boat carried fire. Most blessed of all, they were Telluir, they were troublecrew. For the first time since Mid-summer night, I could feel almost safe.

I HAVE SHIRKED the rest of it. Even now. Even here. Merely to think of it sends my mind broadside. Gods, if there are gods, what is anyone to make of this? Am I to laugh, or curse, or cry, or . . .

Attempt, then, to compass the impossible within the rational. Begin when they had thawed us out and fed us, when Tellurith had been examined, and the physician judged moving her a bearable risk. When

Tez had summarized the—night—or as much as could be borne of the night. It was then that Zuri said, out of her trouble-Head silence, "Who is this?"

Tanekhet. In the first press of rescue, the only one unaccounted for. Wrapped in a blanket, teeth still rattling on the soup-cup. And as he looked up, pushing back elf-locks with a still bloody hand, nothing but a great noble. Even yet.

Zuri bristled without moving. That deadly, viper stillness she and Alkhes share.

Tez looked wildly to Tellurith, who was beyond speech. At Alkhes, still too clearly stupefied. At me.

And I heard myself croak, "Tellurith brought him. From Riversend. His name is Tanekhet—"

Zuri said, "Tanekhet?" and stood up. At the bare tone Azo and Desis turned in their tracks with light guns out and charged.

She was trouble-Head. Of course she would know Tanekhet and all Tanekhet had been. Far better than me.

"Zuri," I said desperately, "he knew what to do last night. He saved her life . . ."

Zuri's jaw was granite, the eyes an executioner's. Tanekhet stared back at her. He has a great lord's courage, no doubt of it. He did not try to be airily witty. He did not so much as move.

Only, after a moment to make it clear he had no foolish intentions, he said, "It is a long story, Ruand. But I am no enemy to Iskarda. I can swear that now."

Zuri's eyes never moved

I looked helplessly at Tez. Who swallowed and got out, "It's true. About last night."

At which point the physician, no clod with atmospheres, put in coolly, "I would like to have the Ruand out of here."

Zuri's suspicion held another endless moment. Then, warily, she looked to Tez. Who swept a responding look over the sky, oh, that magical House communication, and answered, "It'll rain before dark."

They had shot the Narrows in the first dawn-light. They had seen wreckage upRiver, ship-beams, drowned men, they had been searching frantically, when some sharp-eyed soul glimpsed our beached table. The River, their captain considered, was still passable for such a small, light boat, and nobody had to stress the deadly urgency of getting out of Verrain. It was that, I think, which tipped Zuri's scales.

She gave Tanekhet one last slit-eyed stare, then grunted and gestured to Tez. "Your surety." Her eyes came round and she jerked her chin. A command gesture. "Your ward."

And that, she said to me.

In retrospect, it was the kindest thing she could have done. It forced me to action, it drew me back into a former self, it obliged me not to think. And if I was shaky-legged to the point of impotence, Tanekhet was no better: if he had been an enemy at all.

In fact, he just wanted to oversee Tellurith. So we were all hovering like first husbands as they got the blanket litter under her, fastened it to the oarblades. As four hefty Marbleport water-women eased her slowly off the ground.

Then only debris remained: broken branches, blood-stained rags, the aftermath of a battlefield. Clotted, red-brown mud. A desolate memorial to a night's hell, the wreckage of so many, such exquisitely agonizing hopes.

Alkhes was at my shoulder. Still too numb for speech, but I felt him staring with me, both of us shrouded in the suffocation of first grief.

Then Tanekhet said, "What . . . ?" and bent toward the mud.

"What the—" He straightened, bringing his hand up. Something glittered sharply between his thumb and finger and with a yell he threw it wide and high.

"What in the River-lord's hell!"

He wrung his hand, too stung and disbelieving to panic yet. The mud glittered where the missile had come to earth.

Alkhes' eyes opened as if he was going into a convulsion. He made one sound and lunged.

Strung troublecrew reflexes had jerked them too. We were already surrounded. Desis snapped, "What—" and stopped.

It had not stung Alkhes. He had it cupped in both hands, nursing it, as if it were a treasure more precious than a child. His face was not numb any longer. It was the face of a man dazzled beyond belief; who seems his most impossible dream fulfilled.

"Tel," his lips shaped. His eyes were a night beyond fathoming, shot with unknown stars. His cheeks ran with tears. "Tel?" he said, and his voice broke. "Oh, Tel. . . it remembers me."

It was Zuri who jumped that time. She knocked the other troublecrew spinning, if she did not tear his hands apart it was pure miracle. I never heard anyone shout in a whisper before.

"*What did you say?*"

He never heard her. He turned and walked straight through them, hands still cupped, went like a sleepwalker to Tellurith's side and sank on his knees before he whispered, "Tel—Tel . . . look."

She cannot have been more than half-conscious. But her eyelids moved. When she found his face her eyes opened. Ruand, House-head, lover, how could she not have answered? When she tried to sit up the physician knew better than to protest.

At Tellurith's look I found I myself had moved. Was staring down, over Tanekhet's and Zuri's shoulders, to whatever Alkhes cupped within his palms.

Smaller than a seed, purer than moonrise, perfect as a seed-pearl. It gleamed as it had shone in the cutter-panel when he hazarded his hand, as it burned when Zariah slashed a rapist's head off, as it had shone in the great bulwarks above Amberlight.

Qherrique.

Spring. The River.
Tellurith's Diary

To LOSE a child . . . A lover is a lesser bereavement. Heart of your heart, but not blood of your blood, flesh of your flesh. Losing a lover is not to find your soul, your heart as well as your body empty; to feel that center of all that makes you woman torn away.

To find . . .

To feel that touch again. My dear, my darling, the surety under my heart, the life rising to my fingertips; the blood to my heart-beat, the voice in my silence, the measure to my song.

But not the future of my child.

BLESSINGS UPON the Mother, then, who gave me another gift—how am I to say a lesser? with which to tip Her scales. That very evening, as I lay in the musty upstairs room of the inn at Marbleport, after that doubtless lung-bursting trip up through the Narrows, with my men safe—all my men safe—and the impossible returned to me, nested like an altar-light on my palms; and the rain, quiet now as a world's weeping, on the sodden roof.

What anguish is it, to be torn between equal enormities of joy and grief?

I doubt I would have slept, even with the comfort of my husbands next to me; except that the door opened, on the faintest of taps.

"Come in," I said, trying not to let my voice husk. "Is it a report?"

She came up to the bedside; pale, dour, with old prison-pallor and new privations inscribed under the grief. Stood staring down at me, the daughter of the rival I could no longer hate; the daughter I had never had.

"Is there some trouble . . ."

Swiftly, she shook her head.

Then sank down on the bedside, as no Navy officer, as hardly any House woman would have dared; not Iatha herself.

"Do you want to see it?" I could uncup my hands, if I could not bring myself to let it go. "It's true."

She shook her head again.

Though laid as weak and flat as six feet of untroubled water, I can read my folk well enough to hear, Shut up. I lay and watched her mother's, her sister's sharp-cut jaw work; the shadows shift on her austere face.

She put her hand over mine and said, "Ruand, I came to ask . . ."

I waited again.

She went on, all but lost in her throat. "I am his daughter by blood. I am yours by marriage tie. I would ask to be—your daughter in truth."

She is Navy, and in whatever extremity, or at least, in less than the previous night's extremity, she did not cry. But I felt her gulping, as she cradled me; I did get her to do that. And I managed to set the qherrique down, in the little coffer that will be its traveling nest, to put my arms about living flesh and blood.

A daughter. A freely-given daughter, bone of his bone, flesh of his flesh, bred of our House. The daughter I never had, the daughter, even now, I would not have had—

Amid this surpassing doubleness of joy and cruelty, the Mother has been kind, after all.

Spring. The River.
Meditations. Alkhes-Assandar

If I could have given her a child.

Even then, would it have equaled that gift? Could anything, anything I ever did have equaled that? To watch her face, lying there. To know what she felt. To be part again of that communion, to know it was not dead, not destroyed, not driven from the world forever. To feel yourself more than human. Become part of, known, recognized by what was never human.

Welcomed home.

There are questions. There are a great many questions that I—I'm—I was—a soldier, I am troublecrew. The gods witness, I'm not a seer or a philosopher, I don't even see into things as far as Tellurith. This—this—cleavage—this—confusion—

I do not know how to unwind.

Spring. The River.
Journal kept by Sarth

So now we come to it: not the questions that sent Zuri to us so providentially, that is an easy speculation. News of some plot against the Ruand when she headed home, generated downRiver, to be sprung from Cataract. Zuri thinks that if we had not met that timber-raft so unexpectedly, we might well have met by anything but chance. It is quite possible, she says, they were risking the Narrows because they feared to miss their prey. After all, once above that, it was a mere fifteen miles to Marbleport, their plot would already be near unstuck.

Which explains why Zuri and her crew deserted Iskarda and consigned themselves to the River's luck, intending to patrol above the Narrows until they found either Ruand or raft. And their sharp-eyed lookout feared something had gone by in the early dark.

As for the instigator . . . if Tanekhet did have the means, let be the motive, he would not risk his own neck in the trap. Zuri is inclined to plump for Nessis' family.

It is as good a candidate as the Emperor.

I am dodging the issue again. As I know Alkhes is dodging it, has dodged it all the way to Marbleport: all that blessed night with Tellurith safe inside the inn's best bedroom, and shelter from the rain. All next day . . .

When she called us in, Alkhes and Tez and I together, to tell us about her new, her other gift.

How can one say "second?" or "lesser?" Even now, I take the thought out at night sometimes, more precious than any heirloom. More precious, to me, than the qherrique. More precious, perhaps, than anything thing except Tellurith.

And Tez herself.

A solace then, an anodyne, to ease the road that seemed ever more interminable, the road I did not remember, and have wondered so many times if I would ever travel again. With the ranges rising slowly round us, and the unfamiliar prospects shifting slowly, slowly, to become the hill's butt; the quarry-gate; the marble's flare; the crowd, every soul in Iskarda, filling, blockading the road.

To be welcomed. To be truly, finally home.

To see the bare fields rimmed with crocuses, to feel winter's last nip in the sparkling air, to know we are a mere week behind the Sowing-rite. To sit by the kitchen fire, among the remembered, beloved faces, and draw new music, the one sweet fruit of Riversend, from the heirloom flute. To savor long-recalled reality, deeply as the spectacle of Darthis managing a close copy of delight.

To sleep at last, the three of us together, in the great old bed, and watch the window traversed by a silver curve of waxing moon.

Or the nights in Zuri's den.

But in hers or Tellurith's bed, there are questions no one has asked. And affliction strike Tanekhet, the most urgent ones are his.

AT FIRST, of course, hardly anyone had time for him. The Ruand safe home, the treaty, and that most miraculous benison of all. Rejoicing, celebration, thanksgiving, it took a week to subside toward routine. So he knew them, at first, far better than they knew him. Rising from her bed with weak imperiousness, Tellurith dispatched him to Hanni's assistance: records, intelligence—Zuri suffered that a single day. We did not discuss him, and they had the wits, yet, not to send him chopping wood. But Roskeran was more than glad to resign me house-command, and there was troublecrew training. So I had barely laid eyes on him before that eighth morning, when he waylaid me at the washing bay door.

"Sarth—I need to speak to you."

It was not ten valets and a street of tailors after all: the fastidiousness is Tanekhet's own. Shaved, hair tied back, the dark Dhasdein clothes clean. And a most uncharacteristic darting haste, a hunted look as he caught my sleeve and tweaked me inside again. "Now."

It had exercised the House as much as anything beyond the qherrique, to stow an unmarried, unattached, adult man. In the end they gave him yet another cellar store-room. He yanked me in the door, leant against it, all but panting, while I stared.

"Zuri stonewalls. Hanni will not let me near Tellurith—the Ruand, I mean. The Crew-heads won't heed, I can't get any sense out of Alkhes. You must listen to me, Sarth."

Close to a flaw of desperation in that perfectly modulated, that now absolutely anomalous noble Dhasdeini voice.

I said, "I'm listening."

He straightened off the door. "The qherrique. What will they do with it?"

That he went on himself, when I did not answer at once, was a measure of his stress.

"Yes, it's pure miracle, all they can talk about is new cutters, a mother-lode, maybe statuettes. Tellurith doesn't hear. I know she swore never to use it again, but they think—!"

"Tellurith is Head."

He drew breath. "I know that. But . . . Do they mean to—to—*plant* it, or . . . ? How does a motherlode . . . come about?"

I could only shake my head. "The oldest stories say Amanazar—Hafas, the first House's Founder, chanced on the original bed. I suppose that was Hafas House's—outcrop. This one . . ."

He gave his head a shake. But his wits were Tanekhet's.

"Then gods know how long before this, whatever it is—is fit to, to crop, or cut, or whatever they do. Sarth, does nobody understand?"

And I, born and bred in Amberlight, proxy to that communion's ecstasy that I know meant more to Tellurith than the power, the City, her House, even Alkhes and I—I was too lost in that tradition's dream to say more than, "Eh?"

"Even if this can be planted or whatever they do—the River knows. The River knows *now*. Why do you think Antastes hunted Assandar? You think one renegade general mattered so much? Sarth, this thing can't give them so much as a cutter panel, and in a couple of months the whole River will be up here!"

I gawped at him, while the political universe fell on my head.

Antastes will hear of this, yes, nothing can stop it, such news travels on the ambient air. Shuya and Cataract know their statuettes will fail, and before Dhasdein's. They will descend like the griffins in old fairytales: because if none can afford to give the others possession, neither can anyone afford to leave us alive.

"I have talked at Zuri till my face is blue. The other Heads rave about their crafts. Hanni thinks I'm trying to assassinate the Head or something. Iatha told me, if I plagued her again, she'd throw me back here in chains."

He tore his hand back through his still beautifully cut hair. "You," he said, sounding exhausted. "Will you tell them, Sarth?"

"I'm out of my place, I know that." He misunderstood my silence, my shame. "But this is what bought me to begin with. This is the value I have for them. Sarth?"

The desperation was open now. Not simply, I understood, for the risk to Iskarda. But because we were hazarding his own hope, his dear-bought second life. His new world.

"Sarth." He had his hand up. His right hand, without thinking perhaps. Rubbing the fingers together, first finger and thumb.

Where the qherrique had stung.

"I know—it rejected me." Even Tanekhet swallowed on that. What can it have been, to know yourself denied by the miracle that is your new world's rediscovered heart? "But. . ."

The eyes came up. Hooded, and steady now, and piercing as the great lord of Dhasdein's, loss denied, pinning me through the brain.

You know what you owe me. You know that without me the lynch pin of your happiness would be forever broken.

Tellurith would be dead.

"I'll tell them," I said.

So now I cannot prevaricate any more. And who is there to answer *me*?

Am I to credit a Mother who could afflict any of Her children with such a commerce as this?

To lose the child of your flesh, and recover your soul's love in its place?

For Tellurith that bargain may truly be a recompense. For her, after all, it was the greatest loss. But for us?

Who have lost yet again the child we could at last have had, the flesh of our heart's desire. The healing, the making good, of the worst wound that plagues my life.

Alkhes, at least, got back the qherrique.

Not the fundament, even yet. It is the other questions that linger, sinking into my flesh, rising in my mind as I wait for sleep.

Why, of all places, did we find it *there*?

Did it wash downRiver? Was it a—seed—a spore—however the qherrique reproduces, was it the heritage, unimaginably preserved, of Amberlight's ruin?

Then why, of all chances, did *we* wash up there?

If that is chance, it is a chance too long for any god's disclaimer. And if it was not chance . . .

Is the River itself subject to qherrique?

And if it was not qherrique . . .

Is there a divinity's hand in this, after all?

IT WOULD be far more comfortable to accept that. To rejoice, as wholeheartedly and unthinkingly as Tellurith, that we have it back, how it happened was unimportant, the qherrique's doing.

Or the Mother's in all truth.

Except . . .

What if we had *not* found it there?

It has haunted my thoughts. It lingers, a shadow, over all my nights. It is a ghost I exorcise a dozen times a day, and it will not be laid.

What if it *was* no mere coincidence?

What if we *were* meant to meet again—or *it* meant us to meet again—

Or She meant us to meet?

And given all that—given it was not some impossible manipulation that conjoined us on that River bank—

If we brought it with us—

How did it come?

Spring. The River.
Tellurith's Diary

I HOPE—I hope with all my heart, that it was an accident.

If I carried it, as I must have carried it, even a divinity would not trust such ramshackle chains of happenstance—even a divinity, surely, would take the simpler way. After all, qherrique lives, if it is not as plant or flesh; it would need a haven, it would need some nurturance.

Unless it was carried as a seed.

If that is so, the likeliest way is with Alkhes.

He was in rapport, at the end he was closest to physical contact, he was wounded. The Mother knows, perhaps it rode, like a fever spore, in the very patterns of his blood.

Or is it as likely that the spore came with Sarth? That it was latent, as the bleeding sickness can lie, in the blood of every man in Amberlight?

The Mother defend, it might as easily have lain in mine.

Assume then, whoever the original carrier, that it—

That it shared my womb.

Assume the kindest, the kindliest thing, that it was meant to come to term ...

That it would have been born with

That it would have been born with, not instead of

An hour of a Head's time wasted there, and a page ruined as well. Blessed Mother, I am truly grateful for what you redeemed for me. But, even with another daughter—

Did it have to come at such a price?

Thank the Mother, there is life to occupy a Head, from dawn to moonset if she chose. The latest decisions for the pipe-makers, the dovetailing of Tanekhet's ships and exports with the work of Marbleport. The news upRiver, where winter has muzzled Cataract. The disposition of Tanekhet.

The disposition of the qherrique.

It cannot not simply sit in Zariah's plundered jewel casket, or under the pillow of my bed. It is not a bauble, it is a living thing, perhaps our world's—god.

A peculiar, a most peculiar thought. I have been avoiding it, I see, all my life. Nevertheless.

We are meant to do something with this.

And I swore, long before I vowed it to Antastes, that I would not enslave it. Never again.

The questions open out of each other like puzzle balls. It had won its freedom, it killed itself and Amberlight to win that freedom. For what inconceivable reason would it come again within the reach of humankind?

Consider the consequences. For us alone.

No need for Tanekhet's panic to warn me of that. A greater power than Amberlight's. A worse danger, a deadlier cynosure, than a dozen Tanekhets. How, with one small seed that cannot so much as drive a cutter-blade, am I to protect Iskarda?

What in the Mother's name are we intended to do?

As the Mother sees me, I am an idiot. Again.

So if I was an idiot, what does that make You? Or it, or whatever—whoever—is Ruand of this lunacy. Because if I sat down, as I can now in all sober sense, and took your visible presence in my hand, and woke all the dear life, sentience, weight and substance of the qherrique as I knew it in Amberlight, if I asked: What are we supposed to do?

If I asked: How am I to protect Iskarda?

If I asked as, whether or not I have the courage, I do at least have the right: Did you kill my child?

You—whoever You are—could at least have answered me.

Spring. The River.
Meditations. Alkhes-Assandar

Be hung if I'll ever get used to this. Why in all the pantheon's name can't we do it like before, why can't Tellurith just ask, and get an answer, instead of all this—this—

An hour past, and I'm still shaking. It's so strong. So present. So *real*—

That first time I all but tore the bedroom down. It frightened the brains out of the three of us, and considering the nightmares I—we—have had in that room, that is no mean feat. Gods, I can feel it now, heart in my teeth and hair on end, shaking like a leaf and sweat all over me, out of bed trying to strangle the clothes stand with Tellurith clawing my back and Sarth trying to smother her—

We sorted it out finally. Lit the lamp. Crawled back into bed, hung onto each other, thanked heaven we hadn't roused the patrol and had to tell Zuri we all ate too much dried-raspberry pie. Shia makes the best raspberry pies . . .

Trying to run out again. Gods witness, it's not my place, not my calling, why does this have to happen to me?

Perhaps I should be grateful it doesn't just happen to me. I can imagine trying to explain. I still hear Tel, sitting up between us, with the half-grown moon in the window and that sweet, sweet mountain-night so quiet outside. I still hear how she had to hold her voice steady. As she said it, for the first time.

"I had a dream."

CLEAR AS CRYSTAL, every detail. I can see it now. How can I help but see, what is this, the tenth, the twentieth time?

"Mountains. Mountains high up over us. No mountains I ever saw before. Snow peaks; none of that maiden's breast thing, these are like triangular teeth. Snow mountains, whiter than anyone can imagine; and a quarter moon going down."

She all but lost her voice there. While she swallowed—

I still hear the tremor when Sarth's dark, deep voice—like mahogany velvet—picked it up.

"It is very close to sunrise. On my right hand, there is a counter-flush in the sky already. It will be reflected soon, out on the lake."

He paused. I'm not sure if it was waiting, or sheer lack of words. But I couldn't speak.

"Quite a small lake." Meditatively now. "A mountain lake. I can see plains, a long way out. Tremendous . . . Flat, and tawny. Like a lion's winter hide. But there are trees here, going a long way down. Jungle, I think. The way it sounds in stories about the Heartland. The trees are very thick, and they are not pines."

Another long pause.

"Something is calling. I doubt it is a bird. More like some sort of— moving—troop of beasts. It looks . . ."

A very long pause. Then, softly, "It looks very beautiful. The sky is clear, so it has not rained, but the—the forest is sparkling. I can see the nearest trees, just beyond the lake. There are orchids on them. Purple, I think, as big as a man's hand. The outer leaves are a sort of—midnight green, and they are sparkling. I think it's dew."

"And it smells," said Tellurith dreamily. "It's as quiet as a dream, nobody was ever here before. There's just the little wind, and I can smell the—forest? It's like—mushrooms, like dozens of different plants in a nursery, like Heartland cinnamon sticks and—I don't know how many other things. It smells like soil, and forest and—spice."

That was when I knew my last chance was gone. We could all have imagined it, could have made the rest sound the same.

But not the spice.

"The lake . . ."

Curse it, I've been a god's messenger if I don't remember it, I have been the Mother's Chosen, I have felt the weight of a people's will behind my own. Why did I feel it was too sacred to put words around, let alone being there; in the flesh?

The other thing grabbed me then. Like a night ambush. Like a wrestler jumping you. I thought my heart would spit out between my ribs, I swear the hair shot straight up again on my head. Pressure, demand, the most terrifying urgency, like it was when I burst the dream just now, somebody screaming at you just under hearing, Get here, get here, get here.

Like it screamed then. Tell, tell, tell.

"The lake . . . has a spring in it. The water's—so smooth, it's like—pale, pale jade, right across to the tree-shadows, just starting to flush, with the—dawn. Except right here—where I—we're standing. The water's coming up, bubbling, at the shoreline. Sweet water, must be, it's grown the bulrushes, and they're flowering, they must stand ten, twelve feet high. It comes down—comes down—"

When I stopped, Tellurith and Sarth whispered it together. Like dreamers, like a forsaken oracle. Like they didn't even know what they were saying.

"From the snows."

THE FIRST THING Tellurith did was to get back out of bed, kneel down on the floor and pray.

"Because," I heard her saying softly at the end of the invocation, "this time You have set it right."

Then she wanted to prove it. So in the middle of the morning watch I had to light the lamp, she dug the casket from under her pillow, gathered up the—seed—and ordered Sarth, "Hold out your hands."

Sarth all but swallowed his tongue. Tellurith just repeated, impatiently, "Hold out your hands."

"Sarth," she said, when he did not move. "I know what it means. But I want you to see, as well."

I saw Sarth's eyes get big. Like me, he must have been remembering Tanekhet picking it from the mud. But after all, he's Sarth, and her husband, and a tower man. He cupped his hands.

And his face, when it lay there. When it did not sting him away, when he, too, must have felt, must have understood . . .

THE FIRST THING Esrafal said was, "It's the Source."

Golden-brown eyes, brindle-brown hair. Hanni's sister, the House's drummer. The last, Sarth explains to me, of the Music-makers' Guild; which was not actually a Craft, because it didn't work qherrique.

No, they just preserved the lore.

So after we'd split our brains, and Hanni's, and Iatha's and the rest of the Craft-heads' and house-Heads' and Iskarda's lore-keepers', right up to Darthis' own, when after three whole days Tellurith, at her wits' end, told the dream to the night-time kitchen, Esrafal sat bolt upright by the hearth-stone and said, "It's the Source."

It's old lore. Very old, Iatha thinks maybe older than Amberlight. And as I did not say, it may just as well have been warped, deformed, downright fabricated in Amberlight. Of course they'd have stories about the River-source, there are stories clear to the Delta coast and no two the same, and nobody knows the truth because nobody ever crossed the Heartland and lived, and *none* of those match with this!

I said that to Esrafal. I worked very hard at being tactful. So I consider Tellurith and Iatha had no business to look nonchalant, or Sarth to try not to laugh when she gravely turned her eyes to me—she's a very sober woman, for a drummer—and said, "Of course."

"What," I managed, "do you mean?"

"Only Amberlight's folk came down the River. Verrainers are desert folk, and Dhasdein always draws from the sea. But we came down in the days of Amanazar. The Heartland was our place."

"Musicians," she added complacently, "are the only people who tell the story now. It's of no interest, except as lore."

Except as lore. Ha.

THE FIRST THING Zuri said was, "You're not going."

Tellurith turned her eyes sidelong, and no more.

"Cataract," said Zuri. Her flattest growl. "*The* cataracts. No boats. The Jump-up cliffs. They've killed River folk even with ropes. The Heartland. Lynxes. Tigers. Herds of stampeding—wild-beasts. The cattle-people, the cannibals. The jungle. It's a story. At best."

Everything I've ached to say. Except . . .

She hasn't felt this—thing—in the middle of the night. I swear there are times I could have run straight down to the River and swum to the cursed place.

Zuri let silence weight out the rest: You are Ruand, the House's Head, we can be your proxies for a time, but the vision, the only true steering, has to come from you.

Tellurith said, "I'd be back."

Zuri's only answer was a snort.

THE FIRST THING Tanekhet said, with the most intense relief and more intense thankfulness, was, "Ruand. Thank the gods."

Before he got out of his chair, his absolutely unprecedented chair at the council table, walked past me and Sarth and before an audience of gaping Craft-heads, with the fullest of his inimitable grace, kissed Tellurith's hand.

When he sat down again, he read their faces: Quetho, Zdana, Charras, Hanni, Zuri, Hayras. Darthis.

"Ruands," he said carefully. A gesture of Tanekhet's indescribably graceful respect. "Naturally, you will have followed the Ruand's reasoning?" He looked at Tellurith. She nodded him on.

She is such a conniver. It wasn't just a council to install men, to install Tanekhet. It was to use all his wits, all his skills as a great lord and ruler and public speech-maker, to lay out what he has naturally seen. Pushing the political nightmare down their throats, the deadly threat of Dhasdein and Verrain and Cataract, the impossibility of keeping the qherrique secret, "when you have already celebrated it all over Marbleport?" The trumpeted removal of temptation as our only alternative, and what better, what more impossibly perfect choice? "We can spread that story, and it will travel to the River's end, believe me." The only hope of saving Iskarda was for the qherrique, and Tellurith, to leave Iskarda.

Spring. The River.
Journal kept by Sarth

THE SECOND THING Zuri said, after she hurled herself out of bed and nearly knocked my head off when I grabbed for her, after she stood shaking a good minute with her breathing like the Narrows-rush, was, "Mountains. Mountains. Oh, Mother's love."

It—She—whoever, whatever is in charge of this has its own choices, and it does not mean to be gainsaid. They have dreamed it all over Iskarda and beyond. Ahio, Esrafal. Azo and her husband Herar. Dhanissa at the signal tower. Caitha's apprentice, short, intense Quiran, the innkeeper's second son: enrolled in his trade last autumn, and, says Caitha, soaking it up like a sponge. His betrothed, Darthis' lanky second daughter Keraz. And two of Tez's best water-women, ex-Navy, with the husbands they have taken in Marbleport. A fine selection of necessary skills and crafts, plenty of volunteered cutter blades. Nine women to six men. Sacred numbers,

Zdana tells me, fifteen, five threes, six, twice three, nine, thrice three: all the numbers of courage, enterprise, consummation, luck.

And every man has had the dream as well.

AND ONCE you have felt that heart-paralyzing, impossible urgency, you no longer wonder about perils or legends or impossibilities. Or even political necessities. You are going, and that is an end to it.

To have come home so hardly, to stay so briefly, to resign Iskarda again into others' hands . . . But even Zuri has had to shed her manic troublecrew need for certainty before she jumps. As those left behind have had to swallow their queries and their quibbles—and I must admit, I would give much to watch that government at work.

Darthis. Iatha. Charras and the other Craft-heads.

And Tanekhet.

Oddly enough, I think the clashes will indeed be unimaginable. Tanekhet has won his way from an emperor: what chance has Darthis? And he is shrewder than any Craft-head, and he knows the River well enough to play the role she destined him for. Most of all, as Tellurith said to the council's incredulous faces, "My lord Tanekhet is committed to Iskarda, heart and soul, body and blood."

To believe that, you only had to watch his face.

Far harder, to bear the look from Tez, when she understood she was not going.

"I can't spare you," Tellurith said, holding both her hands, and looking almost as distressed herself. "We need the River. We need the marble-trade." Under her breath, "We need an heir. And," she glanced aside, "I need someone to work with Tanekhet."

Because with Zuri gone, the burden of gathering intelligence, of collating and exploiting his knowledge, of using him as he can best be used, will fall on Tez.

She swallowed and set her teeth in best Navy fashion, before she too looked at Tanekhet. Who gave her one of his best bows and murmured, "It will be a pleasure to work with the lady Tez again."

She grunted. "I told you not to call me that." But her second look was scrutiny of a different sort.

Something tells me that she will not find it so very difficult to work with Tanekhet.

Something in Tanekhet's eye tells me this was not a good idea, from my own point. But against a Lord of Riversend, and a Navy officer of Amberlight, and the compulsion of this—call—what can I do?

TEZ HAS given us the best patrol-boat at Marbleport. We will be escorting a freighter to Cataract. One of Tanekhet's freighters, which, with Tanekhet's ever-alarming efficiency, was due past Marbleport in what one might expect, and rightly in this case, to be the first good weather of spring.

So we are back on the River, lying to, this evening, under an island so close to Amberlight that half the crew are fidgety as fleas. With a full moon glossy and superb in the east, and a lamp to write this on deck. The patrol-boat is, perhaps, a little crowded, but with so many couples among us, things have sorted out quite well.

Esrafal is tightening her drum. Some freighter people have come across in a skiff; they are from the Kora themselves. In a minute or two I shall have to set this aside for the flute: and probably, later tonight, I shall dream.

It happens somewhere every night. The commotion, the stifled cries, the slow settling, as someone receives the message we are not allowed to forget.

When we get there, will there be answers also?

I have so many questions. How did this chain of destiny fall out, and what has forged the links? Is there a divinity involved here, or have we held divinity, all of us aboard here, in our close-cupped hands? How, in my mind, my soul, am I now to shape the world?

And can the way we came here ever be justified?

Spring. The River.
Tellurith's Diary

IN ALL MY DAYS at Amberlight, I never went to Cataract, let alone contemplated going beyond. There are so many questions I have never had the answers for.

Not the questions Sarth has shown me. As the Mother sees me, I have married a philosopher.

Or a seer.

What else was lost, was buried in the towers of Amberlight?

Or the tap-room of Iskarda.

From one end of the River to the other. Already it has been a long, a harrowing journey; and at its end, maybe there will be yet another—an inconceivable—rebirth.

What other questions will be answered, what fresh proposals will be made? What new world will we bring back?

Because we will be coming back. Throw in Cataract tyrants and cliffs and man-eaters four or two-legged, that is one question I do not have to ask. I have no idea whatever why it or She has decided that it—She—wants humankind, but I have no doubt of it. We are called. We will be taken care for.

We will be coming back.

Sarth has put his pen up and unwrapped the flute. The moon is limning his profile, and lighting bronze sheens down his plait. I can see Zuri beyond him, a granite vigilance. Ahio is by the mooring ladder, flirting with freighter-crew as they come aboard. Alkhes . . .

Is beside me, that silky black wing of hair merging his face into the night as he looks quietly, absently, upstream. Knowing Alkhes, it will not be great questions, but the problems of tomorrow that fill his thoughts.

Or perhaps, the memories of yesterday.

Time to call him back then. To take his hands, to take both their hands, and draw them with me. Into the community that Tanekhet saw, into the expectation which is both trial and joy, into the greater community that is going forward with us. Into whatever is waiting for us at the River's end.

THE END

About the Author

Sylvia Kelso was born and lives in North Queensland, Australia, where she was telling stories almost before she could write. She has published poetry in Australian literary magazines and a national anthology, and has a Creative Writing MA for an alternate history/SF novel set in alternate North Queenslands. Novels in her fantasy series The Rihannar Chronicles include *Everran's Bane* (2005), *The Moving Water* (2007), and *The Red Country* (2008). *The Moving Water* was shortlisted for the 2007 Aurealis Award.

Riversend is the sequel to her acclaimed novel *Amberlight*, also an Aurealis finalist, published by Juno Books in 2007.

Kelso's fantasies most often use an analogue Australian landscape, where bushfires and gum-trees appear along with dragons, mages and bards. In the Riverworld of Amberlight the gumtrees are less obvious but landscape draws on more southern Australian states.

The author teaches at James Cook University in her home town, and has published academic articles on science fiction and fantasy. She lives in a house with a lot of trees but no cats, and likes to play Irish whistle, and sometimes fiddle, with her friends.

Sylvia Kelso's Web site: http://members.iinet.net.au/~sakelso/

BASEMENT

LaVergne, TN USA
18 February 2010
173499LV00002B/126/P